# The Forever Queen

# BOOKS BY ASHLEY METZLER

THE AISLING TRILOGY

*The Mortal Queen*

*The Savage Queen*

# The Forever Queen

## Ashley Metzler

SECOND SKY

Published by Second Sky in 2025

An imprint of Storyfire Ltd.
Carmelite House
50 Victoria Embankment
London EC4Y 0DZ

www.secondskybooks.com

The authorised representative in the EEA is Hachette Ireland
8 Castlecourt Centre
Dublin 15 D15 XTP3
Ireland
(email: info@hbgi.ie)

Copyright © Ashley Metzler, 2025

Ashley Metzler has asserted her right to be identified
as the author of this work.

All rights reserved. No part of this publication may be reproduced, stored in any retrieval system, or transmitted, in any form or by any means, electronic, mechanical, photocopying, recording or otherwise, without the prior written permission of the publishers.

ISBN: 978-1-83618-319-8
eBook ISBN: 978-1-83618-318-1

This book is a work of fiction. Names, characters, businesses, organizations, places and events other than those clearly in the public domain, are either the product of the author's imagination or are used fictitiously. Any resemblance to actual persons, living or dead, events or locales is entirely coincidental.

*To the forests and their flowers and the legends they hide.*

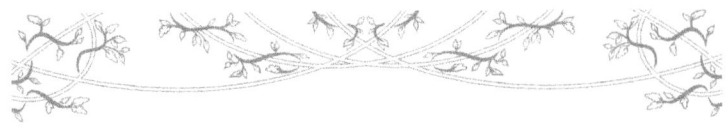

# PROLOGUE

Beginnings are born from the womb of an ending. They will scream as fate pulls their strings taut, dragging them into the light from the den of their ashes for the first time. And once they huff their first breath, lungs rattling, their ending has already been woven into the fabric of the loom. This is the collective, inescapable fate of all: one day, all will end. And only then can something new begin.

The Lady, a gory specter, rose from the cobbles of Castle Neimedh's central tower. She moved strangely, joints popping and snapping as she propped herself up on needle-thin bones. The storm above trickled from the gaps in the steepled ceiling, washing over the Lady's body and remaking her.

The high king of the mortals and the North stood by his son. Nemed's dagger was still slick with red, dripping onto the stone.

Both father and son watched with terror and awe: the Lady's torn, sinewy flesh, her eye sockets exposed and empty, her heart fluttering from an exposed chamber like a bleeding bird.

"Do not be afraid," Nemed whispered to Starn, his tongue clicking where his mouth had run dry.

Starn looked up at his father like he was a child once more, nodding his head. His hand gripped the haft of his blade more tightly—a sword bewitched by the aberration rising before both him and his father now.

Starn was breathless, wondering how his sickly, feeble wisp of a sister was capable of *this*. Of breaking the Lady, this wretched bane, with the strength of undeserved power.

Starn's knuckles burned white, digging his nails into the leather of the hilt. His anger fed off the feast of his horror, growing more swollen, larger, hungrier inside him.

"Are you certain of this?" Starn asked his father.

"Fjallnorr is red with the blood and ichor of my men and yet, despite the cost of our ambitions, I hold neither Aisling, the curse breaker she hoards inside, nor victory over the Aos Sí. My hands are empty and left wanting," Nemed said. "And so, we're left with little option. The Lady is going to help us."

Reflexively, Starn's eyes shot to his enchanted blade. Thanks to the Lady, Starn could wield the sword with nothing more than the will of his mind. A token the wretch had gifted Clann Neimedh to better defeat Aisling. Still, he'd failed.

"The Lady cannot be trusted," Starn said.

"No," Nemed agreed. "But there is poetry to reclaiming what is rightfully ours—magic, strength, immortality—with the hand of those who stole it."

"It was Ina who forsook us," Starn said.

"Aye," Nemed said. "Yet, they are all the same. Their blood is magic and ours is not. It is us against them, and if victory requires devilry—a siding with the enemy—then so be it."

Nemed sucked in a breath, his expression more severe at the cost of both age and exhaustion. His father's reign was a dwindling fire Starn would soon restoke once the last ember dimmed. He, the crown prince of the mortals and the North, could almost feel the blood dripping down his forehead in anticipation of his father's crown being laid atop his brow. He would be king, almost. A reign he intended to punctuate with the conquest of magic, of monsters, of nightmares he'd bury into history. Almost.

"She's almost reborn," Nemed said, ripping Starn from his reverie.

Starn's attention turned to the Lady, snapping her neck into position. No longer was her body broken. Before them both, she stood statuesque and queenly. Her chin tipped up, her shoulders back, the obsidian of her flesh glowing softly beneath the moonlight that shot like arrows from the holes in the roof.

At her feet, lay the bloody corpse of a mortal knight, awkwardly bent at unnatural angles.

Starn resisted the sudden urge to bow. He ignored the weight of her magic or its rotten smell, leveling his glare with hers.

"I will forgive this once and once alone," the Lady said, her voice like nails scratching till they bled. "To summon me with the blood of mortal man is sacrilege."

"I'd forgotten the dark spells whispering between the pages of the Forbidden Lore. It is those very practices that both brought you here and remade you," Nemed argued, not a trace of fear in either his words or posture.

"Those spells do not belong to your kind," the Lady quipped, considering the mortal knight dead at her feet with disgust. "To let such spells crawl off your human tongue is a perversity."

"That's true regarding most magic," Nemed conceded. "But there are those practices even my kind can wield."

"The Sidhe call such practices *scull draiocht*, or shadow magic. It takes not from the breath but from within oneself. Power given to those desperate enough to forsake their souls in exchange," the Lady said, as countless spiders skittered up her gown and settled in the hollows of her eye sockets. Starn shuddered.

"There is no soul left in me to forsake," Nemed said. He spoke matter-of-factly, his voice void of emotion. He was warlike, carved by the scarred hands of every high king before him. And one day soon, Starn would be etched similarly.

"There is a soul left in you yet," the Lady said. "For it is the soul that wants."

"You understand why I've summoned you then," Nemed said.

"So long as the Forge bubbles, you will want. So long as magic exists ungovernable by humankind, you will want."

"End my wanting, Lady," Nemed said. "For your want and mine are the same."

The Lady pursed her lips. She stood still for a long while—her empty, spidery glare uncanny.

"I have already shared with you that which I am forbidden to share," the Lady said, her attention shifting to Starn's enchanted blade sitting on his hip.

"You, too, have committed sacrilege then," Nemed said. "Our hands are sullied equally. We've both measured the tails of fate and have found one to be both worse than sacrilege and worse than death." Nemed's eyes drifted to his knight lying face down on the cobbles in a pool of his own blood. "If Aisling and her barbarian lord are ungoverned and unbridled, we are both denied our want: order, the will of fate, and the continuation of all that currently is and will be."

The Lady seemed to hold her breath, mulling over the high king's words with the patience of eternity.

At last, she spoke.

"Do you wish to destroy or to rule the Forge and all its creation?" she asked, her voice bouncing off the walls of the tower.

The corners of Nemed's lips curled and he exchanged glances with his son.

"There is no satisfaction in conquering the dead. I wish

for mankind to rule," Nemed said. "But if—to stop my daughter's will and that of the Forge—I must destroy... then so be it."

The Lady tilted her head back further, the spiders in her eyes squirming amongst one another.

She sucked in a ragged breath as if her lungs were still not fully remade.

"What do you know of the gateway?"

Nemed and Starn shifted.

The Lady studied him until he spoke.

"The Forbidden Lore claims it's the entrance to the Otherworld—locked to mankind," Starn said, his words falling off his tongue before he could think better of it.

"The Otherworld has many doors through which to slip in and out of the spirit realm. But the first created is the most powerful. Conquer it, destroy it, hide it, and all other doors will follow in kind," the Lady said.

Nemed swallowed hard, forcing Starn to wonder if his heart was thudding as violently as his own.

"Where is this gateway?" Nemed asked, his voice suddenly thick and wet.

The Lady smiled.

"It moves," she said. "Hunt it, find it, and Aisling will be stopped. Our wants will be fulfilled."

"But how?" Starn asked. "Aisling destroyed nearly every northern fleet at Lofgren's Rise. We are dwindling and crippled."

"Aisling is weak after expending so much fury. It's why hers and Lir's bond hasn't scorched the earth yet," Nemed said. "She is useless in battle and more pitiful with a blade. But once her magic returns to her—"

"*Wystria*," the Lady called. In the palm of her hand, a sparkling ball of flame bloomed. It spun slowly and glowed brightly, gilding all that felt its warm gaze. Neither Nemed nor

Starn blinked, transfixed by her magic. "*Wildfire*," she translated.

The Lady lifted her palm to her lips and blew on the flame. Softly, it floated to the high king and his son but stopped a pace short. It bobbed for a moment, crackling as it burned. And then, it cleaved itself in two, one half drifting to Nemed and one to Starn.

"Eat and be filled and spit flame," the Lady said, but it rang throughout the tower like a curse.

Starn's stomach flipped, but he mirrored his father regardless. After Nemed, he took the flame in his hand, brought it to his mouth, and swallowed it whole.

The Lady watched, her fingers moving as if working thread on an invisible loom.

> "Hear me Forge, hear me fate,
> let man and magic meet at the gate.
> A curse will be a boon,
> A king to knight is hewn,
> And a memory returned beneath a storm moon.
> Let this prayer cleave like a sword.
> Let mankind spare the world."

Her words bounced off the walls of forever, sinking into the mind of the Forge and all its creation. Magic crackled like a flame, stinging the inside of Nemed's and Starn's nostrils.

*Scull draiocht.* The heat of its enchantment scalded his tongue, his throat, and his stomach where it sat to burn, hollowing the high king and his crown prince.

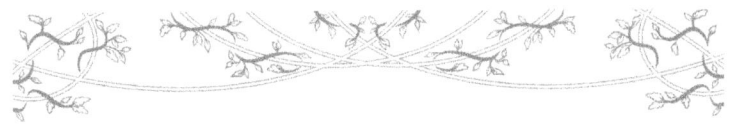

# CHAPTER I

## AISLING

Where Aisling once believed Lir to be a nightmare, tonight he donned the trappings of a dream. He rode Flaithri, the largest white stag in all Annwyn, both of them dripping with Connemara beads, braided blackthorns, and emerald clovers. His antlered crown mirrored Flaithri's own; a tangled diadem of polished ivory, glistering in the firelight of *Imbolc*. But just as a dream unspooled at the edge of potential midnight horrors, so, too, did the Sidhe king of the greenwood.

Lir raised a goblet of mortal blood to the sea of trooping fae and feral beasts. The crowd roared, their jeers vibrating through the wildflowers beneath Aisling's bare feet. Bears soaked the earth with their frothing pints of mead, goblins shoved one another in jest, and toads croaked through the clouds of smoke, puffing from their pipes like old chimneys.

Lir drank, his throat bobbing as a scarlet stream escaped his lips and slid down the muscled curve of his neck. And when he smiled, it was a grin stained with warm death. The death of those whose blood still, in some way, ran through Aisling's veins.

"*Drink!*" Lir shouted in Rún. "*Drink and indulge for this season's Imbolc will not only presage the dawning of springtide but the dawning of a new age."* Lir's eyes flicked to Aisling.

Aisling stood beneath Huriel, a colossal ash tree whose branches cradled the clearing where they reveled, bejeweled with troll-mined gems, cedar cup mushrooms, snowy owl feathers, and lush garlands of sugarberries. Galad hovered protectively at Aisling's side and would likely have kept his hands gripped to his blade if it weren't for Gilrel's reassuring presence —the pine marten as quick with her sword as she was with her tongue.

Galad translated for Aisling. Some words and expressions Aisling already understood, but Galad's guidance connected those phrases she wasn't yet familiar with. Aisling was committed to becoming fluent, and with every flame conjured by the *draiocht*, she found the divine language effortlessly slipped into her mind. It was as if she'd always known it. Like an old road home, Aisling simply needed to remember the way back.

*"Alone, both Seelie and Unseelie have fallen at the knee to the mischief of mortal man. But should we forge-born unite, mortal men will find their blood pooling atop the earth, lapped by the fanged mouths of our forests. Together, Seelie and Unseelie will bind this plane and the Other—the Forge, our own. All thanks to my—"* Lir hesitated before grinning like a wolf. "*Our new queen.*"

Annwyn erupted into cheers. Triumphantly, the fireflies danced in great spells of light; the drums mirrored every racing heartbeat; Huriel swayed in rapture, and every honeysuckle trumpeted in honor of both Lir and Aisling's glory. Together. Together, they were invincible. Stronger than iron and more potent than magic.

Peitho lifted a goblet of her own and her sleeves of embroidered cornelian glittered. She the sun and Filverel the moon in all white robes, smiling to himself as he leaned against one of Huriel's great roots.

"To Aisling!" Peitho said, and the creatures of Annwyn repeated the words, raising their chalices, their pipes, their glasses, and their petrified pixie bubbles.

Aisling bowed her head, a lump growing in her throat. She wasn't certain where to look, so she found Lir's gaze across the glen.

The sage of Lir's eyes flashed with want, exploring Aisling lazily as though they'd just shared thoughts. As though they were alone beneath Huriel, the world fizzling into silence. His regard alone, an enchantment few bore the strength to resist: to not fall in the worship of his blazing, bright darkness.

And as Aisling fantasized Lir's hands would slide up her pearl-white gown, flowers bloomed there instead. Vines of *ellwyn* bubbled at the hem of her dress. An almost translucent slip, sparkling with morning dew on a northern field. Her shoulders were cloaked by a cape of giant luna moth wings that powdered the air when Aisling swayed to the music and dusted the *ellwyn* that climbed her skirts.

Torturously slow and at Lir's will, the flowers grazed her bodice, caressed her neck, before cupping her jaw, and, at last, tangled themselves in both her hair and her antlered crown: a counterpart to Lir's own. She, dressed in spring itself and the rebirth of not only Lir's rule over Annwyn, but Lir and Aisling's sovereignty over everything.

"And to Lir," Filverel added. "*May their reign be eternal.*"

At the advisor's words, the crowd parted, forging a path for Lir to approach Aisling. The winds grew restless the nearer he and Flaithri moved, every tree dancing in the howling winds of *Imbolc*.

"Approach, *mo Lúra*," Galad whispered from behind. Aisling and Gilrel exchanged glances before she took a step forward. Magic hung thickly in the air, rising as the distance between Aisling and Lir closed.

Before a great felled oak, Lir leaped off Flaithri and reached Aisling. Aisling inhaled sharply, holding her breath as he pulled her close and held her waist. Every press of his fingertips scalding her flesh and shuddering through *Imbolc*, Annwyn, and all the North. And by the darkening of Lir's gaze, Aisling knew he felt the *draiocht* roaring, howling, screaming on the inside too.

Without a word, Lir lifted Aisling onto Flaithri side-saddle.

All Annwyn watched her, their chatter hushing into silence.

"Burn, *ellwyn*," Lir said, his hand lingering on her thigh before sliding away. Aisling, despite herself, shivered, left watching as Lir reached for one of his twin axes and raised it before him.

"*Seliac niv lenelle santi lelluna, te mes crai sen shetek duachte my frei lewen*," Lir shouted.

*Despite bitter winter and its formidable blade, even death's knee will bend to the bloom.* A phrase the Sidhe expressed to one another often enough that Aisling had become familiar with its translation.

Lir slammed the axe into the felled oak, vines bursting from the blade upon impact. Aisling's nose burned with his magic, his *draiocht* moaning against her own, the forest tossing madly as the felled oak grew back to life and bloomed as if anew; a creature to rival Huriel's great size and age; Castle Annwyn, grumbling at the weight of Lir's spells in the distance.

Once the oak stood as a giant before them, straight and proud, Aisling closed her eyes and inhaled like she and Lir had practiced in preparation for this occasion.

*I summon the fire*, she said to the *draiocht*.

Racat, the *dragún* who embodied her magic, laughed beneath his breath inside her, wasting not a moment to burst upward and from Aisling.

The oak's leaves grew not green but violet and licked with flame. Both Lir's and Aisling's magic of life and death, intertwining, braiding, knotting until all the north and beyond held its breath at their splendor. An oak of wood and flame, blazing in the heart of Annwyn.

It was unheard of. The *draiocht* and fire were irreconcilable. As antithetical as day and night, mixed by the spoon of Lir and Aisling's power. So, in addition to Annwyn's splendor, there was horror. Fear bleeding across *Imbolc* like blood on linen. A myth few would believe, born before them.

Annwyn roared more loudly, the realm itself juddering with the force of their excitement. But even so, Aisling still heard Lir's voice rise above the others.

"Asн!" Lir shouted.

Aisling found Lir's eyes amidst the elation. But Lir, without warning, reacted with wicked speed, and Aisling watched their celebrations shift into shock—into panic—before Aisling felt hot sap seeping into the fabric of her gown, just above the heart.

Blood.

She hadn't felt the arrow pierce just below her collar, nor the sizzling and popping of her blood against the iron arrowhead. The shock had protected her against the initial waves of pain. Her ears ringing so loudly she could scarcely hear the chaos. Aisling touched the arrow sticking from her chest, eyes drifting from the reed to Lir before her. He stared at Aisling's wound, but his left hand clutched his opposite bleeding shoulder. He was hurt. A wound to match Aisling's own. Except, the iron arrow responsible for the wound in Lir's shoulder was gone. Gone, having cut through the fae king and into Aisling.

Iron had teeth. Or, at least, it felt that way ever since Aisling's mortal blood had thinned to a whisper. Even its stench, its rust, its texture bit into Aisling's flesh and needled its way into the marrow of her bones.

Aisling lay in Lir's arms, pulling the arrow from her chest as chaos blazed around them. Lir hissed something beneath his breath, bloody poppies sprouting madly at her wound where the fae king's attention struggled to think of anything else, ignoring his own violent injury.

Aisling cared little for her pain, horrified by the devastation that surrounded them. Iron arrows showered *Imbolc* as well as both Seelie and Unseelie screams. The scraping of swords being released from their scabbards was a symphony of promised death—from either the Seelie or mortals, Aisling was unsure.

Galad, Gilrel, Peitho, and Filverel twisted with their blades, slicing and cutting shadows. Shadows that grew and warped, growing larger as they surrounded *Imbolc* and the frenzy of forge-born creatures. Their stags lay lifeless at the edge of the wood, Sidhe were staked through with iron spears, and the Sidhe animals that raised their weapons lay horns, hooves, and paws down, vacant eyes void of their Forge blood.

"Mortals," Aisling said between her teeth.

Lir pulled her possessively against himself.

"We need to leave," Lir said, scooping Aisling into his arms as he stood.

"No," Aisling said, her heart hammering. Or Lir's, she wasn't certain.

"*A trevus noralla in cept*," Galad shouted to Lir, slicing through a mortal knight and spraying them all in his fleshling stench. The human collapsed next to Aisling, his armor chinking, the weight of him making a gruesome thud as he hit the earth. Aisling didn't recognize him, but his trappings spoke for themselves. This mortal stranger, clad in Tilrish tartans: the scarlet wool that once belonged to Aisling's mortal clann.

Smoke billowed from the corners of his mouth, an ember

dimming between his teeth. As if his mouth were a furnace hungry for more coals.

Aisling smelled it before she spoke its name beneath her breath.

"*Draiocht.*"

Aisling's chest tightened, her heart hammering madly. She was weak from her injury, her complexion paling.

"Starn was behind this," Aisling hissed, smelling the Lady's influence. "And my father." An indescribable anger simmered within her at the realization.

"Galad!" Lir shouted, capturing his knight's attention. His voice was rougher, darker than it'd been before. "Escort Aisling to the castle." Galad nodded his head, gently taking Aisling from Lir's arms.

"No," Aisling bit, struggling in Galad's grip. "No, I must find them."

Lir opened his mouth to speak but was cut short, swiveling on his heel and cutting through another mortal attacker. Their human screams piqued something in Aisling she couldn't quite describe but longed to hear again. And again she did, Lir conjuring fledgling trees that sprouted and overturned the soil, the flowers, the moss-soft grass beneath their feet. His *draiocht*, teasing her own despite the blood that flooded from his arrow wound, doing its best to heal whilst Lir expended more *draiocht*.

To the Sidhe, magic was breath. They inhaled it, filling their lungs with the primordial sighs of the Forge, and without it, they couldn't survive. Without the *draiocht*, they would suffocate. But too much of the *draiocht* and they'd grow breathless, gasping for more, insatiable, unable to catch their breath, and the weight of their power would be enough to crush their chests and cease their eternal hearts. The more powerful the magic, the greater the cost.

"Lir will deal with them," Galad whispered in Aisling's ear, holding her firmly in his grip.

"They're mine to deal with," Aisling growled, averting her eyes from the corpses of three Forge badgers and a hare piled atop one another, blood dripping from the corners of their gaping mouths.

This was an ambush. An onslaught. Devilry on behalf of humankind. On behalf of her father. And Aisling knew Starn was nearby. She could smell him. So close and most likely the wielder of the arrow that'd struck both her and Lir. It'd been too precise, too perfect not to have been aided by the Lady's sorcery.

Aisling jerked free of Galad's grasp.

"Ash!" the knight cried, but it was too late.

Aisling felt Racat's excitement before her own, boiling in her gut and whistling through her teeth like steam from a cauldron.

*Is this what you want?* Racat asked inside her mind, his voice echoing.

"Aye," Aisling said aloud. And it was done.

The oak's leaves of violet fire grew alongside Lir's fledglings, his vines, his brambles of thorns and needles. Every lick of flame devouring the world that it touched, magnified by Lir's power. So while the Lady was well versed in trickery, she'd told one truth: Lir's and Aisling's magic, side by side, was devastation incarnate.

Both mortals and forge-born creatures became swathed in her flames, in Lir's magic. Their world was the crackling, raging flame of a candle whose wick was too long. Too persistent and too eager to burn.

*More*, Racat growled. *More!*

Lir shuffled backward, alarmed by the magnitude of their combined power. Aisling and Lir had performed brief spells together, played in the woods with flames and flowers between their lips and teeth, but never had they toyed with battle magic to this degree. And it was ruinous.

"Enough!" Aisling screamed at Racat to no avail. She'd let the *dragún* go too far. He was a garland of flame, wicking through *Imbolc* and destroying everything in his path, nearly including the Sidhe themselves.

"Enough!" Aisling ordered Racat, falling to her knees, her entire body possessed by the fire.

*It is never enough, dear friend*, Racat replied.

Lir raced toward Aisling; Galad struggled through hordes of burning mortals; Gilrel screamed her name, but it was out of Aisling's control. And now, Annwyn would burn.

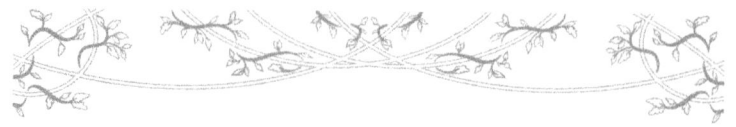

# CHAPTER II

## AISLING

"Stop, Aisling!" Gilrel wailed, landing lithely beside Aisling. Burning tears slipped from Aisling's eyes as she met Gilrel's horrified expression.

"I can't." Aisling closed her eyes, and she cried more embers that floated up and into the fire that engulfed them. Galad, Lir, Peitho, and Filverel were among the hundreds that battled both Aisling's fire and the mortals for their lives.

"You can," a voice said, but it wasn't Gilrel's. It was a male's, as soft and lilting as snow falling. "Just say the word."

Aisling and Gilrel both whipped their heads in the voice's direction.

Fionn.

He appeared without forewarning. He stood silver and sparkling. Boots jagged with ice and the angry, angled perfection of frost. A snapping wolf at his side.

Aisling sprung to her feet awkwardly, staggering backward and away from the son of Winter: Lir's brother and he who'd both imprisoned Aisling and dulled her *draiocht*. Attempted to unbind her and Lir so that Fionn and Aisling might come into union and rule over both Seelie and Unseelie in Lir's stead.

"Another step forward and I'll have your head, sovereign or not," Gilrel said, pointing her blade at Fionn. Frigg, his silver wolf, snapped his jaws at the pine marten. Gilrel gripped her hilt more tightly, glaring down at the hound with her beady eyes.

"Be my guest," Fionn said, cool as the permafrost. "And together, we'll burn in Aisling's *draiocht*."

Gilrel hesitated, the devastation around them proof enough of Fionn's words.

"What do you want, Fionn?" Aisling growled through the *draiocht* seeping from her pores. The vibration of her magic unbearable.

"To help you."

"To what end?"

"To no end," Fionn said, slipping his hands into his pockets. "If the Seelie and Unseelie burn because of yours and Lir's recklessness, then you burn what is rightfully mine. Including yourself."

"Watch your tongue!" Gilrel hissed, leaping into the air.

Fionn ignored Gilrel. "You're running out of time, *mo Lúra*. What will it be? My help or the mortals' victory over Annwyn on the evening of your precious *Imbolc*?"

Aisling glanced over her shoulder at Lir, at Galad, at Peitho, and Filverel. They were losing. The mortals' ambush alone was enough to jeopardize their lives, but coupled with Aisling and Lir's blazing, uncontrollable flames... they were struggling.

*Do not trust him.* Racat chuckled as he continued his havoc. *Speak no more with the son of Winter lest those words be your last.*

Aisling swallowed, the trust between her and Fionn, thinner and more elusive than the wispy spirits haunting the corridors of Castle Annwyn.

"Very well." She nodded, her voice unrecognizable and laced with Racat's growl.

Fionn smiled, handsome and wide, and snapped his fingers.

Without hesitation, his wolf, Frigg, bounded into the mayhem, a trail of ice dragging through Huriel's cradle from the tip of the hound's tail. Like crystals and quartz and spiderwebs beaded with rain, winter spread through the glen, freezing over the piles of dead and those on the precipice of being rocked to eternal sleep in the warm hull of the Other's death galleon.

Those mortals still standing gaped in terror at the unadulterated magic dueling Aisling's own. Two opposing forces battling for supremacy between fire and ice. And so the humans fled, picking up their heavy iron boots and slipping into the surrounding trees as the ghouls, the fauns, the Cú Scáth chased them, still eager for a taste of their mortal flesh.

Everything became ice. The antithesis of spring and *Imbolc*. Of Lir. It was beautiful in its nature, albeit painful.

*No, stop this. Please. Please*, Racat begged. The *dragún's* guttural voice gasping for breath as Fionn and Frigg, together, stamped out the flames. Fionn's careful, ancient practice of the *draíocht* was enough to counter Aisling's reckless, youthful efforts. Lir's power dwindling as he defeated hordes of mortals, all the while bleeding out and surrounded by his vulnerability: flame.

So the son of Winter draped *Imbolc* in silence as the crackling and raging of flames, the beating of blades upon shields, the agony-filled hollering, the plucking of bowstrings, and the final slushy cuts of death chilled to a stop. Until those left standing huffed translucent clouds of frost, themselves silhouettes of sloppy, violent red in a landscape of twinkling ivory.

Castle Annwyn's gates flew apart.

Lir tore through the courtyard like a comet on Flaithri. Aisling lay in his arms, both lit aflame like violet wicks atop a bleeding stag. Many of his knights followed shortly behind him, sinking themselves into the weepy panic of the courtyard. Every castle hare, toad, bird, and forge-born rushed about in a frenzy, shouting, crying, and escorting the injured and wounded to the infirmary. They cut knights from their twisted stirrups, their armor, and their boots. They carried buckets of water and baskets of gauze. But nothing could mask the distant screams, the smoke-stained sky, or the grief of the forest.

Peitho and Filverel rushed to Flaithri's side. Immediately, they reached for Aisling, wet with both hers and Lir's blood.

Lir cursed, pulling Aisling closer to his chest.

"Don't touch her," he growled, his eyes flooded by the black of his pupils. His expression was inhuman and touched by fury. Fangs glistering despite the blood, mud, and soot smeared across his face.

"She needs to be sent to the infirmary," Peitho argued, standing despite a gruesome wound bubbling at her shoulder.

"As do you," Filverel added, looking the Sidhe king up and down.

"Bar the gates, line the northern gorge with swordsmen and the western canopies with archers." Lir ignored them both, barking orders at every and any knight well enough to heed his commands.

"Lir." Galad approached, eager for his lord's attention—an iron reed still lodged and sizzling in his bicep.

Lir turned Flaithri away who was dancing in place on blackened hooves.

"Sift through everything that lies beneath Huriel's shadow," Lir continued. "Collect the injured and bury the dead. Bring every resident outside of Castle Annwyn's gates inside. Room, and feed them. Lock the gates and let none enter or leave until daybreak."

"Lir." Filverel tried again for the Sidhe king's attention, but once more it was futile.

"Gather the owls." Lir started toward Castle Annwyn's

main threshold as he spoke, his knights tripping behind him and Aisling. "They'll be sent to the other sovereigns immediately."

"Lir, Aisling needs proper care." Peitho's voice broke through the chaos.

"She needs a healer's attention," Galad agreed.

"I'll heal her myself," Lir bit, pressing Aisling to his chest.

"You're injured yourself, sire," Filverel said, moving to help Aisling off Flaithri once more.

Without hesitation, Lir reacted, his anger and *draiocht* flaring. Yet, his magic manifested differently. Together, he and Aisling lit with dazzling fire. Flame that threw Flaithri back in a panic and sent the surrounding forge-born scurrying for the edges of the courtyard. Even the Sidhe took several steps back, their king swathed in flames they believed, not long ago, belonged only to the mortals. He and his witch queen, tangled by fury, by magic, and by power.

All the courtyard turned to witness the spectacle. Their eyes bulged red and wet, lips parting with terror.

"*Easca*, Lir," Filverel scolded, holding his arms before his face to shield his eyes from their violet light.

"I will not relent," Lir said. "None shall touch her save for I." His voice echoed as if all the forest spoke from his lips simultaneously.

"Look at yourself," Filverel pushed. "Look at the ruin you both reap! If you do not relent, you will destroy all that you've sought to protect."

An uncomfortable silence hung in the air.

Lir swallowed hard. Aisling sat quiet in his embrace, but her eyes glowed with the strength of his magic pulsing through her as well.

"Look what they've done," Lir said, his voice thundering through the courtyard. "They've come with *scull draiocht* between their teeth. They've ripped my forests with their iron. I will not hesitate to react."

Filverel swallowed.

"And so, you've seen their newfound strength," Filverel said. "You've now witnessed what they're capable of as well as the influence of yours and Aisling's magic combined. Neither will ensure the survival of the Sidhe. They will condemn it."

Lir's expression hardened and their flames grew larger, but he did not speak a word. He clenched his jaw tightly.

"What do you suggest?" Lir asked, his voice void of warmth. Enough to make Aisling shudder with fear herself.

Filverel shook his head, wiping blood and sweat from his brow with the back of his sleeve. They all exchanged glances, but not a word was uttered. Not an answer given. Only the ghost of war howled and Annwyn cried.

∽

"Bring him in," Aisling commanded, her ivory, satin sleeves dragging across the marble floor as she raised her arm in gesture. Wincing, Aisling had forgotten her still-tender arrow wound. For although she healed more quickly now, with Sidhe blood racing in her veins, Gilrel had insisted she gulp down pints of Leshy's tears to quicken her recovery. Especially after having expended so much *draiocht* at *Imbolc*.

"He isn't welcome here regardless of his aid at *Imbolc*," Filverel cautioned from the bottom step of the dais in the throne room.

"Filverel is right," Rian said, one of Lir's closest and most trusted Sidhe knights standing before both Aisling and Lir in the throne room. "Any favor Fionn grants is always followed by a debt."

"Then it's a debt we must pay," Aisling said, half surprising herself. For Aisling wasn't ignorant to the truth of *Imbolc*'s tragedy; perhaps the Sidhe would've survived and slayed the mortals despite their ambush had she not intervened with such irresponsible magic—magic magnified by their consummation. *Draiocht* that she didn't know how to wield just yet. And had it not been for Fionn, one of hers and Lir's most despised adversaries, perhaps they'd all be nothing more than ash beneath Huriel.

Lir's jaw tightened, but he said not a word. In his great, antlered throne, Lir was larger than life. Terrifying and beautiful, king of the greenwood. And today, the morning after *Imbolc*, Aisling felt the same black guilt making sticky his every breath as it did her own.

"Both Fionn and Frigg have agreed to allow Lir to shackle their magic whilst inside Castle Annwyn," Tyr said, another one of Lir's knights. "Without their *draiocht*, there is no danger in hearing what Fionn has to say."

"Words are no blunt blade." Galad set down his pint and crossed his arms. "At times, they are more cutting, more insidious, more dangerous than any sword, leaving behind wounds even Leshy's tears cannot heal."

Lir's closest knights—Yevhen, Aedh, Tyr, Hagre, Einri, Rian, Cathan, and Galad—sat along the length of a thin, live edge table, their expressions carrying the weight of *Imbolc*'s tragedy. Peitho and Gilrel were in attendance too, braiding glowing flower bulbs around the branches of the surrounding trees that framed the interior of the throne room. Every bulb commemorated a forge-born death, either Seelie or Unseelie, and shone white: the Sidhe color for death and mourning.

"Fionn will stop at nothing to dethrone Lir," Peitho piped. "Any 'favors' or acts of compliance should be seen as nothing more than a mask for his trickery and deception."

"Are we so afraid of the son of Winter that we deign not to let him speak?" Hagre asked.

"In times like these," Filverel said, "after we were taken off guard by a mortal advance and nearly bested, it's best to practice the utmost caution. Our enemies are multiplying: Danu and the Lady have been silent, meaning the moment they decide to launch an assault of their own, we must be prepared. Not drunk on mortal blood and wine as we so carelessly chose to celebrate *Imbolc* during wartime. Nemed and the mortals at large will see this 'almost victory' as a beacon of hope for further destruction. We've gifted them confidence at the cost of our arrogance. And what's more, they've come with new power."

"Yet, we cannot subject Annwyn to constant paranoia," Galad said. "We cannot forget to live the lives we fight for, to act boldly in the name of the Forge, and not behave simply out of fear."

"Out of *caution*," Filverel corrected.

Aedh shook his head. "Caution is the bane of the brave. We are Sidhe—warriors of the Forge and the gods."

"You speak with the same arrogance Filverel warns against," Rian said.

Hagre scoffed, stabbing the table with his knife. "And you speak not as a knight but as a coward."

"Enough," Lir said, his voice commanding silence. "Caution. Bravery. Our approach will vary in result, but most important is our harmony as we lead together. Don't let them divide us."

The room exchanged glances, the quiet buzzing in each of their pointed ears.

"Let my brother speak," Lir commanded, and the room thickened with alarm.

Aisling turned to Lir, surprised herself by the fae king's words despite knowing the depths of Lir's hatred for Fionn. She herself wished her elder brothers would meet some semblance of justice as well. Even if said justice was a bloody one, dealt by Aisling's hands. Her clann, her túath, had taken her life, given it away, and attempted to reclaim it once more for their own mortal ends. Now, it was Aisling's turn to reap all that'd been stolen from her.

Lir and Fionn, on the other hand, bore a different dynamic. One where Fionn, the eldest child of Bres and Ina, felt Lir had taken all that was rightfully his: Annwyn, Racat, and now Aisling.

Two armored forge-born bears nodded their heavy heads in response to their sovereign before exiting the throne room, off to retrieve the Sidhe king of Winter and his bestial hound, Frigg, from Annwyn's dungeons, deep below the mountain.

The rest of the chamber, including Lir's knights, Peitho, and Gilrel, continued to stew in silence.

"More wine," Lir said, tipping back yet another chalice. Aisling had barely touched her own considering this vat of fae wine was more potent than most, the berries having been harvested by brownies in the depths of Annwyn's eldest brambles.

"Is that wise, *mo Damh Bán?*" Filverel asked, arching a brow.

Lir ignored him, raising his glass to be filled once more.

A rabbit scurried over with a pitcher, eagerly pouring more of the sticky syrup into Lir's goblet while they awaited Fionn and Frigg's entrance. But they waited not long, for the great doors at the end of the throne room creaked open and the son of Winter entered.

Immediately, a chill possessed everyone present. The crackling of ice spidering from Fionn's boots with each step made the hairs on the nape of Aisling's neck stand straight. For despite Lir's magic-dulling spells, the cold was Fionn's nature, and one couldn't strip breath from body quite so simply.

Frigg followed shortly behind him, the fur of his haunches spiked with malice as he struggled against the thorny muzzle.

"Is this the thanks Annwyn bestows upon its heroes?" Fionn

spoke first, his wrists bound in the same knot of thorns as Frigg's muzzle.

The corners of Lir's lips curled slightly, his eyes flashing a brighter shade of green. "Most self-proclaimed heroes journey to Annwyn on their iron-hoofed steeds to die. And you, Fionn, will be no exception."

"Always so barbaric, brother. You're in no position to be turning away offers of peace and good faith truces."

Lir laughed, leaning back slightly and setting a murder of silver-eyed ravens loose in Aisling's belly. The surrounding trees swayed with similar excitement. Lir rarely laughed, but when he did, the world felt it: either overgrown and wild with joy, lush, velvety, and dark with amusement, or a ghostly growl laced with bloodlust. Right now, it was all amusement, enjoying the invisible noose he was tightening around Fionn's throat with every passing breath.

"Go on. Humor me with your eleventh-hour attempts at self-preservation."

Fionn tipped his head back. "Very well, I'll start with a more lighthearted approach then: a spar." Fionn's eyes darted toward Aisling. Lir followed his line of sight, a muscle flickering across his jaw the moment his eyes also arrived at Aisling, heart pounding in her chest. Resisting the frigid claws Fionn dug into her *draíocht* even from where he stood. "Would the queen of Annwyn accept a simple duel?"

The attention of the room darted toward Aisling and lingered.

Filverel rolled his eyes. "This is nonsense. Let Aisling burn his tongue for wasting *mo Damh Bán's* time."

Lir set his glass down, but before he could grant Filverel's request, Aisling spoke first.

"You mean to challenge me to a fight?" she asked, her curiosity taking hold. She steeled herself against the otherworldly freeze he wove, refusing to wilt beneath the weight of his ancient, arcane magic that tasted of wintertide spells.

"Indeed," he said. "Yet, I'll need full use of my hands to stand a chance," Fionn said, gesturing toward his bound wrists. Frigg lifted his muzzle, demonstrating he, too, wished to be freed from his thorny shackles.

"Are you mad?!" Aedh piped, standing from his seat with an abrupt screech of wood sliding against marble. Cathan and Tyr stood too, their tattooed hands wandering toward the hafts of their weapons.

Lir only smiled. He glanced at Aisling: an invitation for her to decide whether Lir should unbind Fionn and allow him full range of his magic. A risk, one that could cost them greatly. Aisling wasn't ignorant to Fionn's mischief, his games, or his tricks. However, one glance around the room and it was obvious. Fionn was outnumbered and outmanned despite his icy gifts.

Nevertheless, the image of Fionn's smile just before he extinguished her fires at *Imbolc* was a promise in Aisling's eyes. A gesture of goodwill from the moment his presence in Annwyn was made known. And now a debt Aisling was bound to repay. Not to mention, Aisling hated the thought of refusing a duel, especially if the challenge came from the son of Winter's lips.

"As you wish," Aisling said.

Many of the knights and Gilrel audibly growled, looking to Lir and even Filverel for a rebuttal. For someone—anyone to stop what was unraveling.

Yet, Lir leaned fully back in his throne and did as Aisling commanded.

The dark lord of the greenwood need not move to weave magic. Lir was powerful beyond measure and with Aisling beside him, his *draiocht* was boundless. It was rather the smell of the forest after a heavy rain, the humidity, the pressure of his *draiocht* popping their ears that presaged the shriveling of the thorny shackles around Fionn's wrists and Frigg's muzzle. The sinew of each vine collapsed to the floor and eventually vanished.

Freed, Fionn nodded his head, bowing to Aisling in gratitude. His silver hair, sparkling as the braided strands fell over his shoulders. Fionn was somehow more beautiful and more resplendent with his *draiocht* returned.

Lir, however, dug his fangs into his bottom lip, poison gorse tangling itself around the stem of his goblet.

"Let us begin," Aisling said. She stood from her throne, the satin of her gown spilling down the dais as she moved. Slowly, she descended, until she stood across from the son of Winter at the center of the hall.

The room held its breath, the knights dropped their forks and spoons, newly freed hands settling on the hafts of their weapons. Peitho and Gilrel stiffened themselves, dedicating their full attention to both Fionn and Aisling.

Fionn inhaled and snowflakes flurried in the wind of his breath.

"Have you dueled a Sidhe before?" Fionn asked.

"No," Aisling admitted.

"Well then." Fionn smiled. "First, you bow to your opponent. Once you do, you've accepted the duel and cannot forgo the challenge." Elegantly, Fionn bent at the hips, lowering his head as all subjects of Annwyn and elsewhere were required to do in Aisling's presence. The *draiocht* popped and crackled in the air, waiting for Aisling's response to seal the duel.

Aisling mirrored the movement, never once releasing Fionn from her sight.

"And now?" Aisling asked.

"Now, we gather our weapons," Fionn said.

A jolt of excitement shot up Aisling's spine. She tasted the plum-sweet flavor of her magic on her tongue and the burning potential it fanned inside her, coaxed hotter by Lir's proximity.

And, without vocation, her *draiocht* flared like twin comets on both of her fists.

"Ah ah ah," Fionn said, smiling like a fox. "This is a sword duel. Weapon to weapon. Blade to blade. No *draiocht*."

Lir audibly shifted behind Aisling.

"You overestimate our patience for your foolery, son of Winter," Galad spoke immediately.

"The queen of Annwyn has already bowed," Fionn said.

"Because of your deceit," Gilrel piped.

"It's alright," Aisling said, her voice a contrast to the slick tip of Gilrel's and Galad's angry tongues. "Let me duel him by blade."

Aisling dared not glance over her shoulder at Lir, but she felt his anger. Saw his fury climbing up the edges of the hall in thick, sticky thorns and dense weeds.

Gilrel and Peitho exchanged glances, speaking without saying a word. At last, Gilrel grumbled a string of curses beneath her breath and accepted Sarwen from Peitho's keeping: Aisling's blade.

Aisling kneeled to accept the blade from her handmaid. Fionn watched her closely as she familiarized herself with its weight and balance. Aisling wasn't entirely sure how to ready herself for a duel of swords, but she'd seen enough to know a knight always tested their blade before the first strike.

Sarwen hummed softly between her fingers, equally measuring Aisling.

"You're in luck," Fionn said. "Your *Faerak* friend stole my beloved blade and so, I'll need a replacement." Without hesitation, Frigg leaped onto the dining tables and wrapped his fangs around Tyr's blade resting beside his plate.

"You filthy—" Tyr growled, almost staking Frigg's tail to the table with his dinner knife. The wolf carried the double-edged longsword to his master, proudly placing it in Fionn's palms.

"Now we may begin," Fionn said, spinning Tyr's sword as if

he'd known it all his life. The Sidhe knight stood from his seat at the table, crossing his arms as he pleaded silently with the fae king to intervene. Aisling, however, prayed her *caera* would not. If she was to prove herself as rightful queen of Annwyn, Lir couldn't undermine her strength nor her courage.

"First to render the other prone wins," Fionn explained.

Aisling swallowed.

"Begin," she commanded the son of Winter.

The corner of Fionn's lips curled as he shot forth with wicked abandon.

A gasp escaped Aisling just as she stumbled to the side, clumsily avoiding the onslaught. Instinctively, her *draiocht* rose like a midnight bonfire at the center of Annwyn's wine-muddled evenings, but she swallowed it down. Racat flailed, whipped back as if yanked by a leash only Aisling held.

From the corner of Aisling's eye, she saw Lir stand from his throne. His broad shoulders cast a shadow across the floor of the hall, swathing Fionn's swing as he turned on his heel for another attack.

This time, Aisling wasn't so quick. She stumbled back.

"Your blade, Aisling!" Gilrel shouted from the side. "Sarwen is as much a shield as a blade!"

Aisling, understanding, lifted Sarwen above her head and braced against the impact of Fionn's next blow. Fionn swung down and hard, the force of his strike rippling through Aisling's arms as she gritted her teeth to withstand it.

Lir stepped forward, but Aisling steeled herself, her feet sliding back across the floor as Fionn continued to push. Aisling wrenched her eyes shut, gathering the mettle to withdraw her blade and release herself from Fionn's hold. She sucked in a breath and pulled Sarwen back, stepping to the left in the same movement. Fionn flew forward, rolling onto the ground before he found his feet. But it was not enough.

Fionn threw Tyr's blade and the sword spun.

Aisling's eyes grew wide, but her feet were rooted to the floor. Aisling raised Sarwen once more. This time, the force of Tyr's blade against her own knocked her off balance and onto her back. Aisling hissed in pain, her fingers searching for her sword in the chaos. Sarwen clattered beside her, vibrating as Aisling's *draiocht* bubbled inside, begging to be released.

Fionn defeated the distance between himself and Aisling in no more than a single breath. Before Aisling could fumble for Sarwen beside her, the son of Winter was already atop her, Tyr's blade collected once more, and its tip poised at the center of her throat.

Aisling had lost.

The duel was complete, and Fionn had easily bested Aisling in no time at all. The great commotion followed by a moment of equal violence: silence.

Before a word could be uttered, black vines coiled around Fionn's hands and wrists, forcing Tyr's blade from his grasp.

Aisling looked to Lir, quiet, unpredictable rage storming beneath his stoicism. His anger flaming against her *draiocht* inexplicably.

"You've all seen it for yourselves," Fionn said, despite his struggle against Lir's bonds. "Aisling is a knight only by the law of magic, but not by blade."

"Is that why you've come?" Lir asked, his voice frighteningly calm. "This was Aisling's first duel, and it will be your last. In Aisling's eternity, she will carve you bone by bone with her blade."

"Perhaps," Fionn said, clenching his teeth as Lir's vines grew slender, needle-sharp thorns. "But not today. You see, brother, I have something you need."

At this, Lir's smile broadened, yet his grin was joyless. The hall shuddered as the Sidhe king of the greenwood and his brother locked gazes.

"You have nothing," Lir said, his voice vibrating darkly through Castle Annwyn.

"There's rumor the Seelie king and the queen of Annwyn intend to venture into the Other to win the gods' favor," Fionn said. "A necessary requirement to reign over both this plane and the next: harness enough power to defeat not only Danu and the Lady, but the mortals as well and turn the tide of destiny. I believe such ambitions can be achieved, should you not first destroy yourselves and, as a result, the world."

Aisling arched her brow, unfurling from the floor as Gilrel and Peitho both raced to stand on either side of her.

Fionn continued, "Niamh, the Seelie queen of the Isle of Rain, is the fabled keeper of the Goblet; a token of the gods' favor."

Legend claimed Niamh lived in the Other; a supernatural plane where the Forge bubbled and the gods slept—both the beginning and the end of everything, the cradle of creation, and the cauldron of magic itself. The Sidhe were ripped from the Other in the beginning of time, forcing them to make a home in the mortal world between the wind, within the waters, through the trees. The responsibility to stay and watch over the mortal plane, heavy on their shoulders even as they yearned to return. Which forced Aisling to wonder *why* Niamh and the rest of the other Sidhe of the Other, stayed behind. Why they still reigned in the world of magic, of dreams, of visions, of the afterlife.

"The Goblet of Lore." Filverel repeated the object's full name. "A chalice said to hold the bubbling brew of the Forge of Creation itself. Whosoever sips from its lip, can build, write, create at the limit of their own imagination but only beneath the light of a storm moon."

The room swelled with wonder, eyes wide and mouths parting.

"The Goblet could win this war," Galad said, bringing his fist to his mouth in thought.

"Why doesn't Niamh use the Goblet herself?" Aisling asked. "She, a queen of the Other, assisted by the Goblet, could change the course of ill omens and prophecies herself. She could save us all."

Lir inhaled before speaking. "*If* she knew its resting place," the Sidhe king said.

"Few know where the Goblet lies—even its keeper," Gilrel said, speaking directly to Aisling. "After the gods lent Niamh its power, they hid the Goblet between the folds of the Other—a token not to be found by the unworthy."

"Find the Goblet and we find Sidhe victory of the mortals, Danu, and the Lady," Filverel said.

"And should Aisling wield it, alongside the power fomented by hers and Lir's union—ultimate sovereignty is within our grasp," Fionn said, his voice strained and almost pleading.

Aisling's ambition grew hungry inside her gut, her tongue wetting at the words against her own volition.

"But such an opportunity won't be granted if Niamh believes Aisling and Lir to be the harbingers of ill omens, the inevitable death of the Sidhe, and ill-equipped to unearth the Goblet," Fionn said.

Aisling considered Fionn where he stood. His silver hair and embroidered robes were more disheveled than she'd seen them before, having spent the evening in Annwyn's dungeons. Nevertheless, his eyes held Aisling's stare with the same cool confidence he'd possessed when they'd first met. Held her gaze even as Aisling approached. Yet, a single glimmer of hesitation in the twitch of his jaw was enough to betray his nerves.

"Perhaps it's whatever human ghost remains inside me, that finds your every gesture so—"

"Aos Sí?" Fionn finished for her, a reference to how her clann referred to the Sidhe.

Aisling nodded. "Like a tea steeped far too long."

Fionn smirked, but Aisling saw the way he hung onto her

every word. How he listened for its tone, for its mood, wondering if this conversation would be his last.

"Ash," Lir said, taking another step toward her till his boots reached the edge of the dais.

"You've said it countless times before and yet," Aisling spoke to Fionn, "your silver, Sidhe tongue finds another way to express it; Lir and I, despite being pulled to one another by fate's fickle threads, are destined to bring ruin. Like we did at *Imbolc*."

The corners of Fionn's lips twitched upward. Hope blooming around the frost in his iris.

"Like you did at *Imbolc*," the son of Winter repeated.

Aisling held out her hand, palm up. In response, Frigg's expression bore the suggestion of an unsung growl, but he dared not voice it in Lir's audience.

Aisling's *draiocht* fizzled and popped, rising up her spine till it blossomed in lush bouquets of flame, dangling from the oaks Lir had grown centuries prior.

Lir's knights, Peitho and Gilrel, and everyone in attendance held their breath, glossy eyes reflecting the violet of Aisling's fire. Spells that Castle Annwyn had never sheltered within its walls. Spells that, by their nature, contradicted all that was forge-brewed or born. Fire and magic together was blasphemy. And they all knew it.

Aisling's breath hitched.

"Every moment the two of you spend together, is another pace closer to the destruction of our world," Fionn said, stepping closer to Aisling. "Your union is lawless. There are those elements in either this plane or the next that long to be together—"

"The sun and the moon, the fox and its star, the moth to the flame..." Aisling trailed off.

"Aye, yet, by the bounds of the natural world, never can their love be. Despite how much either might desire it."

Aisling, against her own volition, met Lir's gaze over her shoulder. Immediately, her heart took off, beating against her rib cage as though its rightful home was with the beast, fury and all, behind her, standing before his throne. Still, she sank into the sage of his eyes and wandered deep into their grisly forests.

The magic between them electrified every breath she and Lir shared, every glance, every touch, every thought one had for the other. Lightning webbing between them like the threads of their *caera* bond, twisting painfully, hauntingly, till Aisling found her obsession with the Seelie king all-consuming.

"And what's your solution?" Aisling returned her attention to Fionn.

The son of Winter glanced at Lir. Frigg flattened his ears against his head.

"That depends," Fionn said. "On which path you choose to take: I believe you can fulfill the omens that presage the desolation of the Sidhe or you can spare us. The road is cleaved by your potential and fate is shackled to your decision. So, what will it be?"

"My allegiance is with Lir and the Sidhe," Aisling said, her voice laced with the echoing ring of prophecies spoken aloud. Aisling resisted the urge to meet Lir's eyes. She felt him watching her, but she needed to stand on her own, without his strength to guide her. A sentiment he understood despite the muscle that leaped across his jaw as he withheld his violence.

"Then let history remember Oighir and Winter's support in the sparing of the Seelie race." Fionn snapped his fingers and a belt sparkled into existence around his hips.

Immediately, Peitho sucked in a sharp breath, her shoulders going rigid beside Aisling with recognition.

The belt was seemingly made of solid gold. Plate by plate, the belt hung on the son of Winter like a chain of shields, braided together by silver threads. It clinked when Fionn moved and flashed brilliantly when graced by the light. But it was the eerie, near-intangible ring of its magic that unsettled Aisling most of all. As if a gong had been struck and the noise was trapped inside the belt, echoing into oblivion. And if Aisling listened to it closely, the ring became a scream—desolate, hopeless, and angry.

"This is Anduril," Peitho whispered beneath her breath, just loud enough for Aisling to hear. "The Blood Cord of the Dark Sun."

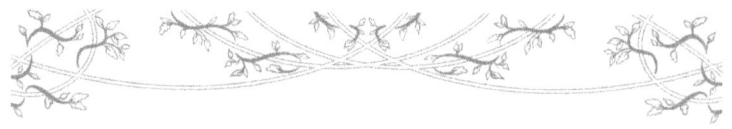

# CHAPTER III

## AISLING

Fionn took another step closer to Aisling, and Lir shifted, his hands balling into fists at his sides.

"Thief," Peitho snarled, her face twisting into hatred. "How dare you don an artifact that rightly belongs to Niltaor and the southern Sidhe kingdom?"

The room inhaled, heads leaning against one another to better hear their muffled chatter.

"You misremember, princess," Fionn said, unflinching. "This belt was given to Oighir on behalf of Niltaor and Lugh, one of the original Sidhe sovereigns."

"It was stolen!" Peitho shouted, cheeks flushing with her temper.

"It's irrelevant," Fionn said. "The belt is what Aisling needs to spare the Sidhe and so, Niltaor."

Peitho opened her mouth to speak but shut it swiftly thereafter, her words caught in her throat.

"A belt will find no Goblet," Galad said, scoffing at the glittering artifact winking against the son of Winter's robes.

"Aye, no ordinary belt could aid Aisling and compensate for her..." Fionn considered, "lesser talents. After all, the path you'll carve to find the Goblet will be laced with monstrous guardians tasked by the gods themselves." His eyes darted toward Sarwen in her porcelain, uncalloused hands.

Aisling resisted the urge to avert her eyes—to look away in shame or embarrassment. Physical strength, athleticism, and a knight's prowess with a blade had always eluded her. She had scarcely lifted a blade before having wed Lir.

"But this is no ordinary belt," Fionn said.

"Anduril is an enchanted object," Peitho chimed through clenched teeth. "Whosoever wears the Blood Cord is transformed into a warrior of legendary prowess."

Aisling's eyes glittered a shade brighter.

"If I wore the belt, it would render me a proficient swordswoman?" she asked, studying Anduril anew.

Fionn smiled, watching Aisling's expression intently.

"You'd be unstoppable," Fionn said. "Worthy of the gods' favor, of sovereignty, and of the Goblet."

Aisling's stomach knotted. Her heart took off racing. The belt rang more loudly, tearing through the fabric of the Other and swelling inside Aisling's ears.

Aisling exchanged glances with Gilrel, Galad, Peitho, and finally, Lir.

"And the cost of the belt's magic?" Lir asked.

Fionn hesitated, eyes darting back and forth.

"Impossible to know exactly..." Fionn's voice trailed off.

"Then it's no option," Lir said, his voice booming through the hall.

Fionn took an instinctive step forward, almost a pace from Aisling and Lir, not far atop the dais. The son of Winter reached for Aisling, but Lir reacted quickly, summoning mighty roots before his brother's boots. The marble floors cracked before they exploded, debris flying across the hall.

"Lir, wait!" Fionn called above the mayhem. "Anduril does have but one condition."

Lir turned slightly, indicating Fionn to continue. In response, the Winter king sucked in a breath and swallowed hard.

"Lugh's spirit remains trapped within Anduril, animating the object with desire, thought, and ambition. And so"—Fionn swallowed again—"whosoever wears Anduril will share their spirit with Lugh."

The green of Lir's eyes turned an inhuman black. His attention darted to Anduril, glowing hotly on the son of Winter as if eager to be removed.

"*Bind him*," Lir said in Rún. "*Bind him and offer him to the bocanach, limb by limb.*"

Fionn turned to Aisling, searching her expression. A silent plea in the pinch of his brows.

"Or to Racat's physical body in the gorge," Lir continued, switching tongues effortlessly, "whoever will relish his death more."

"No," Fionn hissed so softly, only Aisling could hear. The panic in his voice, splintering something inside her. "You provoked me!"

"Take him now!" Lir yelled, his temper growing as each of his knights hesitated. Hands on the hafts of their age-old blades, yet their boots firmly planted on the ground.

Aisling gritted her teeth, forcing herself to meet their terrified expressions. Their fae features riddled with the haunting future Fionn described. That the Lady described. That Danu described. Each and all, forewarning of Lir and Aisling's union. Of Aisling's inability to save them. And a part of Lir's knights... believed it.

Galad, Gilrel, Peitho, Filverel—all had witnessed what Aisling and Lir's magic was capable of when they were together. Immense power but also inevitable destruction. And yet, *Imbolc* hadn't yet shown what a full release of either of their *draiocht* would look like. Perhaps, such a demonstration would be the last, Aisling realized to her own horror.

"Take him now!" Lir shouted again, the surrounding trees groaning with his rage.

"Wait," Aisling said as Galad charged forward first, his jaw clenched even as he bit through the paranoia. Their enemy's words that'd slipped through the cracks of Castle Annwyn like a vine between stones.

Aisling dared not meet Lir's gaze, afraid as any other of his wrath.

Galad grabbed Fionn—Cathan and Einri shortly behind. They pinned Fionn's arms behind his back, thorns climbing up his legs and around his wrists.

They tied Frigg's muzzle too, even as he clawed, and his barks were smothered. And if the belt could've aided Fionn in escaping Annwyn altogether, he never used it. Instead, he surrendered to Lir's knights and looked to Aisling until Anduril broke from the son of Winter's hips, slithering down his robes like a snake till it clinked against the marble of Lir's hall. Aisling eyed it, compelled to approach it by its otherworldly humming. A siren's call, enticing her nearer.

"Lir, stop," Aisling said, at last mustering the courage to spin on her heel and face the fae king.

His expression promised violence, tattooed hands white at the knuckles. And Aisling thanked the Forge the axes crossed at his throne weren't in his grip.

"He speaks only in mischief and tricks," Lir said, his voice terrifyingly soft as the fog before the storm.

"And yet he speaks the truth," Aisling said.

Lir's face shuddered, eyes widening with the horror of Aisling's words before he settled, once more, into quiet, shadowy rage.

He turned from Aisling and faced his throne, broad shoulders eclipsing him. This was Lir's way of ignoring—of *willing* the existence of this one, tragic truth into black oblivion. A gesture that shattered something in Aisling she couldn't quite describe. His back to her, a door slammed in the face.

"This might be the answer we've been searching for! My father has made use of dark spells and magic, we've all seen it and experienced it for ourselves!" Aisling yelled at Lir. "If we're to survive, we must also make use of every advantage possible. At whatever cost."

The Seelie king didn't react, didn't move, didn't speak. His mood thinly veiled by the groaning of the surrounding trees. So, Aisling climbed the steps of the dais, her skirts in one hand and the other reaching for Lir's arm so she could force him to face her. Her shoulder aching from her still tender arrow wound.

Lir turned and leaned toward her, dipping his chin as though to kiss her. As though to slide his hands around her waist and pull her close. To press his lips against her own and feel the rise and fall of her breast against his chest. To run his fingers through her hair.

Still, Lir didn't move further. Didn't flinch. He didn't need to. The maple leaves blooming from the antlers of their thrones, the redslips hanging overhead, the bark of every surrounding yew, and ash, and pine, and oak, bursting into flame, spoke for him. Every lick of flame rising toward the rafters with the pace of Aisling's heart.

"The world will burn if we continue this way," Aisling whispered, watching as he focused on her lips. "And then, we will have nothing."

"Then let it burn," Lir said. "Let it burn so long as you do not."

Aisling shut her eyes, the ache in her chest budding painfully.

"Perhaps," Aisling began, "perhaps, there's a future where we can have everything."

*Everything.*

The word hung between them, dripping with meaning like honey.

Lir's knights held Fionn firmly in their grip, his thorns digging into the flesh of his wrists and Frigg's muzzle the more they struggled.

"Perhaps we won't need to choose between each other and ruling—bearing dominion over everything. Perhaps, there's a way we can have both. But we cannot continue as we have... lest Danu, the Lady, and mankind use our recklessness—our weaknesses against us," Aisling said. "My father is more powerful than ever. You've seen the smoke in their eyes, the fire between their teeth, the strength of their iron."

Lir searched her violet eyes for what felt like an eternity, weighing her words in his mind. He ran his fingers through his dark hair, biting his bottom lip with his fangs.

"Is this what you want?" Lir asked at last. "In a few decades, I intend for your clann to perish—mortal flesh and bone no more than the ash from which they were born. On the other hand, what you covet is everlasting, and the risks... costly. If this is merely vengeance for the crimes of your father, your brother, I'll capture them for you, bend their crowns with my bare hands, and make them sing their apologies to you through pained and gnarled voices..."

"It's more than that," Aisling said. "It is who I am. I ventured through the North only to discover that who I am was nothing my hands could grapple externally, but rather the feral bloom within and present since birth. Since Ina hid it there. It is a hunger born in my blood and come alive with the will of Racat. It is the oak that my seed is destined to grow into. It is the reflection I desire. The 'me', I desire. And I fear I'll perish if this hunger is never slaked. If my bones never grow. If everything I've ever wanted and never had—power, sovereignty, the world —is never mine."

Lir's face grew shadows, and there was something animalistic in the way he studied her. He watched how her lips moved, listened to the clicking of her tongue, the sound of her blood running through her veins. A certain sadness clouded his gaze and poisoned the words that fell from his lips.

"If you continue to chase desire, you'll be in pursuit all your life," Lir said.

Aisling turned from him. The same sentiment had crossed her mind more than once. Aisling was indeed fearful that, like Racat, she'd never be fully satisfied. She'd once blazed through Unseelie-ridden forests, ran from the dark lord of the greenwood, escaped Fionn's ice fortress, and burned fleets of mortal men to discover who she was. And now that she knew, she couldn't help but seize it. Seize all her potential and never let it slip between her fingers like a dream she could wake from. The very possibility, spine-chilling.

And what's more, Aisling feared vulnerability. Feared being subject to another ever again—capable of being sold, of being traded, of being imprisoned. And so, she'd stop at nothing to harness who Ina intended her to be and ensure her clann, the world, never made her feel weak again. Aisling would stop at nothing to witness the regret in the eyes of those who'd wronged her.

"Perhaps," Aisling conceded. "But a wolf will never catch its prey if it ceases to hunt."

Lir rubbed the back of his neck—a habit he'd developed from reaching for his axes even when they weren't there, in times of need. But no blade could fight this battle for him. Once Aisling's mind was made up, all were aware that little, if anything, could change it.

"Very well," Lir said at last. "Whatever you covet, shall be my heart's labor."

And for reasons unknown to Aisling, the *draiocht* sealed the promise with an incorporeal laugh, punctuating Lir's words with a finality Aisling couldn't understand.

Aisling approached Anduril, still lying on the floor. She bent to collect it, admiring it in both hands.

The belt rang, vibrating through Aisling's palms, up her arms, and into her chest. Her *draiocht* responded immediately, flickering to life like a fire stoked. Its magic filled her, reaching out and familiarizing itself with her spirit with the belt's darkly gilded fingers. It was alive, Aisling could feel it. A heartbeat thrumming through her till it fell into pace with her own.

Slowly, Aisling clipped the belt around her hips. The belt was heavier than Aisling anticipated. And what's more, the belt's mysterious ringing ceased the moment Aisling took possession, followed by a ghostly silence.

Aisling shivered, every hair on her body standing straight.

# CHAPTER IV

## LIR

At the edge of the Isles of Rinn Dúin, the waves of the Ashild beat against the crags without reverence to their age-old songs. Only those taught to listen to the melody of the storm, the wind, the northern cliffs could hear their sad lullabies wailing for sorrow's sake.

Lir dismounted Flaithri and left him to stand guard between two rather self-pitying pines. Down he climbed, using the basalt columns to reach the hidden grotto where the ocean's edge frothed like a rabid animal.

Lithely, he leaped into the waters where he stood hip deep, the leather of his belt, his trousers, his boots absorbing the foam of its freshly stirred waters.

Lir closed his eyes, listening to the Ashild's moans. He took a deep breath, concentrating on its words and the story it longed to tell. That's how he knew he'd find her here, in this grotto. The ancient, gravelly voice of a being whose throat had been scraped with salt for millennia.

It was perhaps one or two heartbeats before their scales glittered beneath the surface. Ivory creatures that slithered like eels, their laughter echoed by the bubbles boiling like a cauldron around Lir.

Sakaala, a powerful merrow of the Ashild, emerged. Her slimy hair plastered to both her head and her bare breasts as she skulked up the jagged rocks to fully face Lir, the end of her tail twirling seductively, eager for his admiration.

He could smell her *draiocht*: charms of lust, of desperation, of need that sank more than its fair share of iron ships and mortal sailors. Its texture as smooth as obsidian pearls and its voice spilling from the gaping mouths of conch shells.

"*Mo Damh Bán*," she said, ruby lips enunciating every syllable, savoring his title on her tongue. Her pod of merrow were still dancing beneath the surface of the grotto.

"*Did you receive my owl?*" Lir asked in Rún.

"*Aye*," Sakaala replied. "*The Ashild is swarming with mortal galleons that carry some eternal flame on their masts.*"

Lir's mind flashed with the memory of *Imbolc*. The mortals had come with iron, with vengeance, and something else. Something burning between their teeth and simmering in their bellies, gurgled from the throat of shadow magic. *Scull draiocht*; a practice Lir had only ever witnessed once before in all his years and for good reason. In Annwyn, *scull draiocht* wasn't forbidden, but it was frowned upon. Nevertheless, the parasitic nature of such spellcasting—feeding off the soul instead of breath—was enough to deter most Sidhe from ever attempting it.

Lir bit down, his chest tight.

"*Both around the coast of Fjallnorr and all the Isles of Rinn Dúin, they sail*," Sakaala continued. "*Yet, they stay stagnant. Bobbing on the eager crests of waves that cannot break till the autumn storms arrive. Storms capable of crushing those manmade vessels into splinters. Three storm moons will pass shortly, and then the seas will be calm enough for mortal conquest.*"

"They have no intention of waiting so long," Lir replied, thinking out loud.

"*What* are they waiting for then?" Sakaala asked.

Lir hesitated, despite having toyed with this very question within the forest of his mind. The mortals had been silent since Aisling destroyed the majority of their fleets in Fjallnorr, most likely rebuilding their armies and licking their wounds until they were once more prepared to strike. So, Lir and the rest of the Sidhe hadn't expected an attack so soon—a mentality that'd cost them greatly at *Imbolc*.

Yet, the question remained: Why had they struck so soon after such a great defeat? And why riddle the northern seas when they could just as well attack on land?

"*I don't know*," Lir confessed, eyeing Sakaala carefully as she slithered off her rock and swam circles around him.

"*Then this is cause for concern indeed*," she said.

"These mortal fleets," Lir continued. "What colors did they bear?"

Sakaala thought for a moment, conjuring more bubbles in her wake.

"*Mortal tartans, crests, and sails from each of the seven continents; the Isles of Rinn Dúin, Centar, Bethel, Lilina, Ri, Shuilan, and Rolum.*"

Lir's heart dropped. This was no longer a feud between the northern Sidhe and mortals. The whole of the Earth was now embroiled in this conflict. And he should've known—should've anticipated quick mortal retaliation after everything Aisling had taken from them. Aisling, once the princess ambassador for their kind and now the destroyer of their people.

With hindsight, it was now obvious that not only the fire hand of the North, Aisling's father, but the whole of humankind wanted both swift vengeance and the realization of visions: Danu's and the Lady's claim that mankind would celebrate a final victory over the Sidhe.

Lir bared his fangs. He'd been too blissfully distracted by Aisling over the past weeks, and even now, he couldn't bring himself to regret the attention she stole. Was this a portion of how he and Aisling's union would inevitably destroy the world? The Sidhe king shuddered, the *draiocht* of the Lady's and Danu's prophecies spinning through the fabric of time and space to birth a life of its own. A first cry, shrieking into the caverns of the universe. Insidiously, their words, their visions, their prophecies, were already taking root. And Lir felt powerless.

"*What will you do, mo Damh Bán?*"

Lir fixed his eyes on the merrow, coming up for breath from the depths of his thoughts.

"*Aisling will win the gods' favor and bring an end to this within the fortnight. Long before autumn's storms or the mortals play their next move.*"

"*And then what?*" Sakaala pushed. "*Power and power and power and power. One wave rises as quickly as it breaks. No matter how often it swells and storms and the ocean churns, the waves will always break. Power is not the answer. It is fleeting.*"

"*No, but it is a tool. One I'd rather have than not.*"

"*At what cost?*"

"*Everything.*"

"*Because you desire such ambition?*" Sakaala said. "*Or...*" She paused, the corners of her lips curling knowingly. "*Because the not-so mortal queen desires it?*"

Lir flared with annoyance, doing his best to resist Sakaala's provocations.

"*Tell me, mo Damh Bán,*" Sakaala continued. "*What is it the dark lord of the forest wants?*" The merrow flicked her tail, playfully splashing Lir. "*What is it your heart desires above all else?*"

Against his own volition, exactly what Lir coveted most was summoned to the forefront of his mind. Violet eyes and raven-black hair filling him to the bone with the flames of fathomless longing. With obsession. He, spellbound by her courage, her ambition, her will. By the savage, wild magic her smile conjured. The way her body moved when she danced after too much wine. The way she glanced at him when she believed him unaware. The personification of a prayer turned poetry, sung to those whose soul bled darkly.

Before Aisling, he'd wanted power for the sake of Annwyn; the legacy of his mother and father. A child for the sake of Annwyn. He'd wanted the extinction of the human race. He'd wanted the fire hand's blood at the edge of his axe. The wings Danu had ripped from his back, returned. And while he still yearned for—*needed*—all of those, there was something else—*someone* else—that'd become a priority.

A part of Lir could've blamed this shift on his and Aisling's consummation. Magic two *caeras* shared that bound them tightly by threads of fate. But the Sidhe king was more honest with himself than that. His utmost desires had changed long before then. Perhaps when he'd first set eyes on a mortal princess beneath a crimson veil.

"*Mo Damh Bán?*" Sakaala, once more, burst the enchantment. Lir whipped his attention toward the merrow.

"*Keep an eye on any and all mortal fleets, especially those closest to any Sidhe kingdoms,*" he said, redirecting the conversation. "*If anything changes—if there is any movement at all—send a message to me.*"

Lir turned, climbing back toward Flaithri and out of the grotto.

"*Very well, mo Damh Bán,*" Sakaala said, bowing her head.

"And Sakaala," Lir called out before the merrow submerged again, "*there's a new village being built off the coast of Aithirn. They're new to the land and haven't yet become acquainted with the legends that might've otherwise advised them against building a coastal community. Feel free to indulge in those waters.*"

Compensation for Sakaala's efforts that undoubtedly endangered the aquatic Sidhe.

The merrow grinned, ear to ear.

*"Seliac niv lenelle santi lelluna, te mes crai sen shetek duachte my frei lewen,"* she said.

*Despite bitter winter and its formidable blade, even death's knee will bend to the bloom.*

A bidding of good luck the Forge knew Lir needed.

Lir and Galad descended the spiral staircase, greeted by a chill far more potent than even Castle Annwyn's dungeons were accustomed to. A century-old badger guided them through the dimness, carrying a lantern of brightly glowing flower bulbs that shuddered with the cold. The hoop of keys, dangling at the badger's belt, jingled every step further into the abyss.

*"I thought you bespelled his draiocht,"* Galad said, eyeing the frost that stuck against the stones and their coats of moss.

Lir worked his jaw. *"Aisling requested the enchantment be broken. If it were my decision, my brother would've suffocated under such spells the night of Imbolc."*

Galad grimaced at the ice glazing the steps thickly now.

*"It isn't like her,"* Galad continued. *"She's usually more..."*

*"Merciless?"* Lir asked.

*"Unforgiving."*

Galad, Lir, and the badger exchanged glances.

*"Fionn is a tool for Aisling,"* Lir explained. *"And if Aisling is anything, it's clever. She's well adept at compartmentalizing her feelings to find an advantage in favor of her ends. Something more of the Sidhe, including myself, would do well to mirror if we're to rewrite prophecies."*

Galad nodded in understanding, opening his mouth to speak but thinking better of it. The winter Lir's dungeons were now possessed with, was more than enough to herald Fionn's growing presence. For wherever the air grew cold, Fionn would be listening.

At long last, the badger shuffled onto sheets of ice in the pure dark, nothing but his lantern to shed light on the wooden boat, frozen where the pools of a cistern once rippled. Pools bewitched by Angharad, a water nymph from Niltaor, who Bres —Lir's father—commissioned to enchant the waters so that whosoever stood within their depths, suffered from a mind lost between clouds, a soothed spirit, and an eagerness to both stay and rest. A brew one yawn short of a sleep potion. However, such *draiocht* was petrified by the same winter that froze a forest solid.

Lir reached for a nearby flower. He blew against its petals once, twice, thrice.

The flower's petals floated away, multiplying into billions of new buds, brightening the room till the impression of daylight was given and all could be seen.

Colossal pillars, carved in the image of bucking stags carried the barreled, mosaic ceilings on their antlers. They protected the willows that grew upside down, branches plunging into the waters of the cistern and forming various cages with their limbs. Here, in Castle Annwyn's dungeons, prisoners would rot waist-deep in both the pitch dark and Angharad's enchanted waters.

Yet, the behemoth willow—that caged the son of Winter at the far end of the cistern—was frozen solid. Now, it resembled an ice giant's hand, punching down to protect Lir's elder brother from the summer green of his forest kingdom. Fionn and Frigg were shielded between the giant's fingers.

Lir buried his irritation and Fionn's silvery eyes twinkled with interest, his chin lifting the moment Lir and Galad's boots set foot on the ice, forgoing the boat they would've once sailed to access each cell, and approaching on foot. The badger was shortly behind.

"*I expected to see you sooner, brother,*" Fionn said, listlessly reclining on jagged ice as though it were cushions and pelts. He didn't move, didn't so much as stand, the image of a king interrupted whilst relaxing in his throne room. Yet, the hollows of his eyes betrayed him—the hungry curve of his lips when he flashed his fangs.

"*How long has it been?*" Lir asked, feigning sincerity. The other prisoners they passed, nothing more than piles of bones, half-submerged beneath frozen waters.

"*Three days give or take,*" Frigg snapped.

"*When Aisling convinced you to let me aid you both and the Sidhe at large, I didn't realize that meant my accommodations would remain those that once imprisoned me,*" Fionn said.

"*And after three days in these dungeons, I anticipated more enthusiasm at our arrival.*" Lir stopped a few paces from Fionn's cell. Galad and the badger following suit.

"*Let's see.*" Fionn, at last, straightened, studying Lir and Galad more closely.

"*Your hands are empty. So are your pockets stuffed with fog pastries, yule gelatin, or twelfthtide rolls?*" Frigg asked.

"*If not,*" Fionn added, "*then our indifference at your arrival is better exchanged with the disappointment you aren't your caera.*"

Lir grinned, flashing his fangs like a wolf before it bites. That familiar, warm shadow spreading beneath his skin with violence.

The Sidhe king crouched beside the cage. Now, he met Fionn's stare where the son of Winter sat, lazily unsheathing one of his axes and lodging its blade into the ice beside him in the same movement. The cistern juddered with his strength. "*So, tell me what you have planned.*"

"*I've said it before, yet I'll say it again: my plan is the same as yours,*" Fionn replied, dusting the chips of ice from Lir's axe off his shoulder.

"*A death wish then,*" Galad said.

"*To prevent Danu's and the Lady's visions from manifesting,*" Fionn corrected, holding Lir's glare. "*If you're thinking what I'm thinking...*" He smirked. "*I was the Sidhe's and all of the Other's best chance at ensuring the mortals' defeat once and for all. That their prophecies never came to fruition. Yet, as the Forge would have it, now we're left with you and must make do with the spells dealt, lest all our skulls rest on iron pikes a decade from now.*"

Lir studied his brother, listening for signs of deceit. Of word play, of charms, or vulnerabilities. The light of his eyes was so like their mother's—Ina's—it was terrible. Painful to behold and more torturous to recognize.

"*I cannot rewrite a loss,*" Fionn continued, "*but I can still endeavor to never repeat one. As of right now, you and Aisling bear sovereignty over the twelve Sidhe kingdoms and the Unseelie as both wielders of Racat and rulers of Annwyn. Despite our differences, I'd say—given the current climate—you're better positioned to prevent that which is the death of the Sidhe, of Oighir, and of myself. So call it self-preservation, call me your fair-weather friend, but, by the Forge, let us put the past behind us.*"

Lir straightened. Unfurling from his crouch, he lifted his axe from the ice and rested it on his shoulder.

The badger, Galad, and Fionn all hung on Lir's every breath. Aisling had chosen to accept Fionn's aid to defeat a common enemy, but nothing was etched in stone nor any bargains sealed.

"*I'd rather not,*" Lir said flippantly. "*But I'll honor Aisling's choice regardless.*"

The Sidhe king turned and started back across the cistern. Fionn's expression flashed with panic, before swiftly collecting itself.

"*You're expected in the great hall by dusk,*" Lir called back, Galad and the badger on his heels. And as the dark lord crossed the threshold to ascend the stairwell—Fionn and Frigg staring up at him—the flowers dimmed and the dungeons plunged into oblivion once more.

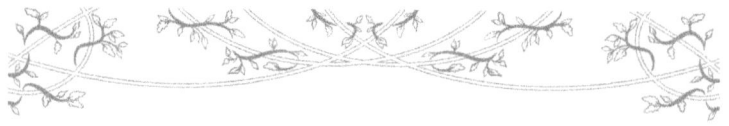

# CHAPTER V

AISLING

Beyond Annwyn's gorge and past the oak tree meadows, grew a grove of willows. After *Imbolc*, Spring had arrived and the swaying branches flowered, dappling the blue pond beneath them in a confection of petals. The edges of the pond foamed and bubbled with lavender and indigo soaps. The water sprites that lived here were generous, always eager to share their lotions, their clay, and their perfumes with Aisling and Peitho when they'd come to bathe.

Gilrel stood watch just outside the veil of weeping leaves, blade at the ready.

"Turn over every stone until the Goblet is found," Peitho said, running her fingers through Aisling's wet tresses, careful to avoid the butterflies that crowned her.

"How will I know where to begin looking? I imagine the Other is vast—near limitless. Is it even possible to find that which was hidden by the gods themselves?" Aisling asked, Anduril's metal growing hot at her hips at any taste of her *draiocht* waking with anticipation. Aisling hadn't yet received an opportunity to test the belt's effectiveness. It neither hummed nor rang. It neither glowed nor shone when Aisling summoned her *draiocht*. It was silent as if waiting for something. A fact which bred unease in Aisling.

"Most legendary objects enjoy discovery," Peitho said, eyes flicking to Anduril at Aisling's waist before swiftly turning away. "Half their power is born of its master's attention and desire to wield. If you seek the Goblet, so, too, will it seek you."

Aisling swallowed looking down at her nakedness—she was dressed in nothing but pond waters and Anduril, shimmering in the sprites' soap bubbles.

"And how should the gods find me worthy then? Will they measure my worth by the hunt or the discovery of the Goblet alone?" Aisling asked.

"It's up to the discretion of the gods," Peitho said, her work effortless and graceful. "According to the Lore, Niamh was gifted the Goblet. But as for the gods' favor—"

"She found the Goblet once herself?" Aisling asked.

"Not quite. The gods lent Niamh the Goblet temporarily. She was allowed a single sip before the brother gods tucked the Goblet away once more, beyond even Niamh's knowledge. My mother and father have little first-hand recollection. But the tales passed down from Lugh are remarkable," Peitho said. "It's said Niamh went in pursuit of the Goblet even after the gods had snatched it back and buried it in oblivion. It was in this search for the Goblet that Niamh first learned to bewitch her sword, Sarwen. The only reason she returned to her castle alive. No ordinary creature traverses the Other's darkest corners without facing its wilderness nor the lesser gods it hides."

Aisling shifted.

"In that case, gods bless this belt," Aisling said, aware she was no fighter nor swordswoman, and without Anduril, Aisling stood less of a chance of earning the gods' favor.

Peitho, however, didn't mirror Aisling's relief. Instead, her cornelian eyes narrowed, and her lips pursed.

"You should remove that belt from time to time," Peitho said, brows furrowing as she turned from Aisling.

"I want to familiarize myself with it and allow it to familiarize itself with me," Aisling said, speaking her thoughts aloud for the first time.

Peitho's expression flashed with horror before recovering once more. She smiled, but it never reached her eyes.

"Be careful with enchanted armor, weaponry, and tonics, Aisling. They aren't to be used recklessly."

"I treasure Anduril," Aisling protested.

"That's what concerns me," Peitho said.

"Is this because Oighir stole Anduril from Niltaor?" Aisling asked, cutting straight to the point.

Peitho stuttered, taken aback but swiftly collecting herself.

"Aye, the history of Anduril is complex and far from agreed upon in legend," Peitho confessed.

Anduril grew hotter, almost scalding Aisling's hips whenever its name was spoken aloud.

"Tell it to me," Aisling said, lifting her chin so the sprites could scrub down the length of her neck, her clavicle, and her shoulders while the butterflies pinned her dripping curls.

Peitho exhaled, muttering something in the divine language Aisling couldn't quite understand.

"As with most magicked objects, Anduril was once ordinary," Peitho began. "Anduril was a lover's gift given to a trooping Sidhe of the wintertide court from the armor of Lugh. During the Wild Hunt, the lover returned the belt to Lugh hoping the token would breed good fortune for Lugh and Niltaor as a whole. At the time, Niltaor was a kingdom of gold—unconquerable. Until..." Peitho's voice trailed off, her fingers toying with the suds falling down the angles of her tattooed arms.

"Until," Aisling encouraged her.

"Until a *dragún*, Muirdris, was within reach and Lugh was driven mad by its proximity—its spear-tipped tail always just outside his grasp. Lugh grew obsessed with victory, with war, with the hunt, stopping at nothing to at last capture the *dragún* for himself and for Niltaor. And so, when he believed he could trap Muirdris within the confines of Niltaor's walls as it feasted on his baited soldiers, he called upon the sun for every morsel of its blazing power in honor of the South."

"Did it work?" Aisling asked.

Peitho nodded her head. "Aye. The skies turned black while Lugh drained the sun of its light. But its power went not to Lugh but rather Anduril, slung across his armor and reflecting the very light he sought for himself from the polished faces of the belt's metal."

"And so, Anduril became enchanted," Aisling concluded.

"This is what the Sidhe refer to as *scull draiocht*. Magic that takes not from the breath but from the soul."

Aisling repeated the name silently to herself.

"Some say Anduril wields the power of the southern sun," Peitho continued. "Others claim it trapped Lugh's spirit for eternity. The latter being why his lover claimed Anduril after his subsequent death, stealing and hoarding it in the North so they might be with Lugh in some capacity."

Aisling turned to face Peitho.

"Lugh perished?" she asked.

Peitho exhaled. "No creature, man or Sidhe, is forged to carry such power. It is the pursuit of such might that has led to the fall of various men and Sidhe alike. And it's the reason Niltaor is nothing more than rubble now—a ghost of its previous glory."

Anduril pulsed with heat and for the first time since Aisling had clipped the belt to her waist, the Blood Cord hummed again.

"Have caution with Anduril," Peitho warned again. "Creatures that cannot speak are masters of secrecy—others' and their own."

At this, Anduril winked, gleaming more brightly the longer Aisling considered it. Anduril would do what none other could: make a warrior of the sorceress. And so, secrets or not, Aisling couldn't bring herself to remove it—even for a short while.

The Lady kissed Aisling's cheek when she slipped into her bed chamber. Aisling slept before dinner, draped across pelts and quilts and lost to the world of dreams. So the Lady dug her nails into Aisling's mind and scratched.

*An iron blade speared a great tree. A river of blood spilled from the open wound as the tree swayed back and forth, screaming in agony and eager to lift its roots from the earth so it might run.*

*The tree managed to turn itself upright, daring a glance over its shoulder before it dove into the hollows of the greenwood once more. Its ancient eyes glimmered with fear.*

*Incorporeal, Aisling watched like a lesser god from above, stuck somewhere in between reality and the land of dreams, recognizing the beast immediately.*

*Leshy.*

*It made one, two steps before the blade flew once more. Soil was upturned, stones, leaves and debris showering the mortal as the tree walked on thick roots like writhing snakes. Needle-thin, the sword shot through the smoke-dense air, seemingly wielded by an invisible knight. But Aisling recognized both the sword and its master before either were near enough for the sorceress to see closely.*

*Starn followed his enchanted sword—one gifted by the Lady.*

*A group of mortal knights followed shortly behind, heeding her eldest brother's orders with impressive obedience. Eyes red with flame that spread wildly through the forest like hunting dogs. They climbed atop the writhing tree, poking the beast with their iron weapons, chains, and torches. A shadow of dark magic pressing down on the forest.*

*Their every movement was uncanny. Eyes bright with strange flame and teeth stained with soot. There was magic at work here. Something dark. Something wrong. Something stolen.* Scull draiocht.

*"Keep it alive!" Starn shouted to his men. "It cannot give us what we want if it's dead."*

*The tree flung itself to the side and the mortal men atop, including Starn, flew like ants across the forest. They groaned as they collapsed against the earth—some caught in trees.*

*"Again!" Starn shouted in a fit of coughs from the smoke. He staggered to his feet, bidding his blade dart for the tree once more. It swung its great body further into the forest, desperately trying to disappear. It moved quickly, awkwardly, roots and branches breaking as it shoved itself through the densest corridors of the greenwood.*

*Starn's men pursued it, shouting at one another, but it was futile. Leshy moved quickly despite its injuries.*

*The tree left a trail of blood in its wake. Every droplet stank and steamed, but where it pooled on the forest floor from Starn's violence, flowers, clovers, and fruit grew in its place. Vines bloomed from the blood and wrapped themselves around the limbs of prone mortals, eager to prevent more mortal destruction.*

*Still, Starn hunted Leshy, devoured by the forest as he sunk deeper into its depths in pursuit, his blade just ahead.*

Aisling knew not what chaos her clann was brewing. Only that the Lady teased her with glimpses of their progress from time to time, eager to watch Aisling squirm.

For as long as Castle Annwyn remembered, sylphs haunted their passages. And the great hall was no exception. A sylph flew between branches tangled in the rafters and squeezed their berries between its fingertips. Juice dribbled down their fingers and into Aisling's glass, the consistency of blood and the taste of seed-filled marmalades. The Seelie queen gulped until it stained her lips red. The sylphs above giggled, searching for another bottle to offer Aisling.

Galad and Gilrel sat on either side of her while Peitho and Filverel ate quietly further down the table. Two chairs left empty.

Their quiet was louder than usual considering the great hall wasn't booming with music, the laughter of tipsy animals, nor the rustling of skirts and wings as the Sidhe danced till they were left breathless. Annwyn still mourned the tragedy of *Imbolc*—a celebration meant to herald life but that was now tainted with so much death. And what's more, Lir requested this meeting be kept private, only inviting the members seated around the table. A request made after Aisling had learned that Lir visited Fionn in the dungeons.

Aisling nodded and the sylphs unstoppered the next bottle.

At long last, the entrance was pulled open by seven or so owls—ribbons in their beaks tied to the gold hoops embroidered along the doors' edges.

Unceremoniously, Lir walked into the great hall.

The sylphs sucked in a collective breath, eyes of fog, glistening. And every clover, every bluethorn, every bat sleeping behind the beams and branches, perked up, buzzing with the presence of their sovereign.

"*Mo Damh Bán*," Filverel said and the room pushed back their chairs to stand. All except Aisling who kept her eyes fixed on the Sidhe king, measuring his every gesture. She hadn't seen him since they'd all spoken in the throne room the day following *Imbolc*. Lir was usually elusive, but when chaos unraveled—especially within his kingdom's walls—he was a ghost vanishing from room to room, his attention demanded by everyone and everything.

Lir took his seat beside Aisling, a swarm of sylphs darting to be the first to fill his glass.

He glanced at Aisling. The moment their eyes met, Aisling's heart ached. She realized she'd die of such pain if it meant waiting all her life to endure it again. Yet, something was different. Aisling could feel Anduril taking in the sight of the Sidhe king as well. The belt observed, watching and listening closely to the way Aisling's heart raced in Lir's presence.

"*Ellwyn*." Lir greeted Aisling, a playful smile brushing across his lips. Lips Aisling's gaze lingered on a moment too long, for Lir's smile grew wider, collapsing shortly thereafter when Anduril caught his attention, beaming from where it wrapped around Aisling's waist.

Lir frowned but said nothing. Aisling felt Lir's obsession with her as richly as she felt hers for him, and yet, Lir was still the nightmare legend spoken of around the hearth and creeping into the sweet dreams of children taught to fear the woodland and the wilds. He, the brutal, barbarian king of the Aos Sí—and no amount of lust, of want, of affection, of obsession could let Aisling forget it.

"Should we begin?" Filverel asked.

Lir leaned back in his seat, eyes flicking to the doors he'd just entered. The flowers released a collective "brr" as all attention centered on Fionn's silhouette, Frigg a pace behind. Lir's thorns were still tightly wrapped around Fionn's wrists and Frigg's muzzle.

Peitho huffed, crossing her arms. The rest felt similarly—

perhaps having hoped that Lir had killed Fionn regardless of Aisling's wishes—but none said a word as the son of Winter took his seat around the table. Silver eyes searching for Aisling's and locking into place once they had.

"Now you can begin," Fionn said as Frigg paced behind his chair. "Unless you'd like to remove these first." Fionn raised his hands, gesturing toward the thorny shackles.

Filverel, instead, exhaled, exchanging glances with Peitho before, reluctantly, continuing. "Tonight, at the stroke of midnight, is Niamh's own version of *Imbolc: Là Brear*."

"The Isle of Rain's welcoming of the storm season," Gilrel explained to Aisling, stabbing her potatoes with her wooden fork.

"I've sent a message to Niamh and received a response just this morning," Filverel said, reaching into his tunic's breast pocket. The advisor pulled out a folded piece of parchment, its resplendent seal already cracked in half.

Aisling leaned forward in her chair, eyes locked on the letter.

"Word from the Other?" Aisling asked. Indeed, Niamh, the Seelie queen of the Isle of Rain, lived in the Forge's realm.

"It isn't often we communicate, considering all interaction with the Other is dealt in invitations," Filverel explained. "But once a year, each Sidhe sovereign is invited to the Other for Niamh's celebration. One of the only times of the year one can step into the gods' plane and not be carried away by the Other's death galleon. The second is *Samhain*, of course."

"And the celebrations are always marvelous," Peitho said. "The gowns, the music, Castle Yillen..." Peitho trailed off, eyes sparkling with memories.

Aisling perked up.

"So, why has Aisling received more than one invitation from Ina previously?" Gilrel asked. Ina, Lir and Fionn's mother—the

Seelie queen of the mountains and the reason for the existence of mortals.

"An answer I assume sits with Niamh," Lir said, taking a sip from his goblet. Filverel and Galad nodded their heads in agreement.

Aisling's brow furrowed. "What happened to those Sidhe who chose to return without invitation?"

"Those who snuck into the Other uninvited?" Gilrel clarified.

"They were fed to demons this plane knows not of," Frigg growled. "Monsters your nightmares couldn't fathom, but that roam the Other hungry for fleshling souls, sucking on bones and slobbering over rotting corpses."

Aisling's stomach knotted.

"He's toying with you, *mo Lúra*," Fionn said, hissing something beneath his breath to Frigg.

"So, there are no monsters?"

"No, there are," Fionn confessed and the pit in Aisling's stomach deepened. "But no one knows what happens to those Sidhe who venture uninvited. Only that they never return. Most believe they're either slaughtered by the gods themselves, boiled in the Forge, or, in my opinion, stuck between worlds."

*Stuck.*

Aisling shuddered. "Then for what reason would Ina summon me to the Other in the past?"

Glances darted back and forth across the table, perhaps searching for the answers none bore. Indeed, Ina had invited Aisling on several occasions—the first being a few weeks after she'd first arrived in Annwyn: a garden snake had led her down Ina's wing and revealed the previous Seelie queen's fountain and portal to the Other.

"Ina was clever enough to hide Racat and thus, the curse breaker, in the den of the thief himself: Nemed, his utmost desire buried deep inside his daughter's heart," Galad said. "He who leads the race Ina created by accident from the bones of her very people."

Both Lir and Fionn bristled.

"Surely she never anticipated he nor his son would be willing to carve such victories from the chest of their only daughter and sister," Peitho rationalized.

"No," Gilrel said, "she didn't. Aisling is Ina's gift from the gods by nature. She wouldn't have ever subjected her to such a fate."

It felt likely enough and yet, the uncertainty all felt toward Ina's intentions vegetated in the room—stank until every nose wrinkled with the anxiety of the unknown. The inevitable fear of what they were willingly stepping into.

Lir cleared his throat.

"What does the letter say?"

The room's attention returned to the parchment in Filverel's hand.

The advisor unrolled the letter and pinned it to the table with an ivory knife.

*When the days lengthen and the wildlings crawl from their slumber,*
*Woke by warm breezes, by berries, by nuts—your hunger,*
*They'll come with the rain.*
*When the ice melts and the forest thaws, crying out in pain,*
*The clouds will gather and break,*
*And the seedlings will be slaked.*
*So I pray,*
*That you'll come with the rain.*

-Niamh-

Another invitation.

This time, one for everyone who'd read Niamh's quill strokes.

The table exhaled, eyes darting back and forth across the parchment as though it hid more than a mere invitation. As though whatever trickery—real or not—would be exposed by glaring at the letter long enough.

"What does one wear to *Lá Brear* on such short notice?" Peitho said, the first to break concentration.

"Whatever you choose. We'll need to gather in Ina's wing when the last star joins the night sky," Filverel said.

"That's not long from now." Peitho stood from her seat, inspecting the cornelian embroidered gown she already wore—a garment far too humble for a celebration, especially by Peitho's standards.

"That's too soon," Galad said. "We haven't prepared. Haven't planned—"

"We ask for Niamh's compliance," Gilrel said. "It isn't so complicated; so long as Niamh allows us the opportunity to earn the gods' favor and, in turn, her Goblet of Lore, then our task—for the moment—is complete. At that point, we need only wait for whatever hoops she wishes us to jump through."

"You drawl as though it's simple," Fionn said, setting his shackled wrists onto the edge of the table. "Niamh, now, is most likely curious as to our motives considering Lir's and Aisling's choices going forward will affect all the Sidhe whether they reside in the Other or in the mortal plane. That's why she's invited us. We cannot overestimate her affection for us. Especially as word of *Imbolc*'s tragedy has no doubt already reached the Isle of Rain and other Sidhe might fear Lir's and Aisling's power."

"It matters not. She'll stand to help against the mortals," Galad said.

Aisling looked down at her hands in her lap and then at Anduril, glowing softly as if listening intently. Lir's eyes flicked to the belt, turning to slits as he considered it. And in response, Anduril seemingly growled at the fae king and his oppressive attention.

"Regardless," the son of Winter continued. "Aisling and Lir shouldn't be near one another at all unless absolutely necessary."

Now Lir did move, grinning from ear to ear wolfishly. But it was absent of its playful nuance, filled to the bone with a cruelty that sent the sylphs above cowering.

"How convenient," the dark lord said. "But I won't be separated from Aisling."

"Just until we obtain the gods' favor and the Goblet," Galad said, gesturing toward Niamh's invitation.

"You agree with him?" Lir asked Galad, a glint of betrayal sweeping across his features before fading behind his facade once more.

Galad pressed the heels of his palms into his eyes. "Your *draiocht*, together, is unpredictable, uncontrollable. Every touch between the two of you encourages whatever power your union bears. Until we better understand it, isn't it wise to abstain from provoking it? Or at the very least, allowing it to mature when the fate of our worlds depends upon it?"

Lir cursed beneath his breath, seeming to dare a look at Aisling.

Anduril grew hot, warming Aisling's flesh beneath her gown with an intensity she couldn't understand.

Whatever Aisling and Lir's union was, the mere mention of it sent Racat writhing inside her. Her *draiocht*, alive and humming to the potential of Lir's whenever she was beside him. And touching him... every day the sensations, the magnitude of their connection grew, and a part of Aisling wondered if she could withstand it. Similar thoughts, Aisling imagined, ran through Lir's mind as well.

And yet, there was something more. Something she desperately tried to untangle in her mind whenever the Sidhe king appeared in her thoughts. Anduril hummed more loudly, growing heavier at her hips.

"Very well," Lir said to everyone's surprise. Lir stood from the table and started toward the door. The room, the forest, the sylphs all staring after him and the night beyond, twinkling from the corridor's balcony. A single star short from joining the moon's procession; the time to leave was nigh.

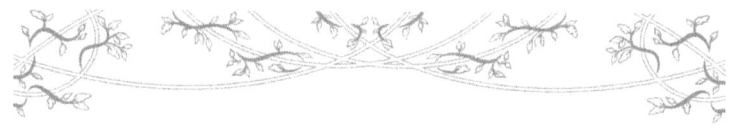

# CHAPTER VI

LIR

Heartbroken, Annwyn's wolves howled. Just as the alders soaked themselves in the blood of its berries in mourning, so, too, did the wolves cry, remembering *Imbolc* and all that was lost. Lir tasted Annwyn's grief like one drank from a chalice, gulping until every drop slid across his tongue and the burden of Annwyn's sorrows was made less. So was his responsibility as high king of the Sidhe and wielder of the twin blades. Lir, the forest, and the *draiocht* were one; his despair, mirrored in the inky veins from the five-pointed leaves sailing into Castle Annwyn on the current of evening's breath.

Lir stood bent over a table. Both palms were pressed into its edge while his eyes wandered across its surface again and again, memorizing the pieces scattered across a map of the mortal plane. The emeralds, carved into ash leaves, represented the Sidhe, their kingdoms, and their legions. The rubies stood for the mortals, spreading across the map like embers in a summer forest.

Only that morning, Lir had received three owls. One from Niltaor in the south, Sheka in the far east, and Reili farther west. Each spoke of mortal sightings just beyond their kingdoms, creeping closer with their scarlet torches crackling in the dead of night, their steel clanking, their boots marching. Stepping nearer and nearer to enemy territory, yet just out of reach. The seas were swarming with fiery ships that left tendrils of smoke in their wake, bobbing before the storm moons. They were everywhere, marring the world black with their influence.

Lir and each of his knights had organized the gems across the map to identify a pattern. Something—anything—to give insight into the mortals' minds. And yet, Lir couldn't decipher their movements. Thus far, Annwyn was the only kingdom that had been directly attacked... but for how long? The question weighed heavily on Lir's mind. He'd assigned all the bears and wolves to guard Annwyn's borders whilst every fox camped in the canopies, reeds at the ready for another assault. But the mortals remained silent, fleeing back to their iron bastions and naval fleets to prepare for more bloodshed, Lir imagined.

Lir leaned back for the first time in hours, pressing the heels of his palms to his eyes. The rest of his knights had retired long ago and now, only Lir remained.

"Staring at this map will not grant insight into the fire hand's mind," Filverel had said when he'd clapped a hand to Lir's shoulder before taking his leave. This much, Lir knew. And still, Annwyn needed his strength, his cunning, his protection. Lest what occurred at *Imbolc* repeat itself.

Lir stepped back from the table. From the corner of his eye, beyond the arched windows, a flock of strawberry finches burst from their nests down below and shot into the sky. Lir felt their alarm as they took flight and their relief as they beat their wings against a starry sky—at last, to safety.

Heart racing, the Sidhe king approached the windows and looked down.

From where Lir stood, he could just see the stained glass bridge that connected the base of Castle Annwyn's mountain to the forest, nestled over an angry, foaming river. And inside the bridge, was the shadowy silhouette of a maiden.

Lir took another step closer to the window, narrowing his eyes to better make sense of the vision. From what Lir could tell, she was beautiful. Artfully, she moved the feminine lines of her body like a willow in a storm. And, despite the weight of her blade, she stepped with all the grace of Lir's swordmaidens, the tenacity of his woodland vipers, and the bite of his wolves. Lir took another step closer, his *draiocht* thrashing inside inexplicably. He hummed the beast inside into acquiescence and still the spells of enchantment this maiden cast with the arch of her blade did not break. This stranger, brandishing a sword as well, if not better, as any of his knights.

Light-footed, Lir tore through Castle Annwyn till he reached the dank depths of the mountain. Here, the moisture from the surrounding rivers, the rain, and the inside of the mountain curled his hair and dressed the walls with moss. Lir's and Aisling's chambers were in the tallest tower and so, Lir rarely ventured this deep into his castle, nor cared to. Nevertheless, his boots—seemingly bewitched—led him nimbly to the stained-glass bridge that veiled the maiden's identity.

Like a shadow, Lir leaped onto the bridge's landing. The constant roar of the river would've masked a mortal's footsteps and so, a Sidhe king was practically invisible to any knight—Sidhe or not. And this swordmaiden was deep in concentration, facing the mouth of the bridge that led into the feywilds, her back turned as Lir came into sight.

Lir froze.

Moonlight spilled through the panes of stained glass, coloring the inside of the bridge in blood reds, royal blues, forest greens, and treasure yellows. Still, Lir recognized the maiden at first glance. Felt the rhythm of her heart, beating against his own before he laid eyes on her. Understood the pace of her breath even despite the colors that masked the signature ink of her tresses or the violet of her eyes.

Aisling moved like a creature loyal to the order of the moon; always shifting with the shadows, elegant, lovely, and bitingly attractive reflective eyes seducing those weak-willed enough to venture into her keep. And although Lir's will was far from weak, Aisling's presence rendered the lord of the greenwood's character inconsistent.

Lir forgot himself. He stood like an oak on a windless day, watching her practice with a gleeful Sarwen. Every step was made with the wisdom of a knight who'd battled for centuries and yet, only yesterday, Aisling had struggled to lift Sarwen from her scabbard.

Without thinking, Lir stepped closer. And as though he'd snapped a branch in a quiet wood, Aisling turned, her body going rigid. She shouldn't have been able to hear him, but perhaps their bond signaled his proximity the way it did him.

"*Ellwyn*," Lir said, his gaze softening in greeting. Aisling's lips bent strangely, her eyes studying him with Sarwen still poised in her unyielding grip.

Aisling glared at Lir like a fox considers the hunter—a foreign intruder whose presence was wholly unwelcome. As if she considered locking her jaws around his throat or scurrying into the forest. Without recognition.

The belt—Anduril held her body, but Lugh watched the Sidhe king through Aisling's eyes, staring down the grooves of the blade.

"Ash," Lir said again, hoping it would burst the spell Anduril had woven. And yet, the light of recognition Lir hoped would shine in her eyes instead came from Anduril hanging at her hips, flashing as if its own name had been spoken.

An unfamiliar dread filled Lir to the bone. Something dark

and sticky growing beneath his skin. This was more than Lugh's spirit merely joining Aisling's own.

The Sidhe king shifted, and it was the first mistake of many.

Aisling lunged for him.

The tip of Sarwen aimed for Lir's heart, so the Sidhe king stepped to the side. Aisling turned on her heel without hesitation, catching Lir off guard. She swung her elbow back hard, aiming for Lir's jaw before turning the opposite direction with her blade. Lir leaned back, narrowly missing the blunt of her elbow before angling himself away from Sarwen's edge once more.

"Ash," he said, and Anduril glowed brighter. Aisling raised Sarwen and jabbed, forcing Lir's axes from their bandolier and into his hands. The Sidhe king blocked the strike, blade upon blade ringing through the bridge and into the forest.

"Ash, what are you doing?" he asked as they stood nose to nose, an axe and a sword between them. Aisling's eyes flared a brighter shade of violet. Her cheeks flushed red, and her lips parted the way they always did when she wanted to kiss him. Lir shuddered, transfixed by the supple curve of her ruby frown the angrier she became. She was feral. The heat of her magic crawled up his boots, his legs, his chest until it gripped him and held him—invisible to the eye yet scalding to the soul.

Lir leaned forward, starving to feel her mouth on his own. His second mistake.

Aisling shoved him away, spun low, and struck him in the legs with the head of Sarwen's pommel.

Lir lost his balance, staggering backward.

"Aisling," he said, almost breathless—in shock. He lowered his axes.

"Who are you?!" she shouted at last. "Why do you speak my name?!" Her voice was animalistic, wild.

Lir inhaled sharply. He searched her expression, desperate for a sign of recognition, for a symptom of trickery or mischief.

But only Anduril spoke, shining brightly as if freshly pulled from the molten fires of the Forge. The Sidhe king swallowed, his tongue almost turned to ash. That tar-black, sticky dread, bleeding him from the inside.

Lir opened his mouth to speak, but the words fell from his tongue in silence. His mind was overwhelmed with questions, thrashing like a muzzled wolf dying to bite. How far away was Aisling's spirit now and could he speak to her? His mind spun with concern, with anger, with confusion, whipping back and forth and unable to produce anything tangible enough to speak aloud. Until he recognized the answers before him for what they were. Aisling stared at Lir without recognition, and Anduril glittered mischievously at her hips, winking at the lord of the greenwood.

"I am your king," Lir said at last. "And you are my queen."

Aisling straightened, lowering Sarwen for the first time. She breathed steadily, comfortable with the dense quiet.

"I am beholden to no king," she answered at last.

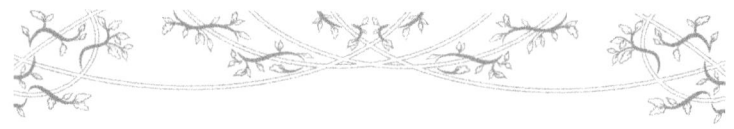

# CHAPTER VII

## LIR

The Sidhe king cut through the corridors of Castle Annwyn.

Aisling was gone. One moment she'd been his and the next... the fire of recognition in her eyes was extinguished. Like the petering out of a night's old fire or a plume of smoke. Not the blazing, destructive magic he understood flamed around the hollows of her heart. Lir searched for their connection—that intangible cord between them—and felt nothing. Instead, there was only a profound emptiness that clawed at his throat for a scream, a curse, a malediction to darken even the life heart of his forests.

Lir raced up the spiral stairwells, wishing for his mother's wings. He was a blur of darkness as he moved, and still, he wasn't quick enough. "Aisling," he repeated beneath his breath. A prayer, a spell, a means to keep her close to him when he felt out of control.

Lir burst through the doors of Ina's chamber. Fionn, Filverel, Galad, Gilrel, and Peitho stood inside the room, heads whipping toward their Sidhe king as his silhouette came into focus at the threshold.

"What have you done?" Lir asked, almost a whisper. His

reflective eyes addressed Fionn from across the room, eliciting a conspicuous gulp from his elder brother.

"I'm sorry?" Fionn replied dubiously.

"You have one opportunity to speak the full truth, here and now," Lir said, eerily calm. "Or," he continued, "I'll bleed you dry and cut your tongue from your mouth."

The room darkened and even the stone statues shuddered.

Fionn glanced around Ina's chamber, exchanging expressions with Peitho. The princess of Niltaor turned away quickly, abandoning the son of Winter to explain himself.

"I don't know to what you refer," Fionn said, planting his boots onto the stone floors. And in response Lir flashed a wicked grin.

"I was counting on your dishonesty," Lir said, spinning his twin blades.

"Wait—" Fionn began, but it was too late.

Lir tore past the rest of the room and pummeled into Fionn.

Both brothers crashed into the chamber's windows, shattering the glass with their force.

Winter against green, they fell. Plummeting through the night like twin stars, just before slamming against the mosaic-jeweled towers. Castle Annwyn shook, stones and debris crumbling into the river and flying buttresses below.

"Anduril—Lugh—has entirely consumed her," Lir shouted, fangs lengthening and dripping with rain. Lir pinned Fionn to the tower's steepled roof, pushing his head into the chipped gemstones. Fionn shoved his brother back, but Lir had always been the stronger of the two. The dark lord's hands tightly coiled around Fionn's throat while he seethed.

"The belt is meant to aid Aisling so she might stand a chance in the Other!" Fionn yelled back, summoning his *draiocht*. The magic huffed awake, climbing up and out of him. Fionn's iris was swallowed by the white of his eyes. "You must surrender to the magic that aids her, even if it is against your will."

Ice climbed up Lir's hands where he held Fionn. Sharp and sparkling, the ice grew, devouring Lir's limbs up to the shoulder. The Sidhe king of the greenwood roared, breaking his arms free yet also releasing Fionn.

Wet ice spread across the turret, allowing Fionn to slide down its side and away from Lir. Fionn rolled onto his side and down the side of the turret, plunging further down Castle Annwyn with Lir shortly behind.

Fionn crashed into a nearby pine in one of Annwyn's courtyard gardens, his arms flailing as he reached for branches to break his fall. His hands blistered and broke, at last, catching a limb that snapped almost immediately. He fell through the pine, sliding down until he slammed into a tiered lily-pad pond, shattering the stone fountains that moved when they believed none were watching.

Lir, on the other hand, caught himself with his magic, the pine's branches cradling him as he descended. Lir hit the cobbled path of the garden in which they stood, rolling with momentum till he lithely found his footing.

Lir wasted not a moment, starting toward Fionn as he unsheathed and threw one of his twin blades. The axe was wicked, cutting through the rain like a silver star.

Fionn reacted, quickly turning his head to the side. The axe brushed his cheek, carving a cut across the son of Winter's face.

"You're wasting our time fighting me, brother!" Fionn shouted, raising his hand in a gesture of magic. Winter rose from the cobbles like spears, almost knocking Lir off his feet. Lir steadied himself, catching the axe he'd thrown like a boomerang.

Lir threw both axes this time. Mid-flight, they curved inward, careening toward Fionn like sparrows.

Fionn slammed against the ground, avoiding his brother's

axes by less than a sylph's width. Hastily, he leaped to his feet, walking backward to increase the distance between himself and his brother.

"I will make the time to gut you," Lir growled, but the voice was not his own. It was dark; the sound of blades dragged across bite-sharp stones. "To cut Aisling's name from your mouth like a sacrifice."

Lir caught his spinning blades again, throwing one and then the other, his entire body lunging forward.

Fionn's spears of ice blocked both blades the moment they converged. Yet, Fionn's heels were now bending over the edge of Castle Annwyn.

"Let Anduril make a warrior of her," Fionn shouted, teetering at the edge. "Your selfishness—your bond—will only bring the Sidhe to their knees."

"Perhaps, but the decision was not yours to make."

The dark lord continued, throwing his blades again. Fionn dove backward, flying off the edge and down.

Lir leaped shortly after, plummeting with reckless abandon. Vines and roots tangled themselves around his limbs, carrying him as he fell.

Both lords crashed into a floating bridge. The center cracked and burst with stones upon impact, immediately tilting onto its side. Fionn and Lir reached for the balustrade, gripping its edge and climbing till they balanced on its side.

Lir wrapped the bridge in vines, hungrily climbing and reaching for the son of Winter.

Fionn clawed through them, spraying the stairwell with the blood of his palms.

Lir's lips curled. His magic swallowed the son of Winter with its thorny limbs. They squeezed, sucking the air from Fionn's lungs.

"Lir," Fionn struggled, grasping for his *draiocht* without breath. "I did not make such a decision. You did."

Lir's smile widened: the image of a wolf raising its bloody muzzle from the belly of its kill.

"Beg for it," Lir said. "Beg for your life."

Fionn shuddered, filled by the same goblet of thousands before him: fear. Lir's expression was monstrous. The nightmare shadow that slipped between the rooms of your mind.

Even so, Fionn couldn't speak if he wished to. His complexion was purpling, his body tightening, his life fading while Lir continued.

"Li—"

One, two, three more breaths...

"Enough!" Peitho's voice shouted from above. A beam as bright as sunlight crashed into the bridge in a flash of gold. The bridge split, severing Lir's *draiocht* and freeing Fionn.

They fell further this time, slashing through the moonlight. At some point, their paths met; a tangle of magic spinning as they plunged, fighting fist to fist, and magic to magic.

They crashed into the angled side of a turret, but still, they did not stop. Both slid down the jeweled shingles, reaching for something to break their fall. Everything they touched fell loose, sending both the son of Winter and Lir down the edge of Castle Annwyn's mountain where nothing rested below save for the river's rapids.

Fionn caught onto the rim of the turret, stopping his descent.

Lir's hold on the rim, however, broke loose, sending Lir further down the tower's side. Lir unsheathed his blades, slamming them into the side of the tower. They took hold, ripping through the side of the mosaicked edge.

Finally, Lir stopped, a few lengths short of the bottom of Castle Annwyn altogether.

"So long brother," Fionn said, finding dark amusement in his brother's misfortune. He looked as if he'd happily leave Lir stuck at the edge of Castle Annwyn, shivering till daybreak.

Lir's mouth bent with agitation, pulling one of his axes free and slamming it into the tower further up its side. He repeated the movement, climbing up and toward Fionn.

Peitho struck once more from above, tearing Fionn's hold. And so, the son of Winter flew off the edge and toward his death. An end written in the hand of his brother.

Fionn seemed to brace himself for the fall. He closed his eyes, jerked open almost instantly by the violent tug from his shoulder. Fionn inhaled sharply, glaring down at his boots dangling above the clouds.

The son of Winter looked up and at his brother.

Arm to arm, they hung from the side of Castle Annwyn by the blade of Lir's axe.

"I'll tear the belt from her body myself *after* Aisling finds the Goblet and the Sidhe have been spared," Fionn said through gritted teeth.

"No," Lir said. "Such honor will be mine. If we survive this war, you'll be banished to Oighir for eternity." It was a promise. Oaths, secrets, and bargains were no thoughtless vows. They were soaked in the Forge's wax, sealed, and locked until the end of time. No more impossible to break than the truth on the tip of a fae's tongue.

"Anduril has possessed her," Lir said, leaning against the stone wall with his arms crossed. Lir, Peitho, Filverel, Galad, and Gilrel stood in Ina's wing, beside the crowned owl fountain with ruby eyes. Eyes that studied and watched as if Ina herself saw through those very jewels from whatever depths of the Other she was laid to rest.

Aisling had been allowed inside this chamber once before, by Ina's spirit or will, none were certain. Only that Aisling had been guided there by a garden snake, the door unlocked, and

Ina's fountain waiting. Every stone head watching with keen interest. The waters themselves still and eager in an otherwise empty room, buried in the depths of Castle Annwyn.

Lir believed in Aisling—in her power, ambition, and potential to become the Sidhe's salvation. Aisling was the key to spare the Sidhe from extinction and, Lir speculated, Ina somehow had known that all along.

"I feared this," Peitho said, brows pinching. "Anduril has been locked and frozen away at the edge of the world in Oighir for good reason."

Lir's temper flared, but he swallowed it down, biting his tongue with his fangs.

"And still, my brother lent it to Aisling. Where were your fears when Fionn offered the belt to your queen?" Lir asked, his voice descending into the gravelly depth of a primordial creature waking at a curse's summons.

Peitho's gaze fell to the floor.

"Aisling knew it would possess her and chose to wear the belt regardless," Peitho swallowed. "Which is why your brawling is of little use to either Aisling or the Sidhe at large."

"You lecture me while Aisling suffers at the cost of your double-edged gifts?" Lir's nose scrunched in annoyance.

"*Easca, mo Damh Bán,*" Galad chided gently.

"The belt is a token of legends as slippery as your brother's tongue, *mo Damh Bán*. There are endless versions of the same tale, and all told differently. This outcome was one of countless potentialities," Peitho said, brow knotted with both fear and guilt alike.

Lir clenched his fists at his sides, turning from the princess of Niltaor to calm his rage. And yet, Lir knew it wise not to further divide the Sidhe by condemning Peitho altogether.

"And what is this outcome?" Lir asked, running the tip of his tongue across his fangs in frustration. "What legends speak of what's possessed Aisling?"

Peitho hesitated before exhaling. Her shoulders rose and fell as if physically relieving a burden. "Anduril was a lover's gift, taken from the armor of Lugh. During the Wild Hunt, the lover returned the belt to Lugh as a token of good fortune. However, when Lugh was driven mad by the sound of Muirdris's wings just out of reach, he channeled the sun for every morsel of its blazing power in honor of the South."

Lir cursed beneath his breath.

"And the skies bled black while Lugh absorbed the strength of the sun. But it was Anduril who took the sun's magic," Lir said, remembering this version of the legend he'd heard in passing over the millennia.

Peitho swallowed.

"Aye, and now—without a morsel of doubt—I believe Anduril trapped more than the sun's strength inside its metal," the princess said. "As Fionn suspected, I believe it also trapped Lugh's spirit."

"But for what reason would Lugh intend for Aisling to forget our bond?" Lir asked.

Peitho bit her bottom lip before speaking. "Enchanted objects are most formidable when they find a wearer or master with a like-minded spirit. Lugh's obsession and pursuit of strength is not so different from Aisling's own. In which case, Anduril views yours and Aisling's connection as not only a barrier to her potential and focus as a warrior, but to the Sidhe and Aisling's success at large."

A muscle flashed across Lir's jaw. The gums of his *draiocht* bled inside, snapping and biting as if tethered and scraped raw by invisible shackles. The thought—the mere possibility of Aisling forgetting their bond—was unthinkable. And although the Sidhe king knew such agony was selfish, it mattered not. In every lifetime, he'd condemn his soul for her.

"We remove it," Galad piped from his dark corner for the

first time. "I'll break my blade if I must," the first knight offered, unsheathing his sword.

Peitho's eyes grew wet with remorse.

"It cannot be done," the princess said, no more than a whisper. The entirety of the room turned to face her.

"My blade has cut through iron chains, bled Unseelie hearts, and tasted the armor of kings," Gilrel said. "A belt is no match."

"An ordinary belt, perhaps," Filverel said, eyes drifting toward the Sidhe king. "But this is no ordinary garment."

Lir glared at his mother's fountain, imagining different ways to destroy Anduril either by the strength of his bare hands, his *draiocht*, or the godsforsaken Forge.

"Only the master of Anduril can remove the belt," Peitho said, this time louder. "It must be a choice from Aisling's will and not another's."

Lir's heart sank, rage and despair alike filling his throat with unswallowable stones.

"What is there to be done then?" Galad asked, his mouth bent with frustration.

The room exchanged glances. The answers eluded them, and the silence mocked them. Lir thought he would descend into madness if there weren't a seedling of hope. A single root could bloom into an oak.

*Despite bitter winter and its formidable blade, even death's knee will bend to the bloom.*

Lir sucked in a breath and straightened, reaching for his axes. Ina's fountain rippled and the ruby eyes of the owl blossomed to life.

It was time.

"Aisling will find the Goblet, earn the gods' favor, and spare the Sidhe from mortal destruction," Lir said. "And then, I'll remove the belt myself."

"It's impossible—" Peitho began but was swiftly cut short.

A silhouette appeared in the doorway. As elegant as long-cast shadows, Aisling stood at the threshold to Ina's chamber considering each of them closely. Her violet eyes gently swept from one face to the next until, at last, they met Lir's eyes and stayed. The Sidhe king's heart stuttered, but he held her gaze.

"I'll make it possible," Lir said beneath his breath, his knuckles bone-white against the wood of his axes.

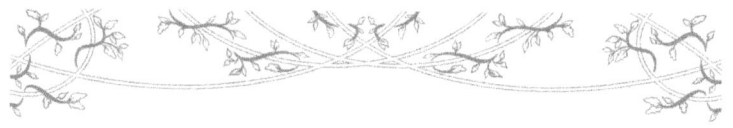

# CHAPTER VIII

AISLING

Aisling remembered her lungs on fire, skidding to a halt at the end of Annwyn's bridge. Her mind was filled with dense clouds, muddying her thoughts and feelings. She remembered wandering through the castle confused and delirious. And then, she remembered there was a new voice inside her mind.

*Aisling*, it had spoken to her. Strong and steady, it had filled her chest with warmth. It was an anchor in a tossing sea, a light amidst the mist, and a beacon in the storm. So, Aisling had listened.

Aisling remembered the bear's armor scraping her cheek when he moved to draw his blade. The boar on his right side had followed shortly after, prepared to end whosoever pursued Aisling down Annwyn's bridge. Aisling remembered shouting for her guards to kill the intruder, her hair flying into her eyes as she spoke and moved. Instead, they'd lowered their weapons the moment the intruder came into view. Both the bear and the boar had fallen into bows, lowering their heads to the cobbled floor of the bridge.

"What are you doing?!" Aisling remembered screaming,

Sarwen spearing toward the intruder and keeping him at large. "End him!"

Lastly, she remembered his eyes. Her intruder shed the darkness and padded into the light. Aisling had sucked in a sharp breath despite herself, gasping in either horror or awe, she was uncertain. He was beautiful and horrible all at once—hideous in his perfection. Heartbreak incarnate, he moved lithe as a shadow but not without some unspoken, elegant violence. His eyes green and bright as blades.

"*Mo Damh Bán*," the guards said in unison, falling into bows before her intruder.

*Mo Damh Bán.*

Aisling clawed at her mind, swatting through thoughts shifting in both shadow and light. She remembered and then she did not. So whilst her memories piled high, toppling over with their growth on one side of her mind, the other was empty and dark. A void she couldn't enter if she dared.

"Seize him!" Aisling had yelled, but her guards kept their eyes lowered to the floor and their knees bent. Statues before the intruder who'd stood slick and tall, armor licked by shadows.

"Bow before your king," the intruder had said, his voice deep and wet with a fae accent. The corners of his mouth curled, but it didn't meet his eyes. Instead, his gaze was annoyed, cold, and sharp. His disdain for her clear enough if his words weren't already.

Your king.

Aisling had stepped backward. Her mind spun and her heart raced. Anduril squeezed her tightly, ringing with heat.

"But I'd prefer you take my hand," the intruder had said, watching Aisling intently. He offered a hand, palm to the sky above. "Bri—

Anduril had flashed with light before the world fell dark.

And then, Aisling remembered collapsing against the cold stone of Annwyn's bridge. The final part of the memory.

Aisling snapped back into her body, the vision fading.

The sorceress swallowed, focusing on all those standing before her, here and now.

Tonight, Aisling was clad in a gown sewn by mourning banshees and collected during twilight's fog. Her only accessories were watercress and Annwyn's antlered crown to match the Sidhe king's own; a dark rogue himself, dressed in leather and an artfully tailored jacket without a tunic beneath. And yet, Aisling scarcely remembered his name. For all that she remembered of her time in Annwyn and her ascension to queen, she did not recall Lir. But she recognized his eyes as those of her intruder's and shuddered.

His place in her memory was empty despite what the sparrows insisted as they braided her hair around her antlered crown. And the more she heard his name, the more she disliked it—Anduril burning through her gown and into her flesh at the mere mention of the Sidhe king.

"The time to enter the Other is nigh," Aisling said, ignoring their gawking.

Filverel cleared his throat. "Aye," he agreed, stepping toward the fountain.

Filverel, Galad, Peitho, and Gilrel were resplendent in their attire: embroidered tunics, leather jackets and boots, and polished pauldrons. But Peitho glimmered more brightly even in the dank atmosphere of the forbidden wing, clad in a ball gown made from autumn leaves dappled in pond water.

"Shall we get on with this then?" The southern Sidhe princess approached Ina's fountain with no hesitation, the others shortly behind—too eager to wait on greeting one another.

Aisling wondered to herself what they thought of visiting the Other. Returning to the plane of their making, where their blood and bones were forged yet rejected from all the same, unable to return lest invited this one time of year.

Filverel pulled out Niamh's invitation. He glanced at the Sidhe king, a silent conversation passing between them. The dark lord of the greenwood was as stiff and stoic as a lone pine, arms crossed before his chest and his jaw clenched. A silent sort of fury he donned. He despised her, Aisling felt. His eyes studied her with palpable disdain, flicking away the moment their eyes accidentally met as if repulsed by her attention.

Aisling chose to ignore her intruder—*the strange king* until he spoke suddenly.

"Wait," he said. The room froze, the tension between them inexplicably high. Aisling studied their expressions, their postures, the way their hands fidgeted when her eyes lingered too long. "Aisling and I will go forward alone," the Sidhe king said.

Aisling whipped her head at her intruder.

"We will do no such thing," she bit. Her *draiocht* rose up her throat with an energy Aisling hadn't anticipated. She hushed Racat, digging her nails into her palms. The Sidhe king unsettled her, and because she couldn't remember him, Aisling questioned why. Nevertheless, if Aisling chewed on such questions for long, they were swiftly beaten out of her mind. It was as if another occupied her thoughts, guiding her again and again to Sarwen strapped to her back and nothing more.

"My mind will not be changed," the Sidhe king said, his face expressionless. He was as inhuman as the myths claimed and more nightmarish in his beauty than Aisling allowed herself to admit.

"It is my will that ought to be convinced," Aisling said, the violet of her eyes glowing more brightly with her temper.

"Perhaps it's wise to enter the Other with us all," Gilrel said, cautious as she pleaded to the Sidhe king and not Aisling. At this, Aisling fumed. She was queen of Annwyn and soon, she'd earn the gods' favor as well. This strange wolf who crowned himself in antlers and struck fear in Aisling's allies was an imposter. This much, she knew in her gut.

Anduril vibrated with magic, confirming Aisling's beliefs immediately.

"My word is done," the fae king said and, as if a bell had been rung, the room descended into obedient silence from either fear, respect, or both, Aisling couldn't tell beyond her own frustration.

Filverel, Galad, Gilrel, and lastly Peitho, met Aisling's eyes with a silent apology. They'd chosen to stay and obey the strange king.

Aisling rolled her tongue to one side, chewing on her anger lest it seeped through fangs like the flames from a *dragún*'s mouth.

Filverel cleared his throat and repeated the invitation in Rún.

> *When the days lengthen and the wildlings crawl from their slumber,*
> > *Woke by warm breezes, by berries, by nuts—your hunger,*
> > *They'll come with the rain.*
> > *When the ice melts and the forest thaws, crying out in pain,*
> > *The clouds will gather and break,*
> > *And the seedlings will be slaked.*
> > *So I pray,*
> > *That you'll come with the rain.*

-Niamh-

In response, the stone owl's ruby eyes glowed more brightly, casting a cloak of red across the chamber. The fountain rippled and every woodland statue with a spigot in its mouth spat Annwyn's gorge water, babbling with excitement. Its *draiocht* groaning awake after decades, perhaps longer, asleep. The sensation of a bear turning over after months of deep-winter dreams. The smell of mildew and moss thickening the air, ancient, primeval and born of a bygone era.

Aisling shuddered.

The doorway to the Other was open.

The fae king moved toward the waters as if to enter. Aisling jolted forward, reaching the lip of the fountain.

"I'll enter first," she said. It wasn't a question, yet the fae king considered her words for longer than Aisling anticipated. His eyes—darkest of greens—growled like a nightmare forest, hoarding monstrosities spoken of only in fairytales. But there was something more. A strange glint, like the nick of a blade, sparkling before vanishing once more. Something harrowed, something desperate, something afraid.

Aisling pulled back, aware she'd stared at the strange king too long and shuddered.

"Very well," he said mercifully, stepping aside for Aisling to pass. He brought his arms closer to himself as if disgusted by the prospect of touching her. Perhaps repelled by the stench of what mortal blood ran through her veins still.

Aisling turned away, unable to stomach his expression or the tugging of her thoughts.

She sucked in a breath, already leaning forward to plunge into the Other when Gilrel jumped atop the edge of the fountain. The pine marten's blade, tucked at her hip, was made bloody by the light of the owl's eyes.

"Wait for my return," Aisling said to her chambermaid, clasping her paw between her hands. "Don't wander nor attempt anything half as wicked as dueling a den of neccakaid without me."

The pine marten's eyes shone with unwept tears, her whiskers quivering as she recalled the memory. The den of neccakaid had been the final trial before reaching Lofgren's Rise —one they'd scarcely survived.

Gilrel nodded, swallowing hard as Aisling released her paw.

Aisling turned her attention back to the fountain, her *draiocht* popping like a gleeful flame at the edge of a wick. A cauldron, the waters churned and the owl's ruby eyes sparkled.

Anduril tugged her closer, gleaming and eager. It burned, humming an unsettling song that echoed into the caverns of oblivion.

And so, Aisling plunged into the gateway.

# CHAPTER IX

AISLING

*Starn was familiar with the fleshy sensation of his blade sinking into the tree. It felt more alive than most trees, and that was before he'd looked the beast in the eyes. Or so, that was what the Lady allowed Aisling to hear from Starn's thoughts as he crouched in a blackened clearing of a coastal forest. Blood, sap, and mud sat in his cupped palms, turned over by earthworms as he thought.*

*That single moment of hesitation had cost him. The tree slithered from his grasp for the second time, bloodied and wounded but escaping, nevertheless.*

*Starn cursed beneath his breath. His men were shouting at him from behind, at last, catching up with the pursuit.*

*Next time.*

*Next time, Starn would kill it.*

∾

Gasping for air, Aisling emerged from a pond.

Lily pads stuck to her arms and algae caught between her fingertips while she clawed for dry ground. Rain showered upon her as she toppled over the edge and onto flagstone, heaving, and lungs on fire.

Immediately, she staggered to her feet. Aisling's heart thundered inside her, her fingers still trembling with adrenaline—with *draiocht* crackling inside her veins. Her vision blurred, focusing in and out without her consent, the world tilting side to side on its axis.

Aisling gripped the edge of *something*, quickly realizing it was a balustrade. She held her head in both hands, doing her best to focus.

"Lir," her lips spouted before she could think clearly. Not a soul replied but Anduril, buzzing like a gong and tightening painfully around her hips.

*Lir*. Her mind pawed at the name, unfamiliar with its presence. Her *draiocht*, however, warmed to it, sung awake by the magic of a memory. She knew it belonged to the fae king and so she banished such warmth, grimacing at its rich taste on her tongue.

A moment ago, Aisling was falling into the fountain, its warm, supple waters embracing her, wrapping their limbs around her and pulling her under. Then, everything became cold, dark, and *in between*. And when the light returned, Aisling was swimming up and toward the surface of water.

Aisling's eyes widened, devouring the view before her.

A kingdom of slick stone bridges, gardens stretching into the clouds, flying buttresses, and thousands of spindly glass-like towers, was neatly squeezed between two floating cliffs—its bottom suspended in the air as a waterfall wept over the entire kingdom. A mirror to the cloudburst that descended from above.

A castle in the sky.

"The Isle of Rain," Aisling said, breathless.

She stood alone, suspended on a moss-covered turret somewhere at the center of the kingdom, floating bridges both below and above her, carrying figures Aisling couldn't focus on well enough to recognize.

Aisling turned on her heel, her heart regaining its rapid pace.

Where *was* the fae king? He'd claimed to follow her into Ina's gateway, but was it possible he'd deceived Aisling into going alone? Aisling soured. Of course it was possible. Aisling bore little memory of the fae king, but she remembered the tales she'd been taught as a child: he, a blood-soaked nightmare incarnate. His mischief was unmatched, and his mind was centuries old. There was no telling what he intended or didn't. Regardless, Aisling was glad to be rid of him and certainly, he of her.

"The not-so mortal queen in the flesh." A voice sounded from the threshold to the balcony. A steepled entryway, that'd been tightly closed until now, opened wide with three figures at its center.

Aisling jerked her body upright, disturbing the pond in which she stood.

The stranger was resplendent. A Sidhe creature forge-born with pointed ears, long limbs, large eyes and an eerie, fearfully beautiful face. Yet, there was more. More to the female who flashed her fangs, a gown made entirely of wispy clouds transforming, constantly moving as the rain and the waterfall touched it. Her crown, a delicate circlet of water beads, framing her braided, blue tresses. Her flesh, sparkling and shimmering wet.

Niamh. The Seelie queen of Rain and the keeper of the Goblet of Lore. Two mares made of what appeared to be flesh and bone stood beside her, but upon closer inspection, it was running river water purling through their manes, their hooves clacking against the flagstones, and their flattened ears. Both elegant and wild at once.

"*Elliati merla tu sakka. Sarwen,*" she said in Rún, but Aisling's knowledge of the divine language was not yet so advanced to understand. A fact Niamh understood for she repeated herself.

"I heard her voice and so I came. Sarwen." Niamh's voice was both the timbre of thunder combined with the feminine melody of spring drizzles.

Aisling, without thinking, glanced over her shoulder. Sarwen, the blade Peitho had gifted her at her coronation and Aisling had dubbed Sarwen after Niamh's legendary sword, was still strapped to her back. The mortal reaper.

"Like twin souls, both their halves speak to one another in a tongue only they share," Niamh continued, taking a step nearer. "My blade recognized yours."

"*Your Majesty*," Aisling said, dipping her chin. "We've come upon invitation: the Seelie queen of the greenwood and—"

"The Seelie king of the greenwood, the dark lord of the forest, the barbarian king of Annwyn. Yes," Niamh said, "I know. It was I who invited you, was it not?"

Aisling hesitated, carefully measuring what she wished to speak.

"Although," Niamh said, her dress parting at the top of her thigh as she walked toward Aisling. "I see no Lir."

Anduril hummed softly. The belt, however, refused to glow as it had in Annwyn. As though it were hiding from Niamh and the magic of the Other altogether.

Niamh continued to study Aisling. Pale lips pursing before they spread into a thin, amused smile.

"I've come alone," Aisling said.

"So, you are no bride of Annwyn whilst without your king... for now," Niamh conjectured. "Then what is your title?"

Aisling hadn't thought of this answer. Her mind was a forest veiled in fog; the trees of her mind moved in her periphery only to freeze when she turned to acknowledge them directly. The animals skulked along the forest's bed of leaves, whispering strange incantations to one another the longer she tried to sort through her memories. Pieces were missing and others were replaced. And should she catch a glimmer of what she believed was the truth, Anduril gripped her tightly, sparing her from her madness and delivering her back to reality.

*Sorceress*, Anduril whispered inside her mind.

"Sorceress," Aisling said. "My title is sorceress."

"Court sorceress? Sorceress to the Sidhe? To the mortals? The gods?" Niamh pressed. "Titles establish allegiance. What is yours?"

Aisling straightened, unwilling to let even a Seelie queen of the Other toy with her as though she were a pet.

"I envy those of pure blood such as yourself," Aisling said. "Your allegiance was chosen for you and interlaced with your destiny. I boast no such clarity, for while my love for the Sidhe grows parallel to the growth of my hatred for humankind, wisdom would compel me to only ever stake allegiance in myself."

Niamh's eyebrows rose, the droplets streaming down her cheeks running more quickly.

"What of love?" she asked, an intensity piercing from her pale gaze.

Aisling's heart inexplicably twisted. Her *draiocht* snapped its jaws and Racat's eyes opened from their slumber, alive with a fire Aisling recognized but couldn't understand.

"*My love is a blade,*" Aisling said, but the words were not her own. They were Anduril's.

"Or perhaps a shield," Niamh countered, glaring at Aisling from head to toe with narrowed eyes. "And yet," she continued, "I smell him: the dark lord of the greenwood. He's here—in the Other."

Aisling's heart jolted. So Lir was alive and well somewhere in the Other. He'd made it across, but why had he separated himself from Aisling? The sorceress bit her bottom lip, mind racing. The fae king hadn't lied when he'd claimed to follow

Aisling into the gateway and yet, he was missing still. His absence was reason enough for suspicion.

"Or..." Niamh trailed off. "Do I smell him all over you, sorceress?" Her attention honed in on Aisling. The sensation of a lightning bolt striking the tallest tree in a wood.

"Like lust and want and need and—"

"*I am here to request the gods' favor,*" Anduril interjected through Aisling's lips despite Racat's writhing, the *dragún*'s biting, the *dragún*'s growling. "I understand I must first find the Goblet to prove my worth, and so, I humbly submit myself to the task."

Niamh seemed taken aback, pausing for a moment, the rain falling silver down the straight edge of her nose. As though any deceit might make itself known by staring straight through Aisling's very flesh and into her soul.

Niamh tore her eyes off Aisling. She moved slowly. The urgency of a queen who bathed in the suds of eternity. Ancient limbs carrying the weight of a millennia each moment she so much as blinked or tipped her chin.

"Of course," she simpered, eyes narrowing as she bared her fangs in a toothy, hollow grin. The image of someone who knew not what a smile was but desperately attempted to mimic one.

Aisling shuddered.

"As an honored guest of mine, you're welcome to stay in the Isle of Rain for as long as you please. Tonight, we shall celebrate you as our guest of honor."

Aisling tried to bite her tongue, but it was too late. The words slipped before she could catch them.

"And Lir? Will he make it tonight?" Aisling asked against her own volition, Anduril pinching her the moment the fae king's name left her lips. Aisling, too, despised herself for how her voice cracked the moment his name was spoken.

Niamh quirked a brow, staring down at Aisling. Aisling was

tall for a female and still Niamh towered over her. Larger than life, Niamh was statuesque and made of heaven's tears.

"Fate will decide such outcomes," she said, "but I'm certain the Sidhe king of the greenwood can handle a bit of bad weather." Niamh giggled, turning on her heel with her beasts right behind.

"I'll have you escorted to your rooms," she called back. "Welcome to Castle Yillen," Niamh said just before she crossed the doors.

Panic bubbled inside Aisling's throat, rising to her tongue and escaping from her lips.

"I don't think—" Aisling piped again, but this time, she bore the clarity of mind to stop herself.

"Careful, sorceress," Niamh replied. "Stand there too long and you might catch a chill." Niamh met Aisling's eyes over her shoulder before disappearing into her castle, the roar of the waterfall echoing inside Aisling's mind while the storm soaked her to the bone.

# CHAPTER X

## AISLING

Castle Yillen was not made of brick and mortar but of fabled spells and jinxes.

The chamber Aisling entered was sheathed with emerald moss, dripping with the rain that cried down the walls. A castle pebbled together by an infinity of brilliant river stones and gems, polished by storm and fog. And the passages that weren't artfully mosaicked, were stained glass and bejeweled by every droplet that beat against their panes. This was the style and make of most of Niamh's castle: a labyrinth of floating bridges, suspended turrets, and flying buttresses, all alive with the life heart of ancient forests, drenched with the rain and mist that pressed against every windowpane, eager to hear its keepers' voices.

Although, if the beauty of Castle Yillen wasn't enough, as soon as Aisling's appetite tugged for attention, the vanity, the bedside tables, the terrace, and the tray atop the silk quilts of their giant bed, spilled over with Sidhe treats. Delicacies and desserts Gilrel would've devoured if she'd been staying in the same room.

Yet, even Aisling's appetite couldn't distract her from the

discomfort of her wet and heavy gown. Her dress had been bathed by the gateway and again by Niamh's rain. The ivory of her slip was translucent and clinging to her body. She needed to change.

Aisling wandered toward an extension of her chambers, divided by a sheet of water. As she passed through, the water separated into a steepled arch, revealing a cerulean and sage quilted bed with a night slip prepared and strewn across. Forget-me-nots dangled from the four-poster frame, laughing to one another in voices like Sidhe children. But it was the blue rabbits that busied themselves with steeping a pot of tea, a small basket of leaves, and a plate of steaming sweet rolls, that caught Aisling's attention.

The rabbits jumped when they noticed the sorceress.

"*Mo Lúra!*" the first exclaimed, ears flattening against its head in surprise as it bent into a bow, followed by its companion. The two rabbits rushed toward the sorceress, a clattering tray held between their four paws.

"We've prepared tea for you, *mo Lúra*," the second rabbit said. "So that you don't fall ill with the weather."

Aisling lifted the pot's lid and inhaled. It didn't smell anything like Annwyn's chocolate bark, wolfberry, or jasmine brews. It was far more potent, leaves plucked from trees that didn't grow in the mortal plane.

Anduril rang like the chime of a soft bell the moment Aisling lifted a flower cup to her lips. The belt's vibrations were potent with suspicion, warning Aisling of the brew. But the purity of the blue rabbits' gaze, their delicate handiwork, and their soft voices suggested they could be trusted. Aisling scrunched her nose, temples pulsing as she chose to ignore Anduril.

"That's kind of you," Aisling said. "Thank you."

The belt shimmered with annoyance, hugging Aisling more tightly as a reminder of its influence.

Aisling glanced at the belt before swiftly averting her eyes, eager not to draw attention to it.

The sorceress moved toward the wardrobes carved with the likenesses of various woodland creatures. Every animal glittered, glazed in the slime of various snails and their opalescent shells that inched over all of Castle Yillen. And the moment Aisling opened both doors of the center hutch, several frogs leaped from the shadows, croaking as they scurried toward the terrace.

The blue rabbits followed their leaps, scolding the frogs for the mud on their webbed feet.

The terrace was different from what either Castle Oighir or Castle Annwyn had built—the only Sidhe castles Aisling had entered thus far. Both the balustrade and the floors were made of glass, creating the illusion one was suspended in the air like the thousands of towers that surrounded them, separated only by rain, mist, clouds, and sparkling figures that flew from one part of the castle to another, ignoring the hallways, the galleries, the staircases, or the courtyards that would aid those who otherwise bore no wings. In fact, from this vantage point, Aisling realized their quarters were inside one of the highest suspended towers, the terrace wrapping around the circumference of the detailed spire. But it was Castle Yillen's gates far below that caught Aisling's attention and held it.

A beast of a Sidhe ambled through the gates on the back of an obsidian horse. The hairs on the nape of Aisling's neck stood on end, watching as the rider took in his surroundings. The rider wore black. He and his mount were shadows from the Other, followed by the tattered, wispy tail of his cape.

Badgers skittered toward the hooves of the mount, ears flat against their heads as they fearfully worked to accommodate Niamh's new guest. Aisling smelled the badgers' terror, the sweat beading beneath their furs as they hurried. But it was the silence that followed the rider that unnerved Aisling most of all. A quiet that hung in the air like a throat hung in a noose.

Thunder groaned perhaps hopeful it'd been Lir who'd entered Niamh's gates. Anduril snapped at the thought without hesitation.

Aisling worked her jaw.

"Who is that?" Aisling asked the blue rabbits, looking down below at Yillen's gates. And as though the rider could hear her voice, he tipped his head up and glared straight at her. Aisling held steady, narrowing her eyes, but beyond the sharp, intricate angles of the rider's helmet was darkness. Empty, yet capable of filling whosoever brave enough to stare back with immeasurable despair.

"Percy," one of the blue rabbits said, a muddy frog between its paws. The storm thickened at the mention of the visitor's name.

Aisling placed her hands on the balustrade, leaning forward to better peer through the mist.

"We should go back inside," the blue rabbit said, eager to forget the rider. The rabbit turned on her heel, hoping Aisling would follow. Yet Aisling, uninterested in the rabbit's proposal, didn't move, rather transfixed by Yillen's new arrival.

"Who is he?" she asked.

"One of Niamh's guests," the rabbit said, hoping that would slake the sorceress's curiosity.

"Yes, but who?" she pushed.

"Why do you assume I know him?" the rabbit countered, holding the terrace door open for Aisling to come inside.

"You knew his title."

"I know many titles of many irrelevant souls."

"You won't answer my questions directly then," Aisling said, finally spinning on her heel and meeting the little beast's eyes. The rabbit's chest hitched, the desire to both flee yet sink into her violet magic rendering her paralyzed. A fool to her spells she was quickly learning how to cast on a whim.

The rabbit exhaled. "Centuries have passed since anyone last saw Percy."

"So, he's renowned?"

"In a way," the rabbit said, pushing aside the spiderwebbed curtains and sinking into the warmth of their quarters. "He's Fiacha's, one of the original twelve Sidhe sovereign's sons."

Aisling followed a step behind the rabbit, yet her interest filled the room.

"And his court?" Aisling asked.

"The stars where he hides himself away from the rest of the world," the rabbit explained.

"But no longer," the second rabbit said. "His court was taken by the mortals, and so, he seeks refuge here."

Aisling straightened, eyes widening.

"Father." Aisling spoke her thoughts aloud, despising the sound of his title on her tongue. "But how?"

"I heard the fire hand blew fire from his throat like a *dragún*, lighting the evening sky till every star fell," one rabbit said.

Aisling sucked in a sharp breath.

*Scull draiocht*.

"I heard his men shot flaming reeds into the sky—their fire growing and spreading with unnatural hunger," the second rabbit said.

Dread sank like an anchor in Aisling's stomach while she thought. But it was Anduril that steeled her. The belt buzzed with excitement and the possibility of whetting its deadly appetite.

"Hopefully, he is the last victim of my father," Aisling said, but the rabbits appeared unconvinced. Aisling shook her head, biting her bottom lip. Time was running out.

"I hope as well, m'lady," the first rabbit agreed. "But the hope is surrounded by doubt."

The rain tapped against the stained glass, an eager listener of theirs.

# CHAPTER XI

## LIR

Lir felt the moment that the *in between* shed its leaves and became the Other. The smells were more potent here, every touch more sensitive, the colors, light and darkness all more vibrant. Magic dripped from the trees, the storms hammering from above, and the wind howling, dense and sticky and wild as Lir emerged from a wetland nestled deep in a lush, jade forest.

He inhaled sharply, lungs on fire as though he'd held his breath for millennia.

"*Ellwyn*," his lips whispered before his mind collected itself. "Ash," he said more loudly, spinning in the waist-deep waters.

Lir clawed through the water, fingers coming up with grass and sludge where Aisling should've been. But the Sidhe king couldn't stop. Aisling was supposed to be here. She was supposed to have emerged alongside him. The reminder of Danu's gateways and Annwyn's aqueducts stabbed Lir with dread. So, he'd keep searching, keep digging, keep clawing through the wetland till he found her.

At last, amid his madness, Lir stilled.

He smelled it before he saw it. The stench of its wet pelt, its talons digging into the mud, its snarling muzzle caught the Sidhe king's attention.

Lir swiveled, meeting the eyes of a demon.

A questing beast.

The creature lifted its dragon's snout from the waters, ivory eyes shimmering like pearls despite the dense canopies and dark gray sky. Its haunches rolled back the moment its talons moved, one step into the waters and closer to Lir. A tail like ribbons, dragging behind it.

*Don't move*, Lir thought to himself in Rún. The questing beast was a monster of great strength and magic, known to skulk in dense forests and feast on its prey whilst they still breathed. Whilst their heart still pumped warmly for the questing beast to lap. A monstrosity—the beholding of which had cost various knights their lives before discovering the questing beast's weakness: sight.

The demon cocked its head to the side, its mane dripping down the scales neatly patterned along its neck. It took another step forward, eager to bait another sound. Another clue as to where its next meal lurked.

Lir's body tensed as it approached nearer, his hand drifted toward the axes at his back upon reflex.

But it was too late. The questing beast had latched onto his smell—potent from the mortal plane—the Sidhe king's heart racing and filling the demon's ears with its chorus.

The questing beast grinned, flashing a trap of sharp teeth still stink-ridden with the sinew of its last meal.

"*Easca*," Lir commanded it—out of reflex or habit, Lir wasn't certain. Wild beasts in the mortal plane heeded the Sidhe king's orders, but he knew the laws were different in the Other, if there were any laws at all.

Lir focused on the monster, watching its muscles roll until it was prepared to pounce. To rip its prey's organs from their still-screaming body.

So, Lir lunged first.

Before their audience of trees could blink, Lir cut through the water, axes in hand and swung for the creature. A spell of violence as the demon shrieked in pain, writhing while it snapped in search of the Sidhe king. Nevertheless, Lir was too quick for the seeing eye, much less that which saw nothing at all, hopelessly spearing in the dark.

Lir lunged again, this time with more force, separating the questing beast's neck from its body.

The beast collapsed into the wetland and sank into its depths. Black blood rising to the surface and clouding the waters till nothing was visible.

Lir sheathed his axes at his back and wiped the splattered blood from his face with the back of his sleeve. And as if conjured by the boom of the monster's last heartbeat, Lir's spirit sank, caving in at the chest. A part of him perished with the forge-born. For Lir knew better than most that he boasted no moral high ground to the questing beast. Lir was simply stronger. And so, he dreaded to reap the lives of the creatures who loved the forest's shadows as much as he himself. But this was the nature of the greenwood whether it be in the mortal plane or the Other. Only the deadliest survived. A game forged by the forest's hands and forced its dwellers to play. And eventually, they all grew to enjoy it.

"Did Niamh send you?" an unfamiliar voice called from the forest's edge.

This time, Lir was taken off guard.

The Sidhe king of greenwood turned, unsheathing his axes at the same moment. But before him was not a monster, nor a man, nor a Sidhe. Rather, a fox stood between two gnarled yews, cloaked in a hood.

"Tell me the truth and nothing more for I'm well aware of the tricks your kind spins with a silver spindle," the fox said, holding a humble wych elm staff like a sword.

Lir's shoulders and axes lowered.

The fox was old, speckled with gray around his brows and muzzle. And by the subtle quiver of his left knee, Lir knew the staff was primarily used for walking and not spell-casting.

"What do you know of my kind?" Lir asked, more to toy with the fiend than anything else.

"By the point of your ears and the arrogance of your posture, you're undoubtedly some Aos Sí thief come to steal from me once more."

Lir chuckled beneath his breath.

"You deny your Aos Sí blood?" the fox pushed.

"Call me nightmare, for that is all I am to you." Lir flashed a playful grin, yet still the fox was unamused, encouraging Lir further.

"I warn you!" the fox shouted again.

"We were invited by Niamh to the Other," Lir said, "but she hasn't sent me here. At least that I know of. We were meant to arrive at Niamh's castle in time for *Lá Brear* this evening."

The fox studied the Sidhe king more closely, taking in the sight of him.

"We?" the fox asked.

Although soaked, Lir was dressed for a royal occasion. Splattered red, his formal garments tested and tried by the portal to the Other and then the questing beast.

Lir's nostrils flared, angered by the reality he wasn't with Aisling.

"I've been separated from my queen," Lir said.

The fox considered him for a long while. Their audience of trees swayed back and forth, whispering to one another.

"Friends of Niamh are no friends of mine," the fox growled. But despite his expression, the beast lowered his staff.

"We are neither friends nor allies of Niamh," Lir confessed. "Our business is our own, but we can swear by the Forge that we mean you no harm."

The fox considered, mumbling something grumpily beneath his breath. Most forge-born creatures were hatched or laid with tempers beyond their bite.

"I would, however," Lir continued, "request a map to Castle Yillen. I must reach Niamh's kingdom by *Lá Brear* this evening."

"Those in a hurry are always up to no good," the fox said.

"Perhaps," Lir agreed. "But it's a request I implore regardless."

The old fox huffed, cursing something intelligible as it stabbed its staff into the mud. Its cloak was well soaked and the longer the creature stood in the storm, the more its lame knee wobbled. So, Lir knew it was only a matter of time before the fox, at last, surrendered and offered him aid.

"Very well," the fox conceded, "but I ask for a favor in exchange."

"I don't bargain with beasts," Lir said, turning on his heel to find Niamh's castle on his own, his impatience gnawing the longer he entertained the fox. He was the most powerful fae king and didn't take kindly to being denied or haggled with. Lir had never traversed these woods, but the trees here spoke loudly, their tongues loose and drunk on the Other's magic. However, the Sidhe king knew venturing alone, without guidance, would risk the journey taking substantially longer than if he were given directions.

"You'll never find Niamh's castle on your own, nightmare!" the fox called after Lir. "This is not your mortal plane."

Lir's ears perked up.

The fox wrinkled its muzzle and raised its nose as though sniffing them from a distance.

"I can smell it on you. You aren't from here. If you aren't lying and what you say is true, then Niamh has intentionally separated you from your friends despite giving you an invitation. And so, she won't be found so easily."

Lir blinked slowly, cracking his neck from side to side.

"Very well, what is it you covet?" Lir asked.

The fox grinned ear to ear.

"Seeing as you slayed my questing beast, I'll need another fiend to guard my cottage from your kind. Surely a nightmare of your hulking size can fetch me another," the fox said.

Lir sighed, reluctant to waste any more time than necessary.

"You do, however, look quite cold and in need of some cider. You may join me in my cottage after you fetch me my end of the bargain, nightmare. And perhaps then I'll have remembered the way to Castle Yillen."

Lir ground his fangs into his bottom teeth.

"Very well." Lir surrendered, perhaps because the guilt of killing the questing beast still weighed heavily on his shoulders or because he found he quite liked the old fox. Either way, he'd satisfy this bargain quickly. "I'll bring you another monster."

And then he'd find Aisling.

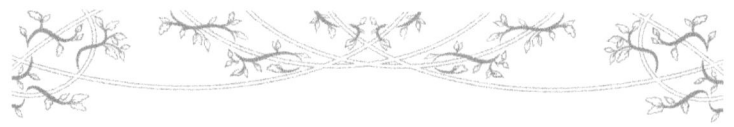

## CHAPTER XII

### AISLING

Once the blue rabbits, at long last, left their quarters in search of supper, Aisling undressed. She stripped off her gown, loosened her braids, unbuckled Sarwen from her back, and slinked off her jewels. All save for Anduril, glittering across her naked hips. For a moment, she considered unclasping the belt. It was both heavy and large, bruising her where it tightened and loosened from time to time.

*You need me*, the belt whispered into her mind. Aisling swatted at the words, but they sank into her consciousness like teeth. So, Aisling forwent removing the belt.

The sorceress sank into a steaming bath prepared for her by three silent sylphs. The bath however, was more of a pool than a tub, located in a separate room attached to her chambers by an opaque, crystal entryway.

Shamrocks grew from the bottom, rising so their beryl-green leaves bubbled at the surface. A fountain carved in the image of a Sidhe poured steaming water into the pool eternally. Water laced with what Aisling believed was star root, silk petals, and mint.

Finally, Aisling was alone. Her thoughts grew loud. Too

loud, scratching at her fears, her anxieties, wondering where the fae king was. He occupied her mind like a haunting, driving Aisling mad the harder Anduril burned the image of him, the name of him, the sound of him from her mind.

Aisling sank further into the pool until only her eyes peered above the surface. She could breathe not with her lungs but with the *draiocht*—a spell someone had taught her when they'd first wandered through Annwyn's greenwood. Anduril bloomed awake and scalded her flesh. Aisling whimpered out in pain, grabbing the edge of the bath. But once the pain had subsided, she couldn't remember what she'd been thinking of.

Aisling closed her eyes, her mind wiped clean as she breathed in and out slowly, hushing Racat back into acquiescence after thoughts of the Sidhe king. But while her mind cleared, her heart remained heavy, filling her dreams with images and voices. Dreams Anduril couldn't seem to prevent from unspooling.

*You and the Sidhe king can never be*, an ancient creature boomed before a spindle. Yet still, Aisling felt the fae king's fingers on her bare flesh. Felt the bliss of him inside her, making her whole once more, wrapped in the dark lord's embrace, hot, heaving, and intertwined.

"*Where are you, Aisling?*" a familiar voice cooed from the corridors of a starry forest.

Aisling immediately recoiled, staggering back but tripping on the hem of her gown. She hit the ground hard, struggling to her feet before *she* made herself seen. Yet, Aisling's body felt both heavier and slower here in this realm of dreams. As though Aisling were once more nothing but a mortal princess, slave to the whim of all those more powerful. Anduril gone from her hips.

"*Aisling,*" the voice called again in a sing-song tone that sent chills up Aisling's spine. "*Where are you?*"

"Enough!" Aisling screamed into the darkness, refusing to be haunted by *her*.

"*Tsk tsk,*" she said, "*Isn't it I who should be furious? Isn't it I who should want your bones deep beneath the earth? For wasn't it you who destroyed my loom?*"

The Lady laughed, high and shrill and wholly inhuman. A sound that challenged neither good nor evil, taking on an alignment of its own. Something of yore that was better left forgotten.

"Go on." Aisling bared her teeth, becoming a feral wolf cornered in a cage. "Bore me with another of your long-winded prophecies, your riddles, your warnings. For your loom will continue to break, your threads will fray, and your shears will grow blunt."

"*Perhaps.*" The Lady's voice filled the emptiness of her starry forest, vibrating through Aisling's bones. "*But at what cost? You've already lost so much, child.*"

"I've become Sidhe queen of the fae and before long, I'll rule over the Other. I have everything."

"*Poor Dagfin would beg to differ if he bore a life to protest your arrogance.*" The Lady laughed louder as though overcome with joyful tears. "*He'd despise what you've become. By the gods, I'm certain he wouldn't even recognize you.*"

Aisling stilled.

Her tongue turned to ash, a bloody wound in her heart slashed open once more by the mere mention of Dagfin's name.

"*Where are you, Aisling?*" the Lady asked again, but Aisling could barely hear her. "*Where are you, child?*"

∼

"What did she say to you?!"

Aisling was jerked out of water, gasping for air. She floundered at the edge of a pool but no longer was she in her chambers. She was somewhere else, somewhere thundering and flashing with lightning, yet still deep within Niamh's castle. Aisling must've fallen asleep while bathing and the Lady hadn't wasted an opportunity to violate her dreams.

Aisling choked up water, reaching for the edge of the pool. She pulled herself over the brim, hands lit with flame in her panic.

"What spells did she cast?!" Someone spoke again. And when Aisling bore the strength to focus and address who spoke to her, she spotted the cloud-like hem of Niamh's gown.

Aisling coughed, struggling to her feet and entirely nude from her bath earlier.

"You are referring to the Lady."

"Aye," Niamh said impatiently, glaring at Aisling as though she herself was the primordial creature bound to the threads of her loom of fate. "Did you tell her where you were? Did you let her needle her way inside your mind?!"

Aisling wiped the hair sticking to her face, still processing her surroundings. This must've been Niamh's bathing chambers for the ceiling was dense with dark clouds, lightning spidering down the slick, obsidian walls that opened at the center of the room into a pool as black as night, crowned by steam. And what's more, petrified rain hung in the air like glass beads, bursting when touched.

"I told her nothing. She knows not where I am nor how to reach me," Aisling said, her voice still rough where her lungs burned.

"Do not grow overly confident. If I hadn't pulled you out of your careless dreams, she would've dug deeper, clawing inside your mind for where to find you."

"She must know I'm in the Other," Aisling said, looking down at her bare form and Anduril that Niamh wholly ignored.

"It's likely," Niamh said, the clouds of her dress gathering more thickly. "But we cannot assume she knows anything. Give her nothing, allow her nothing, gift her no advantage." Niamh stepped closer to Aisling, her words spoken more quickly, more urgently, and sharper the longer she spoke.

Aisling took a step back. A gesture that didn't go unnoticed.

"You speak as though we're allies, yet I know nothing of your intentions," Aisling said, her voice clear and unmuddied despite the whiplash.

Niamh searched Aisling's expression, her mind undoubtedly determining what information to offer in exchange for Aisling's. Her face flashed wildly with several emotions. Heartbeats ago, the Seelie queen of Rain had behaved as though she'd known Aisling for a millennium, yet they'd only just met. She'd been angry, concerned, fret with worry as Aisling stood dripping and nude before her, only Anduril returned to her hips after the Lady had stripped it from her body whilst inside her realm of dreams.

"You're right," Niamh said to Aisling's surprise. Her earlier anxious rage clearing like the sky after a cloudburst. "Let's remedy that. Will you dress with me for *Lá Brear*?" Niamh's lips softened, her uptilted eyes foregoing their serrated edge in exchange for something warmer. Something almost familiar.

Aisling hesitated, eyes darting around the room as though in search of an answer. She understood trust was a luxury she couldn't afford. Both the mortal plane and the Other bore a stake on Aisling's life—she, both the prophesied doom of the Sidhe and the curse breaker for the mortals. Wartime loyalties were fickle, and strangers were threats. Especially powerful ones. Even if Niamh welcomed her to the Other, Aisling knew better than to find comfort in the den of a creature more fabled than most. And yet, the legend before her was necessary to the Goblet of Lore, to gaining the gods' favor, to preventing mortal victory. To everything.

So, Aisling steeled herself. Anduril singing softly in her ears.

"I'd love to," Aisling said at last, offering Niamh her prettiest smile. Deception was more effective when its bitter intentions were masked with something sweet: a smile, a glance, a kiss. More effective as a weapon than most blades or jinxes. Indeed, this much Aisling had learned.

The Seelie queen of Rain watched intently as the corners of Aisling's lips curled, her own expression mirroring Aisling's. The smile was still cold but in the uncanny, otherworldly manner the Sidhe moved. Not in cruelty. In fact, it gave Aisling the impression of two serpents slithering side by side, neither allies nor enemies but alike just the same.

"Follow me," Niamh said, starting for the door.

They slipped into an adjacent room inside another spire. Petrified rain bejeweled every inch of this room as well, hanging in the air, on the thick moss that clung to every wall, the river stones, the mosaicked floors, and the oak leaf garlands that bulged from the rafters. A trove of crystals, a spiderweb dressed in morning dew, a room that smelled of freshly wet soil and cool, woodland breezes.

Dozens of winged sylphs flew through this room, carrying gowns and jewels and crowns, but Niamh paid them little attention as she grabbed Aisling's hand and gently tugged her toward a mirror in the center of the room.

Aisling took in her bare form. Raven-black hair sticking to her back, her arms, her hips, and Anduril's supple gold. Her cheeks and chest were red from coughing and her violet eyes were ringed with dark circles. And somehow, standing beside Niamh and her forget-me-not-blue hair, her perpetually wet skin, her dress of clouds, Aisling looked more otherworldly than she ever had in Annwyn. As though a part of her belonged here in the Other.

Racat hummed gleefully, stirring inside. Anduril glittered with approval.

"I've been dying to dress you for several centuries now," Niamh said.

*Centuries?* Aisling thought to herself, but before she could speak it aloud, Niamh stepped behind Aisling and ran her fingers through her hair. Immediately, Aisling flinched. She wasn't accustomed to being touched at all and certainly not by those she'd only just met. Nevertheless, Niamh wasn't discouraged, moving closer to Aisling as she untangled her tresses. So, for the sake of the Goblet of Lore, Aisling let her.

"This belt, however, is ancient and unfit for your beauty," Niamh said. "May I remove it?" she asked, hands already starting toward its clasp.

Without hesitation, Anduril hardened to stone, coiling around Aisling like a snake. The sorceress's eyes lit like embers and before she could think better of it, her hands snatched at Niamh's wrist.

*"The belt remains,"* Anduril spoke through Aisling's lips—a primeval growl lacing her voice.

Niamh bristled, slowly taking back her wrist. Her lips pursed tightly, but she eventually nodded her head in understanding. The Seelie queen cleared her throat and continued her work. Anduril settled back into place on Aisling's hips, quieting once more.

The sensation of Niamh's long, slender fingers against Aisling's scalp, combing through her knots, was too comforting. Too maternal to resist. A touch Aisling had barely, if ever, felt. Her life had been shaped by the rough hands of men and not the sensitive touch of a woman who cared deeply for her. Yet, against her better judgment, Aisling sank into Niamh, allowing herself the affection.

Niamh's touch straightened Aisling's hair till it fell like the waters in Annwyn's gorge. Her fingers traveled toward her scalp, dancing through the strands but leaving behind beads of rain as she worked. They grew along her collarbone, along the edge of her ears, speckled around the crown of her head. And at last, Niamh traced the edge of Aisling's arms and a dress took form. A gown made entirely of water hugged and draped around her every curve till it spilled atop the mosaicked floors. Pearl-tipped crests protecting her most precious parts.

Aisling's eyes burned, glossing over with unshed tears. She'd almost forgotten what she looked like in gowns that didn't burn mourning-white.

"Is everything alright?" Niamh asked, brows arching with genuine concern.

Aisling blinked away the tears, nodding her head.

"The dress is lovely, is all," she lied.

A sylph darted from the rafters and pressed a scarlet cherry to Aisling's lips, staining them red. Niamh smiled, admiring her work before she plucked a single bead of rain from her clavicle and blew.

The bead of rain grew, splashing upward before falling and forming a whirlpool around their feet. The churning of the waters akin to the gentle stirring of tea.

"Ina and I were close friends," Niamh said, eyes reflecting the spinning of the waters beneath them. "She and I were like sisters. I cared—*care*—for her deeply. And although her soul is lost in the fogs of death beyond my realm, my heart finds a piece of her in you, Aisling."

Aisling's brows pinched. She felt the sincerity of Niamh's words weaving between them. She felt the Seelie queen's love for the fae king's mother as potently as she might've felt the love for a sister of her own had she ever been blessed with one. And what's more, Aisling wanted to believe Niamh. She wanted to believe in her kindness, in this newfound warmth, in this... affection Aisling hadn't realized she'd craved all her life.

"I remember the day Ina found you amidst the folds of the

tapestry of time. How she searched for decades for the perfect hiding place for her most cherished gift. She knew her end was coming swiftly.

"We wept together when she placed her gift inside an iron, Tilrish keep." Niamh's voice thickened, lost to the memory. "And so I vowed to watch over you. Vowed to keep you as safe as I knew how. Bringing rain to Tilren, beating it against your windowpanes, finding you in the neighboring loch, watching you from the brim of every goblet of wine."

Aisling's head whipped toward the pool below their feet. The waters reflected not themselves, rather Aisling as a child, Aisling as she grew older, Aisling as she grew lost in Annwyn's feywilds, swimming with Lir in the hot springs the day he taught her how to summon her *draiocht*. Aisling gasped, her mind stretching before Anduril dug into Aisling's flesh with anger, distracting her from the visions and instead, biting Aisling with a venom of equal rage at the sight of the fae king. Aisling fought the feeling, bending the thoughts in her mind to make sense of them, but Anduril insisted, muddling Aisling's mind further.

Just as Danu's Isle of Mirrors used water to watch, to travel, to speak, so did Niamh's. Water was transformative. Water was magic. And water was a part of the *draiocht*.

But the memories the water chose to reveal were not all pleasant. Some were shameful, some were dark, and some were better left unremembered. The image of Nemed locking Aisling inside her chambers, forced to watch Starn, Iarbonel, Annind, and Fergus from the iron teeth of her window while they were raised to be kings.

"It wasn't Ina who invited you to the Other at Lofgren's Rise or in Castle Annwyn," Niamh said, meeting Aisling's eyes. "It was me."

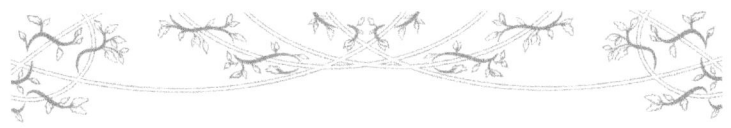

## CHAPTER XIII

*The sun bled, its wounds swathed in the black gauze of smoke-stained skies. Nemed lifted the visor of his helmet, too satisfied to acknowledge the burning of his eyes or the weakness of his body as he trudged up the hill of the main thoroughfare.*

*Hours before, Tahsman was glittering. A copper chalice settled at the center of the southern wastelands with a singing, laughing, merry heart of a kingdom at its center. Winds ran dry and hot, brushing the branches of skeletal, spindly trees and the cracked earth. They blew from the north, scraping up the sides of Tahsman's sparkling gates and into the kingdom itself, billowing below the wings of Aos Sí as they darted between the corridors of their home. Bridges, walkways, and towers stretched and pulled like hardened honey or melted sugars—amber and trapping the light of the sun. All of which fell at the knee to the fire hand.*

*Nemed swallowed* wystria *daily, curled before the hearth like an incubus atop a body. The fire hand spread the* scull draiocht *from knight to knight. Their eyes lit like hot coals, the corners of their lips curled with smoke and the heat of the Lady's wildfire inside. They spat, they screamed, they spoke, and fire bred quickly. It grew and multiplied as if alive. As if the wystria,* nestled inside the chasm of mortal man's heart was as hungry for Aos Sí's destruction as Nemed himself. This was the nature of shadow magic: it ate from the will of its master.

Nemed sucked in a breath, relishing the taste of the Lady's dark magic. It growled inside his gut, stuck to his insides like tar, and clawed at his throat to be released. He bit down on its overzealous whims, finding strange satisfaction in harnessing such powers. But none of that was as fulfilling as what the wystria did.

The Aos Sí screamed for their lives like a symphony of birds crushed slowly. Their whimpering dimmed to muffled cries within the first hour and by the fifth, only the crackling of the flames popped and snapped atop piles of Aos Sí bones. This was conquest. This was war. This was power, Nemed realized, as he tickled the wystria's dark desires between his teeth with his tongue.

The fire hand walked forward, taking in the image of his triumph—ichor crunching beneath the iron soles of his boots. He dragged his left leg, his limp less noticeable with the strength of the wystria inside him. And had it not been for the mortal knight, dead atop the cobbles, Nemed would've explored every death-marked alley, every blood-soaked chamber, and every splintered bone to indulge his victory—his fae genocide. Instead, he stopped short and knelt beside his knight.

The man had been dead for some time, a gem-encrusted fae spear impaling his chest. He was young, perhaps not even past his fourth decade with a blade still firmly clutched in his right hand. Nemed knelt beside him, brushing back hair stuck to his face by both blood and sweat.

The fire hand had ventured to Tahsman with only a handful of men. Aisling had destroyed most mortal fleets, but it'd been the wystria that offered humankind power over the Aos Sí at long last. The ability to venture into the feywilds and their kingdoms one by one and reclaim all that was rightfully theirs despite their *small numbers. And so, Nemed had done just that: Tahsman was the third Aos Sí kingdom the mortals had taken, pillaged, ravaged, and destroyed in every violent capacity war allowed.*

*The wystria thrashed inside Nemed's mouth, eager for release. He clenched his jaw but thought better of it, his hand hesitating on the knight's forehead. Slowly, he opened his mouth and let the wystria slip off his tongue. It fell from his mouth like a floating lantern, falling gradually toward the knight. It hesitated briefly, before diving down.*

*The wystria nestled into the cavity of the knight's mouth. It burned more brightly, biting chunks from Nemed's soul to complete its work. The fire hand winced—a combination of pain and pleasure rattling through his body each time the* scull draiocht *took what it was owed.*

*The knight's eyes opened, but they burned not with human life, only with the will of shadowed magic—Nemed's* scull draiocht *and the bits of his soul it'd eaten.*

*The knight rose to his feet, pulling the spear from his chest with a slushy release. He stood dead but tall, waiting on Nemed's signal to continue the destruction they'd already wrought over Tahsman. Starn's raven, a letter in its beak, landed on a statue lithely.*

# CHAPTER XIV

## LIR

The smell of warm milk cider floated from the old fox's cottage in a wispy tendril, teasing Lir where he crouched in the rain. The cottage was overgrown with ivy and wildflowers, sprouting atop the shingled roof, the cracks between stones, and even the smoking chimney, nestled between a family of pines.

"*Through the wetland it comes, hungry, hungry for more than crumbs, mo Damh Bán,*" the trees said between the groans of thunder overhead. "*Not too long from now.*"

Lir didn't trust the trees here in the Other. They spoke in riddles, spoke too loudly, and too often. So had it not been for Lir's own sense that what he was attracting was indeed coming, he wouldn't have relied on their messages that his waiting was almost over.

Lir dipped his fist back into the wetland and exhaled. The *draiocht* howled inside, summoning a rich magic that vibrated with the surrounding storm. Wetweed bloomed inside his fist and then spread throughout the body of water. It grew dense and lush, transforming the wetland into a feast.

At last, the waters rippled and moved, forming a mound of water as the monster approached.

Lir stood from his crouch and watched as the creature lifted its head, springing for the Sidhe king. Lir anticipated this. Most Unseelie were chaotic in nature, driven by hunger and hunger alone.

Lir didn't flinch. Instead, roots rose like tentacles, reaching and grabbing for the slippery fiend. They tangled around its head, its throat, binding the massive creature in a bed of wetweed.

It shrieked an unholy cry, squirming for its life after having fallen prey to Lir's trap. Yet, its struggle was in vain. And once it stilled, Lir could see the green of its slimy flesh, the coarse mane that grew down the ridge of its head, its neck, and its back. Its square teeth and glowing red eyes.

A kelpie.

"*Asteria missto pastera lek*," Lir said. It was a command for the Unseelie to bow to its sovereign: a necessary display of subservience to the more dominant between the pair. And so long as the kelpie understood Lir was in control, it would obey.

The kelpie wailed, thrashing in Lir's vines. The more it struggled, the more tightly Lir held it with his roots, inspiring the wetweed to grow bountifully.

"*Asteria missto pastera lek*," Lir repeated, and after several painful heartbeats, the kelpie surrendered.

Lir untangled his roots, slithering away like a nest of snakes. The smell of the kelpie's wounds from its skin having been rubbed raw, stained the air where milk cider once had.

"*Protect these waters and the old fox who lives here*," Lir continued, "*and you shall not want for your next meal.*"

Both cautiously and weakly, the kelpie took its first bite of wetweed. One bite became many, and soon the Unseelie was devouring what Lir had grown with ravenous gulps. And with every swallow, the bargain between the old fox and Lir was satisfied—the *draiocht* stirring through the surrounding forest in great howls of wind.

So, by the time Lir entered the fox's cottage, doubling over to fit inside the small door, the fox had already sensed the completion of Lir's debt as well.

"Take a seat, *mo Damh Bán*." The fox greeted Lir, leaping from his stool to fetch another for the Sidhe king. The fox was dry now and wrapped in a woolen shawl, cupping his pottered bowl filled generously to the brim. "I'd offer for you to remove your weaponry so you might be more comfortable, but considering who you are, I'll abstain. Simply know that welcoming a sovereign, even an Aos Sí king, is my utmost priority."

"So, you know my title then," Lir said, scowling at the bowl the fox offered him. The fox's understanding of Lir's identity was a risk considering information of such a caliber could jeopardize their role here in the Other and, more importantly, jeopardize how quickly Lir could find Aisling.

"Don't be cross with me, *mo Damh Bán*. I recognized you the moment I saw you emerge from my wetland," the old fox insisted from the far end of the cottage, ladling cider from a cauldron still bubbling over a fire. It was a small abode, made smaller by the plethora of herbs, spices, flowers, and weeds hanging in bundles from the rafters, the stacks of pots and pans, and the jars of pickled dragons, pixies, and newts lining the shelves. Bookcases stuffed with dusty, jewel-encrusted tomes were pressed against the walls while the windows fogged with the heat of the cottage's interior.

The old fox was wise and skilled, that much Lir could tell. There was a millennium of experience with shadowed magic, with potions, and charms behind the forge-born beast's red-bright pelt. And proficiency, talent, ambition, and potential were virtues Lir both admired and respected. Qualities he sought in those he held closest.

"Yet, you feigned ignorance?" Lir asked as the fox placed his bowl on the table.

"I wasn't certain if you'd skin me for such knowledge. I can only assume your presence here in the Other is of some importance. Especially considering you weren't offered a royal welcome upon arrival. Instead, you emerged from my wetlands like a ghoul."

Lir pushed his wet hair from his eyes and cleared his throat, "You mentioned earlier that our separation from our friends was intentional? You believe Niamh did this?"

"Sshh!" the old fox hissed, leaping from his stool and racing for the windows. Startled, he watched as the fox shut every window and bolted their padlocks, drawing thick, velvet curtains till the only light bloomed from the crackling hearth. "Apologies, *mo Damh Bán*," the fox said, taking his seat once more. "So long as the rain falls, Niamh will be listening, watching, wondering. Even sipping cider is a risk we can scarcely afford."

"You're afraid of her," Lir conjectured.

"I am too old to fear Seelie queens or kings," the fox said, eyes fixing on Lir. "And still, too old to underestimate their reach. Niamh had no reason to keep a watchful eye on myself or my cottage... until you arrived. You see, Niamh breathes through every droplet of moisture in the Other and so, she controls the passage between our realm and yours. You can rest assured she intended for you to arrive here in the wetland and not in Castle Yillen. For what reason? You'd have to ask Niamh yourself."

Lir toyed with the edge of his fangs with the tip of his tongue, considering. The Sidhe king had never met Niamh and never harbored any ill will or a reason to consider her an enemy. But purposefully separating himself from Aisling would make an enemy of Niamh quicker than most other crimes.

"Whatever you know about Niamh and are willing to share, I encourage you to do so," Lir said, the green of his eyes gilded by the hearth. "My court's intentions are to spare the Sidhe from extinction at the hands of the mortals and other powerful adversaries."

The fox snorted, abruptly realizing his place and collecting himself.

"Do not appeal to my sympathy for the Aos Sí if you request my allegiance, for you'll find such empathy has long turned to apathy. A sentiment I'm surprised the forge-born beasts in your realm do not share." The old fox exchanged glances with the covered windows, perhaps thinking of the creatures that scurried between the trees just outside his cottage.

"Many of my knights are beasts such as yourself, swearing oaths and dedicating their blades to Annwyn," Lir said, thinking of Gilrel as he spoke. "If you cannot trust the Sidhe, then trust my oath to my blade, to my honor, and to the Forge when I say that the victory of fae folk is the triumph of the Forge at large, including Seelie, Unseelie, and all forge-born beasts like yourself."

"The arrogance of the Aos Sí will be their downfall. When the last thread is spun, the Aos Sí can no longer blame the mortals nor any other race," the fox said. "Niamh and her court have banished most forge-born beasts to the mortal realm despite their equal claim to this land. Only those who've proven useful were permitted to stay and so, here I am, called upon when Niamh needs my use of spells, of herbs, of knowledge, and of history. Even so, she has no appreciation for those she uses to achieve her ends."

Lir's brow furrowed as he leaned back in his chair and crossed his arms. The chair squeaked in protest to his great height and weight.

"When the realms were divided, the gods slept. But before the gods laid their heads to rest, they allowed some Sidhe and forge-born creatures to remain for the purpose of guarding over the Other in their stead. This includes beasts of all make and nature, no matter their size or stature," Lir said.

"Aye, you know your history well, *mo Damh Bán*," the fox said. "But Niamh grew restless, grew bored sharing such a responsibility. And so, she stormed and stormed until, at last, the gods gifted her the Goblet of Lore and their favor, making Niamh the sole keeper of the Other. The queen and guardian of gates between worlds."

"And then she banished your kind," Lir said. "At least those who didn't prove useful to her ends."

"Indeed." The fox took a sip of cider. "And at the cost of my skills, I lost my family. I, one of the few forge-born creatures cursed to live in the Other alone. Separated from my companions and forced to live alongside these *draiocht*-maddened fae."

There was silence for a long while. Niamh's tempest pounding against the windowpanes as though eager to eavesdrop but unable. Her presence was palpable. Lir could almost hear her heartbeat in the surrounding woodland, her influence affecting the nature of the elms, the willows, and the birches that grew wild and crooked and gnarled here in the Other. Every leaf veined with secrets.

"Then we're aligned," Lir said, breaking the silence. "As king of Annwyn and of the Sidhe at large, we plan to replace Niamh as the favored child of the gods. Your loyalty would be both greatly valued and rewarded."

The fox did a double take of Lir.

"If Aisling is successful, defeating our greatest threats, her will is that of the Forge; for one day, Seelie, Unseelie, and forge-born to live all united in one plane."

"The mortal plane?" the fox asked.

"So it is believed," Lir replied.

The warm glow of the hearth inspired shadows that danced across the planes of the Sidhe king's face. His soaked leathers and armor still dripping onto the floorboards.

The old fox's ears twitched, beady eyes glossing over with an expression Lir found difficult to read. His whiskers shook and his wet nose scrunched up.

The fox stood from his stool and buried himself in the pile of books tossed beside the slanted shelves. And when he at last emerged, he carried a tattered scroll in his paws, spreading it onto the table so that all could see its illustrated map.

"Niamh's castle is here: Castle Yillen," the old fox said, pointing to the drawing of a floating fortress at the center. If you begin your journey now, you'll arrive before the end of Niamh's *Là Brear*. But make haste. The rains and the beasts of the wood are no small obstacle."

Lir gathered the map and stood from his chair, remembering last minute to duck his head before he hit the ceiling beams with the back of his head.

The ramshackle cottage still huffed from its chimney as he braced against the outside storm. The old fox's newfound kelpie was deep within his wetlands no doubt devouring the wetweed that grew plentifully there, thanks to Lir. Bound to protect the cottage until the end of time.

"Farewell, nightmare," the old fox said, waving at Lir before he disappeared into the wilderness.

"Not '*mo Damh Bán*'?" Lir asked.

"I've neither witnessed myself nor overheard the presence of *mo Damh Bán*," the old fox replied mischievously, winking at Lir. "You'd best find him in Annwyn."

Lir smiled, recognizing the trust weaving between them, thread by thread.

"Until we meet again, Cara," Lir said, addressing the old fox by his name.

The forge-born beast, taken aback, widened his eyes. He hadn't told Lir his name, but the trees had, and Lir would remember it.

"And, nightmare, take the left wing of the forest by the cliff edge of the river. You'll reach Castle Yillen more quickly avoiding the storm floods and the rot that spreads," Cara called after him.

Lir nodded his head in thanks, recognizing—not for the first time—Cara had proven himself a worthy ally.

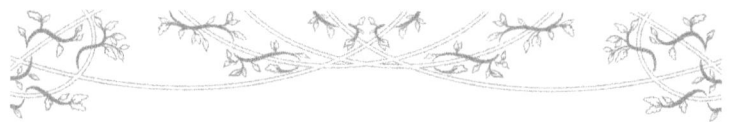

## CHAPTER XV

### AISLING

Niamh and Aisling slipped through Castle Yillen like spirits, the blue rabbits following closely behind. They wandered past the kitchens spilling over with sweet plumes of freshly baked cakes and breads. They passed the chapels, glittering with candlelight reflecting off the stained glass and blessed by the dense ghosts of incense waging holy battles by the rafters.

"A haven for prayer," Niamh explained as Aisling's gaze lingered.

"Do sleeping gods hear prayers?" Aisling asked, wondering if Niamh would take offense to her inquiry. As far as Aisling understood, the twin gods had forsaken both the mortal plane and the Otherworld, choosing to sleep in place of reigning from their primordial thrones. This was why the twelve Sidhe sovereigns ruled—their power, now, divided and insufficient to prevent the prophecies all-seers witnessed.

Niamh, however, smiled. "Time will tell."

They continued their passage through Castle Yillen until Niamh approached the steepled doors. Aisling smelled the alder tree the doors were carved from. Still, its heart thumped, pumping sap through the veins of its gnarled surface. But it was the face around it, born from the same tree, that unsettled Aisling most of all.

The alder bent and twisted, taking the form of a colossal king. The doors were his gaping mouth. The king's hair was long and braided, beaded with leaves and blackberries that bled along the ridges of its roots. His beard was thick and cloaked with moss, spilling around the doorway like snakes.

Aisling's ears popped with a change in pressure. A sensation similar to being in the presence of magic for the first time: an invisible enchantment made old, timeworn, and immortal by the pressure of eternity.

"Breka," Niamh said, staring up at the colossus herself. "The eldest of the god brothers."

Breka. Anduril vibrated as if trembling. As if disquieted in the presence of a god's likeness. Aisling had never heard the gods' names spoken before. The Lore—the library of collective history—was referred to as the Forbidden Lore in the mortal world. And so, Aisling had scarcely sipped from its well of knowledge.

Niamh raised her arm and as if summoned awake, the doors opened of their own accord.

"*Lá Brear* is on the other side of this room," Niamh said as she stepped forward. "We must pass through."

Aisling peered into a darkness like oblivion. But the moment they crossed the threshold, every rain droplet froze in mid-air like suspended crystals, sparkling with luminous light.

Aisling inhaled.

Tomes, novels, bibles, and the entire Forbidden Lore were stacked on shelves, forgotten on desks, or pressed against the sky-high rafters. The ceiling was made of stained glass, flashing colorfully each time the lightning outside craved attention.

Poetry scrolls, ballads, and fireside tales floated of their own accord, aimlessly flipping through their own pages as they whispered the stories they yearned to tell. The room was a hushed chorus of murmuring, of humming, of words unread and beautiful.

Detailed and ornate statues of winged Sidhe knights lined the walls alongside gargoyles, dragons, and owls. Each furious, blades in hand, fangs bared, and talons eager to strike.

Niamh chose the center thoroughfare, entering the labyrinth. Aisling followed a pace behind, careful not to knock into the flying, self-reading books.

It was a dark corner where the end of the Forbidden Lore section rested; the collective history of their making written into a series of great opuses charmingly tokened as "forbidden" thanks to the mortals' censorship of the past they shared with the fae.

But it wasn't the books or the shelves or the statues that alarmed Aisling.

It was the singing books, eager for Aisling to appreciate their voices.

"Ignore them," Niamh said as she continued forward. "Lest they never leave you alone."

Aisling nodded her head, but she couldn't resist the rich hues of their leather bindings, the smell of their dusty pages, or how they flapped their covers like a bird's wings. The sorceress tucked her hair behind her ears, listening a little closer to their words.

They sang songs, chanting titles in their choruses like "Niamh's Storm Cloud," "The Book of Sarwen," "Legendary Objects of Other," "Chorus of the Gods," and more. Aisling listened more intently, hoping to hear a melody written about the Goblet of Lore.

> *Seven storm seasons come but never go.*
> *Come child, I hear the wild horns blow.*

Aisling paused, intrigued by the melody of this book.

Niamh however, looked straight ahead, uncaring or unaware of Aisling's growing interest despite her warnings.

*Psalms of Rain*, was inscribed on the front of the book in a humble, cerulean binding.

"A collection of nursery rhymes," Niamh said without turning. Aisling shuddered, wondering if Niamh had eyes on the back of her head. "A useless tome."

Aisling plucked the book from where it flew regardless. Niamh didn't react, approaching the door at the opposing end of the library where they'd exit.

Aisling hurriedly opened the book and flipped through its pages.

"Spring's Herald", "Teardrops of Tempest", and "The Architect of Yillen" were among the various songs the book sang if Aisling hesitated on a page for more than a breath. And perhaps it was "The Architect of Yillen's" haunting melody that encouraged her to wait a breath longer than the rest.

> *Seven storm seasons come but never go.*
> *Come child, I hear the wild horns blow.*
> *A western faerie weeps, broken by a lonely heart,*
> *Cursed to the Other, destined to live apart.*
>
> *Listen to the rain, child*
> *But don't be beguiled*
> *For a faerie will drown you in her tears*
> *Or she'll steal you away for years*
> *Just so that she might not be so lonely.*
>
> *'If only, if only,'*
> *The gods watched in horror*
> *As the Other stormed for her.*
> *'A gift will bring you joy, faerie,'*
> *The gods said so she might, at long last, be merry.*

*'Gift me a friend only,'*
*The faerie said, 'so that I might not be so lonely.'*

*So the gods, with tearful eyes, gave her a Goblet*
*Ruby, red, scarlet.*
*Cast in the Great Forge of Creation*
*A magic that fed on the limits of the imag-*
    *ination.*

*'Be wise,'*
*The gods advised.*
*So the faerie built a home,*
*A castle, stone by stone*
*For she and her friend to live in the Other, only.*
*Just so that she might not be so lonely.*

*Be wise, child,*
*For the faerie's wish was wild*
*'Bring my friend to me in the Other.'*
*She wished and wished, one night after another.*
*Just so that she might not be so lonely.*
*If only, if only.*

*The Goblet brought the faerie her friend*
*And so came her friend, alive, alive until she met*
    *her end.*
*Death, the boat that crossed the waters*
*From the mortal plane and to the Other, in*
    *slaughter.*
*Just so that she might not be so lonely.*
*If only, if only.*

*Seven storm seasons come but never go.*
*Come child, I hear the wild horns blow.*

*A western faerie weeps, broken by a lonely heart,*
*Cursed to the Other, destined to live apart.*

*Listen to the rain, child*
*But don't be beguiled*
*For she'll drown you in her tears*
*Or she'll steal you away for years*
*To her castle in the sky*
*Just so that she might not be so lonely.*
*If only, if only.*

Niamh abruptly shut the book. The Seelie queen snatched it from Aisling and held the book close to her chest—the melody, silencing itself. Nevertheless, the echo of the song tormented them long after the last note had been sung.

Niamh's eyes glared at Aisling.

"In the Other, curiosity might come at the cost of your life, sorceress," Niamh chided, eyes narrowed into slits even as she started to turn on her heel.

"What was that?" Aisling asked. "That song."

"I've already told you. A nursery rhyme," Niamh bit back.

"The faerie," Aisling continued, nevertheless. "The faerie—"

Niamh spun on her heel and looked Aisling in the eye with a ferocity like gathering of storm clouds.

"Enough," she said, and lightning webbed across the sky above Castle Yillen.

Aisling clenched her jaw, but she uttered not another word. The faerie was Niamh and what's more, Niamh didn't want Aisling to know.

Aisling bowed her head in feigned obedience, keeping the knowledge to herself.

Niamh smothered the book till it could no longer sing. The Seelie queen tossed the book to one of the blue rabbits escorting from behind. The rabbit held the tome gingerly before reshelving the book tightly between two other red tomes. The book seemed to protest the rabbit's efforts, humming to be opened once more. But it mattered not if the rabbit reshelved the tome, burned it, ripped it apart, or tossed it into a lake. Aisling had already heard its song.

Niamh, indeed, staked claim to a kingdom in the west nestled in the mortal plane but never had she actually reigned from such towers. The book could've sung of any western faerie... but even as Aisling's thoughts trailed off, she didn't believe their reasoning.

Niamh built Castle Yillen with the Goblet of Lore. A gift from the gods to cease her sorrows that endlessly stormed over the Other. Alone, she wished for her friend to join her and join her she did. Yet, one cannot enter the Other even with an invitation lest it be *Samhain* or *Lá Brear,* Aisling knew. Even with the Goblet of Lore.

Aisling bit her bottom lip as they left the library in silence.

In order to complete Niamh's wish, the Goblet killed Niamh's requested friend: the only way to deliver her friend to the Other, Aisling realized.

*At the last blood moon, you'll howl once more before you drift into the Other and join your brothers and sisters beyond the fog.* Aisling repeated a tale the beasts in Annwyn recited often. A way to look forward to death and its quest.

A sinking feeling formed in the pit of Aisling's stomach. The Other was vast, limitless: a world of spirits and magic. The cradle of creation itself. But there was a half of the Other that was sanctioned for the dead. The home of the afterlife where souls whose bodies no longer served them drifted into eternity. Beyond the fog on a ghostly galleon.

Aisling shuddered but not from the cold.

So, who was this "friend" the song spoke of? Aisling asked

herself as Niamh quickened her pace. Eager to leave the library as swiftly as she was able.

The answers to Aisling's questions eluded her. And yet, she knew the Goblet of Lore was more powerful than she realized. Aisling could create anything she dreamed of by the bidding of the Goblet.

Anduril lit gleefully, as though basking in warm showers of sunlight.

*Perhaps the solution to ending the war with the mortals, and now Danu and the Lady, lies elsewhere,* Aisling thought. Perhaps she was still spooked by the haunting melody or perhaps her intuition was telling her something. The tale felt wrong and so did her search for the Goblet.

"Arawn," Niamh said, startling Aisling from her thoughts, "the second brother god."

Aisling looked up, greeted by the giant face of Arawn. He was monstrous, weeping thick streams of dark syrup from his eyes. His branches grew richly with sharp pointed leaves and his expression was warped with madness. The first god was silent, was still, was ordered. But the second god was chaos and discord, prickling with thorns as sharp as teeth.

Aisling swallowed, relieving the pressure in her ears where the weight of the god's likeness and *draiocht* pushed down on her head.

Magic enjoyed giving and it enjoyed taking. Only by the law of the *draiocht* did it ever give in return for something and only to those capable of dominating it. This was what all Sidhe children were taught when they first learned to fly, to breathe beneath the waves, to sing with the wind, or wield a weapon. And each was reminded of such laws on more than one occasion when casting spells or charms or jinxes felt too "easy". It was a lesson they did well to remember even as they aged into oblivion. Even as Aisling glared up at one of the fathers of magic himself. Or so, Lir—Anduril tightened—the fae king had taught her. Hadn't he? Aisling struggled to remember, doubt budding in her mind like weeds. More and more she felt like she couldn't trust herself. Uncertainty, her constant companion.

Their attention wandered back toward the tome on the shelf, still humming between the crimson bindings of its silent neighbors.

But it was the blowing of horns on the other side of the doors that broke the spell of their silence. A muffled concert boomed from the chamber beyond the door.

*Lá Brear* had begun.

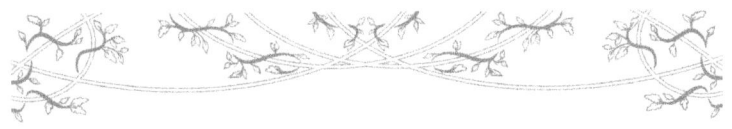

# CHAPTER XVI

## AISLING

Niamh took Aisling's hand and squeezed it tightly. Their hands fit perfectly together, the warmth of the gesture giving Aisling reason for pause. A part of her wanted to pull away. To snatch her hand back. And another part found she craved this affection. It made Aisling feel as if she belonged. The Other, a home she could grow to love: a realization that only made her ends that much more desperate.

And as if Niamh read her thoughts, she dipped her chin and looked Aisling in the eyes.

"You could belong here," Niamh said. "Forever."

Aisling focused on Niamh's expression, studying the swelling of her pupils as she considered the sorceress with an unnerving intensity.

"My home is Annwyn," Aisling said without thinking. She hadn't given much consideration to what would become of her life after she'd taken vengeance against the mortals. She'd been so focused on achieving everything she'd ever desired that she hadn't spared a moment to wonder... what then?

"And from that throne you'll rule beside the Sidhe king for eternity?" Niamh pushed. Aisling's brow furrowed and suddenly her mouth grew dry. The premise felt correct: Aisling and the fae king would rule from the heart of the Sidhe and heat the Great Forge of Creation until both this plane and the next bubbled with the *draiocht* and their power. The images fluttered through Aisling's mind like visions seen through the rippling surface of the Isle of Mirrors.

Anduril growled softly as if warning Aisling of its temper if her mind wandered too far. Her mind snapped like burning braids and the visions collapsed into dread that filled her chest.

*Nightmare king, deceiver, villain,* Anduril chanted inside her mind, reminding her why she despised the fae king.

"*From that throne,*" Anduril spoke through Aisling's lips, "*I'll rule alone.*"

"Mercy be upon your Sidhe king," Niamh said, barely a whisper. Aisling shook her head, ripping thoughts like gossamer—either hers or Anduril's, she could no longer tell the difference.

"The Sidhe king?" Aisling asked, grasping for clarity.

"Lir—your *caera*," Niamh said, speaking his name like a bygone curse better left forgotten.

Racat whimpered the moment Anduril muzzled him quiet. Aisling felt her heart tear in two, her mind muddled. Anduril's voice and her own warring for attention as she desperately tore at the tangles of her thoughts. The longer Anduril settled on her hips, the more Anduril felt as essential to her body as the bones that built her. Yet, the longer Anduril armored her, the more Aisling couldn't differentiate its voice from her own—its thoughts from her own.

Something was wrong. Aisling couldn't put her finger on it, but Niamh bore some responsibility for separating herself and the fae king.

Wondering about Lir's whereabouts was starting to bubble between Aisling's thoughts, conscious or unconscious, swiftly punished by Anduril's intensity.

Niamh's words had struck a chord in Aisling. The tone of Niamh's voice suggested the Seelie queen found *joy* in the fae king's misfortune or potential for it. Niamh wasn't being entirely forthcoming. And while the Sidhe couldn't tell a lie, they could tangle you between words until the truth was no longer so evident.

Aisling would expose Niamh's intentions soon enough whether they be aligned with her own or not. But she couldn't forget to tread lightly. Aisling still needed Niamh's adoration if she were to convince the Seelie queen to bless her pursuit of the Goblet and replace her as the gods' favored one.

"Think no more of it as we celebrate this evening," Niamh said, "my sorceress champion."

Aisling nodded her head, doing her best to convince Niamh she believed her. Widening her eyes with the same naivety that'd consumed her when she was a Tilrish princess traded to the Aos Sí. And had Aisling been the woman she'd been before she'd met the Sidhe, she might've believed the Seelie queen.

"Let us welcome the storm season together," Aisling said.

Niamh grinned and the great doors opened wide.

A storm of starlight descended silently as far as the eye could see.

Aisling stood atop a checkered, glass floor suspended far above Castle Yillen, still floating like a leaf in the wind. Transparent, Aisling could just see the earth far, far below, past a confection of clouds and mist and falling stars. The water from Niamh's showers spilling over the edge of the floor in cascades of light.

Winged Sidhe danced through the sky, glittering ball gowns ballooning like buds blooming come spring. Ethereal, they moved with such grace, every step rhythmically aligned with the orchestra of wild beasts playing harps, fiddles, lutes, and beating drums. The music rapturous.

And if there were a single guest more, Aisling worried there wouldn't be room for the tables that stretched endlessly at the center of *Lá Brear*, overflowing with steaming rolls, chocolate puddings, plum candies, sweet moon cakes, hot wines, and apple roasted pigs among much, much more, gloriously displayed beneath chandeliers of pulsing lightning.

Aisling couldn't help but smile. Couldn't wait to take off dancing. To sip wine until her feet were numb and she could twirl endlessly until morning. But the moment Aisling and Niamh emerged from the doors atop a platform that split into twin staircases, the celebration stopped. Even the droplets of liquid starlight froze mid-descent, streaks of light illuminating the Sidhe's glorious faces as they beheld the two Seelie queens.

Aisling's stomach flipped. A sea of faces devoured the sight of her, yet she recognized not one. The sorceress was reminded she was alone in this unknown realm.

Anduril burned her hips as if reassuring Aisling of its power. But it was too late. The image of the fae king bloomed inside Aisling's mind like a wildflower during *Imbolc*. He was always on her mind, especially when she felt vulnerable. It was nonsense. He was the enemy and no protector, and yet, here and now, when she felt pinned beneath the light, her mind searched for him. Aisling ripped the petals of her thoughts apart but still they remained, digging their roots into her soul.

*Blood drinker, barbarian, mortal reaper, nightmare, dark king*, Anduril spat like hot coals leaping from a flame. The words melted with Aisling's own, impossible to tell Anduril's spirit from herself. Aisling wrenched her eyes shut, clawing for clarity when at last Niamh tore her from the labyrinth of her mind.

"Welcome all," Niamh said, gently slipping her fingers from Aisling's so she could raise her hands in greeting. Her endless, sparkling sleeves spread like wings on either side of her, as though she were a bird of rain, lightning webbing in great cracks of light down the length of her arms and endless legs. She, half tempest incarnate. "I could think of no better way to welcome the storm season than to celebrate with you all this evening."

The crowds erupted into cheers, heads bobbing back and forth as they laughed in one another's pointed ears.

"And so," Niamh said as Aisling emerged from the fuzz, "let the rains baptize the earth!"

Niamh clapped and thunder roared. The skies flashed brilliantly as the rain broke and fell once more, continuing where it'd left off, followed by the orchestra and its euphoric melodies.

"Thank you for your patience," Niamh whispered in Aisling's ear, tickling her neck with her breath. "Come and sit with me on the throne before the evening truly begins."

Niamh snapped her fingers, and the rain clotted at the top of the staircase into two matching thrones of rippling, splashing water. The queen of Rain took her seat and invited Aisling to take hers.

The festivities continued to swell around them, growing louder, brighter, and more barbaric as the evening aged. Various Sidhe approached their thrones one after another, greeting Niamh with thanks and enthusiasm. Most, however, stared unapologetically at Aisling—the once-mortal princess turned Seelie queen—seated before them in the flesh.

"The fae here are happy," Aisling said to Niamh between conversations. "They are safe from mortal retaliation and the confines of the mortal plane."

"Aye," Niamh said, a glimmer of pride in the tip of her chin. But it was the quiver of her bottom lip that focused Aisling's attention. "But no one is safe."

Silence sat between them, dense and oppressive.

Aisling's heart beat a few paces quicker, stropping the blade of her mind. "And to think, had Ina never betrayed the Sidhe and cursed either plane with the mortal race, the fae would be spared from the fate that bleeds from us now."

Niamh's attention whipped to Aisling. Her eyes pierced Aisling like twin reeds, darting for the soul. Aisling held her ground, leveling her gaze with the Seelie queen's. Aisling had successfully provoked Niamh. A victory. And so, Aisling pushed farther.

"Ina was a bane to the Sidhe who sealed her death—"

"Quiet your tongue," Niamh snapped. The lagoon-blue of her complexion drained to white while her fangs grew noticeably sharper. Her chest rose and fell with each great breath, the clouds above gathering like armored giants.

Aisling had known Niamh and Ina were close friends, but testing and seeing Niamh's reaction to Ina's death, confirmed Aisling's suspicions: Niamh was the faerie and Ina's death came at the cost of Niamh's wish. To cure herself of loneliness, she'd inadvertently delivered the Seelie queen of Iod to the Other on death's galleon.

Niamh stood from her throne, furious.

Aisling opened her mouth to speak but was cut short.

The orchestra of wild beasts screeched to a halt. The melodies of their instruments collapsing into a caustic, irritating mess of noise till half the room covered their ears.

Aisling spun on her heel and Niamh stepped closer to her side.

From Aisling's vantage point, she could just see the crowds parting at the entrance to the ballroom, the height of the Sidhe obscuring what lay beyond.

While the evening burned, guests arrived and departed beneath a great arch curtained by rain, but now, the area was cleared as though death itself had stepped beneath the waters and into *Lá Brear*. A drop of oil in water. A shadow of fear cast across the merriment.

Lir had come.

## CHAPTER XVII

### LIR

The Sidhe king of the greenwood could inspire life at the beck of his slightest whim. And yet, it was the blood he shed, his violence, and his appetite for brutality that preceded him. A fact which Lir enjoyed, his *draiocht* purring at the terror glossing the eyes of those who beheld him. The bitter smell of their dread, sweet to the taste.

Lir wicked his wet hair from his eyes and stepped into *Lá Brear*. Still blood-splattered from the questing beast, Lir was a grisly contrast to the lustrous opulence of Niamh's gathering. The sound of his boots on the glass floors, echoing into oblivion. His carnage-stained axes winked where they sat crossed at his back.

"*Dark lord of the forest, mo Damh Bán.*" Slowly, Niamh took her seat on her throne once more, a maiden draped in piles of dewy spiderwebs and the glow of lightning bolts. Her powder-blue hair dripped onto her shoulders.

Niamh smiled knowingly, inspiring something tempestuous in Lir's gut.

"How wonderful of you to join us," Niamh said. "Albeit so late and ill-dressed." Her narrow eyes looked him up and down as though disgusted by his heathendom. Lir's shade of violence, more barbaric than her own.

"I wouldn't have missed it," Lir said, unable to help the wolfish grin that swept across his face. "Although I'll admit, my intentions, for once, are less focused on the wine and more so on the fate of our worlds."

"How dramatic," she simpered.

Lir laughed under his breath. "Aye, the end of the Sidhe's existence would be. Which is why I'm here to prevent it."

Gradually, Niamh's arrogance faded with each of Lir's words, her irritation rising. The surrounding Sidhe and forge-born beasts whipped their heads between the Seelie queen and Lir.

"You'd have me believe in your kingship if it wasn't you who broke the Sidhe's alliance with the mortals and caused this mess in the first place," Niamh said, crossing her arms over her chest and tilting her chin up. The first transparent blow.

The crowd erupted into frenzied chatter, stirring like birds taking flight from a juniper.

Bemused, Lir walked further into the room, aware of the guests who staggered back in a panic, eager to clear his path.

"Do I sense compassion for the mortal race?" Lir asked, the corners of his lips curling further. "Or perhaps you'd rather place your trust in those who will make myths of us yet. It is by blood we will win this war. Not mercy."

Every Sidhe and forge-born beast fell quiet, the potency of Lir's words sobering the celebration, the reality of their approaching doom as tangible as the first leaf turned come autumn. Death's approach, a surety.

Niamh's complexion grew flushed and mottled, eyes widening until the whites were visible and her nails dug into the arms of her throne.

"You disguise your lust well, *mo Damh Bán*," she bit, "for every choice you've made since the day you accepted an offering from the mortals has been with your *caera* in mind and not our people. A *caera* whose consummation with you will not only bring the mortals to their end, but the whole of the world as we know it." Niamh beamed, but it was cold and void of emotion, eerie to behold. "Do not think that I, the gods' favored child, does not know of the prophecies spun between the threads of fate. You, *mo Damh Bán*, are not the savior of the Sidhe. You are their unmaking."

*Lá Brear* froze, panic bubbling in each and all's expressions. *Lá Brear*, *Imbolc*, any and all Sidhe celebrations were designed to inspire hope, community, and strength. And yet, war had rotted even this. Had diseased its way into even the fae folk's frivolity, their savagery, their wonder.

"I do not stand with the Sidhe king of the greenwood," a voice called from among the throng. The voice was distorted; a melding of two spirits into one. Nevertheless, Lir already knew who one half of the voice belonged to.

*Aisling.*

Lir's heart leaped.

His flesh caught fire.

The words of vitriol he'd intended for Niamh caught in his throat. Eyes glazing over with his *need* to be close to her. An unholy flower, plucked from the earth by rain's right hand. She was devastating to behold. Cloaked by spring's showers, she shimmered beneath the light of Niamh's flashing chandeliers. Eyes as violet as cauldron potions and lips as red as stolen hearts. Lir was paralyzed by her beauty. By the way she tilted her head like a beast of prey, considering him. By the way she swallowed her fear and armored herself with a resolve Lir had scarcely witnessed in battle-worn knights. And when she met his eyes, her magic was enough to bring the Sidhe king to his knees.

"*Whilst our ambitions are aligned,*" Aisling continued, "*our coupling is no longer.*" Anduril glistened smugly from Aisling's hips, beaming brightly each time Niamh's lightning webbed across the sky.

Lir bit the inside of his bottom lip, tasting blood.

At Aisling's words, *Lá Brear* released a collective gasp, voices rising until they were no longer whispers. Every Sidhe and forge-born beast among them shouting amongst one another, polarized by the news.

Lir, however, hardly heard them booming. Aisling stood at the center of his world, the rest a blur.

*Anduril,* Lir repeated to himself. *It's not real.*

But the sight of Anduril clasping Aisling's waist inspired something feral in Lir he didn't know how to contain. Wasn't even certain if he wanted to.

"And this," Niamh concluded, tearing her eyes from Aisling's to stare into Lir's, "is why you are not welcome here."

The attention of the room flew from Niamh to Lir like a dart. The Other held its breath. The *draiocht* thickening the air as history was being written. The threads of fate braiding, weaving, waiting on a confirmation from Lir to begin its work.

"Is this true?" Niamh asked Lir. "You're no longer bonded to the sorceress?"

Lir clenched his hands into fists. Every muscle wrung taut.

*Whatever you covet,* Lir reminded himself again, *will be my heart's labor.*

"It's true," the king of the greenwood said, avoiding Aisling's eyes lest his anguish spill forth in violence. And still, he caught Anduril's self-satisfied glint from the corner of his eye.

The Other released the breath it'd been holding, and the tension burst like a cloud before the squall.

Niamh, straight-backed and lips pursed, broke into sudden laughter. Ear-splitting, the sound broke the champagne flutes and chalices circling the punch fountain. The badgers and tortoises enjoying their drinks, leaped in surprise, staggering away from the broken glass.

"Then you aren't welcome here," Niamh said. "Return to Annwyn before the mortals invade your borders once more."

Lir's temper rose, but he stifled it quickly. He needed an excuse to stay in the Other. A reason—an *obligation*—to protect Aisling that even Niamh couldn't argue with. He needed an excuse to stay by Aisling's side.

"Even so," Lir continued, "I've come as an ally to the Lady Aisling." The Sidhe king found Aisling's eyes across the room and held them. Anduril's cruel sheen glossed her expression, shielding the sorceress behind its magic, but the Sidhe king continued nonetheless, speaking to Aisling and Aisling alone.

The Sidhe king cut a path through the crowd. A wolf, he lithely took his place before the dais and knelt on the ground.

Lir bowed his head. Slowly, he unsheathed one of his twin axes and crossed it before his heart.

"I swear my fealty and my blade to the sorceress," Lir said. The Sidhe king raised his head, fixing his eyes on Aisling. She sat still—a dark lake hidden by the forest. Lir held her stare regardless. At last, a spark of recognition flaring across her expression before returning to stone. "She will need a knight and a protector if she's to spare the Sidhe. I can think of no better option than myself."

"And what authority do either you or Aisling boast that's capable of liberating the Sidhe from impending doom?" Niamh asked Lir, dabbing at her amused, tear-filled eyes with the edge of her sleeve.

Lir held his ground.

"I understand Aisling was introduced to the Sidhe as my bride, the mortal princess, the daughter of the fire hand; the bane of the Sidhe with a legacy of fae blood packed between the mortar of his iron keep," Lir said. "I understand that her proclivity to the *draiocht* is strange and unprecedented, and that the nature of her fire is darkly poetic in its relationship to the Sidhe. I understand Aisling was introduced as the enemy. As a casualty." The room stilled. "But that is not the sorceress that stands before you."

The hairs on the nape of Lir's neck stood on end. The universe leaning closer to better hear his spell.

"Ina chose Aisling as a hiding place, a home to shelter her gods-blessed gift. She is the keeper of Racat and the personification of magic. And as both sorceress and the reaper of men, Aisling wields the power to ensure Sidhe victory and to unwrite prophecy. Her only request from those she intends to fight for..." Lir said —The whole of *Lá Brear* waiting on his every breath—"Is a chance to earn the gods' favor and obtain the Goblet of Lore. Of this she will agree."

Like an oak felled, Lir's words hit the earth with a thunderous crash, the Sidhe flaring into hysteria like birds taking flight.

Aisling's expression flashed with a flurry of emotion, her breath hissing between her teeth, the angrier Anduril shimmered. And still, her eyes stayed locked on Lir, studying him closely.

It was chaos.

Madness and confusion spreading and rising into the clouds above.

Niamh's crystal eyes stared deeply at Aisling, flecked with—what looked like—betrayal.

Aisling exchanged glances with the Seelie queen of Rain, a silent conversation passing between them that Lir couldn't decipher.

"Enough," Niamh said at last, silencing the crowds.

"This is lunacy!" a fox yelled. "A mortal and the enemy's daughter endeavoring to win the gods' favor?!" The beast snorted in disbelief, shaking her head.

"It is the Forge's will," a Sidhe knight argued.

"Impossible!" another said between clenched teeth.

"Since when have the Sidhe been averse to change?" a bear

asked with sincerity, the toads beside him nodding their heads in agreement.

"The not-so mortal queen has never asked for the Goblet nor the gods' favor," another Sidhe said.

Lir's throat grew thick. In the wake of *Imbolc*, in the angst over Aisling, in his focus on their journey from the mortal plane to the Other, and in his desperation to find Aisling, he'd forgotten about this drawback to their schemes.

"Let her search for the Goblet then," a winged Sidhe said, his crown of fruit wobbling atop his ebony curls. The majority of the crowd nodded their heads in agreement.

Aisling whipped her attention to their audience, but her gaze was inward, churning with thought.

"To pursue and find the Goblet for the gods' favor..." The fox shook her lovely head, concern pinching her brows. "Such a task is a death sentence."

"She's no longer mortal," Lir said, his voice more biting than he'd intended.

"And yet," said the bear, "she is neither Sidhe."

"Whosoever seeks the Goblet and the gods' favor with their will, is eligible to hunt it," said Lir. "It matters not our opinion, nor her race. So, it is written in the collective lore of our history and in the nature of our power."

There was silence as every guest, as every bead of rain weighed Lir's words. Lir hoped it wouldn't come to this. He'd hoped that asking Niamh for the Goblet would be enough and that the gods' favor would follow shortly thereafter. Perhaps he'd allowed himself this measure of denial; to blissfully ignore Aisling potentially risking her life in the pursuit of the Goblet to secure everything she desired. And yet, standing here now, Lir realized it was always an inevitability. Without thought, without hesitation, Lir would protect Aisling from the wild and from the dark. Any who wished her harm, sadness, terror, would be repaid tenfold by his hands and his alone. But Lir realized to his own dread, that he couldn't save her from herself.

Anduril, dappled in rain, shone like a trove of gold.

Aisling rolled her shoulders back and balled her hands into fists at her sides.

"Through trial or test or task or quest," the sorceress said, "I'm prepared to do whatever it takes to *earn* the Goblet of Lore, the gods' favor, as well as all of yours."

Aisling's gaze found Lir across the celebration. He tore his eyes from her, head falling so he stared at his bloody boots, wet with rain.

Niamh broke the silence, clapping loudly and slowly.

"How valiant, the both of you," she said, but her tone was biting. "Very well then. If Aisling is to earn my crown and favor, then so, too, should her oath-given knight. Prove yourself, great king, by the tradition of the first knight, and battle your queen."

"What?" Lir asked, eyes suddenly going wide.

"This is my kingdom, *mo Damh Bán*," Niamh said, cold as sleet, "and if you wish to maintain your welcome, you'll follow my rules." As if prompted, several of Niamh's knights shifted where they stood along the edges of the festivities. Their hands and paws drifted to the hafts of their blades, eyes pinned to the Sidhe king.

A muscle flickered across Lir's jaw, but he didn't move.

"If you wish to stay and aid Aisling, then prove yourself her protector, her guide, her knight as you claim," Niamh said, lips cutting into a grin.

Aisling's and Lir's eyes met. The room inhaled sharply and Anduril exploded with excitement, glowing at her hips like a blade dipped in the Forge.

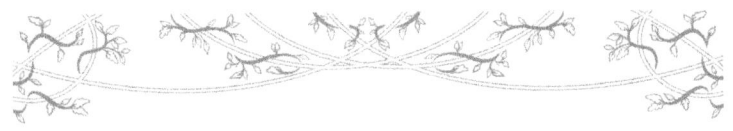

## CHAPTER XVIII

AISLING

The fae king held Aisling's gaze like a dagger staked through the heart. Aisling's expression turned cold, tugged by two sides of the soul. She felt both a strange melancholy and an eager excitement. Her fingers twitching at her sides to draw Sarwen from her back and slake its thirst for the fae king's blood. And yet, inexplicably, she hesitated. Her body stiffened, torn between divided thoughts.

"Step forth and begin," Niamh said, commanding both Aisling and Lir. She gestured for them to approach the center of the celebration. The crowds parted like bunches of flowers searching for sunlight in the creases of the room.

"Step forth," Niamh repeated when neither Aisling nor Lir moved. Her saber-sharp eyes cut to Anduril at Aisling's waist, pulling the sorceress forward with fiery intent.

"*Gladly*," Anduril spoke through Aisling's lips.

At last, the sorceress stepped down the dais. Niamh hemmed Aisling's beaded raindrop gown as Aisling descended, transforming her elegance into a battle-ready beauty. Aisling unsheathed Sarwen from its scabbard as she walked. Tendrils of water braiding through her hair until her inky tresses were pinned behind her.

Aisling and Lir met at the center. The few paces that separated them, dense and prickling with energy.

"While I'm certain Lir knows the law of first knight combat duels, I'll repeat them for Aisling," Niamh said. "To protect, first you must attack, and any first knight must best their liege in combat and prove their strength, their cunning, and their will. The first to draw blood, wins." Niamh clapped her hands and lightning snapped like a whip across the star-embroidered sky.

Both Gilrel and Galad had explained this law to Aisling before. By now, the sorceress was becoming well accustomed to the culture of the Sidhe—traditions drunk with mischief, tricks, games, and bargains. All bloody, violent, and steeped with magic.

"Address your opponent," the Seelie queen of Rain said.

Lir frowned, but he stepped closer regardless. He fixed his eyes on Aisling. Had Aisling sunk beneath the surface of their Connemara oblivion before, or did the fae king bespell all and any who dared to meet his gaze?

*Wicked stranger*, Anduril seethed in her ears, the belt's determination running thickly through Aisling's veins.

Aisling forced herself to lock eyes with Lir. Her *draiocht* lashing inside like a bridled horse, gums bloody where it ripped at the bit in its mouth.

*Hush*, Anduril hissed at her *draiocht*.

The fae king lowered his gaze and Aisling drew a breath. Regally, he bowed. Aisling mirrored the gesture. Her blood, hot, rushing through her ears till she could scarcely hear the anxious susurrations of their audience.

"Begin," Niamh said, and Aisling tasted the plum-ripe taste of the *draiocht* from a duel begun. Aisling's stomach jumped into her throat.

Lir drew his twin axes, spinning them between his fingers.

Anduril chuckled, the sound clawing up Aisling's throat until her lips bent into a smile.

"I'll go easy on you, sorceress," the fae king said, tilting his head back. The edges of his lips curled like a fox—his easy arrogance provoking Anduril further.

Aisling felt the belt's ache to fight and then she felt her own reluctance. Her own fear. A warrior of legends standing across from her. He, who for centuries, defeated mortal legions, brought the Unseelie to their knees, and defended his keep by the edge of his twin blades.

On her own, Aisling could scarcely lift the blade she now tested, tossing it gently to familiarize herself with its balance and poise. But with Anduril thrumming at her hips, she could defeat him. This much she knew.

"And here I was," Aisling replied, "hoping for a challenge."

At this, Lir's eyes lit like embers. His smile cutting further across the sharp edge of his jaw.

Aisling lunged first, Sarwen's tip spearing for the fae king. Lir stepped deftly to the side, swinging and knocking Sarwen's blade to the right. In the same movement, the fae king moved forward, snaking his arms around Aisling till he held her from behind, locked behind the cross of both his axes.

"You can do better than that," he whispered just loud enough for Aisling to hear. His breath hot at the crown of her head.

Aisling's stomach twisted, her *draiocht* bristling like wool at the edge of a flame. Anduril possessed her, compelling her ambition, her resolve, her hunger to its will. The sorceress stabbed her right elbow into the fae king's ribs while her left foot slammed into his boot. The fae king tightened his grip, startled by the strength of her struggle. It was enough.

*Burn*, Aisling commanded her *draiocht* with the intention of lighting like a match. Instead, her *draiocht* exploded, flaring like wildfire and ripping the fae king from her body. Lir reeled, staggering back to escape her violet flames.

Aisling inhaled sharply. The hair on her body standing straight with the intensity of her *draiocht*'s excitement. Racat and Anduril clashing inside her with wild abandon.

"Like that?" Aisling asked, turning on her heel to face the fae king as he collected himself.

"Just like that," Lir said, eyes darkening as he deepened his glare. The forest-green of his attention bleeding shadow-black as he considered her, chin dipping with wolf-like hunger. All need as he defeated the distance between them, spinning like the nightmare of myth Aisling recognized.

Their blades struck against one another, ringing into the fabric of the Other. Nose to nose, their blades crossed between them. Aisling cursed. Her *draiocht* relished the fae king's proximity. It hungered for his scent: pine needles, wood smoke, and summer woodland sighs. The strength of his Sidhe arms pushing against Anduril's force left her breathless. His great height casting a shadow atop her whose darkness fed the ravenous appetence of her heart. The *draiocht* purred in the rattle of their heaving breaths. Half-lidded, the fae king's eyes dropped to Aisling's lips. His fangs lengthening with a hunger Aisling understood. A tease, for she wished to be closer still, but by the way Lir clenched his jaw, she imagined he'd rather be anywhere else. His hatred for her tangible in Aisling's eyes.

Three beads of blood fell from Aisling's nose. Her *draiocht* was pushing at her lungs, begging to be unleashed, and Anduril was struggling for sovereignty of both her body and mind. A fact Lir recognized, for his eyes flicked to the Blood Cord at Aisling's hips. He smiled, pushing his blades harder against Aisling's own.

At last, Aisling severed the tension and slipped to the left, lowering her body and rushing into the fae king's legs. Knocked off balance, Lir nimbly caught himself before blocking

Aisling's second swipe of the blade. He crashed his axes into Sarwen's curved swing, snatching Aisling's wrist with vines of *ellwyn*.

Aisling ripped herself free, throwing her weight into the next jab. Lir dipped low, striking Sarwen's edge and loosening the sorceress's grip. Aisling took a breath, flowers sprouting in her hair, around her gown, her hands, her legs, crawling around her neck, her waist, and gripping tightly—till Aisling tore petals between her nails. *Ellwyn*, blocking her vision as she struck again and again, her *draiocht* seeping between her clenched teeth like pipe smoke.

Anduril roared from Aisling's lips, slamming Sarwen into the Sidhe king. At last, the vines swarmed her, burying her in the life breath of the woodland.

Aisling summoned more of her *draiocht*, lighting like a torch. Lir's magic hissed against her own, screaming as she burned. Lir pulled his magic back, jerking at Aisling's ankles and throwing her to the ground.

The sorceress smacked into the glass floor. Cracks spidered across the surface, reminding them all of the descent the cloudburst underwent to slake the earth below. The glass platform higher than Aisling remembered as she swallowed the stone in her throat.

Aisling, still burning, rendered the fae king's magic to ash. She started to her feet, but Lir was quicker.

Lithely, Lir climbed atop her, his vines holding her prisoner. For every flower, thorn, or liana burnt, two more grew, shackling the sorceress to him. He held a blade to her throat.

"First taste of my blood," Lir said as he held her eyes. Anduril screamed, feral and raging. The words were familiar. Painfully so.

The fae king lifted Aisling's hand with his vines and brought one of his axes to her palm. A nick, he scraped her palm and a bead of blood bloomed.

The Other's *draiocht* giggled into the caverns of oblivion, smacking its lips.

Aisling hissed, snatching her hand back to little avail. Lir held her tightly, watching her with curious eyes. She felt the heat of his attention and found herself drawn to its warmth. He was a stranger and yet... familiar. He blew on the embers of her soul, fanning their fires with the nearby humming of his magic. This close, Aisling could believe she'd once been in love with the fae king. But how? How when he despised her so, the mere image of her seemingly painful for him to behold?

The Other smelled her blood, then tasted it, sealing the duel and the fae king's victory.

# CHAPTER XIX

"We're close," Nemed said, slapping Starn on the back. He'd arrived from Tahsman with his group of mortal knights, alive with the power of wystria. His scar bent oddly where he beamed at Starn as he dismounted his black gelding—an expression Starn would remember, filling him with pride. His hands eager for more fae blood when the reward was his father's approval.

"We've thought that on a few occasions now," Starn replied, careful not to get the fire hand's hopes up.

"We've done it considerable damage," Nemed said. "Surely it's only a matter of time."

"Perhaps," Starn said. "Once we stop it, we'll gut it or break it... but it still remains to open it."

Nemed nodded his head, understanding.

"Can you not request the Lady's aid once more?" Nemed asked. "She favors you and her goals are aligned with our own. I cannot see a reason—"

"No," Starn said. "I will take aid when necessary. The rest of Aisling's justice will be served by my hand alone."

Nemed's lips thinned into a line.

*"The end is near," the fire hand said. "Fae territories are falling each day as we apply pressure on their kingdoms. The gateway is within our reach. We're close. Don't forget that."*

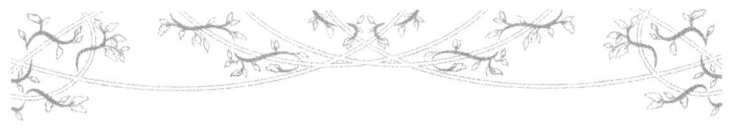

# CHAPTER XX

### AISLING

Outside the glass dome of Niamh's throne room, thunder cracked.

The boom vibrated through the wooden archway, the steepled doors, and the stained-glass panels. Every mosaic portrait wept rain filled tears before the altar of the twin gods, Breka and Arawn.

Aisling inhaled deeply, standing below the marbled statues of Breka and Arawn, bewitched to breathe incense smoke from their nostrils as they loomed over Niamh's court. Trooping fae solemnly surrounded the hall's arcade, hands clasped before their jeweled robes.

"*Protector of my blade and my breath,*" Aisling addressed the fae king in Rún, "*By the Forge, I dub thee my knight.*" The sorceress gently laid Sarwen's tip on Lir's right shoulder and then his left.

Anduril rang angrily at her hips, searing into her flesh, but Aisling ignored the Blood Cord. She was compelled by duty, duel, and bargain to honor the fae king's victory whether she liked it or not. Even Anduril's protests, its hissing, its temper could not prevent Aisling from fulfilling the accolade as

Niamh's court bore witness. Fate cackling like bats set loose from the chasm of eternity. And whilst Aisling would never admit this truth even in the privacy of her own mind, for once, she and fate were aligned—Aisling needed the fae king's strength, his power, and his bloodthirst if she were to successfully find the Goblet. He'd proven his mythic might in their duel, for no other soul could wage battle against Anduril and win. A fact that enraged the Blood Cord, grinding its metal-like teeth in a monster's mouth.

A warren of blue rabbits carried a quilt of midnight blue and draped it over the fae king's shoulders. The supple velvet spilled in folds of embroidered stars, shimmering like lanterns in the dark. And upon his neck, a wreath of bluebells was laid honorably by a flutter of butterflies.

"Rise," Aisling commanded the fae king.

Lir unfurled from his kneel and met her eyes. Sage and sharp, they cut past her defenses and pillaged her heart. His left brow twitched in the same moment, forcing Aisling to wonder if he felt the same: if he, too, felt the magnetic pull, mercilessly drawing them closer together. And as if summoned by her thoughts alone, a trickle of blood escaped the fae king's tear ducts as it did Aisling's.

"Stand and take your first breath," Aisling said, her voice thick. Her temples throbbing from Anduril's voice screaming and grating against her own. "And join me in my quest for the Goblet so that we might spare the Sidhe from mortal desolation. My knight," Aisling addressed the fae king.

The court burst into applause. Petals showered from the vaulted ceiling, the glass dome, and the gallery whilst the storm outside gathered more thickly. Their Sidhe wings fluttered with excitement and the forge-born beasts howled, croaked, and hooted with celebration. They blew their spiral horns, plucked their fiddles, and cast pretty charms of sparkling light. It was a feverish glimpse of joy that warmed the room sweetly. And yet, the deep groans of Niamh's tempests reminded Aisling that such magic and merriment was fickle—easily squashed by the iron boot of mankind should she fail to successfully obtain the Goblet. Easily ground into the earth by the will of her clann.

The fae king bowed and the court grew more joyous. Still, his gaze remained locked on hers. His distrust for her tangible.

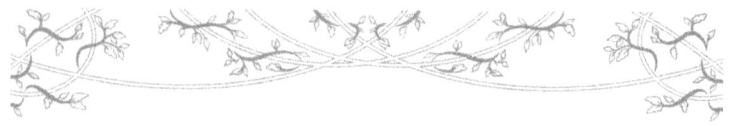

# CHAPTER XXI

## LIR

Once the ceremony was complete, Niamh wasted not a moment before cleansing her throne room of every courtier and forge-born beast. Even Aisling was sent to her chambers to rest for the evening despite her protestations and the fiery temper in which she left the hall.

Yet, the moment the doors locked behind Aisling, Lir's heart steadied. His mind cleared. The murder of ravens in his stomach settled. The torture of her nearness abated until they'd be together again. And yet, he mourned it. Yearned for the suffering her presence afflicted.

"Thank you for remaining a while longer so we might speak in private," Niamh said, "Sidhe sovereign to Sidhe sovereign."

Lir flicked his eyes to the Seelie queen.

"We both seek the triumph of the Sidhe, Niamh," Lir said. "What else is there to speak of?"

"You were once bound to Peitho," Niamh said, taking a seat on the steps of her dais.

Lir arched a brow, curious as to the direction of the conversation.

"She's still a valued member of my knight's guild."

"Aye, because your affections for her were never near what you shared with a mortal princess," Niamh said, the corners of her lips curling.

Lir rolled his head back, his throat working. Speaking of another felt strangely intimate to Lir. Words were powerful spells and if spoken just right, carried weighted magic. So for an enemy—or at the very least, someone untrusted—to speak of Aisling, made Lir's canines sharpen to a point.

"I fell in love with a mortal princess, traded to the fae," Lir said.

"And you still love her?" Niamh asked.

Lir hesitated for a moment. He couldn't lie, but he could twist his words.

"She is formidable," he said instead.

"That isn't an answer," Niamh pushed, her gaze hardening.

Lir exhaled, annoyed. "I carry no apathy for her."

"Answer my question, *mo Damh Bán*," Niamh said, her voice like a chorus of many, shaking the stained glass.

Lir ran his fingers through his hair, disheveling it.

"I cannot love her," he said.

"If love required permission, few among us would experience it," Niamh said. "You love her."

Lir crossed his arms, his heart pounding inside his chest.

"Aye." He spoke the truth, the confession blooming primroses and bluebells around the arcade like piles of gold spilling onto the marbled floors.

Niamh laughed, tipping back her head. Her voice was as shrill as sleet.

Gasping for breath, she spoke: "Unfortunately, your love is unrequited."

Lir remained stoic—his face expressionless as he endured Niamh's blows. For while Anduril's possession of Aisling enraged Lir, he was no fool, and even anger wouldn't make him one. Niamh's motives were ulterior to his own, this much was evident. And conceding even a morsel of emotion to the Seelie queen was to make oneself prone before the edge of a blade. Regardless, Lir wasn't certain whether Niamh was aware of Anduril's possession or if the Seelie queen believed Aisling's change of heart to be in earnest. For now, it was a boon Niamh didn't know: they couldn't trust her and she seemed to align more closely with Anduril's will than Aisling's when it came to the Sidhe king. Either way, he'd unearth the truth through Niamh's recklessness and not his own.

"I serve and honor the Lady Aisling as queen," Lir said matter-of-factly. "Whether or not I remain a lover, is at the Lady Aisling's discretion."

Niamh smiled coyly, brushing a raindrop from the sharp cliff of her cheekbones.

"What devotion," she cooed. "The legendary barbarian king of the greenwood leashed into such obedience for the likes of a sorceress."

"For our salvation," Lir corrected, but he'd made certain not to speak in a full sentence lest the Forge identify his lie for what it was. Lir had feared Aisling from the moment he'd laid eyes on her. Not on account of her hands, her iron, or even her magic. But on account of the spells she cast so effortlessly around his heart—enchantments prayed to life by her mettle when she'd dueled him, her elegance and posture whilst she'd stood before the supernatural court of the Other, and the steel of her voice when she'd laid her blade on both his shoulders.

"Does this not pain you? To see Aisling *use* you to obtain the world she wishes to rule?"

Lir licked his lips, patiently waiting for the correct response to come to mind. Every word exchanged with Niamh needed to be perfect. He couldn't make a mistake. Not when everything—when Aisling—depended upon it.

"I'm no stranger to pain," Lir said, his first *caera*, Narisea, and his late child sprouting inside his mind like poison gorta.

"And as for Aisling's ambitions, they align with my own. We both wish to see the supremacy of the Sidhe and the triumph of the Forge above all else."

"You believe Aisling, once a mortal princess, to be capable of leading the Sidhe to victory?" Niamh asked. "Only a few years prior, these very words would've been curses on your tongue."

"Just as the seasons change, so do our minds, our desires, our spirits. It's the nature of growth, as you well know," Lir said. "Regardless, I don't need to believe it. Ina believed it. A fact you're well aware of."

Niamh stilled, fixing her pale eyes on the Sidhe king.

"How long I've waited to hear you speak your mother's name."

"I understand you were both close," Lir said. "She mentioned you often, taking a vow of silence for your friendship during the storm seasons in Annwyn. I shared only a few memories with her before her passing, but those were amongst them."

Niamh's eyes glazed over with tears. She bit her bottom lip, hands balling into fists. The rains roared outside, cascading against the floating tower in which they stood. The vibration of her *draiocht* thrumming beneath Lir's boots.

Lir leveled his breath, shielding his thoughts. Studying Niamh's every nuance to understand hers instead. Indeed, Lir had known of Niamh and Ina's friendship at the dawn of creation, yet he hadn't anticipated such despair, such mourning a millennium later as the Seelie queen displayed now. The depth of her emotion caught the Sidhe king off guard and gave him reason for pause. Niamh was hiding something.

"Aisling reminds me of your mother," Niamh said. "Ina never spoke of her visions with me nor did she ever reveal *why* she chose Aisling to hide her gift and Racat. But I imagine she saw what we all see in her: the courage to dream greatly and the strength to seize it. Aisling may have been born a mortal princess, but long has her heart raced with the makings of legends."

Lir ached for he didn't need a reminder of all he loved but couldn't have. The Sidhe king shifted, resisting the urge to clear his throat and expose the emotion Niamh had wrought from his spirit.

"So we agree." Lir forced himself to speak past the lump in his throat. "Aisling will bring victory to the Forge, and my heart won't break in vain if it is the Sidhe she spares in her destiny to rewrite prophecy. To force the hand of fate that might've once forced hers."

"Aye," Niamh agreed. "And yet, you are still afraid."

Lir scoffed, his expression stretching into an amused grin.

"Afraid?"

"Ah yes, even the dark lord of the greenwood finds himself fearful," Niamh replied with a smile in her voice. "Especially, of a sorceress."

Lir's heart stuttered, but he masked his feelings well, refusing to give Niamh the reaction she craved.

"You fear losing that which you love," Niamh continued. "You've lost so much already... your first child, Narisea, your wings... Almost Aisling herself at one point in time..."

"Your point?" Lir asked, his patience thinning.

"Your fear of losing Aisling will prevent her success. You hold her too tightly, too close, too afraid of everything and everyone that you block her destiny from manifesting."

Lir shook his head.

"I have done everything in my power to aid Aisling and her path."

"This might be true," Niamh said. "However, there is fear still to be released. The great Sidhe king of the forest has only ever allowed one other to reign supreme above even him: fear. And so, it is time to let go."

Lir shifted, not stubborn enough to ignore the truth of her

words. The Sidhe king feared the end of the Sidhe, the fall of Annwyn, the loss of Aisling—any and all heartbreaking loss he didn't believe he bore the strength to survive. Still, he'd never confess such fears to Niamh.

"You must promise me this," Niamh said, the words cold and bitter between them.

Lir straightened. Promise: a word that always yielded suffering. A word more binding than chains or dungeons.

"Promise me you'll never love Aisling again. Promise me to heed the prophecies of your destructive coupling," Niamh said, her voice strained and quick. "Promise me you'll let Aisling go. And once your fear has been released, you'll find a weight lifted from your back and your feet lighter."

Lir staggered backward, his hand reaching toward his heart against his own volition. He shuddered, horrified by the venom spilling past her ancient lips and the screaming of the storm.

"Promise me and I'll return to you—with what magic I boast —something you once lost," Niamh said, standing. *Something you once lost.* "Promise me you'll let her go and spare the Sidhe the violence your union would otherwise wreak."

Lir's heart pounded in his ears, his throat, his hands, thorns spiraling around the gallery, the arcade, the statues of winged Sidhe that glared down at him with such intensity he believed they'd come alive to pry the promise from his lips if he didn't speak it willingly. And still, Lir would fight. Would rip his agency to love Aisling from the pits of the Forge if he must.

*I want everything,* Aisling's words echoed in his mind. *And I fear I'll perish if such a hunger is never slaked. If my bones never grow. If everything I've ever wanted and never had— power, sovereignty, the world—is never mine.*

*Whatever you covet,* Lir had said, *will be my heart's labor.*

A promise.

A bargain his heart had sealed.

To break it, would be to break a vow. To break it would be to undermine Aisling. To break it would be to lose the gods' favor and the Goblet. To lose the war against the mortals. To break it, would be to lose Aisling wholly.

Lir's soul grew vast and dark. A cavern of sorrow that cannibalized itself, scratching at the walls of his body alongside his writhing *draiocht*, begging to be unleashed.

"I promise," Lir said, and the Forge boomed like a drum, snapping lightning and thunder in its fury, threatening to crack the skies in half. The Other and the mortal plane, both trembling with the finality of their high bargain.

*Something you once lost.*
*Promise me.*
*A weight lifted from your back and your feet lighter.*
*Something you once lost.*

The spell echoed.

Lir fell to his knees. His soul was bloody where it had been ripped and left behind a gaping hole. A decision made for him by the events of the past; every moment imprisoning him against his knowledge.

The Lady's laughter echoed in the thunder.

"And should you break such a promise," Niamh said, "your love may throb and beat, but never shall you exist together again —Aisling's heart, my own."

Lir had suspected Niamh wanted to deepen the divide between himself and Aisling but now he was certain of it. Perhaps she feared their power when they were joined. Perhaps she wanted Aisling all to herself. Perhaps she enjoyed toying with the Sidhe king she feared and envied all at once. Regardless, she bore power over Lir because she recognized his greatest vulnerability: Aisling.

Just like that, fate stabbed its needle into the fabric of the universe and began to sew.

## CHAPTER XXII

LIR

Lir scaled the side of Castle Yillen, invisible to all but the trees that thrashed in Niamh's rains. Even her tempest couldn't sense him as he worked his way toward Aisling's chambers, gripping the slippery stones. Lir could have walked the corridors of Niamh's castle, but he preferred the Seelie queen knowing as little as possible of his whereabouts and movements.

At last, Lir jumped atop the balcony attached to Aisling's chambers. The doors were left ajar, the wych lace curtains a veil that separated Lir from the warm glow of Aisling's rooms.

Aisling sat atop a mound of velvet quilts, moving Sarwen in shapely formations. Anduril buzzed gleefully from Aisling's hips—its magic rippling from its metal and through Aisling's veins.

Aisling's hair was entirely undone; thick rivulets of ink spilling over her shoulders, framing the whisper-thin chiffon of her ivory night slip and robes. Her slender fingers slid over the grooves of Sarwen's hilt, both the blade and its sorceress familiarizing themselves with one another.

The Sidhe king held his breath. Lir was still invisible, having cloaked himself with his *draiocht*, yet still he approached with caution. Aisling hadn't yet sensed his presence, so he stood outside the wych lace for a heartbeat longer than he'd intended, watching his sorceress through the veil.

At the center of his chest, a familiar pang of jealousy struck him. Jealousy that anyone else had ever laid eyes on her. Jealousy that everything she was, could never be his.

A crack sounded at the other end of the room.

Lir jolted, instinctively stepping back.

Several blue rabbits entered the chambers from the corridor entrance, carrying porcelain pots. They hopped over to Aisling's bed and began mixing syrup into Aisling's tea. Even from where Lir stood, he smelled the fir needles, the ground spruce, the shards of starlight, and the crisp tongue of evening breezes: a night balm intended to deepen sleep and prevent night terrors.

Lir's shoulders stiffened.

"I plead with you, Your Grace," one of the blue rabbits said. "Take your tea lest Niamh grow angry you deny her hospitality."

Aisling winced at the steaming cup offered by one of the rabbits.

"To prevent the Lady from entering your dreams once more," another rabbit said.

Lir perked up, listening more closely. Nightmares and terrors were no stranger to Aisling, and Lir had known the Lady invaded her dreams on darker nights. Yet, he'd assumed the Lady's connection with Aisling was severed upon entering the Other. A hope quickly disproven.

Aisling turned her head from the teacup like a child, refusing the brew. The sorceress sheathed Sarwen instead, draping the blade on one of her bedposts as she sank into the quilts.

"I prefer to know if the Lady infiltrates my mind—the balm does not protect me. It only blinds me to her intrusions," Aisling said.

The rabbits sighed, setting the tea on a table beside her bed. Each rabbit hopped off, busying themselves with tidying her chambers, washing her gowns, folding, or organizing her jewels until, at last, they retired for the evening.

"Rest, Your Grace," the last rabbit whispered as they shut the door behind them and vanished into the hall.

Aisling's chambers were black with shadow, brushed by the storm breezes sweeping from the terrace where Lir stood.

Slowly, quietly, he slipped into the room.

A rogue, Lir slinked against the walls to the rhythm of light cast only by a stormy moon. He made not a noise as he approached Aisling's bed to wake her. But where the Sidhe king anticipated the soft, feminine figure of his sorceress possessed by sleep, instead he was met with a blade to the throat.

Lir jerked back, unaccustomed to being caught off guard. He hadn't seen nor heard Aisling move from her slumber, reach for her blade, or poise it at the bobbing of his neck. And once he had, it was too late.

"My knight," Aisling bit between clenched teeth, her violet eyes fixed on him like a bird of prey. And at her hips, behind the mounds of pelt and quilt, Anduril shone mischievously. Lir cursed to himself, raising his hands in mock surrender.

"Get dressed," he commanded her. "We leave in search of the Goblet at once."

Aisling, too slow for Lir's liking, lowered Sarwen.

"I am dressed," she said, matter-of-factly.

"Hardly," Lir replied, swallowing despite himself.

Aisling sheathed Sarwen and laid the blade at the foot of the bed. Like a flower inspired by spring's bloom, Aisling rose from her bed, shedding her outermost robes till nothing but the slip remained. Lir hadn't meant to stare, turning from the sorceress only to find her once more in the mirror at her vanity. Lir's lips parted and the room grew several degrees hotter. He felt his *draiocht* snapping its chomps inside him, begging to sink its teeth into—

"Do I distract you, *mo Damh Bán?*" Aisling asked. Lir straightened, rolling his eyes in frustration with himself, carelessly caught by the object of his full attention. Aisling, on the other hand, smiled like a cat with a mouse between its teeth.

"You test my patience," Lir said. A half-truth.

"Some privacy then while I ready myself," Aisling said, disappearing behind a curtain of twinkling sapphire and azure beads beside her wardrobes. Fireflies fluttered from their perches the moment she stepped behind the veil and began fully undressing. Her purpled wine voice rising above and gracing Lir's ears.

"In what direction does our hunt take us?" Aisling asked while she worked.

Lir needed a distraction and so he drew one of his twin blades from his back and tossed it idly in his grip while he waited. Still, the reflection of her silhouette in the vanity mirror haunted him. His eyes latched onto the supple shadow of her figure, reminding him what it felt like to slide his palms against her skin. She was his wife, and all at once, she was not. Anduril's influence had bled her heart of anything she seemingly felt for the Sidhe king, and each breath he underwent, tolerating the Blood Cord's spell, would be a breath spent destroying the belt with his bare hands once he discovered a way to remove it. For even now, her feminine silhouette was interrupted by the jagged prominence of the cursed object seated on the throne of her hips.

Yet, he couldn't forget the promise he'd sealed with Niamh in Aisling's name. What he coveted most, was never his to have.

"Toward a friend," Lir said, but his voice betrayed the emotion he felt inside.

Aisling was silent for a moment, perhaps contemplating his response.

"Here?" she asked. "In the Other?" Every word thinly veiling the suspicion that laid beneath.

"Aye," Lir replied. "Not far from Castle Yillen, so make haste."

"Duty-bound knight," Aisling addressed him, "make use of yourself and help me clasp this."

Lir's heart leaped, his body moving a step in her direction as though it bore a will of its own. Cautiously, he approached the beaded curtain—he, the hunter and she the creature he pursued with uncharacteristic desperation. What he felt for her, what her presence inspired in his body, left him breathless, foggy, and weak. Made his every step heavy and slow as he rounded the beaded curtain, squinting from the light reflecting off the beads, and allowed himself the indulgence that was the sorceress.

Clad in owl-white banners, drapes, and a sash that cinched her waist, her body was armored with silver plates that reflected the violet of her eyes till she stood like an aberration—a monstrous beauty that struck fear in the Sidhe king like no creature ever had. She was at once regal and feral. Both lovely and cruel. Both the star-drunk night and the sun-bright dawn.

"My commands must be met more quickly," Aisling bit through the unholiest of ruby lips.

Lir straightened, realizing to his shame he'd been gaping. The Sidhe king cleared his dry throat and moved toward her as she turned, lifting bundles of curls from the nape of her neck. Her perfumes of lavender and dusky pollens, weakening his knees as he found the clasp to her breast plate.

Aisling had never been able to assemble a suit of armor on her own, always misplacing gauntlets for grieves and pauldrons for knee cops. It was a reminder that somewhere beyond Anduril's influence, Aisling still lived.

The Blood Cord thrummed as Lir neared her, trembling fingers taking the clasp and beginning his work.

"Do you remember me?" The words slipped from Lir's lips

like a secret. It was a selfish question. He hadn't meant to speak it, but his spirit had, forcing his body to comply with its insatiable demands for her.

"I know who you are," she said, her voice laced with the growl of a wolf. "You're the terror evening champions as its haunt. And never have you hidden the full face of your nightmare nor boasted any redemptive light."

Lir ground his fangs into his bottom teeth. So, she recognized him. Knew him as she once did before they'd been handfast. But no longer did love or affection pulse at the mention of his name. He was only a story, an image, a myth that was breathed to life and placed in her life the moment Anduril locked at her hips.

"Tell me, sorceress, of the stories your clann told of the barbarian king of the fae. The ghoulish monster that sucked on children's bones inside caves, between the forest's claws, in the dead of night," he asked.

Aisling was quiet for several breaths, her face concealed where she still stood with her back to Lir. The Sidhe king worked slowly, biding his time with his hunt at last cornered and rendered prone.

"Tell me," Lir pushed. "Tell me a tale of my infamy." He wanted to hear her speak of his terrors, of his villainy, of his demonic appetite, and condemn him. He wanted to hear her confess her hatred for him and perhaps, if the Forge was willing, he'd know it was Anduril and not Aisling who spoke. *Perhaps*, he pleaded in his mind.

Aisling remained silent, her hands curling into fists at her sides. Anduril rang hotly, seemingly glowing a brighter shade of Niltaor gold.

Niamh's rains beat down, yet they both stood still as Lir clipped the last fastener. Aisling turned on her heel and faced him.

"Describe to me the monster you see," Lir said.

Her violet eyes explored him, brightening and widening the way they once had when she was fully mortal. She tipped her chin up to see him fully, so small in comparison to the broad shadow he cast over her and yet, boundless courage as she faced the legend she'd been born to despise. And Lir knew such bravery was no work of Anduril's. Even before Aisling could lift a blade much less wield it, she'd stood before him at their handfasting with the same determination she did now—fury and all.

Aisling took a single step toward him and then another. Her heart beat like a rabbit, fluttering beneath the shadow of his attention. Lir's chest tightened, but he did his best to conceal the power she held over him. He closed the remaining distance between them until they stood chest to chest. Her breath mingling with his own. Her hands, her arms, her lips, just within reach.

Lir didn't believe in monsters. Neither did he believe in heroes. There was only *want*, and Niamh was right: Lir *wanted* Aisling more than anything. Yet, for the first time, no manner of strength, of cunning, of dominion, would win Aisling for Lir. It mattered not the wildness of his wolf nor his reign overall. His soul and his word had been bargained. Their fate together was a lightning-struck oak, alive at the roots but burning to a taper. So if Lir couldn't have her, he'd give everything of himself for her, to her, in honor of her. Just this time, despite the rage, the jealousy, the frustration scratching inside, he'd bite his tongue.

"I don't believe in monsters," she said, as though she'd stolen the words from his heart and spoken them as her own.

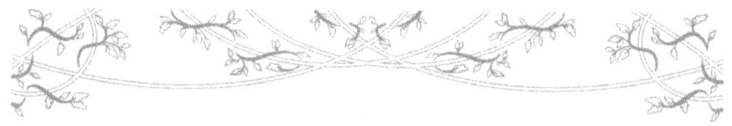

# CHAPTER XXIII

## AISLING

Castle Yillen floated between the thunderclouds of the Other, traveling like a petal in the wind. At Niamh's whim, the castle moved, casting a shadow atop the Other's forests, lakes, canyons, and fields, all sparkling with bygone magic. And if one looked hard enough from the flying towers of Castle Yillen to the emerald earth below, one might catch the shifting of giants, of demons, of a world alive and throbbing with power.

Aisling held her breath the moment she peered over Castle Yillen's edge. The drop below appeared endless, stretching further away from her the longer she looked. Aisling gulped, doing her best to ignore the quivering of her knees.

"Ready, *ellwyn*?" the fae king asked.

*Ellwyn*.

The word elicited a growl from Anduril but a purring from her *draiocht*. He was mocking her with sweet titles, his arrogance thick.

The Sidhe king stood a few paces behind Aisling, tightening the saddle of an ebony stag. Aisling glanced at him over her shoulder, careful not to meet the glimmering sage of his eyes. For each time they locked gazes, Aisling's heart raced, her *draiocht* thrashed, and Anduril pressed against the walls of her mind until her temples ached. Even so, Aisling could hardly help it. The fae king was a dark rogue, dressed in battle leathers and armor forged by the nimble fingers of mountain trolls. Every edge of metal was etched with garlands, runic symbols, and blade scars. Each nick, a memory of the violence the fae king had both endured and inflicted.

Dark jewels and metals winked from his pointed ears. His usual wind-tousled hair was combed neatly back, curling at his nape and ears from Niamh's storms. Aisling watched the veins in both his hands and forearms cord around his limbs like the roots of an oak. His muscles rippling beneath the sticky layer of soaked leather and fabric as he secured the saddle. But it was the way he whispered to the stag beneath his breath, soothing the beast in Rún that silenced Anduril's screeching to a whisper, leaving only the beating of Aisling's heart drumming in her ears.

At last, the fae king caught Aisling staring. He studied her closely even after she nervously averted her eyes.

"*Ellwyn?*" he repeated.

*Ellwyn.* Aisling rolled the name over her tongue again and again. Anduril spat the word like poison, gagging and heaving for breath.

"I'm ready," Aisling said. The sorceress approached the stag and took hold of the saddle's horn. The stag huffed, prancing in place nervously. It appeared to smell her *draiocht*; its nostrils flared and the wiry hair at its haunches rose like needles.

"*Easca,*" Lir hissed at the beast. Still, the stag eyed Aisling warily—her magic both potent and unfamiliar. Some creatures slithered, crawled, or flew from their nests, dens, and burrows to breathe the same air as Aisling. Others reacted as if Aisling were a wolf herself, biding her time till she snapped her maw shut and devoured them whole.

"Perhaps we need another mount," Aisling suggested.

Aisling looked around. It was the dead of night and most of the blue rabbits that tended to the stables were off drinking in the tavern hall at the base of Castle Yillen.

"Geld is strong enough for the both of us," Lir said, and while Aisling knew the fae king understood that wasn't the issue, she didn't protest.

Aisling grabbed the horn of the saddle once more. Ignoring Geld's protests, Lir held Aisling's waist and lifted the sorceress onto the stag. His hands, large and firm, carried her as though she weighed no more than an owl's feather, setting her gently down. His touch was tender whilst still bearing the promise of untold might. Aisling swallowed her yelp, swinging her leg over Geld's back and sliding closer to the horn to make room for Lir. The fae king leaped atop the stag behind her.

Aisling tensed. She felt the warm brush of his thighs, the solid wall of his chest, and the strength of his arms as he reached his hands around her and grabbed Geld's reins. Aisling swallowed. Had she ever been this close to the fae king before? Suddenly, she couldn't remember.

*Skin like thorns, words like venom, hands like claws*, Anduril snarled. *Hate, hate, hate.*

Aisling wrenched her eyes shut, holding her breath. Were these her words? Her thoughts? Her feelings? Her mind despised the beast, but her body relished him. Needed him closer still. Even as Anduril chimed hotly against both Aisling's hips and Lir's thighs. And if the fae king noticed, he said not a word, pressing his palm against her abdomen and pulling her closer.

"Is that necessary?" Aisling asked, her voice betraying the heat she felt building inside.

"The closer your body to mine, the easier to shield you," Lir said, his lips tickling her ear where he bent to whisper. The storm was loud, competing with his words.

Once, twice, the fae king wrapped the reins around his wrist and flicked, encouraging the mount forward.

"Your excuses grow tired," Aisling said, straightening her back. She became needlessly stubborn in his presence, impatient, and cold. All of which appeared to encourage the fae king further. "The only creature I need to be shielded from, is you."

Lir laughed. The sound rattled inside Aisling like the first notes of an organ seated in the righteous mouths of chapels. Deep, inhumane, and coupled with the echo of forgotten gods. A being whose age—whilst invisible to the eye—shone through his elegance, his violence, the wisdom and intelligence behind his every glance, and the burden born heavy in the slope of his shoulders.

"What are you suggesting?" he said, and while Aisling couldn't see his face, a smile was apparent in the amused lilt of his voice.

"I do not know—or care to know for that matter—the history that lies between us. For whatever reason, your influence in my life is tangled, knotted, and fraying. Both difficult to understand and more frustrating to unravel. And so, you are a weakness to me," Aisling said. "Even if you despise me."

This inspired a strange noise from the fae king. He twitched, doing his best to hide his surprise at Aisling's forwardness.

"You flatter yourself, sorceress," Lir said. "You'd have to occupy my mind for me to despise you."

Like a club to the face, Aisling felt the blow of the fae king's indifference. She shouldn't and didn't care, she reminded herself, embarrassed she was hurt at all.

Geld approached the steepled gates of Castle Yillen veiled like a bride with the tempest. Two vast, armored bears stood on either side of the portcullis. They crossed their spears before the gate, still as statues.

"You deny that which my senses determine easily," Aisling

said. "I hear your heart jolt when you see me, I smell your anxiety when I'm near, and I taste your nerves when you accidentally touch me." All truth. But none of that made Aisling so certain of the fae king's disdain as her own. Whatever strange bond they shared sank its teeth into the marrow of her heart, and fed off the blood of her obsession.

*Parasite, deceiver, distraction!* Anduril screamed, squeezing Aisling till she feared the bruises that would follow shortly after. *Seek the Goblet. Seek the Goblet. Seek the Goblet*, the Blood Cord chanted like a mad man wailing through cobbled streets.

Lir said nothing. His silence, formidable.

The fae king nodded his head at the two bears, and they uncrossed their spears. Slowly, the portcullis released its teeth from the flagstones of Castle Yillen and heaved open.

Aisling and Lir passed through the gate like ghosts, laced in the supernatural mist of the Other as they stepped onto the jeweled stepping stones that spiraled toward the earth far below.

Aisling's tongue turned to ash and her stomach knotted tightly. One small misstep from Geld and they'd all three plunge to their death.

Geld's hooves struggled to adjust to the slick edge of the floating stones, the rain, and the moss that mischievously coated each step of their descent. Geld's hooves slid off the edge of the fourth stone, sending the stag into a panic.

Aisling screamed, her dinner rising up her throat.

Without hesitation, Lir grabbed Aisling and pulled her tightly against him. His magic flared out, manifesting in vines like ropes that caught Geld's hooves and straightened the stag. The stag whimpered and whined, prancing in place despite the vines that stuck the beast to the stones. At last, Geld calmed and continued, each step secured by Lir's vines as they descended.

Nevertheless, Aisling's heart fluttered as quickly as a cornered hare's. Her body firmly pressed against the fae king's.

Racat shrieked inside Aisling as if pierced by an iron reed. The *dragún* whipped back and forth, struggling for breath as if the fae king's proximity had made it manic. Anduril, on the other hand, smiled. The belt stifled Racat's energy, smothering her *draiocht* till it collapsed against the caverns of her soul—its chest rising and falling with brittle breath. The Blood Cord loosened and cooled, shimmering with satisfaction.

She didn't love him, didn't know him, nor remember him and yet, her *draiocht* shriveled and smoked like a wilted flower, crushed beneath a boot.

*You see? You see?* Anduril said inside her mind. *This is why we hate him.*

Aisling clenched her jaw and matched the fae king's silence. She'd mistaken their connection for obsession. It was only hatred. Enemies by blood once. Enemies by heart now. This much, Aisling knew.

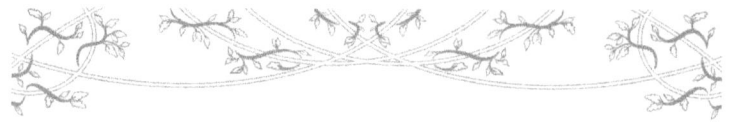

## CHAPTER XXIV

### AISLING

"*His bride, he brings,*" the forest prattled in Rún. Aisling understood every alder, every yew, every ash perfectly as if they spoke inside her mind.

*Lies, lies, liars, liars,* Anduril said. Aisling ground her teeth. She knew the mischief of the fae world, but still her *draiocht* huffed weakly, reaching for the trees' words. Aisling shook away the warring of her thoughts, biting at the dissonance for the truth.

*Ellwyn* bloomed beneath Geld's hooves as they climbed off the last stepping stone and moved across the meadow before the forest. Every step summoned a bloom of violet petals and their sparkling pollen. Aisling wasn't certain if Lir had intentionally or unintentionally grown *ellwyn* or if the forest had done so in his stead. But she marveled at the cloud of glittering dust following their wake.

"*Over the threshold of a castle made of trees, they come, they come,*" the forest sang.

A muscle flashed across Lir's jaw.

"Do they speak to you like this often?" Aisling asked him, so softly only he could hear.

"Always," he said, staring straight ahead as they wove through the gnarled, ghoulish aisle of bone apple trees. "When I wake, when I sleep, when I can't think of anything else but..."

The Sidhe king's voice trailed off. Aisling considered asking him to complete the thought but decided against it.

The forest groaned as their trunks bent and bowed when their sovereign passed. The vision unsettled Aisling. In the mortal plane, the trees, the forest, and the *draiocht* were phantoms—always most visible when caught slipping at the edges of one's vision. But if looked directly upon, the magic vanished. Popped like a soap bubble. Here in the Other, on the other hand, the magic was fully alive, proud, and eager to be seen. The trees were behemoth beasts themselves, moving with the strength of storm-blown giants.

"That's enough to render anyone mad," Aisling said. "Which explains the lunacy of a centuries-old forge-born lord."

"I've grown accustomed to it," Lir said, not biting the bait Aisling had laid with her teasing.

"*I vow to you the first cut of my heart, the first taste of my blood, and the last words from my lips,*" the forest cooed.

Anduril objected immediately, but Aisling couldn't deny how familiar the words sounded. As if she'd once treasured them.

"Were you born with such an ability?" Aisling asked. He'd told her the answer before, but she'd forgotten.

"No," Lir said. "Upon coronation, the Sidhe sovereign of the greenwood inherits the ability to speak to and, in turn, listen to the whole of his kingdom—including the trees themselves and the animals they shelter."

"So, why can I hear them too?" Aisling asked.

Lir tilted his head back, avoiding her eyes.

"Because as my bride, you, too, are sovereign to the greenwood, Aisling," he said. "No matter bargains, enchantments, or legends, you are queen to my kingdom by the law of our oaths. And the forest recognizes you as such."

Aisling looked around the woodland.

She remembered handfasting the fae king. She remembered her crimson gown, the ring of fire, the three blades, the nightmarish barbarians that burned Fiacha's evening with their hedonism. She didn't remember Lir's face, his voice, or the way she'd felt afterward. The memories were distorted and complex, drifting in and out of clarity.

Yet, from the moment she'd handfasted the Sidhe king, she'd felt the rush of her mare beneath her, the mood of the trees, the whims of the owls that hooted from their perches. Even then, she and Lir had been bound in a way she didn't entirely understand and didn't think she ever would. How could she have forgotten their marriage was a union tied only by a duty to their people and nothing more?

Eventually, the trees thinned and the dense carpet of hollow grass spilled into wetland where wetweed grew rampant. The aspens dipped their spidery roots into the waters, overgrown with moss and colorful fungi. And beyond, rested a cottage that puffed clouds from its toppling chimney like an old man and his pipe. The shingles of its roof reminiscent of a tattered, pointed hat, protecting the weathered face of the home from the rain.

Aisling smelled the herbs and spices that cooked inside. The cottage's warmth, steaming against the windowpanes decorated in salt gems, small brownie skulls, and wind chimes.

"We're here," Lir said. He guided Geld to the cottage's entrance before jumping off the mount first. Without hesitation, the fae king turned and carried Aisling off the stag, setting her gingerly on the ground. And had Aisling still believed the fae king held any affections for her, she might've thought the lingering of his hands at her waist was a token of his attraction. But she knew better.

*Yes, yes, yes*, Anduril encouraged her.

Aisling found her footing, peeling strands of wet hair from her face.

Lir knocked on the door, but he didn't wait for an answer. He grabbed the knob and pushed the door open.

"Wait," Aisling said, touching his elbow. Lir's eyes shot to her hand on his arm, lingering for a moment longer than Aisling anticipated. "Shouldn't we be invited inside first?"

Lir shook his head. "It's alright."

And so, Lir entered, Aisling a step behind.

Immediately, the heat of the cottage rushed toward Aisling like a banshee intent to possess. Her bones and flesh thawed where she'd been too afraid to use her *draiocht* to warm herself from Niamh's rains. It was as if Lir and Aisling had stepped into the belly of a beast—bubbling, hot, and ripe with all manner of unidentifiable objects. A plethora of stacked jars, hanging pots, bundles of sage, sugared bones, and shelves stuffed with books whose spines changed titles when you looked too closely.

"*Mo Damh Bán*," a voice said from behind a curtain of garlands, obscuring a room that tunneled deeper into the cottage. An old fox emerged from between the leaves, first his nose and whiskers and then his orange face, speckled with gray above his beady black eyes. He held a stack of ornately embroidered quilts, decorated in silver constellations that reminded Aisling of a cloak she'd once been gifted.

The fox bowed to Lir before noticing Aisling as well. Taken off guard, the fox sputtered something unintelligible before bowing swiftly to Aisling.

"*Mo Lúra*," he said. "It's an honor to at last make your acquaintance."

Aisling smiled softly. "The honor is all mine."

The fox blushed, muzzle scrunching as he gathered himself. His beady eyes darting toward and hesitating on Anduril, gleaming happily on Aisling's hips.

"Please, please, make yourselves at home," the fox said.

"Had I known you were coming, I'd have tidied up." Frantically, the fox gathered scattered scrolls and stuffed the frog aimlessly hopping atop the floorboards into his cloak's pocket. "And to what do I owe the pleasure?"

Lir pulled out a chair and fell into it. Lithe as a cat, he reclined, crossing his arms over his chest as his long legs nearly reached the other end of the cottage.

"*I need a favor,*" he said in Rún.

The fox set down the stack of quilts.

"*I cannot thank you enough for the kelpie,*" the old fox said. "*Already the fiend has done away with a horde of orcs twice over. So, mo Damh Bán, name your favor and it's yours.*"

Lir popped his knuckles, flexing his lean, elegant hands. "*We're in search of the Goblet of Lore.*"

The fox paused, considering Lir more closely now.

"The Goblet of Lore," the fox repeated, tasting the words himself. His whiskers twitched as he moved his teeth, licking the tips with his pink tongue. "You've piqued my interest."

"What do you know of it?" Lir asked.

The fox's frog sprung from his cloak's pocket. The fox caught the green thing with ease, trapping it between his paws. Idly, the fox stroked its slick back.

"The chalice from which the gods sipped the Forge's brew, capable of mass creation at the whim of those bold enough to sip. To give in exchange for everything they will take."

As if the gods themselves clapped their hands, thunder shook the cottage.

Aisling felt the *draíocht* of the Other stir knowingly, pressing its ears against the windowpanes and its eyes to the keyhole.

"The gods, however, hid the Goblet, afraid of what would become of their world if the unworthy were allowed to sip from its gilded lip," the fox continued.

"No one hides anything without the intent of it being found," Aisling said. "Eventually."

"Perhaps that's what they've been waiting for," the fox said. "Someone worthy enough to find it."

"Yet, the legends, the myths, the fables speak nothing of its whereabouts," Lir said.

The fox patted the frog's head.

"There is but one tale that makes mention of the Goblet's name," the fox said. Both Lir and Aisling leaned in closer, hanging onto the fox's every breath. "The last anyone saw of the Goblet, it was tossed into the mouth of Eogi, the god of beginnings, and swallowed whole."

Eogi.

Aisling had never heard the name, but by the look on Lir's face, the fae king had. Lir exchanged glances with Aisling before clearing his throat.

"Where does Eogi lie?" Lir asked the fox.

"Normally, he rests beyond the fog, watching the death galleons sail across black waters. During the rainy season, however, many claim to have seen his lumbering shadow on the howling Isle of Rokmora," the fox said.

Aisling glanced at Lir, hoping the fae king knew where to find this Rokmora. Lir said not a word, instead, bringing a fist to his lips as he sank into thought. And once the fae king was consumed by the labyrinth of his mind, there was little to release him from its grip.

"How long is the journey?" Aisling asked.

"It is a weeks' long trip," the fox said. "However, with both *mo Damh Bán*'s and *mo Lúra*'s strength, I'm certain you can halve that time. I'd guess three moons will pass before you reach Rokmora. One of which will be a storm moon."

Aisling nodded her head in understanding, eyes wandering around the fox's cottage.

"If there are any supplies you can spare us for the journey, we'll repay you tenfold upon our return."

The fox hopped off his seat, dropping the frog and spreading his arms.

"Of course, of course, *mo Lúra*," the fox said.

He blazed through the cottage, collecting armfuls of leather flasks, herbs, dried meats, breads, pelts, ropes, and more until neither Aisling nor Lir could see his face for the mountain of loot in his arms. The fox organized the supplies and divided them into sacks that would latch onto Geld's saddle as they rode. At the end of the hour, Geld was decorated in the fox's collection. The fox had even tied garlands of four-leaf clovers around the stag's antlers for good fortune on their journey.

Aisling and Lir bowed to the fox.

"Thank you," Aisling said, taking the fox's paw between her two hands. The fox dipped his head nobly in return, beady eyes glistening with unwept tears.

But as Aisling and Lir approached the cottage's threshold to leave, the fae king hesitated at the exit.

"Go on ahead," he said, tipping his head in Geld's direction. "I'll be there in a moment."

Anduril buzzed hotly, but this time, Aisling's curiosity masked the belt's protests. She watched closely as Lir sank back into the heat of the cottage and began whispering with the fox in Rún. She couldn't understand nor hear his voice properly over the screams of the storm, but she inclined her head toward them regardless.

The fox watched the fae king speak with familiar intensity. Of what they spoke, Aisling was still uncertain, but she was determined to find out eventually.

The sorceress, at last, turned and slipped into the rain.

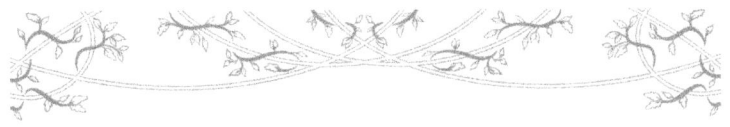

# CHAPTER XXV

LIR

"Is there no way to remove it?" Lir asked the fox.

Cara's expression pinched, his paws fiddling with the edge of his cloak.

"Only the wearer can remove the Blood Cord from their body. It must be of their will and no others."

Lir cursed.

"How can it be by the will of the wearer if the Blood Cord transforms their will entirely?"

Cara frowned. "It is the nature of magic to take as much as it gives. This much, you already know, *mo Damh Bán*."

Lir clenched his jaw, grinding his teeth together. His *draiocht* tossed with frustration, snapping and clawing for release. The forest felt it too—the trees whipping their heads to the rhythm of his anger.

Lir turned on his boot, bidding one last farewell to the fox. Aisling was waiting for him and Anduril's keen eye would breed suspicion in her heart if he stalled too long. He felt the battle the belt waged in Aisling's mind. How it twisted his words, his image, and her memories till Aisling couldn't recognize truth from deceit. It was enough to drive Lir mad by the mere influence of its proximity.

The Sidhe king stepped into the rain and lifted Aisling onto Geld's saddle. She obliged, sitting straight-backed before him so as not to touch him more than was necessary. The lavender of her perfume and soaps mercilessly wafted and overwhelmed his senses. If he could, he'd rip Anduril from her body and crush its metal to dust. If he could, he'd tip her chin up so her lips met his mouth. If he could, he'd remove every plate of armor, every bit of chainmail, every strip of leather, and memorize her. If he could, he'd listen to her speak till the sun rose. He'd watch her cast petty spells in silence. He'd be close to her. If he could, he'd love her.

But he couldn't.

Lir, Aisling, and Geld trekked through the forests of the Other, its cliffsides, and its mountain ranges, making quick work of the path they'd intended to travel. Lir trusted the trees when he bore no other option but mostly referenced Fiacha's stars to guide him. They pointed northward, through the misty planes of what the yews called Kaster: a vast and sparkling meadow, wealthy with cornflowers, *Imbolc* lilies, and bulbs of greenmary. The walnut trees that punctuated these fields slept peacefully, snoring alongside the creatures that hid in its knots and bends—a faith-filled sign Kaster was a safe enough place to rest for the night.

"*Ellwyn*," Lir whispered to Aisling. She hadn't spoken in several hours, sitting silently before him as they rode. "*Ellwyn*," Lir repeated when she didn't answer.

The Sidhe king shifted, peering over Aisling's shoulder and at her face. Her eyes, gently shut, twitched with dreams. He'd wondered why her breath had grown deep and steady, but he hadn't believed she'd be capable of rest on Geld's saddle. Riding was not for the faint of heart, but it appeared Anduril's strength had proven useful in this one capacity.

As gently as he was capable, Lir lifted Aisling into his arms. She stirred and Lir held his breath, watching her lips pucker with conversation. The realm of dreams had ensorcelled her fully, immersing her in another world entirely. She convulsed softly, her body forgetting that only her spirit moved in its parallel realm.

The Sidhe king slipped off Geld, carrying Aisling beneath the arms and knees. Her head rolled back, so Lir adjusted her till her cheek pressed against his chest.

"*Samsaral*," Lir said. Obedient, the *draiocht* responded, blooming a plush bed of mage's moss. He set the sorceress down in the shadow of a walnut tree, crowning her head with violets as she settled into the emerald cushions he'd summoned.

Geld lowered to his knees and rocked himself to sleep as well. Midnight beetles and opal snails climbing up the stag's pelt. They cleaned the beast's furs of dirt and debris from their travels, polishing his hooves and antlers.

Lir lowered himself beside Aisling, leaving a space between them. Still, he watched her, eyes fluttering shut with exhaustion.

The Sidhe king slept hard, waking just before dawn bled across the horizon.

Lir blinked, adjusting himself to morning. The sun was already breaking and spilling across the sky. He'd overslept and he was still groggy. The Sidhe king propped himself up on his elbows, immediately searching for Aisling.

She lay next to him still, sound asleep, but to Lir's horror, no longer was the sorceress uncovered.

Grin mushrooms grew from her skin, from the moss, from the fertile soil of Kaster. Pale as bones, the plant bled from sharp, tooth-like edges, pointed enough to cut. But it was the aroma of its scarlet sap that dealt the greatest damage. A syrup of bottled rot, some called it—if you were brave enough to collect it and stopper the bottle before the first whiff entered the nostrils and began its death-bidden work.

A rot—a disease that didn't belong in the Other.

Lir's chest tightened with dread.

Almost buried, Aisling's chest rose and fell with the fungus bleeding atop her armor. Consuming her. Geld was similarly cloaked by the disease, lulled asleep by its poison. Only Lir had been spared, the grin tracing his body but never touching him—as if afraid of his might should they bite into his life breath. Rot and disease was a mortal machination. The Other suffered no death, only life eternal, and so did the Sidhe. Lir himself was the antithesis of such poison. He, the bloom and not the wilt. Only he, spared.

Lir cursed.

The Sidhe king sprang from the moss and lunged for Aisling. He ripped the bleeding tooth from her skin, but for every mushroom torn, three more grew in its place.

*No, no, no, no.* Lir's fear transformed to anger and then panic, clawing at the disease like a rabid dweller. He gritted his teeth, ignoring the heat pressing the backs of his eyes.

"Not our will, *mo Damh Bán*," the walnut groaned above him. Lir glanced up, staring at the tree for the first time. It, too, was overcome with bleeding tooth. The fungus had overcome everything and all, taking the life of the Other and rendering it to rot.

"This is not of the Other," the walnut choked beneath grisly, haggard breaths. "This is a mortal contagion seeping through the cracks."

Lir blanched.

Mortal contagion.

"What do you speak of?" Lir asked, his voice stripped bare by his fury and fear alike.

"They're coming, *mo Damh Bán*," the walnut said, blackening before his eyes. Darkening like old blood on the belly of a blade. The walnut tree was dying. Its life sucked from its bones by the vampirism of death's grin. "They're coming."

Lir dove into the mushrooms around Aisling and ripped her from the earth. The pace of her heart was slowing and her breath was thinning. Soon, the rot would take her too.

Lir screamed, uncertain what else to do. He bore limitless *draiocht*, unmatched strength, twin blades gifted by the gods themselves, and still he couldn't spare her. Couldn't stop the grin that grew even as he tore their buds from her freckled flesh.

"Aisling!" He screamed again and again with none to bear witness but the meadow of Kaster. Even Anduril's glimmer was extinguished, consumed by the maggots, the spiders, and the infection as was Aisling.

Lir looked over his shoulder, searching Kaster for an answer. There was nothing and no one. The meadow was populated by only chattering flowers, and beyond, only dense forest as far as the eye could see.

Lir leaped to his feet and raced toward Geld. The stag, covered in grin as well, breathed slowly. The great barrel of his belly swelling as the fungus devoured him. Lir tore through the rot, digging for the satchels Cara had prepared for them. Mushrooms exploded where Lir searched, growing between his fingers, crawling up his arms, his shoulders, desperately trying to latch onto his throat, his face, his hair but failing and falling once they tasted a morsel of his life-giving magic. Still, Lir ripped at the rot, diving into the disease until he could curl his fingers around the nearest satchel.

Lir pulled and flew away from the stag with a single bag in hand. He opened it, ignoring the rot that still fell from his body, and squirmed on the ground around him. He dug through Cara's supplies.

Blackberry swords, mint salves, belle figs, wild milk thorns, broad leaf, briar balms. Nothing, nothing, nothing, until Lir's fingers wrapped around a glass box. The Sidhe king almost crushed the delicate thing between his hands in his frenzy, fingertips trembling as he snapped the box open.

A single dose of morning breath: an elixir to cleanse the body of contaminants, infections, and disease.

Lir's heart took flight inside his chest. His cheeks flushed, blood rushing through his veins like frothing rapids.

The Sidhe king scrambled to Aisling, all his elegance and ease gone and replaced with utter desperation.

Lir clawed at the grin once more and once more the grin grew more thickly. No longer could Lir see Aisling. She was a mound of white, bleeding grin. Its toothy smile mocked him, swallowing Aisling whole as he bore witness.

The Sidhe king drew his axes. He swiped at the grin, hacking at the rot with his teeth bared. At last, between the fungus, her face shone. Delicate, sleeping, and serene, she lay in her hungry grave.

Lir moved quicker than he believed possible, adrenaline pulsing through his body as he neared her, reaching for her, until, at last, he could bring the morning breath to her lips. Three droplets fell and slid down her tongue.

Lir waited, watched, fought past the growing grin even now. Nothing was happening. The elixir wasn't working.

Dread filled the Sidhe king, bottomless and black. He shook his head.

She wasn't drinking the elixir, still fast and hard asleep. Several sky-blue droplets leaking from the corners of her mouth.

*No, no, no, no.*

Lir—perhaps driven mad by his desperation—tipped the elixir back and filled his mouth. He cut through the grin one more time, holding his breath as he brought his lips to Aisling and kissed her.

Gently, the Sidhe king spilled the elixir from his mouth to hers. Lir wasn't certain how long they lay in the meadow of Kaster, his lips to hers. He only knew that if they both died there, buried in the forest's death, he'd be happy he'd died beside her.

# CHAPTER XXVI

*Incorporeal, Aisling watched her father limp through clouds of ash. He dragged his iron prosthetic through the charred flesh of the forest, followed by a procession of black knights glimmering in the pale judgment of the moon. Their eyes red with wystria.*

*Torchlight floated amidst the darkness like the hideous, luminous eyes of a succubus, spotting Aisling amidst the stars and pinning her to the ink of Fiacha's sky—the Lady's signature written in the sadistic turn of the blade that pierced her and held her in place.*

*"This way!" her father yelled: Nemed, high king and fire hand of the North. The violet of his eyes as violet as Aisling's own: a cruel reminder of the blood they shared.*

*Aisling grimaced, the gravel of his voice conjuring spirits of her past. His soldiers heeded his orders, emerging from the woodland alongside their sovereign. Behind them, a stain of death was left in their wake—Sidhe and forge-born corpses piled between the mounds of broken oaks.*

*For the most part, the knights were faceless ghouls. A mystery of opalescent blood wetting their garments, their weapons, their boots. All save for Starn, her eldest brother and the crown prince of Tilren, standing behind their father with the crow-sharp scowl of their mother.*

"Are you certain it's this way?" Starn asked. His crooked nose was smeared with blood and ash, and the whites of his eyes were bloodshot from too much smoke. Aisling's chest seized, despite herself, with memory. She'd rushed Starn into the kitchens when Fergus had accidentally broken their eldest brother's nose in a fist fight over the litter of kittens Aisling had found near Castle Neimedh's cisterns. They were so much smaller then —wisps of the men they'd become. Now, Starn's eyes shone with the brutality of war, of death, of violence, and of loss. There was something tortuous in the harrowed glances he cast to the shadows, startling when a branch snapped too loudly in the distance.

"I'm certain," their father replied.

Nemed and his fleet approached the edge of a craig. Vast and storming, a sea sprawled before them, hammering against the forge-made rocks beneath their iron boots. The wind whipped their torchlight till each flame danced, casting shadows across soot-soiled helms. And upon the bone-white crests, bobbed mortal fleets with their cannons and flame and iron. They'd come to meet Nemed, Starn, and his small fleet at the edge of the continent.

Aisling's eyes pricked with heat. This was not the North. They were somewhere else. Somewhere far away, where colossal trees grew from the sands of the sea and stretched their limbs so their canopies might whisper breaths of fresh salt air between the bellies of ships that narrowly avoided their spindly, wooden claws.

"You believe it's run somewhere out there?" Starn asked, eyes studying the steely gray of the horizon.

"I've no doubt," Nemed said.

"Is it possible?" Starn continued, his voice brittle after weeks of inhaling smoke. "Can Leshy truly run so far? Especially with such an injury?"

Nemed laughed. A horrible cackle that sent shivers down Aisling's spine.

"You've seen it yourself," the fire hand said. "You watched it rise from the earth. You held your breath as it reached for you, stumbling on its giant limbs after centuries asleep and rooted to its throne."

Starn's lips pressed into a thin line. His eyes glazed over, focused on the memory his father described.

"Can we trust her?" Starn asked. He referenced the Lady.

"No," Nemed confessed. "And neither can she trust us. But to bury the Aos Sí once and for all, I'll accept the blade my enemy hands me."

"Even if it's laced with their venom?" Starn crossed his arms over his chest.

Nemed turned to his son, meeting his eyes. "You already have."

And as if its ears burned, the sword at Starn's back shuddered, twitching in its scabbard to be unleashed. Indeed, the Lady had lent Starn a pearl of magic—one he'd used to rob Dagfin of his life at Lofgren's Rise.

Aisling's draiocht growled, the hair on its haunches standing at attention as Racat dug its claws into the caverns of her soul and kneaded like a cat.

"Rest easy," Nemed continued. "We'll hunt Leshy down within the fortnight and all will be over. Once and for all."

"And Aisling?" Starn asked.

Nemed's eyes flickered with hesitation. His nose twitched strangely, but it was the reddening of the scar across his face that alluded to any emotion at all.

"There will be no victory without the fae witch bent before an iron blade—without the mortals' birthright cut from her chest."

Had Aisling been more the spirit in the wind, her body would've drained of all blood. She would've bitten fury and

*fear between her fangs and lunged at the fire hand with ravenous claws. She would've summoned her magic like a body from the grave, bones snapping into place as she crawled for him. As she dragged him under and killed him slowly. Slowly.*
*Slowly.*

~

AISLING

Flame was no stranger to rebirth. A story as old as time, a fire collapsed only to be born from the same bed of ash in which it perished. And so, when Aisling woke to the familiar dance of violet flames surrounding her, she knew something was wrong.

Aisling lurched awake.

She straightened like a ghoul in a crypt, heaving air into its lungs after centuries of sleep. Around her, white fungus and rot shriveled to dust, squirming and screaming for mercy. Aisling gave none, devouring every mushroom and insect with her *draiocht*. Anduril burned angrily at her hips, ringing and shaking the last bits of disease from her body.

But once the flames shed their original fury, Aisling focused, blinking till the world regained clarity.

The fae king sat before her, leaning back and propped up by his arms. He looked as if he'd been flung off her, his leathers scorched and his armor blackened by her influence. But it was his face that captured Aisling's attention: eyes ringed with horror and his complexion pale as the bone that lay beneath.

They stared at one another, a silent conversation passing between them. The taste of dawn and him on her lips and tongue.

"Geld," Lir said at last. The name falling from his mouth half-broken.

Immediately, Aisling's gaze darted to the stag. He was still buried and drowning in the fungus.

Aisling summoned her *draiocht* and allowed her flames to crawl up the edges of the stag's body, careful not to singe a single hair on its pelt. Only the rot, she reminded her *draiocht* as it made quick work of every maggot, beetle, and mushroom. Conscious now, she could destroy that which asleep she could not.

Silence followed the chaos while Aisling and Lir fell to their knees beside Geld. Without discussion, the sorceress and the fae king mended the wounds the fungus had wrought on the stag—wounds Aisling and Lir could heal on their own bodies in a few forge-blessed breaths, but the stag could not. They wrapped gauze around his legs, wiped the rust-colored blood from beneath his nostrils, and brushed the withered bodies of insects from his rump.

Perhaps it was a distraction. A means of biding their time as they worked at a glacial pace, accompanied only by the quiet. For the walnut that'd shaded their rest was dead, black, and consumed by the rot that would've otherwise devoured Aisling and Geld whole.

"My father is coming," Aisling said, unable to avoid the inevitable any longer. The nearer they drew to Aisling and the Other—the nearer they approached to achieving their ends, the more the veil between the mortal plane and the Other thinned. Fate eager for a conclusion.

The fae king exhaled, but his expression didn't light with surprise. He knew it too.

While Aisling had allowed exhaustion to gently lower her head beneath the surface of consciousness, the Lady had seized the opportunity, grabbing her legs and yanking her into the depths of somewhere *in between*. A dream she chronicled to Lir, piece by piece.

. . .

Aisling stood shakily, swaying on wobbling knees. The grin had sucked the energy from her body and the Lady's intrusion had left her mind swimming in shadows and fog. Even Anduril hung limply from the sorceress, glowing dimly.

"Ash," Lir said, standing and catching her before she fell. He held her gently, an arm beneath her arms and one behind her knees.

"I can walk," Aisling said. "They're coming. We must continue. We don't have much time." It was true. Aisling's dreams hadn't been mere fantasy or nightmare—the Lady was teasing her, haunting her, proving to the sorceress that she was still in control even if Aisling couldn't see her.

Lir, who'd listened to every detail of her dream, hid his anxiety well. He nodded as she spoke, listening intently but never interrupting. Aisling watched for a long while as the fae king turned her words over in his mind.

"You must rest," Lir said, holding her with both the strength and grace of an oak. "The grin sapped from the marrow of your soul and left you drained, scarcely alive. If it hadn't been for Cara's elixirs—"

"Or you," Aisling added, interrupting the fae king. She wasn't certain why she said it or why her heart jolted when he fixed his eyes on hers. Anduril protested weakly, as feeble and defeated as the sorceress felt.

Aisling felt the quick beating of Lir's heart against her cheek as he held her. His eyes swam with torment, with the green of greatest affliction. It was the look of a man who feared that looked back. It was terror and horror and fascination all at once.

*He despises you, you and your mortal-muddied blood*, Anduril said, but the voice sounded like Aisling's in her mind. Perhaps it was. Perhaps it wasn't. This time, Aisling truly couldn't tell the difference. *He hates you.* Anduril laughed, but it came out broken and clipped by exhaustion. *Did you really think the nightmare king of the forest would like you when your own túath did not? He fears you.*

Aisling swallowed before the rock in her throat formed. He was a stranger. A weed that'd blossomed in the gardens of her memories and disguised itself as a flower that'd been there all along. He wasn't real and neither was the burning of her lips as his eyes flicked toward them.

"They're coming," Aisling repeated like a mad woman. Weakly, she shuffled out of the fae king's arms, but he didn't protest, allowing her to slip from his embrace. "We must find Eogi."

Lir opened his mouth to speak but thought better of it, closing his lips.

The fae king clenched his teeth, a muscle flashing across his jaw. He then readied Geld for the journey ahead. Geld was weak, awkwardly bending his thin, blood-rusted legs till he stood as straight as he was capable. The grin had taken greatly from the beast, and it was possible Geld wouldn't survive another moon or two.

"The grin," Aisling said as Lir unlatched several satchels. He dropped them to the ground, abandoning the supplies on the fields of Kaster for another traveler to stumble upon. "It's an ill omen of my father's approach."

Lir nodded his head grimly, tightening the saddle as he spoke.

"I felt it too," he agreed. "It's the rot of mankind. Their destruction, their vampirism, their poison seeping into the veil of the Other as they approach nearer to their victory. Grin is a rot that grows only in the mortal plane where death is inevitable. Here in the Other, such a species cannot survive."

"But how?" Aisling asked. "How could my father affect this realm so greatly? What is it he nears?"

Lir scowled, his brow lowering and casting a shadow across his eyes in the dim light.

"Whatever he's hunting, they've already injured it badly," Lir said. "It runs, but for how long? Our time is borrowed. Whatever he pursues—whatever he bleeds—its wounds are shared with the veil. All that the Forge births from its molten cauldron is bound through magic. Spells, jinxes, and enchantments tugging at the threads of these connections, these strings, these breaths. Your father has found a thread—the gateway—most likely with the help of the Lady, and he will bleed this realm with rot to get to you and his victory."

Aisling bit her bottom lip, stroking Geld's neck.

"We must find the Goblet," Aisling said at last. "Before it's too late."

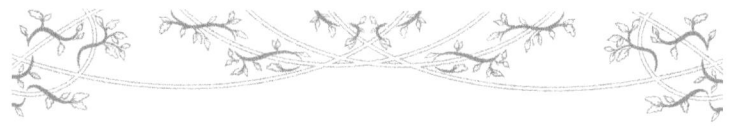

# CHAPTER XXVII

AISLING

The night was dying.

Soon, morning would arrive on a blazing gelding of war, prepared to cast its light across the Other in conquest.

Seven horned owls flew circles above Aisling, Lir, and Geld as they walked. They moved at a snail's pace; Geld was unable to carry a rider whilst he recovered from his crippling injuries. So, Lir wrapped the stag's reigns around his wrist and led the beast, Aisling by his side.

It had been one full day since they'd scarcely survived the grin. Aisling's muscles ached and her head throbbed—her breath a quiver between her teeth. Racat lay on his side within her, eyes half-closed and eager for rest. But Aisling couldn't rest. Not yet. Her clann was coming and if the grin was a forewarning of the destruction the fire hand planned to wreak, Aisling needed the Goblet immediately.

"Let's rest for the hour," the fae king said. He removed one of his gloves and pressed his palm to the bark of a tree. This was how he spoke to the forest when the willows and yews weren't whispering aloud. Aisling wondered about their dialogue, but a part of her—a still mortal part—was too afraid to ask. It was an eerie, unsettling sort of magic Lir shared with the woodland. Something ancient and wild and wholly inhuman. He, himself, a spirit of the bloom.

"No," Anduril said through Aisling's lips, gleaming hotly. "*We continue on.*"

Lir sucked his teeth, shaking his head and muttering something unintelligible beneath his breath.

Aisling wasn't certain how long they pushed through the Other's wilderness, carving a path with the guidance of the trees to protect them as they pressed through. The trail was longer this way, the fae king had explained. To avoid the most monstrous secrets of the gods' realm, they sometimes went around instead of through, left instead of right, and up instead of down. Aisling's strength was dwindling, and their supplies were depleting quickly.

Aisling's vision blurred. Nausea swelled inside her like an infection till black fingertips crawled at the edge of her vision, threatening to toss her into darkness.

*Just a little further*, Anduril said. *Don't be so weak. Don't show the fae king how mortal you still are. How incompetent you are without me.*

Aisling forced one boot in front of the other.

*Farther, farther*, Anduril said.

Aisling lost feeling in her fingertips and toes. Her body was suddenly twice as heavy to carry.

"Ellwyn," Lir said. Aisling tried to look at him, but the weight of her head was immeasurable. The realm tilted on its axis and Aisling's knees gave in. She flew toward the ground, the sky spinning above her in wild, nebulous loops as she grasped for something. Anything.

It was futile. The realm, seemingly made of sugar, dissolved at the edges until nothing was left but the nothing in which it was born.

Aisling woke to the steady thump of the fae king's chest against her cheek. Lir carried Aisling in both arms, holding her tightly against himself as they traveled. Thankfully, Niamh's rains had spread into the misty breath of the mountains. Their mossy peaks rose jagged around them like the spikes atop a crown's palisade.

Geld followed closely behind, head slumped and his hooves dragging against the rain-polished stones.

Aisling tensed against the fae king's grasp. The hairs on her body stood to attention, her skin crawling with the sensation of him pressed against her. Anduril growled at her hips, still weak from the grin but protesting, nonetheless.

"Flasing," Lir said, the sting of the name echoing between the narrow corridors of the mountains. "At the western edge of the Other, there sleeps the eldest sons of the Forge."

"The mountains themselves," Aisling conjectured. Lir looked down at Aisling, but the sorceress swiftly shifted her gaze away. Her *draiocht* was flaring, brightening, pulsing despite the grin's infection that'd left her spirit bloody and bruised. Anduril's temper rising the longer they remained so close.

"I can walk," Aisling said, pulling against the fae king's grip. Gently, Lir released her, setting her softly on the ground. Regardless, Aisling's knees wobbled—nothing but Anduril's strength to keep her propped up on quivering ankles.

"If you'd prefer Geld to carry you—" Lir began.

"I'm alright," Aisling protested, doing her best to stand straight. Her efforts weren't convincing, for the fae king's expression bent with concerned—*annoyance*, Anduril corrected.

*You'll slow him down and he knows it*, Anduril grumbled in her mind.

*I've made it thus far*, Aisling argued with Anduril—herself? She wasn't certain anymore.

*You're no match for the Other. Without me, you'd be dead*, Anduril insisted, burning more hotly.

Aisling shook her head, tangling her fingers in her hair to seize the ache in her temples.

"You need rest," Lir said.

"No," Aisling insisted. The sorceress took a step forward, swaying side to side before balancing herself once more. "But perhaps," she surrendered, "some form of nourishment. Do any of Cara's supplies include Leshy's tears?"

Lir's eyes flicked to Geld before lowering to the ground. There was scarcely anything left, much less an elixir as potent as Leshy's tears.

"We'll rest for the evening here, and by morning, if you're not well, we return to Castle Yillen," Lir said.

"That's not possible," Aisling bit through bared teeth. "My father is coming, and the mortals are bleeding through the veil."

"Then he will come and the veil will bleed."

"At what cost?!" Aisling said, her voice rising. Immediately, the exertion shot through her ribs, forcing Aisling to double over. Lir flinched, his body jolting slightly before catching itself.

"If you aren't well when morning arrives," Lir said, his voice low, vibrating through the stones beneath their boots and into the surrounding mountains, "then we return to Castle Yillen. As high king of the Sidhe, I command it."

Aisling felt her anger crawling up her body and crouching inside her chest like a hissing ghoul. Wisdom urged her to bite it down. To leash it by the snapping shut of her fangs. Anduril, however, goaded her anger further.

*He wants the Goblet for himself*, Anduril said. *He couldn't fathom allowing you, his blood sworn enemy, to wield so much power. Can you imagine?*

Aisling's skin heated.

"You are my knight and I your queen," Aisling said, standing as tall as she was capable. Still, she was forced to tilt her head entirely back to meet his eyes. "I command you."

Lir's eyes flashed a violent shade of green. His lids lowered while a muscle flashed across the sharp edge of his jaw. He stepped closer, their bodies but a breath's width apart. Above, thunder groaned, summoning webs of lightning. Flasing's *draiocht*, waking to the rhythm of Aisling and Lir's combined power. Sparks of energy flaring from their fingertips, between their teeth and their tear ducts.

The fae king opened his mouth to reply, but before he could, a wild horn blew. Hollow, it whistled through Flasing's passages and into Aisling and Lir like a ghost eager to possess. Aisling and Lir fell apart, their attention stolen by the growing wind and the echo of the horn.

"We need to keep moving," Lir said, a sense of urgency in his voice.

"What is it?" Aisling asked.

"Anything. Nothing," Lir said. "But I'd prefer not to find out." The fae king turned on his heel, starting toward Geld waiting patiently to the side.

"Wait," Aisling said. "What if it's Eogi?"

Lir paused, hesitating as he wrapped Geld's reigns around his wrist.

"I don't think—" but before the fae king could finish the sentiment, Flasing shifted, rolling over like a den of bears waking midwinter.

The rock beneath them turned over, stones flying like embers from a fire. Geld reared, huffing and groaning with fear, but it was hardly audible over the roar of Flasing and its shifting granite. Lir drew his axes, cutting Geld's reigns from his wrist. He smacked the mount's rear, encouraging it onward. The stag bolted down the corridors, winding through the mayhem for his life.

Before Aisling could blink, the fae king cut the distance between them and shoved her against one of the cliff walls. The scream in Aisling's throat was cut short by the smack of several giant rocks on the face of Lir's axes, crossed above both their heads.

Lir's breath traveled hotly down the curve of Aisling's neck where both he and his axes bore the weight of the rock above them.

"Wrap your arms around me," Lir said, his voice strained from the weight of Flasing's debris.

"What?" Aisling asked, cheeks flushing despite herself.

"Wrap your arms around me," Lir repeated, his voice more coarse than before.

*It's a trick,* Anduril snipped. *Don't trust him. Don't touch him. Don't—*

"Ash—" Lir hissed between his bared fangs, veins cording in his neck and forehead.

Aisling swallowed, slipping her arms around the fae king's narrow waist and pulling herself against him.

Wicked quick, the fae king released his axes above him, arms falling around Aisling. He smashed their bodies together, swinging them out from under the avalanche that'd nearly buried them alive. Both Aisling and Lir flew to the side, falling against broken stone. Dust powdering the corridors and mingling with Niamh's storm mists.

Aisling blinked, grimacing with the pain of the fall. She lay on her back, the fae king atop the sorceress, a leg and arm on either side of her—shielding her body with his own.

The forest green of his eyes studied the violet of hers. A recognition of the trust she'd laid in his nightmarish hands—the legends she'd grown to fear, fizzing like poison wines between them. The dark lord of the greenwood a shadow, a myth, a horror that had sunk its teeth into her spirit and locked its jaw.

Lir's lips parted; his breath still heavy from the adrenaline even as the dust settled.

"Another faerie king," a voice boomed from above. Both Aisling and Lir bolted upright, searching for the source. "And could it be?" the voice continued. "The sorceress—the queen of Annwyn?"

Around them, Flasing had shifted. The mountain had moved, taking itself apart piece by piece and reassembling into a lantern-lit village around them—grey oaks growing horizontally from the sides of the cliffs, upside down and right side up, braiding their branches to hold the various stairwells and golden-lit rooms dripping with garlands of ripe highland fruit.

It was a tavern, built along the edges, through the corridors, and along the belly of Flasing. Alive with ghostly laughter, music, and the chinking of chalices.

And at the center, a giant body of rock grew from the mountain. Its bones sprouted first, then its muscles, and finally, its flesh. It was seemingly male, large and round like feast kings. It melted back into the mountain, the rock crunching as it receded and regrew elsewhere—this time, closer to Aisling and Lir.

"Welcome, welcome," the creature said, its voice half laughter. "Please step forward."

"We only wish to pass through," Lir said, his voice as cool and arrogant as usual. Soft and lithe in comparison to the gravel of the rock fiend. "Nothing more."

"Nonsense!" the creature said. "I can smell the blood of the summits in you, child, Lir, king of Annwyn and the son of Ina."

The fae king bowed his head curtly.

"I know your name, Dorkoth," Lir said. "My mother spoke various tales of the ill-begotten child of Flasing, born of both the mountain spirit and the wraith of pleasure."

"So, legend has it," Dorkoth replied, the edge of his lips curling, flesh greening with moss and lichen as Niamh's rains made slick his black rock body. "And so, too, does legend speak of my law of requirement: whosoever approaches my tavern, must stay for the evening."

"We've other business," Lir said, his axes still gripped in either hand. Dorkoth's dark eyes darted to the edge of their blades—throat bobbing in response.

"Very well then," Dorkoth said. "But in foregoing my hospitality, you also forego a warm meal, room, and bathing chamber for the evening. All of which, your bride appears to be in desperate need of."

*Bride.* Anduril bristled, pinching Aisling when she shifted.

Lir's eyes flicked to Aisling before returning to Dorkoth. A reflex he seemingly hadn't meant to expose. Dorkoth smiled knowingly, expression brightening as the clouds gathered more thickly above, threatening a storm.

"One evening," Aisling said. "One evening to recover from the grin and then we continue on."

Lir cursed beneath his breath, rolling his neck from side to side. At the mention of the grin, however, Dorkoth's smile vanished.

"One evening," Lir agreed, glancing at Aisling over his shoulder as Dorkoth clapped his hands. Their fate for the night, sealed.

"Dinner will be held once the storm moon reaches its highest peak," Dorkoth said, the stones of his body rippling and scraping against one another as he melted back into the side of the mountain. "I pray you'll join us."

Wedged between two of the tallest peaks, was the central house of the tavern. The rest of its rooms were scattered along the walls of Flasing like hanging bats.

Aisling and Lir approached the central house and entered.

Lir ducked his head beneath the threshold, the weight of him setting the floorboards of the tavern into a chorus of creaks and whines.

The room was warm; a stark contrast to the cool, highland breezes that graced the outside world. A distant plucking of strings calmed the energy of the tavern, accompanied by the smell of freshly baked bread and sweet meads. But where Aisling expected a patron, a keeper, or even Dorkoth to greet them behind the counter of the tavern, none were present.

Aisling and Lir were seemingly alone.

"What now?" Aisling asked, eyes studying the room. There were ledgers, papers, and scrolls, all scrawled and scribbled over with blue ink. Real flame—not fae flower bulbs—danced in their lantern cages made of red, emerald, and sapphire glass. But it was the treasury of keys floating against the ceiling that caught Lir's and Aisling's attention.

There were hundreds, if not thousands, of keys hovering above their heads like petrified butterflies, caught mid-flight. Indeed, most of the keys bore insect-like wings of all color, shape, and form. Even their stems, bows, and bits were forged uniquely, sparkling in the lantern light.

"This is a mountain spirit dwelling," Lir said, eyes wandering across the keys. He raised one arm, tugging on the string of the nearest key. A square piece of parchment was tied to the key's string, labeled with a runic letter. "Meaning, it's alive."

"The tavern?" Aisling asked.

Lir nodded his head. "Aye. Most dwellings owned by spirits develop one of their own after centuries of breathing their spirit's *draiocht*."

"Is it one and the same with Dorkoth's spirit?" Aisling asked.

"No," Lir said. "It's an entity of its own and, the older the dwelling, the more powerful its spirit."

The fae king cleared his throat, facing the center counter of the tavern.

"We request quarters for the evening," Lir said matter-of-factly. Silence followed for several breaths till Aisling shifted uncomfortably behind the fae king, waiting. At last, the treasury of keys above their heads clinked like chimes and a single key descended from the ceiling and dropped onto the counter. A runic parchment tied to its shank. One key for one room.

Lir waited a moment longer, attention drifting to the horde of keys above them.

"Quarters," Lir repeated. "Two rooms," he clarified, swallowing quickly after he'd said it. Aisling's stomach turned when she realized. The sorceress hadn't thought of their room arrangements until now.

*We cannot share rooms with a stranger*, Anduril chided inside her mind. *He will cut our throats in the night. He will trick us. He will ruin us. He will take what is ours.*

*He's sworn to protect and to serve*, Aisling argued.

*Trust will make a fool of us*, Anduril insisted, vibrating against her bones. Aisling closed her eyes, concentrating on her thoughts—ripping at the threads Racat and Anduril braided together inside her.

And yet, the tavern offered no more keys. Only the first, still gleaming on the counter, twitching as if requesting their attention.

"Are there no other rooms available?" Lir pushed. And in response, the key leaped forward and onto the floorboards.

Lir grumbled something beneath his breath—a runic sentiment that bore the stinging lilt of a dark spell.

"Let's find our room then," Lir said, turning on his heel and starting for the door. A vine sprouted from between the floorboards, collecting the key and slithering up Lir's boots. It dropped the key in Lir's waiting palm as he ducked back beneath the threshold. The door shut behind him, nothing but the grumble of the oncoming storm to mirror Lir's mood.

The temperature rose the moment Aisling stepped into Dorkoth's tavern room. Several lanterns, lit with soft flame, draped shadows across the humble bed—fabrics harvested from common cotton clovers that grew along the path Aisling and Lir had recently tread. Hand sewn, the needlework was clumsy and unseemly. The work of mountain spirits and their rigid, stony fingers, Aisling realized as she brushed the surface with her fingertips.

Lir stood at the threshold for several beats. Long enough to draw Aisling's attention. The sorceress, however, refused to meet his eyes. Each time their gazes connected, it was an intimate affair. As if the fae king's undivided attention conjured strange magic, possessing Aisling's body. For whilst her mind battled between her own thoughts and Anduril's, her body heated uniquely when in his presence. Her stomach knotted or took flight, her body shuddered or froze still, her tongue dried or her lips grew wet. But it was her *draiocht*, Racat, who shivered. Who slithered against the fae king's magic, rubbing its scales against his hide. Twin devils, Aisling felt, sinking their fangs into one another and gulping from their vein of power.

Lir took a step into the room. The old floorboards groaned beneath him, bending even as his lithe body moved—a shadow in Aisling's periphery, approaching like death's maven.

"Rest while you can," he said, voice cleaned of emotion like a blade once bloodied. "I'll fetch our dinner."

"We aren't joining Dorkoth?" Aisling said, spinning on her heel to face him at last.

For the briefest of moments, Lir hesitated, eyes catching on Aisling's and trapping his words.

"If I can convince you otherwise," Lir replied matter-of-factly, his expression, once more, void of emotion, "then no."

Aisling frowned. She was starved, her body jittery with exhaustion and hunger alike. But she wanted her meal at a table instead of stones, lit by gold wax light instead of violet flame, with cutlery rather than her fingers, with dishes rather than bones, and wine goblets in the place of her cupped hands. All in the hopes of regaining her strength more quickly.

"You're free to stay," Aisling said, "but I'll be joining Dorkoth regardless."

Lir did a slight double take.

"By oath: where you go, I follow," Lir said, standing straighter. A great shadow was cast from his towering stature and fell across the room. A reminder he was the guardian she'd knighted by blade. The accolade complete as Anduril released a blistering cry.

Aisling swallowed her protests.

*He doesn't trust us*, Anduril hissed, tickling the inside of Aisling's mind. *He wants an eye on us always.*

Aisling's brow pinched, Anduril's intensity squeezing inside her mind.

Lir's eyes darted across her face before falling to Anduril at her hips. His eyes narrowed and his jaw clenched. He said nothing of it; instead, cleared his throat and turned on his heel.

"You should change," he said. "And bathe. You reek. I'll meet you at the tavern center at the strike of the third bell."

*He's up to no good*, Anduril spurted.

Aisling's brow arched. "Where are you going?" she asked, annoyance pinching her words.

"To guard the door," he said, throwing the door open and shutting it firmly behind him.

Aisling stared at the splintered wood for several moments after the fae king left. Her *draiocht* calmed, lulled back to sleep whilst outside his presence. A relief the sorceress was grateful for.

Aisling turned and faced the rest of the room. The boards of the tavern groaned against the cool breath of Flasing, lashing the sides of Dorkoth's tavern as the storm thickened. She wandered through the chamber, at last, pulling apart patchwork drapes that shielded the rusted tub in the corner of their rooms. Rust alchemized the once coppery hue of the large basin to lichen green, shimmering beneath the lantern light regardless. Already, the spirit of Dorkoth's tavern had filled the tub with hot water and soap, suds spilling over the lip.

Aisling eyed the bubbling waters, her expression narrowing. She felt Niamh's watchful gaze and she feared the Lady's influence through water. So, tired and weary as her body was, she pulled the curtains back and forewent the bath Dorkoth's tavern had prepared for her.

Instead, Aisling undressed—all but Anduril slipping off her limbs—and summoned her *draiocht*. She burned every morsel of dirt, of filth, of sweat, of oil, of disease, of the stench of Geld's pelt, and the fresh cologne of the fae king, careful not to singe all that was unsoiled or unsullied.

Fire cleansed her, breath by breath.

Once the work was complete, Aisling rummaged through the broken cupboards, dressers, and wardrobes. They were filled with tattered gowns, moth-eaten dresses, and chipped jewels. All and everything from an age that was forgotten and discarded. Aisling exhaled, surrendering to garments she already donned despite the heavy, biting edges of her armor that weighed heavily on her joints and muscles.

The spirit of Dorkoth's tavern, however, was eager to help. The second wardrobe wobbled on its stout, wooden legs and a dress fell from a hidden shelf at the back.

Aisling knelt to collect the garment, lifting it to better appraise it in the lantern light.

It was plain, as pale as cream and sewn with thick, porcelain threads. The fabric, however, was soft as lamb's wool, cinching at the wrists but flaring till the knuckles. The hem spilled around her bare feet, designed for a Seelie creature much taller than herself—this despite Aisling's great height for a mortal-born.

Aisling considered her reflection for a long while. The mirror, like the rest of Dorkoth's tavern, was old and weathered, clouding and foxing with chips and scratches across its surface. Still, Anduril gleamed brightly, admiring its own reflection with genuine interest.

LIR

Lir leaned his head against the corridor walls of Dorkoth's tavern, just outside his and Aisling's room. And even though the grin couldn't spread nor grow from Lir's life heart, the infection had taken its toll on the Sidhe king, sucking on his energy like a blood bat.

"You need rest, Your Grace," a feminine voice whispered from the other end of the corridor.

"Perhaps some rest, some wine, and a wash," another, similar voice, agreed.

Lir's eyes opened slowly. Not a soul stood at the end of the corridor. Only two artfully sculpted statues, frozen just before kissing. Lir unhooked one of his axes from his back and tossed it. The blade spun, cutting across the hall before sticking to the wall with a thwack. Immediately, the two statues burst apart, squealing with alarm and shuddering to life.

Stone nymphs and daughters of Flasing.

"Forgive us, Your Grace." The first statue fell to her knees, followed by the second. "We didn't mean to alarm you."

"Has Dorkoth sent his eyes to spy?" Lir asked the first nymph, approaching as his axe dislodged itself from the wood and shot back into the Sidhe king's waiting palm. "And his ears?" Lir's attention flicked to the second nymph.

"Of course not, Your Grace," they said in unison.

"We've come to ensure your accommodations are satisfactory. And that you've been serviced, Your Grace."

Lir studied the nymphs, searching for Dorkoth's mischief. Written across the planes of their gray expressions, however, was an earnest desire to serve the tavern and the spirit that possessed it.

The Sidhe king considered Aisling's door, weighing the choice in his mind. She was safe in her rooms and, not to mention, desperate to be rid of him thanks to Anduril.

"Very well," the Sidhe king said, eyeing them both from head to toe. "I'll need a change of clothes and somewhere to bathe."

"Absolutely, Your Grace," they said in unison. Immediately, both nymphs unfurled from their bows. They nervously skittered down a hall to the right, clutching the skirts of their wolf-gray gowns, and gesturing for the Sidhe king to follow.

AISLING

Aisling watched the shadow disappear from the crease below her chamber door before she turned the knob. Lir was no longer outside, guarding her door. In fact, he was nowhere to be seen. Only floating, flickering candles drifted near the creaking beams and gilded the corridor. Colorful wax dribbling from their stems and onto the floorboards beneath.

*Keep your eyes open*, Anduril said, glowing softly. *Who knows which guests Dorkoth keeps.*

Aisling considered the doors as she traveled through the narrow passages, the candles following her wake like curious ghosts. Some rooms were silent. Others rattled with commotion and muffled speech. A labyrinth of strange, age-worn doors that varied in size and color—each and all chipped and splintered. But it was the smell of roasted meats, stewed apples, sweet dough, and dark wines that guided Aisling through the tavern, down the broken stairwell, and toward the front entrance of their tavern lodgings.

Aisling turned the knob, but the threshold was firmly stuck. She shoved the door with her shoulder and the entrance gave way, plunging Aisling into a celebration. The tavern center was not roofed but rather stood at the center of a feverish courtyard.

Seven alp pines grew at the edges of the spectacle, bending at odd angles and perfuming the tavern center with their emerald needles and sticky sap. They carried thousands of lanterns on their arms, their fingers, their heads, dressing the center with warm light. Garlands of highland figs stretched from one end of the courtyard to the other and Flasing's surrounding mountains cupped the music played by bears and wolves alike. And in the middle of it all was a lengthy dining table—a colossal pine, seemingly chopped in half by the axe of a giant—spilling over with a dazzling Sidhe feast. Characters of all shapes and sizes filled the seats and chatted idly by the pines. Unseelie, Seelie, forge-born, all basking in the heat of Flasing's fever storm. Some danced while others sang, cheeks rosy with too much wine. And at the head of the table, surrounded by two nymphs, was Lir. Already, he stared at her—eyes dark as he watched her, half-lidded, from behind the lip of a goblet.

Aisling approached, Anduril buzzing at her hips. The nymphs poured more wine for the fae king, smiling and twirling their white curls. They served his plate, piling it high with all manner of foods, whispering secrets in his ears till he shifted, and they scattered like doves.

*Close your mouth, sorceress,* Anduril said. *Are you really all that surprised?*

Aisling shut her lips, clearing her throat. Both she and Lir averted their eyes in the same moment, turning to the side instead.

*A King's bed is never cold,* Anduril continued. *His might is best inspired by the attention of his attractions—bonded or otherwise.*

Aisling blinked, her eyes suddenly wet. She felt nothing for Lir. He was a stranger and an enemy. He was arrogant, too quiet, too cruel, and a rogue. She disliked him beyond understanding—a distaste that neared loathing. A hatred unprecedented, unusual, and muffled by the thudding of her heart. By the pain in her chest and the sickness in her stomach where she stood now.

*I smell the ghost of mortality in your veins, sorceress. Your mind still churns with mortal thoughts. You hate him. You hate him. Did you really believe the nightmare king of the forest would require only one?* Anduril cackled, its laugh as caustic as chimes hammered together.

Aisling gritted her teeth, doing her best to swallow this strange ache. It was futile, the pressure flaring in her chest and crawling up her throat. She stood awkwardly before the tavern center, afraid to glance at the fae king and find him leaning into the nymph's touch.

"Enchantress," a voice sounded. Aisling jolted in surprise, turning to find someone watching her. "Or violet-eyed wolf girl? Which do you prefer to be remembered by?"

He stood below the fountain carved into one of Flasing's many sharp ridges, bleeding ice melt. A Sidhe of great height and broad shoulders, his luminous eyes flashed gold when a lantern floated lazily by. His face, gilded in the soft glow, was breathtaking—described best in legends of heroes, of kings, of knights, and princes. He padded forward, eating a fig as he approached. The light of the celebration fell upon him fully and Aisling marveled at the cut and style of his leathers, his armor, and of his teeth—fangs sharper than any Sidhe she'd met yet.

"Where are my manners?" he asked, standing a pace from her. He bowed slowly and rose elegantly. "I am Helm of the Howling Winds," he introduced himself.

Son of Siofra, Helm was born of one of the original twelve Sidhe sovereigns. Meaning, Helm was a Sidhe king himself, reigning from the mortal plane over his court.

Aisling eyed him closely. Anduril said nothing, quietly watching from its perch.

"Aisling," the sorceress introduced herself, offering not another word.

Helm smiled, his dark complexion sparkling as two more lanterns floated by.

"They call you faerie in the stories," Helm said.

"A faerie?" Aisling asked.

"An elusive word, slipping between the letters of the Lore like a wisp—growing more potent, more real, betraying its ghostly body." Helm looked Aisling up and down, his dark eyes flashing dangerously. "You're more beautiful than the stories describe," he said, eyes darting across her face.

Aisling denied herself the luxury of blushing, swallowing whatever flattery his comment held.

"So, the tales remark me less than?" Aisling asked.

"You misinterpret me, enchantress," he said. "There are scarcely words that could capture your essence. Which is why I'd be honored if you'd join me for a dance?" Helm's eyes glittered with promise.

Aisling crossed her arms, acknowledging his outstretched hand with a brief flick of her eyes.

"Try then," Aisling challenged.

"I'm sorry—"

"Attempt to describe my beauty, and if your efforts please

me," Aisling offered, "then I'll allow you a dance." She arched a brow. She hadn't meant the challenge seriously but only as a mockery. Even so, if he agreed to her terms, she'd at least be amused. For his empty flattery had done all but describe the beauty he claimed to understand uniquely. In fact, Aisling realized, he'd already lost the challenge.

Helm laughed nervously beneath his breath, eyes darting across Aisling's face.

"Your beauty surpasses description, enchantress," Helm said at last. He smiled to himself, chin tipping upward with transparent self-satisfaction.

"And yet," Aisling countered, "I request one."

Helm hesitated. "I—"

"Be your beauty a blade, let it carve me—violent, cruel, and without mercy," someone piped, approaching their conversation from the side. Aisling didn't need to turn to see who came forward. She and Anduril would both recognize his voice in the darkest shadow, brightest light, and all the glimmers between.

Aisling and Helm whipped their attention to Lir, his posture cool and arrogant even as he held Helm's glare.

*See?* Anduril said. *He watches, he does not trust us. He mocks us with his arrogance.*

"I had a suspicion we might cross paths." Helm addressed Lir, his smile quickly fading.

"You're meant to be guarding your court in the mortal plane." Lir crossed his arms.

But where Aisling anticipated a sharp rebuttal, Helm's expression dimmed with something like shame.

"Tahsman was taken," Helm said. "The mortals surrounded us, their iron hot and their fires hungry. The flames moved quickly—too quickly—spreading over Tahsman until we were forced to seek refuge in the Other."

Lir's jaw flexed.

"Taken," he repeated, absorbing the information.

"We had no other choice," Helm continued.

"And the others?" Lir asked, straightening. "Have the other courts been taken as well?"

Helm shook his head. "Communication has been cut from all courts on the mortal plane. But I assume Tahsman was not the first to fall to the fire hand nor will it be the last. I'm only grateful we escaped in time to spare as many as possible."

Lir cursed beneath his breath.

"Where are the rest of your people?" Lir continued.

"Scattered across the Other and finding shelter where possible. I've been traveling across this plane for the past several days, seeking safe havens for Tahsman and the others that will inevitably follow," Helm said.

Lir's expression flickered with... fear, Aisling realized. It was foreign on his face, catching Aisling off guard.

"And Annwyn?" Lir asked, soft eyes gilded by the lantern light.

Helm exhaled. "No word. But if none from your court have yet to appear here in the Other, there's still hope."

Lir's throat bobbed, his complexion paling.

Aisling fought the urge to comfort him. She was horrified by the sudden reflex to reach out and squeeze his hand, to run her fingers through his hair, to cup his face between her palms and reassure him. The impulses were strong and unwelcomed, burning her flesh where Anduril bristled with heat.

"Come," Aisling said instead. "Let us drink wine."

Both Helm and Lir offered Aisling their arm in the same moment. Aisling hesitated, gulping in the awkward silence.

*Take the Howling Winds king's arm*, Anduril insisted. *He is strong and capable but not more so than you. That is a better match for us.*

Aisling chewed on her bottom lip before looping her arm through Lir's. Her body moved for her, quickly punished by Anduril's squeezing.

Helm bowed his head in silent concession, meeting Lir's eyes briefly.

Lir, on the other hand, straightened, his head held a little higher than before.

They approached the large dining table where Dorkoth took his seat at the center.

"Come, come!" he shouted to his guests. "Come and dine with me."

The festival evolved into a feast, food flying from the table in glittering colors and rich smells. Plates clinking against one another and chalices spilling.

Lir pulled a chair for Aisling, watching Helm carefully as he took his seat beside the sorceress.

Immediately, several plates pushed toward Aisling of their own accord—every poached apple, every lamb leg, every cherry gelatin enchanted and eager to be eaten by Dorkoth's guests. Lir took several plates himself as he sat on her other side, his tattooed fingers brushing against hers as he moved.

Aisling shivered, swallowing the pain Anduril punished her nerves with.

Several strange beasts took their seats around the table as well: a guest with three tails, one with pink curls and moth-like wings draping over their shoulders like a powdered cape, three with toads singing songs from their shoulders, and many more.

"Don't stare," Lir whispered beside her, his eyes never leaving his plate.

"I've never seen creatures like these," Aisling said.

"You wouldn't have," the fae king replied. "They're bound to the Other and only the wiliest of them creep into the mortal plane. Spiritual entities whose deception is beyond our comprehension."

Aisling snuck a glance at the creature with pink hair. Politely, she cut through her dinner, opening her pretty mouth to reveal several rows of teeth.

Aisling jolted back in surprise, knocking her chalice against Lir's with her elbow. Wicked quick, Lir reached his hand beneath the table and grabbed Aisling's thigh. He squeezed gently but firmly—a reminder to keep her composure. Heat creeped up Aisling's body, humming softly in her lower abdomen. She'd forgotten—no, she'd never been touched by the fae king. Had she? Aisling cleared her throat, shifting slightly as Lir released his hold. But it was fruitless, the whole table flicked their eyes to the sorceress.

Both Aisling and Lir stilled like foxes between the trees. Helm's eyes darted between them, a question in his glare.

"I almost forgot," Dorkoth boomed across the table. "But here in Flasing's cradle, the high lord of the greenwood and his sorceress drink our wine, together, here, with us."

*His sorceress.* Anduril flared hot, forcing Aisling to her feet.

Aisling and Lir exchanged glances. Lir exhaled softly.

"The legends speak my name in tongues: for every fire, another version of me is born," Aisling said. The eyes of Dorkoth's tavern bore into Aisling, studying her every breath. Aisling swallowed. But it was Dorkoth who leaned forward, placing both his stony hands onto the edge of the table as he spoke.

"Do you seek a correction of your title?" the tavernkeeper asked, half-baffled. Heat creeped beneath Aisling's cheeks. She knew this pledge was unnecessary, but Anduril hardly cared. Its ambition, its drive, its thirst crawled up Aisling's spine and spoke from her lips.

"*I am faerie,*" Aisling said.

Helm did a double take, lips parting as he studied Aisling anew.

"And I her knight," Lir said, bringing his goblet of wine to his fangs.

Dorkoth and the rest of the tavern guests exchanged glances

and darting eyes, whispers rustling through the feast like leaves in the wind.

"A faerie and her knight," Dorkoth said, brows pinching as he weighed the words in his mind. "And what business do a faerie and her knight have in Flasing's cradle?"

"Private business," Lir bit, watching Dorkoth beneath half-lidded eyes.

"In this tavern," Dorkoth said, lowering his voice in the slightest, "we speak freely."

Lir bristled, so Aisling spoke quickly.

"We're in search of Eogi," Aisling said. Every head in the tavern swiveled to Aisling. Lir ground his teeth but said nothing, focusing on his plate instead.

"Eogi," Dorkoth repeated. "The keeper of beginnings."

"You won't reach him," Helm piped. The tavern switched their attentions.

"Reach?" Lir asked.

"He rests just north of here," Dorkoth said. "Up the spindly steps and through Breka's mirror. Beyond, a cave darkens, chilled like metal without flame. That's where the keeper sleeps. The cool basin of the Forge dusted after years without use."

"However," Helm said, "Eogi is not alone. A guard stands before the mirror with a moon-bright blade prepared to prevent whoever disrupts his rest."

"How do we pass?" Aisling asked.

Helm shrugged. "You don't."

"Unless," Dorkoth suggested, "you kill it."

Aisling and Lir exchanged quick glances.

"So, no one has passed before?" Aisling asked, aware of every guest's eyes studying their conversation. They whispered amongst one another, nodding their heads and hissing replies.

"Few have tried," Helm said. "But no, no one has ever passed before."

Silence filled their mouths, but the foxes and the badgers continued plucking their fiddles and lutes while the lanterns floated across the feasting table.

"What did you expect?" Dorkoth asked. "The caliber of a soul must be high to speak with a forge-old being—nearly a deity itself. And so, few if any, will succeed. Your quest is a death coin, already paid and collected by intent."

"You don't believe me capable?" Aisling asked.

"No," Dorkoth replied. "But perhaps your knight might stand a chance," Dorkoth said, eyes darting toward Lir before returning to Aisling.

"It isn't his challenge to take," Aisling said. "It's mine."

Dorkoth laughed and Helm swallowed.

"I speak with your best intentions in mind, faerie," Dorkoth said, his voice lowering as he pinned Aisling in place with his stony eyes. "To venture forward on this path, is to die."

The table erupted into soft chatter, clinking glasses and plates as they moved to better hear one another.

Aisling leaned back in her chair, a glass of wine in one hand.

"There is no other path," Aisling said.

"They seek the Goblet," Helm said. "Or so the rumors say. A weapon to vanquish the mortals and prevent Sidhe destruction."

Dorkoth tilted back his head, pressing his tongue against the inside of his cheek as he considered. The rest of the tavern's guests awkwardly ate their dinners, ears perked and eyes flashing, waiting for the tavern keeper's response.

"What do you know of the mortals' advances?" Lir spoke first, the depth of his voice rumbling across the feasting table till it sent shivers down every guest's spine. The nymphs shuddered despite themselves, eyes dilating as they fully fixed their eyes on the fae king. Aisling bristled like a wolf with its hackles standing straight up.

Dorkoth cleared his throat.

"Flasing has long felt their approach. Their mortal touch is infecting that which makes the Other everlasting, spreading their fleshling diseases, their rot, and their death into our world of spirits and magic," Dorkoth said. "They are coming."

"You've experienced it yourself?" Lir continued.

"As have you," Dorkoth said.

The grin. A rotting of the natural world that didn't encumber the Otherworld... until now.

"As their mortal influence nears, the Forge heats and bubbles, blistering the veil that once separated us from them," Dorkoth explained. "More and more will we experience evidence of their mortality infecting that which was once eternal."

"Unless they're stopped," Aisling said. "Unless I obtain the Goblet and prevent my father—the mortals—from destroying the Sidhe, the Other, the—"

"From destroying you?" Dorkoth asked. The table froze, swallowing hard as they shifted their attention to Aisling. "You're what they search for are you not?" Dorkoth pushed. "You're the curse breaker, the mortal reaper, the daughter of he who threatens us?"

"What do you ask?" Lir said.

Dorkoth rocked his head from side to side.

The tavern keeper said at last, "I only wonder what they want with you."

"It matters not," Lir replied quickly.

"But it would end the war, would it not?" Dorkoth pressed.

"What are you suggesting?" Lir challenged again, his expression becoming more inhuman.

Silence fell and splattered across the table. Eyes darted back and forth.

"I suggest nothing. Only if you do choose to proceed, you feast and celebrate tonight. No warrior enters a battle without proper celebration—be it death or victory that follows," the tavern keeper said.

Dorkoth clapped his hands, and the lanterns bled a scarlet glow. The music grew louder and quicker, and the food laid across the banquet table multiplied. His guests shrieked with delight, lunging across the table for buttered sweet rolls, hot cookies, charred meats, steaming vegetables, poached apples, and overstuffed pies. Goblets, mugs, and chalices bubbled over with punches, meads, and wines, whilst the trees swayed back and forth excitedly. Flasing hummed joyously, chuckling to itself as it observed the growing temperature of the celebration.

"Enjoy the evening, faerie," Dorkoth said, his voice just loud enough above the frenzy. "For it may be your last."

Plum juice dribbled down Aisling's chin. She'd eaten several plates from Dorkoth's feasts and tipped back several goblets of wine. All and each, enjoyed as she did her best to avoid the nymphs begging the fae king to dance with them. Lir ignored their wandering hands as he wove through the tavern center, speaking with several guests, but every now and again, he'd catch Aisling watching him. His dark green eyes depthless and haunting—both frightening and tempting all at once.

Aisling wasn't certain why she cared or why Anduril's protests were reddening the flesh on her hips. Only that her chest grew tight and her palms sweaty, heart racing several beats quicker each time he caught her looking.

"Your eyes are dimming," Helm said from her right side. Aisling didn't bother turning. She remained still, attention focused on the table before her. "You should retire for the evening."

"I'm fine," Aisling insisted. She stood up abruptly, almost knocking over her chair. Helm caught it quickly, reaching out a hand to steady Aisling by the elbow.

"I said I'm fine."

"You're drunk," he said.

"Wine has that effect," Aisling bit, swaying slightly as she turned to look at him. "Which is why I drank it."

"You should be resting," Helm said.

"I'll rest when I'm dead."

"Which might be as soon as tomorrow if you aren't careful," Helm warned.

Aisling shook her head. "You see this belt?" Helm considered Anduril, his eyes reflecting the gold of its metal. "With this belt, I'm invincible."

Helm shook his head, not understanding.

"It's a shield?"

"No, a weapon. So long as Anduril hangs from my body, I am possessed with the talents of legendary heroes, knights, warriors."

Helm arched a brow, eyes still locked onto the belt.

"None can best you?"

"No," Aisling said before biting her lip. "Except..." Her eyes wandered, finding Lir across the celebration while the nymphs began kissing his neck. He spoke to Dorkoth beneath the lantern light, neither shrugging the nymphs off nor rejecting their advances as he'd done before. Instead, he did nothing. Allowing their tongues to slide against his throat as he ignored their preening.

Aisling bit her tongue.

"Except Lir," Helm surmised.

"Aye, except the fae king."

"And if the belt is removed?" Helm asked.

Aisling wobbled on her feet, tearing her eyes from Lir and the nymphs and returning her attention to Helm.

"Then I become, once more, a sorceress alone," Aisling confessed.

Helm nodded his head in understanding.

"Why don't I accompany you to your rooms for the night?" the Sidhe king offered.

"I'd prefer to stay," Aisling said, crossing her arms clumsily.

"And stare at Lir from afar?" Helm asked. "Or I could help you to your chambers and ensure you're prepared to find Eogi in the morning."

Aisling, surprising herself, hesitated.

"I—"

"You what?" Helm pushed. "He is your knight, is he not? You needn't wait on him."

Aisling glanced at Lir once more. His back was turned to her now and he hadn't met her eyes in some time. The nymphs were flushed on either side of him, rubbing the tips of their noses against his cheeks and begging for a morsel of his attention.

Aisling tore her own attention away, chest tight with a sharp pain.

Anduril, on the other hand, sparkled gleefully.

"Very well," Aisling conceded.

Helm offered the sorceress his arm and, after another brief hesitation, Aisling accepted it.

Gently, the Sidhe king led Aisling away from the tavern center and toward one of the various crooked staircases pressed to the side of Flasing. The colors, the lights, the music, and the smells spun together and mixed inside Aisling's mind, making dizzy and incoherent her thoughts. Anduril held tightly, rifling its fingers through her head till her temples ached.

They pushed open the battered door and ascended the first stairwell. The sounds of the celebration below grew muffled by the old tavern walls. The floorboards creaked beneath their feet as they walked, increasing the distance between themselves and the tavern center.

At last, they reached Aisling's chamber door.

"Thank you," Aisling said, not meeting Helm's eyes. She

pressed her back to the door, staring down at her bare feet. She could scarcely think coherently, and the world was rocking back and forth like a cradle.

"You're welcome," he said, planting his boots before her. He leaned forward, placing a hand against the wall by Aisling's head.

Aisling swallowed.

"Good night," she said, grabbing the doorknob beside her and turning it. Helm abruptly reached his hand out and grabbed hers before she could open the door.

"What are you doing?" Aisling asked, the world spinning more quickly.

"Nothing," Helm said, even as he leaned his head closer, his lips breathing against her forehead.

"You should go," Aisling said, her words slurred and slow. Nevertheless, Helm reached below her chin and tipped her head up. Lazily, he studied her face, his thick, dark lashes half obscuring the sheen of his eyes. Yet, it wasn't his eyes that unsettled Aisling most of all. It was his left hand, wandering toward her waist. He grazed her bodice, his fingers sliding down the curve of her abdomen until he was stopped short by Anduril's hot chain.

"So this is the belt you speak of?" he asked, his fingers grazing Anduril's edge.

"Aye," Aisling said, her throat tight and her body stiff despite the wine that loosened her will. "Don't touch it," she managed. "Or me."

"Or what?"

"Or I'll light a fire in your belly that slowly consumes you from the inside out," Aisling threatened between bared teeth.

"Perhaps I'll call your bluff," Helm said just before yanking Anduril's clasp so hard, it jerked Aisling upright. Without hesitation, Aisling's body lit with violet flame. It hardly mattered.

Helm flew backward, slamming into the side of Dorkoth's tavern with a horrible crunch.

Aisling shook her head, desperately trying to make sense of the past several breaths. Helm groaned, slouched on the ground and rubbing his head.

"She said not to touch," Lir's voice materialized before them both—he, a shadow peeling forth from the darkest corners of the corridor. The fae king reached down and grabbed Helm by the throat, lifting him till his feet dangled above the ground.

"Enough, Lir," Helm wheezed, gasping for breath.

"It's enough when I say it is," Lir replied. "Now answer a few questions for me." Lir squeezed Helm's throat more tightly, his knuckles turning white.

"I didn't mean any harm," Helm choked out, his hands clawing at Lir's forearms, but it was fruitless—Lir was stronger by far, easily holding him in place.

"Yet," Lir said between clenched teeth, "you tried to remove Aisling's belt. Why?"

Helm squirmed, his complexion reddening, then purpling.

"Anduril is a cursed object," Helm said. "It begins like a seed in the mind, but if it isn't stopped, its roots will slither between the grooves of her mind until she cannot separate the belt from herself. Power comes at a cost."

Lir's eyes narrowed, but he held still.

"You know its name?" Aisling said, speaking for the first time since Lir arrived.

"Aye," Helm managed. "My mother witnessed the madness that belt inspires firsthand. Nothing good will come of it. Surely not the salvation of the Sidhe."

"And yet," Aisling said, "that's why I wear it. To defeat all and everything that stands before me and victory."

"What about him?" Helm asked, his eyes shooting to Lir.

"He's my knight and sworn to serve me," Aisling said, but Helm's eyes fell to Anduril buzzing softly at her hips.

"Now I say it's enough," Lir said. The fae king dropped Helm suddenly and turned to move closer to Aisling's side. Helm floundered on the floor for a moment, recovering himself and backing down the corridor.

"Leave now," Lir continued. "And don't let me catch sight of you again."

Helm ground his jaw but said nothing, spinning on his heel the moment he'd reached the end of the hall and took off.

Aisling sucked in a breath, her *draiocht* fizzling into wisps of smoke as her heart rate calmed and her mind cleared.

"Are you alright?" Lir asked.

"I'm fine," Aisling said, straightening her gown and her hair. Lir nodded his head, glancing over his shoulder at the hall Helm had run down.

"You should rest," he said. "When the sun rises, we'll continue to Eogi." Lir bowed his head, already preparing to retreat to wherever he planned to rest for the night. He hardly met her eyes. His expression void of emotion as he started down the corridor, his back to her as he took his leave.

"Lir," Aisling said, his name falling from her lips before she could stop it. "Wait."

Anduril flared but Aisling shoved away the pain, focusing her blurry eyes on the fae king and sinking into their depths.

Lir slowed to a stop but didn't turn. Not right away. He inclined his head toward her, his shoulders hiking with tension.

"Stay with me," Aisling said.

*You cannot trust him!* Anduril hissed loudly, stinging Aisling's ears. She bit through the pain regardless.

"Stay with me here in my rooms," she continued when Lir remained silent. "It's safer that way," she clarified.

Lir shifted, moving to face her fully. Half cast in shadows, he fixed his eyes on hers. Immediately, her heart took flight and her *draiocht* growled hungrily. But it was Anduril's ringing that vibrated through the fabric of the Other with a shudder through her spine. He padded toward her, defeating the distance that once lay between them.

"As you command," Lir said, bowing his head once more. He, the vision of a noble, humble knight born to serve. And yet, Lir was a king—the high king of all the Sidhe across the mortal plane. He, a legend, a myth, a cruel fairytale nightmare painted in the savage hues of barbaric reds and greens.

Lir reached behind Aisling and grabbed the doorknob gently. The gesture brought their chests flush against one another. He locked eyes with her, tearing himself away the moment the door clicked open and warm light spilled into the corridor.

They both slipped into the room. Lir watched Aisling carefully as she approached the bed, her steps clumsy and ungraceful after too much wine.

"You shouldn't have drunk so much," Lir said, standing still at the center of the chamber with his arms crossed. "Especially not now."

"I'm to celebrate before battle, am I not?" Aisling said, doing her best not to slur her words.

"There are better ways," Lir said.

"Like being bedded?" Aisling asked, heat creeping behind her cheeks the moment she had. Lir did a double take, ensuring he'd heard her correctly. His expression flashed with confusion, stoically collecting itself once more.

"That's one way, yes," Lir admitted.

"Is that what you do?" Aisling asked, Anduril screeching with frustration.

Lir's eyes widened, his arms falling to his sides.

"I have before," the fae king confessed. In this light, Aisling couldn't see his complexion well. But when he stepped to the side, shifting his weight, she saw the crimson tips of his ears.

A strange jealousy burned hot in Aisling's stomach,

crawling up her abdomen and into her mouth till it sat between her teeth bitterly.

"Tell me," Aisling said. "Tell me what it's like."

Lir stilled, his muscles visibly tightening beneath his leathers and armor. His head tilted to the side like a wolf appraising its hunt, but he made not a sound as he considered her. Aisling sat back onto the edge of the fraying mattress and forced herself to keep his gaze.

*No, no, no, no!* Anduril screamed. *You are a weak, pathetic, whore and nothing more but a plaything to him. This is a mistake. A mistake. A mistake. A mistake!*

The wine suffocated Anduril's protests and Aisling's inhibitions, clouding her mind further. Her *draiocht* spun madly inside, propelling her heart as it hammered inside her chest. The room grew several degrees hotter, and the lantern light bled violet.

"I can show you," Lir said. His voice thick and rough. The fae king moved closer—a tall shadow creeping nearer. A ghost she'd conjured and invited closer. "For the purpose of preparing you for tomorrow of course. Nothing more."

Aisling stiffened, the *draiocht* flaring and biting till its gums bled inside her.

He stood before her. Aisling tilted back her head and stared up at him from where she sat. Nimbly, he grabbed her jaw and got down on his knees so they were face to face.

Their lips were but a breath apart—the smell of him, of alder ciders, of pine needles, of summer breezes, consumed her.

*Stop,* Anduril pleaded. *Please, stop.*

Aisling shut out the belt's words, wrenching her eyes shut and focusing on her *draiocht* instead. The way it moved against Lir's. The way his magic wanted hers. This was undeniable.

"Please," Aisling said, barely against his lips. Just out of reach.

Lir's breath stuttered before he stilled entirely.

"As you command," he said.

The fae king placed both hands on Aisling's thighs. His palms burning into the fabric of her gown and scalding her flesh. Aisling shivered, her *draiocht* blooming fully awake.

Lir watched her closely. He studied her expression, eyes tracing her lips as his hands slid up and gathered her gown between his fingers. Aisling sucked in a breath, her body flinching with surprise. And in the same breath, Lir touched his lips with hers.

AISLING, Anduril hissed.

Racat lit, scale by scale, with a violet glow. Her *draiocht* shuddered awake and alive, eager to be released and numbing Anduril's fury.

Lir deepened the kiss, leaning closer. The taste of him brought fire to the edge of Aisling's will. She sank into him as he moved his tongue inside her mouth. Aisling was flushed with heat—her breath quick as prey as she rested her hands on his arms. Immediately, Lir tensed, his kiss slowing. Aisling continued, sliding her hands up his arms, onto his shoulders, and loosely around his neck. Lir leaned further into Aisling, pushing gently until she fell onto the bed of quilts.

AISLING, Anduril screamed with all its might. And yet, its voice was cleaving from Aisling's mind as she and Lir kissed, his knee pressing between her legs.

Lir moved his hand around her throat, moving slowly down her body and grazing her breasts. He stopped at her waist, pulling her against him—almost lifting her from the bed.

His hand moved further, pausing at Aisling's hips.

NO, Anduril screamed, and it echoed into oblivion. Lir's fingers tugged on the belt even as it trembled with wrath. Aisling froze, her body suddenly turning to stone. Lir pulled again, this time harder. For him to enter her comfortably, Anduril needed to be removed. And what's more, Aisling wanted it gone in that moment. Wanted him instead. Even if it meant nothing. Even if he despised her, she wanted to feel him, to have him, to be with him for a moment. Especially if this evening was her last.

"Wait," Aisling broke her mouth free of his and grabbed his wrist. Lir met her eyes, something sharp in the shadows of his expression.

"I will not remove it," Aisling said instead. She spoke like a spell, sealing the truth of her convictions into the fabric of the universe.

Lir opened his mouth to speak, but before he could utter a word, his attention was stolen. The fae king turned his head to the side. His body stilled completely.

"What is it?" Aisling asked, her heart racing for an entirely different reason now.

"When I say," Lir whispered into her ear, "leap through that window. The trees will help you down."

Aisling found the window Lir spoke of; steepled, its pane was pushed open and the patchwork curtains drifted on a phantom breeze.

"What's happening?" Aisling asked again. Her *draiocht* still pulsing hungrily and Anduril bright with heat between them.

"Dorkoth," Lir said.

As if prompted, a crackling noise grew near the corners of the room. Aisling bolted upright so Lir instinctively held her tightly against himself.

Stone bubbled from the wood, mossy and dirt-caked. It grew like a disease, multiplying, reforming, and reshaping until figures began to take form. And at the center, materialized Dorkoth.

"Apologies, faerie," Dorkoth said, his voice filled with gravel and still solidifying itself. "I don't usually become so hostile with my guests, but you see you're the answer to all this. Kill you and the mortals' pursuit ends."

Aisling and Lir came apart. They wore the same face of

betrayal and anger, both their *draiocht*s snapping ravenously inside.

"Don't be reckless, Dorkoth," Aisling said. "This is a battle you won't win."

Dorkoth opened his arms and looked around at his stone spirits. There were seven or so, some tall and others short. All broad and heavy, made of rock and mountain's edge.

"I like my odds," the tavern keeper said.

"The cost will be your life, Dorkoth," Lir continued. "Reconsider."

"My apologies, *mo Damh Bán*. But the fate of the Sidhe is more important than any single faerie." Dorkoth's smile cut across his face in a thin jagged line. He snapped his fingers and, at once, his spirits descended.

"Now," Lir said.

Aisling dove over the bed and toward the window—quick as a ghost caught moments before sunrise. Four of Dorkoth's spirits lunged for Aisling, their fingertips almost closing in on the last inches of her hair, her gown, or her wrists as she threw herself at the window. But in the same movement, the fae king unsheathed one of his twin axes and threw. The blade flew in a perfect circle cutting down one, two, three, four of Dorkoth's spirits in one fell swoop.

"Get them!" Dorkoth shouted, but most of his spirits were now headless, stone strewn across the floor of the tavern.

*Burn*, Aisling spoke to Racat and the tavern lanterns raged with violet flame eager to explode. Her *draiocht* was salivating, chomping at the bit to be released in its full glory.

"By the Forge," Dorkoth's eyes widened with horror, watching as Aisling's magic pressed a blade to his tavern's throat. Its spirit screamed, burning alive.

The three remaining spirits grabbed Aisling as she was halfway out the window, knees bruised on the metal edge of the sill. The sorceress lit with fire and unsheathed Sarwen from her back. Two of the spirits flew away, but the third held his grip, digging his rough fingers into her skin.

Anduril frothed at the mouth, gleaming brightly as it reclaimed Aisling's body for its own and swung her arms.

Sarwen cut through the air with unique precision. The sorceress made a ribboned mess of the remaining spirits—her ears numb to their pain-ridden screams as they begged for mercy just before meeting the sharp edge of Sarwen.

"Follow us," Lir said. "And we'll not spare you a second time." He held one of his axes to Dorkoth's bobbing neck, holding him from behind. He shoved Dorkoth off and away, narrowing his eyes as Flasing's child stumbled.

"You'll bring death to the Sidhe!" Dorkoth screamed as Aisling and Lir slipped out the window and into the night. "Your father will find you, faerie, and the whole of the Forge will pay!"

Flasing's cradle hummed like a harp string plucked, echoing between the caverns of creation. It smelled of raw minerals, of stardust, and of the beginning of time. The stars above glittering proudly at the sharp peaks Aisling and Lir wove through, their feet quick and nimble despite growing exhaustion.

After several hours, Dorkoth's tavern was a distant ember still shaking with the remnants of a celebration. Nevertheless, Dorkoth didn't follow—most likely licking his wounds and preventing Aisling's flames from devouring his home fully.

"Let's rest for a while," Lir said, pausing at an intersection between mountains.

"After," Aisling said. "Eogi is close. I can feel it."

"You always say that," he said. "But eventually, your body won't be able to fight."

"With Anduril I cannot lose," Aisling said. The belt beamed with pride, flashing extra bright whilst in Lir's presence.

"Aisling." Lir grabbed Aisling's wrist and held it gently but firmly. The sorceress hesitated, the memory of their kiss lingering on her lips even now. Her *draiocht* prickled with excitement the moment their eyes reconnected.

Aisling opened her mouth to speak.

"I—" She was stopped short.

A shadow drifted by in the corner of her eye. Aisling reacted immediately, drawing Sarwen from her back. Lir followed but slowly, seemingly unalarmed by the movement.

"What was that?" Aisling asked, squinting her eyes to better see in the dark.

Before Lir could reply, another shadow passed on Aisling's other side. The sorceress swiveled on her heel, searching for the source of movement.

At last, several more shadows appeared and revealed themselves to both Aisling and Lir.

They were silver fish seemingly swimming through the dense breath of Flasing. They swam without water, cutting through the currents of midnight air and mountain breezes as though they traveled beneath the waves, scales reflecting the ghostly glow of the crescent moon.

"Glimmer fish," Lir called them. "Born of the bubbles long evaporated from the Forge's cauldron."

Four fish became twenty and twenty became countless as Aisling and Lir stood, mouths open, and watched them swim. They swam together, at the same pace, and in the same direction, diving deeper into the cavernous depths of Flasing's cradle.

"Let us follow," Aisling said, starting in the same direction. Lir hesitated but briefly, eventually swallowing his protests and following a pace behind the sorceress as she continued.

The temperature dropped several degrees until even Aisling's magic couldn't warm her flesh entirely. She paled, the tip of her nose pink after the cold's bitter kiss. Teeth chattering.

The deeper and further they ventured, the more fish swam

by, growing larger, longer, and more friendly. Various slipped by Aisling's cheeks, her skirts, through Lir's arms, and by his boots, their fins stroking them both playfully as they passed. Eventually, thousands bottlenecked at the mouth of a cave veiled by a shimmering, spilling waterfall.

Breka's mirror.

A spindly, floating path led up and into the cave, suspended in the air by magic alone.

Aisling's ears popped with the pressure of dense *draiocht* all around. Her body tingled and Racat moved restlessly inside her. Aisling knew Lir felt similarly, his fingers stroking the hafts of his twin blades in rhythmic motions. The smell of forge-cracked flame, overwhelming to the senses.

Aisling and Lir climbed up the suspended path, careful not to look over its edge at the fall below. From where they walked, the ground was no longer visible but only a sea of fog, whipped like freshly made cream. But once they arrived at the top and stood before Breka's mirror, the plummet was the last thing on Aisling's mind.

Lir stepped in front of Aisling, a shoulder between her and the opening to the cave. He drew both his axes now, peering past the falling waters where the fish traveled densely.

"Is it as simple as entering?" Aisling asked Lir, staring past her knight and into the dark mouth of the cave beyond.

"Only one way to find out." Lir stepped forward, boot by boot nearing the edge of Breka's mirror. Close enough that the spray of the falls soaked his trousers and the fish pushed past him to enter first. Lir moved further, the tip of his nose stopping just short of the waters.

"Lir," Aisling warned, but it was too late.

The fae king flew backward, nimbly catching himself and landing in a crouch like a feline. Aisling and Lir stared at the waters, watching as something stepped forth.

It was invisible at first. The only indication it existed was its strength as it pushed Lir back, and the way the water parted so it could pass. The moonlight, however, revealed its secrets, unveiling the creature before their eyes.

A shining knight clad in forge-cast armor stood before them both. He carried a greatsword that almost matched his great height and build, reflecting the light of the moon spectating from above.

"Do you seek Eogi?" the knight asked. His voice was inhuman. Each word was stiff and unfamiliar, as though it were nothing more than a mimicry of Aisling's common tongue.

"Aye," Aisling replied, stepping forward. Lir's jaw tightened, but he said nothing, his grip hardening on the hafts of his blades.

"It is I who seeks Eogi," Aisling said.

The knight considered Aisling with the patience of immortality. He studied her gown, her tangled hair, and the gleam of Sarwen between her cold hands.

"On what authority do you wish to pass?" the knight asked.

"I seek the Goblet," Aisling answered honestly.

"The Goblet of Lore," the knight clarified, his eyes and expression hidden behind an ornate, detailed helmet.

"To rewrite prophecy and spare the Sidhe from mortal victory," Aisling continued. Perhaps she wouldn't need to battle the knight at all. After all, they were on the same side—all forge-born and made of the same magic the Other sipped from.

"The ink is already bleeding," the knight said. "With every wound they inflict on the gateway, the veil thins, and the mortals bring disease, destruction, war, and famine to the spirit world, infecting eternity and the making of the universe. This is the end."

Silence spread between them. Aisling swallowed, the knight's words bouncing off the walls of Flasing's cradle.

"Inflict pain on the gateway?" Aisling asked.

"Leshy." The knight spoke matter-of-factly. "It flees their

hunt, leaving a trail of blood in its wake. But not for long. The fire hand is nearing and fate cannot be stopped."

Leshy.

The last moon of the storm season.

Aisling shook her head, suddenly understanding. Leshy was a gateway to the Other. A needle her father would violently thread if he could. Would destroy, root by root, if it meant obtaining everything he'd ever desired: triumph, power, Aisling... This is what they'd been ravaging the mortal plane searching for. What they'd been hunting. Leshy, their prey. Sidhe kingdoms conquered again and again as he neared his ends.

"Fate cannot be stopped," Aisling agreed. "But it can change course."

"Your arrogance will be your undoing," the knight replied.

"Better my undoing than the world's," Aisling said. She spoke it without thinking, catching Lir's attention as well. She wanted power between her teeth, yes, but perhaps she was starting to believe there was more.

"The choice is yours," the knight said. He moved like moonlight reflecting off the shallow waves of a lake, readying himself to fight whoever wished to approach. Anduril lit excitedly, thirsty for Sarwen to drink their foe's blood. He crouched, his blade poised in both hands.

Aisling exchanged glances with Lir. The fae king said nothing with his tongue but more with his eyes—bright green and flickering with fear. Not for himself. But for her.

*You are his tool and nothing more. A weapon, a solution, but never could he care for your heart*, Anduril reminded Aisling. Still, his expression weakened her knees and made Sarwen suddenly heavy in her palms.

At last, Lir nodded, a muscle flashing across his jaw.

Aisling swallowed, steeling herself.

"I choose to pass," Aisling said and raised Sarwen before her.

Blade against blade, the first clash rang through Flasing's corridors. Sarwen glinted as its metal rubbed against the knight's. Both fell apart, Aisling's chest rising and falling with new adrenaline, Anduril shining as if dipped in the molten brew of the Forge itself.

"I am bound to this gateway by both Breka and Arawn," the knight said. "I will not show mercy." The knight sped forward, a blur of moonlight as he cut the distance with wicked speed. He jabbed at Aisling with his greatsword, light spidering from the tip of his blade when he moved.

"Neither shall I," Aisling said, lifting Sarwen and blocking the assault narrowly. The blow shoved Aisling to the side regardless, almost knocking her off her feet.

Anduril burned, its magic pulsing through Aisling's veins and spinning Sarwen between her fingers. She moved toward the knight, forcing her opponent to block the flurry as she approached.

The knight lifted his blade and shoved forward with his shoulder, pushing Aisling. The sorceress braced herself. She skidded backward, dropping a hand to the stone pathway to balance herself.

"He out-strengthens you, Aisling," Lir said, his expression tight and his muscles corded. He watched the duel from the edge of the pathway, helpless to save his faerie from the fate she'd chosen. "But strength isn't necessary to win."

Aisling had always known she'd lacked strength—the mettle of a warrior was not in her blood. That was why she wore Anduril. Why she'd accepted Fionn's gift and worn it like armor, like a disguise that allowed her to pretend for a short while she was the fierce fighter her clann, the Sidhe, herself didn't believe she was.

Aisling lifted Sarwen, Anduril her strength as she threw the blade, and watched it dart toward the knight. It pierced the guardian in the shoulder, tasting his otherworldly blood for the first time.

The knight scarcely flinched, unaffected by the pain of his newfound wound. A ghoul with no heart and no true flesh to experience suffering—physical or otherwise.

Slowly, the knight pulled Sarwen from his shoulder and cast it to the side. Aisling watched with horror as her blade clattered to the ground, far from her reach.

"Your *draiocht*, Aisling," Lir said, his voice rough and thick.

Aisling nodded her head absently, closing her eyes to call upon Racat.

The *dragún* woke easily, sliding up her throat and burning inside her teeth. Aisling concentrated on the swelling magic, soaking up its energy like waves building and curling before they were allowed to break. Aisling balled such might in her mind, blooming the spheres of fire in her palms. She threw the violet fire, speeding toward the knight like purple comets with tails on fire.

The knight lifted his greatsword, blocking each throw with ease. Her fires ricocheted off and fizzled into the midnight air leaving nothing but wisps of smoke in their wake.

"Gods," Lir cursed beneath his breath, watching with red-rimmed eyes.

Aisling summoned more magic, allowing the fire to consume Flasing's cradle. The heat built and the flames grew, crackling and popping until both she and the knight were surrounded.

"Your magic is powerful," the knight said. "But it is not enough."

Aisling flinched. His words stabbed her where his blade had

yet to harm her. She felt the sudden urge to fall to her knees. To give in and surrender to the weakness she'd been born to carry. But Anduril, Racat, and the ambition Ina had planted in her bones, compelled her otherwise.

Aisling released her *draiocht*, bottled and bubbling still since Lir had kissed her a few hours prior. Ripples of fire bled from her pores, oozing down her gown and racing toward the knight.

The knight carved a circle around his feet with his blade, shielding himself from her magic.

Aisling growled in frustration, eyes flicking to Sarwen still tossed to the side.

The sorceress raced for her blade.

Now it was the knight's turn to throw his greatsword. He tossed it expertly, finding Aisling's hand and staking it through as she reached for Sarwen.

Aisling screamed, the agony unbearable. It struck her like lightning, sharp and webbing up her arm and into her shoulder. Blood sprayed warm and sticky atop Flasing's cradle as she pulled the knight's greatsword from the wound with a quivering arm.

"*Ellwyn*," Lir shouted, his fangs bared. He paced the edge of the pathway, nostrils flared with the smell of her blood.

*Ellwyn.*

The fae king's voice moved through Aisling and her *draiocht* like an enchantment. An alchemy of souls the Forge toyed with at the beginning of time, come to wake again when she looked at him, touched him, felt him. Anduril's screaming and thrashing locked in her jaw like a beast with prey between its teeth.

Aisling rose to her feet, the knight's greatsword yanked from her grasp by his magic. The blade shot back into his grip, immediately spun and twisted artfully between his fingers. The knight approached steadily and confidently, seemingly unfazed by the duel thus far whilst Aisling wobbled on shaking knees.

Anduril grew angry, its temper slaked only once Aisling collected Sarwen from the ground and poised it before her once more.

"Even with Anduril, I am no match for it," Aisling said, speaking her thoughts aloud. Her eyes pricked with heat and, against her own volition, she looked to the fae king. She wasn't certain why her body was magnetically pulled to his—why her mind struggled to rid him from her thoughts. But, in this moment, she hardly cared.

"Are those your words or Anduril's?" Lir challenged.

Aisling thought for a moment. Was there a difference? Was it all Aisling or was it all Anduril? The sorceress shut her eyes, temples aching with the whiplash of her thoughts.

"Do you feel your magic thrashing inside?" Lir asked. "Do you feel it pushing at your lungs, begging to be breathed and blown like wildfire?"

Aisling held her breath, counting the knight's steps as he grew closer.

"Do you feel your own strength begging to be released and not another's?" Lir asked, his voice coming more quickly as the knight approached.

"Do you wish me to believe I could be capable?" Aisling asked, her words weak and laced with defeat despite Anduril's and Racat's energy—their fury and eagerness to be indulged.

"No," Lir said. "I wish to show you, you already are."

*"We are all beasts, slaves to desire. Mortals, Aos Sí, and all else driven by that which will sate our appetite. You must overpower that which sought to overpower you. Become the predator and not the prey," Lir spoke like a prophecy.*

"You wish to corrupt me," Aisling said.

"No. I wish to show you, you already are."

The memory hit Aisling more painfully than the knight's blade through her hand. It slammed into her consciousness like an unwelcomed guest, pulling the door off its hinges and squeezing inside. Anduril resisted its image, but it was futile. The memory bloomed and stayed, planted in her mind anew.

Aisling found Lir's gaze and held it. She wasn't certain how long they stood watching one another, a silent conversation passing between them as the knight took his final steps and prepared to cleave Aisling's head from her body.

"*Ellwyn*," Lir said.

Aisling turned to face the knight, lifted Sarwen before her and summoned her *draiocht*.

A tendril of flame wrapped around Sarwen like a serpent, biting at the tip with a *dragún*'s mouth.

Aisling pulled back her arms and struck forward just as the knight bolted forth.

Sarwen sank into the knight's heart before the creature could deflect, staked through to the other side with Aisling's enchanted sword.

The knight groaned, touching where Sarwen entered his body with a fleshy, spongy crunch.

"Well done, faerie," the knight conceded bent over and falling to his knees before her. "You may pass."

The knight collapsed onto the ground, heaving one last rattled breath.

Aisling watched, expressionless, as the clouds above shielded the moon's eyes. Darkness fell over Flasing's cradle, and once the light had left, so, too, did the knight disappear. Nothing but Sarwen, lit with flames, before Breka's mirror remained.

LIR

Before the Sidhe king could think straight, his boots were already flying forward and racing for her. He ripped his tunic's hem, immediately wrapping her hand with the fabric and watching with horror as it continued to soak through the linen.

"It will heal with time," Aisling managed, but Lir didn't care. He wanted it healed now.

"Let's keep moving," she said.

Lir tensed, but he nodded in reply. She'd defeated Eogi's gatekeeper and now, they were so close. Close to Eogi and the Goblet needed to fix everything. They couldn't turn back now.

Lir scooped Aisling into his arms. She protested at first, her belt pinching him whenever it touched his clothes or flesh. Eventually, however, she relaxed, her head falling against his chest as he walked forward and toward Breka's mirror.

The waterfall parted like curtains woven from crystal silks. They passed through, following the schools of fish still swimming further into the mountain and its cave.

Inside, the air grew even colder than before. Aisling's teeth chattered, so Lir pulled her closer, holding her as tightly as he could whilst still ensuring she was comfortable. The longer they traveled, the darker the cave grew. Nothing but the shining, reflective scales of the surrounding fish to light the path.

Deeper they journeyed, sinking to the pit of a cold cauldron's belly. From here, Lir could hear running river water coursing through the mountains, but most of all, he could smell Eogi's *draiocht*: alive, bubbling, and sparkling like champagne, eager to be felt beneath the flesh.

"What happens once we obtain the Goblet?" Aisling asked, her voice nearly a whisper. "What then?"

Lir thought for a moment.

"We wait for the first storm moon—its necessary requirement—and then protect the gateway," Lir said. "If Leshy is the doorway they've chosen, we prevent them from taking it. The Goblet will allow us to shield it from mortal aggression. If we make it in time."

"And if we don't?" Aisling asked.

Lir inhaled. "Then we destroy the gate ourselves." It was a difficult truth to swallow. With the future of the Sidhe race and the Forge at stake, Lir was willing to do whatever it took to prevent a mortal victory.

"And if we cannot destroy it in time?" Aisling continued.

"Then we destroy the mortals altogether," Lir said.

Aisling considered for a moment.

"Every last one?" she asked.

"Every last one," Lir agreed. They exchanged glances, communicating without speaking another word.

At last, the pathway reached an end at the pit of Flasing's cradle. The cave's corridor widened into a large room where the schools of fish swam in circles, tracing the walls and ceiling. And at the center was an abyss: a chasm that tunneled further into the earth, filled to the brim with smoke as black as wild cherries.

Moisture dripped from the ceiling, echoing through the corridors of the cave with a haunting rhythm.

Gently, Lir set Aisling on her feet. She wobbled at first, quickly finding her balance and steadying herself. Immediately, he missed the feeling of her body against his own. Felt the absence of her like a piece of him removed.

She stepped forward, peering down and into the abyss below.

"Name thyself," a voice boomed from the dark.

The hair across Aisling's body stood on end. A scream bloomed in her throat, but she kept it locked behind her clenched teeth.

They couldn't see the beast in detail. Still cloaked by darkness, all that was visible was its gaping mouth as it opened wide —the smoke churning in a circle inside its open maw. Only its shape and form rolled below them in the great chasm the rocks and the darkness protected.

The hinges of its jaw screeched from lack of use, and inside sat the pool of smoke stirring endlessly and black as the nothing that came before the birth of everything.

"Name thyself," a voice asked again.

Lir's *draiocht* responded immediately, thrashing inside like a hound leashed by a brittle chain. He sensed Aisling's *draiocht* as well, rising from her throat and into the magic-dense air.

Aisling shuddered, but she stood tall and straightened her back as she replied.

"Aisling," she said. "And you are Eogi, keeper of beginnings."

Eogi laughed.

"It has been some time since I've heard my name spoken aloud," the keeper said. "None have ever passed my gate." Eogi laughed again, choking on the pool swirling in his throat. A deep voice, as though the rocks themselves forced breath after breath through their age-old lungs.

"Eogi," Aisling said again, this time softer, the silk of her voice given new life. "Request it and I'll speak it in multiples."

Eogi chuckled once more, the whole of Flasing's cradle trembling with the keeper's vibration.

"You please me," he said.

"I am a friend," Aisling assured him.

"You'd have me believe it," the keeper said. "Yet, the nature of your arrival is prompted by the death of my knight and guardian. Your hands are bloodied, and you smell of something unfamiliar." Eogi inhaled deeply, blowing and pulling Aisling's hair in the direction of the abyss. "You are strange, Aisling."

The sorceress stood still, watching the keeper think. Lir watched her. He admired her courage for not a moment passed when he forgot the mortal princess she once was. Pride swelling in his chest as he watched her face the guardian knight and now the keeper of beginnings. A desperate need to protect her, overcoming him as he stood a few paces behind.

"You haven't only come to speak my name," Eogi said. "So, why have you come?"

The black waters churned, frothing with pearl tipped waves. Aisling stepped closer to the edge, eyes widening as she stared into the vast chasm of Eogi. Aisling sank to her knees and placed both her hands on the edge of the abyss and leaned further forward. Lir's stomach flipped; the sorceress was too close to the edge for his liking.

"We seek the Goblet of Lore," Aisling said.

Eogi erupted into chuckles, shaking the cave once more. He licked his lips, his open mouth spewing more black smoke than before.

"A chalice of creation, of the Forge, and of the gods; the only artifact in this realm or the next capable of creating from the pits of nothing," Eogi said.

"Aye," Aisling agreed. "The one and the same."

Eogi groaned as he thought, whispering to himself in conversation.

"After a millennium, I, too, wish for new beginnings," Eogi said. "And so, the Goblet is yours if you can answer me this one riddle."

Aisling nodded her head, violet eyes flashing a brighter shade of purple.

Eogi cleared his throat, humming softly to himself before speaking.

"What stretches before you, large and mighty, but can only be seen by a few?" the keeper asked.

Lir tasted the silence, rehearsing the words in his mind. The answer came to him swiftly as he'd contemplated its name time and time again in the recesses of his thoughts.

Aisling narrowed her eyes, watching as Eogi waited. Lir could hear her heart pounding, the rush of blood through her veins, and the stirring of her *draiocht*. He heard it as his fingertips would feel her bare skin beneath his touch.

Aisling unfurled from her kneeling position and stood tall before Eogi's chasm.

"The future," she said, her voice clear and unclouded.

Eogi erupted with laughter. Flasing's cradle shook madly and the fish dissolved into chaos. They swam in every direction, a storm of light and scales swirling around them in angry spirals.

The dark grew darker and the echoes deep. The *draiocht* thickening like a primordial soup heated to a boiling point.

"Correct," Eogi said.

But the keeper of beginnings did not hand over the Goblet. Instead, he widened his mouth, his fangs lengthening and dripping with venom.

"I'm glad you visited me, Aisling," Eogi said, flinging his behemoth body from the chasm in a great shadow of teeth and devouring both Aisling and Lir whole.

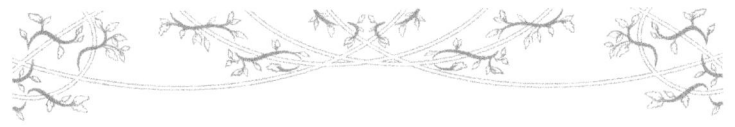

## CHAPTER XXVIII

*In the dark, the Lady tore a hole in the fabric of the world so Aisling could peer into her father's mind.*

*Nemed sat in a dimly lit room, surrounded by candles. Wax spilled down their bent and warped bodies, dripping onto the cherry oak table. And if Aisling looked closely enough, she could see the screaming mouth of the tree he'd cut painfully from the earth and brutally carved without reverence for its life.*

*The fire hand, on the other hand, was also dripping onto the floorboards. Dark red sap fell from the tip of his nose where his head hung, staring downward. His gaze was vacant, ignoring the stains and burn trails across his leathers, his torn tunic, or the wool of his tartans.*

*"When the time comes, will you be capable of it?" a familiar voice piped from the dark recesses of the room. Boot by boot they approached, the metal of their belt chinking as they neared.*

*Starn's angular face was unveiled by the candlelight.*

*"When the time comes, will you kill her?" Starn asked again. "Or must I?" Starn lifted his blade from the scabbard at his hip with nothing more than the will of his mind. The sword, eerily, slipped from its sheath and glittered in the firelight.*

*Nemed considered for a moment. The scar across his face reddened with his concentration.*

"It would kill me to take the life of my kin," Nemed said, his voice more brittle than Aisling remembered it. "I do not fear the grotesque faces of my enemies, the screams of my night terrors, or the unknown of my future," her father continued. "But I do fear her."

"She is a spoilt child given a powerful gift and nothing more," Starn bit, almost jealously.

"I do not fear her strength or her anger," Nemed countered. "I fear the look in her eyes when I tear my life's—and the life of every mortal king before me—labor from her chest. It is my duty, my obligation, and my destiny for mankind. Yet, I fear no sorceress, no fae, no warrior. I fear the little girl that might look back at me. And I fear I'll look back at her and remember."

*The fire hand cleared his throat, clasping his bloody hands together before him. The dark sap and blood pulled at his skin, but he hardly noticed, staring a hole into the floor of the room.*

"We are but a few moons from finding her. We are breaths full away from hunting the gateway, from laying siege, from conquering what is rightfully ours," Starn said, his voice deep and clipped with anger.

"And we will show no mercy," Nemed replied. "We will not wait."

"You hesitate even now," Starn argued. "The softness of your heart makes it easier to strike."

"She is my weakest child, my most useless girl, and my greatest disappointment," Nemed explained, seemingly enjoying speaking lifelong thoughts aloud. *And even here—in this realm in between—Aisling felt the blow of her suspicions come alive by her father's voice.*

"Because I am human," Nemed continued. "Do not forget your humanity, Starn, lest you find yourself more fae than man."

"I could never forget—"

"I hope so," Nemed said, cutting Starn short. "Regardless, the eve of victory is the best moment to reflect. Soon our plane, the Other, and the Sidhe world will bend the knee to me and to you, son. Our harpoons will sink into the gateway, our fiery blades will drive into their chests, and my hand will steal the curse breaker from my daughter's chest."

Starn nodded his head.

"And then?" the crown prince asked.

"And then we take everything. We avenge all those she burned at Lofgren's Rise, every village she let be devoured by beasts after her coronation, every soldier killed in pursuit of our vengeance. We take everything."

"Soon?" Starn asked, his voice rising.

"Soon," Nemed agreed.

"Give me a day," Starn pushed. "Let every day closer renew our efforts, our spirits, our morale."

The fire hand lifted his head, meeting his eldest son's eyes. Violet, they shone brightly, lit with the thought of violence and vengeance alike. The look of a father who enjoyed punishing his children.

"On the last moon of the storm season, we strike," Nemed said.

"Promise it," Starn said.

Nemed sucked in a breath, his chest rattling after decades of inhaling forest smoke.

"I promise it."

## CHAPTER XXIX

"Niamh is coming to fetch her," Lir said, sensing the Seelie queen's approach.

"The time is nigh," Peitho said, pushing the owls aside to wrap Aisling in a tight embrace. She kissed her on each cheek, cupping her face between her hands. "Be strong, *terra*."

*Terra*. Rún for sister.

"Be brave, Ash," Gilrel said, tying her braids to finish.

Aisling couldn't open her eyes, her body limp with exhaustion.

"Rest and regain strength, Aisling," Fionn said, kissing her coolly on the cheek.

"Be patient, *mo Lúra*," Galad said, pressing a kiss to Aisling's knuckles in knightly devotion.

"Be wise," Filverel said with a somber nod of his head, arms crossed as he stood over her bed.

*Where am I?* Aisling asked again and again. Her mind lost in darkness.

Aisling bit her tongue until it bled—physical pain a distraction from the tears that pricked her shut eyes.

But Lir's voice held her steady even in the dark.
"Be merciless, *ellwyn*," he said.
*The last moon of the storm season.*
The words repeated in her mind.

# CHAPTER XXX

## AISLING

*Seven storm seasons come but never go.*
*Come child, I hear the wild horns blow.*

The song carried on like a ghostly chant, echoing into oblivion by the voices of thousands of Sidhe humming despite the rain.

Most of the Sidhe sovereigns stood before Aisling.

Lir, Fionn, Niamh, Katari, Lottie, Tara, Mac Cuill, Percy, and Dagda. Some were original Sidhe sovereigns, whilst others were the descendants to their throne, having accepted the crown after their fathers and mothers passed in similar fashion to Lir and Fionn.

Their *draiocht* together popped Aisling's ears and burned her nose. Their magic tasted ancient and bygone; a beast itself rolling awake since the last moment they were all together in one place.

Katari beamed, sparking with embers of light as though his excitement struggled to contain his magic.

"Will she live?" Tara asked, her voice a midnight breeze as she joined Fionn at his side. Her dark curls were windswept, tickling her lovely features even as she frowned with surprising sincerity. A female whose complexion was richly dark, seemingly kissed by cool breezes, by hailstorms, by blustering nights, and hurricanes. The intensity of her gaze was breathtaking, almost a distraction from the whipping sheets of highland gales that draped across the lovely curves of her figure.

Aisling's heart beat in her throat, but she barely felt it for the booming of the world around her.

They stood around her chamber bed in Castle Yillen, watching her closely.

"Shh, she's waking!" Lottie said. A female of mint complexion, the scales of her gown shimmering like a deep-sea fish before they morphed into the froth of coastal waves near the hem. And when she nodded her head in recognition, her veil of freshwater pearls clicked enthusiastically.

Sidhe, bears, foxes, badgers, falcons, pine martens, tortoises, frogs, and even mice cheered from outside, pelts soaked with the rain that descended from the bed of clouds above and around them. Some Seelie flew as high as the billowing flags and banners, eager to find the perfect spot for spectating what Aisling was certain was a once in a millennium event: this many Sidhe sovereigns together in one room.

"If you aren't the gods' favored one," Niamh said, standing at the center of the Sidhe sovereigns, "then you'll surely be mine."

Fionn shifted, but Lir stood still, eyes void of emotion.

Aisling hadn't the courage to look at Lir just yet, but glancing at Lir now—dressed in form-fitting dark armor, his axes crossed at his back, dahlia-black hair falling into his eyes, and the jade of his gaze, heartless, arrogant, and cold—she struggled to take a breath without blinking tears. Anduril trembled weakly at her hips where she lay.

Niamh noticed Aisling and Lir's stolen glance, nostrils flaring.

Swiftly, Lir averted his eyes.

"Welcome back, sorceress," Niamh said, giving nothing away as to her thoughts.

Aisling could barely hear the Seelie queen over the trumpets and the cheers. The world shook beneath her bed. Sarwen lay beside her, glinting like the high-born knight she was not. Yet, Aisling was done underestimating herself. For who would have faith in her if she did not have faith in herself? She was a sorceress, a queen, and the reaper of men.

Aisling swallowed, straightening her back.

"The Goblet," Aisling said. But as the words fell from her lips and she sat up straight, a glittering object fell onto her lap.

The gleaming Goblet was forged of violet glass, humming with the strange voice of a creature Aisling feared. Something all-knowing, something curious, something alive, and eager.

Aisling gasped, lips falling apart in amazement. She turned to Lir to gauge his reaction. He smiled proudly, genuine joy spreading across the exhaustion beneath.

"You've done it, Aisling." Niamh grabbed Aisling's hand and squeezed it. "You can rest for a time."

"No," Aisling said, almost leaping from the bed. "They're coming. On the last moon of the storm season," she blurted, eyes growing wide with urgency. "They will come."

"The mortals?" Filverel asked, brows raising at Aisling's sudden excitement. Filverel, Galad, Peitho, and Gilrel smiled at her, their presence in the Other bittersweet for it suggested Annwyn, too, had fallen to the mortals—a thought, a possibility Aisling couldn't stomach just yet.

"My father," Aisling said, "my brothers..."

"You need to rest," Tara said, setting a gentle hand on Aisling's shoulder.

"There is no time," Aisling said. "They will come on the last moon of the storm season. They will try to enter the Other."

"How can you know this?" Dagda asked, both anger and panic detailing their voice.

"The Lady," Aisling said. "The Lady showed it to me."

"She cannot be trusted," Fionn said, seemingly unaware of the irony in his warnings.

"No, she cannot," Aisling admitted. "But she hasn't given this information to me kindly. She's done it to scare me—to convince me my defeat has already been written."

"We cannot know for sure," Lir said, his voice blooming and standing out amidst the rest. Aisling warmed to it immediately, lingering on his gaze a moment too long.

"The last moon of the storm season is approaching," Niamh said. "If Aisling is correct, time is fleeting indeed."

The room fell quiet, each deep in thought. They exchanged glances, but the reality was clear: war was on their doorstep and they were unprepared to greet it, each and all of them still licking their wounds from the falling of their kingdoms in the mortal plane.

This was the beginning of the end.

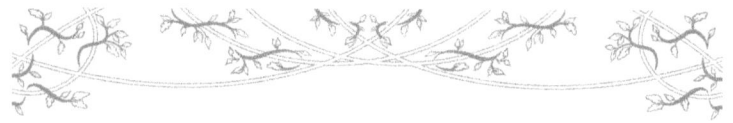

## CHAPTER XXXI

### LIR

The clouds parted and the sun screamed awake. It shook like a prisoner in a cage, reaching through the bars of its cell with its rays.

Niamh watched Lir closely from the largest throne. She was framed by both her water mares, delightedly eating salted candy from a giant daisy's disk. The room was shaped like the moon and as the day faded, so, too, did the light spilling in from the glass ceilings above. Rain tapped against the panes steadily, accompanied by the rabid breath of mist.

"And so we begin," she said, more to herself than any of the other Sidhe sovereigns paying attention. A round table of myths, speaking amongst one another.

The Other froze in suspense, waiting for the Sidhe sovereigns to address the matters at hand.

"This is our last chance," Katari said, opening the conversation. Katari of the Gilding Sun reigned from southern Niltaor with Siwe at his side. Siwe, his bride and Peitho's mother. They ruled by daybright with the brilliance of summer's buzzing heat. And so, Lir knew the sun thrashing up above was no coincidence.

"Aisling must protect each and every gateway," Lottie said. "Not one can be left vulnerable. We must act now. Use the Goblet now."

"It's too soon," Percy said. "The Goblet can only be sipped beneath a storm moon. We must wait for the next. Regardless, it's impossible to destroy every gateway."

"Nothing is impossible with the Goblet," Mac Cuill added.

"Perhaps she should destroy them all," Tara offered.

"And confine us to the Other for all eternity?" Fionn asked, outraged, frost flying from his fingertips as he gestured. "Perhaps it would be better to destroy but a few and not all."

"There may be no other choice," Lottie said. "There's nothing left for us on the mortal plane regardless. Each and all our kingdoms have been taken over, burned to the ground, or destroyed entirely, forcing us here and now."

"Here, we can rebuild," Dagda said, agreeing.

"And yet, there was reason the gods sent us to the mortal plane. We weren't meant for the spirit world alone," Percy said.

"What other choice do we have?" Lottie asked.

The question floated through the room, hanging above all their heads as they exchanged glances in the great hall. Every Sidhe sovereign forced into a corner here in the Other by the hands of Aisling's father.

Tara leaned closer to Lir.

"Your concern distresses me," Tara of the Howling Winds whispered to the king of the greenwood. "I thought your sorceress was well-equipped to destroy the mortals."

Both Tara and Lir looked at Aisling, silently sitting on the other side of the table. She laid the Goblet on her lap, her fingers stroking the stem as she listened to the Sidhe sovereigns discuss back and forth.

"She is," Lir assured her. "She wouldn't be here in Castle Yillen, alive, if she weren't."

"Those were my thoughts as well," Tara said. "But here and

now, with the growing pressure of the mortals and their destruction in the mortal plane... the reality of our losses is fully tangible if not already felt."

"Aisling will go forward as she's done thus far: with determination. Fate will decide the rest," Lir said, his words as sharp as he felt. Lir didn't trust any of the sovereigns; the Sidhe were both truth-tellers and deceivers. If there wasn't mischief afoot, there was something far worse lurking in the dark corners of the rooms they passed through.

"You believe in her," Tara conjectured, studying the Sidhe king's face closely.

Lir considered for a moment. The Sidhe king knew legends, myths, folktales, and prophecies were slippery with the blood of those condemned to worse fates. He knew the loom frayed, broke, braided, twisted, and knotted at the call of its own whims. But with certainty, he knew Aisling was salvation.

"I cannot articulate it well," Lir confessed, running his fingers through his dark hair. "And were it sheer faith I'd doubt myself. But this is different. I feel it in my bones. Aisling will change everything."

"Why not Niamh?" Tara asked.

"It is not in her making," Lir said plainly. "She does not smell of the Forge as does Aisling. Stand close enough to the sorceress so that you can sense her, listen to the pitter patter of her once-mortal heart, taste her perfume on your tongue, and hear the melody of her voice as it blends with the immortal coil of destiny. She was born of the Forge like none before her."

"And yet, is this once-mortal princess, capable of what you claim? Rewriting prophecy by both the Lady and Danu themselves?" Tara asked, eyes darting around the table to ensure none were listening to her's and Lir's private aside.

"I witnessed her courage not long after we wed," Lir said. "a 'once-mortal princess' locked eyes with a Cu Scath and raced a

Sidhe knight on stagback without hesitation. That was only the cusp of what I'd come to witness of her mettle."

Tara smiled. "It will take more than courage."

"Aye," Lir agreed. "It will take more."

"And so, she is our salvation," Tara concluded.

"Are you not yet convinced?"

Tara hesitated, brows pinching. She lifted her eyes to find Aisling still seated across the table.

"Yes, I'm convinced," she answered honestly. "I've long awaited the end to Niamh's reign over the Other."

"You disapprove of Niamh's sovereignty?" Lir asked, his interest piquing.

"Isolation has made Niamh..." Tara considered her words carefully, daring a glance at Niamh in her throne. Niamh was wholly absorbed by Katari's words, back straight as she darted between the Sidhe sovereigns who spoke aloud. "Unhinged," Tara finished.

Lir looked at Tara now.

"What do you speak of?"

Tara shook her head, biting her bottom lip. "Under any other circumstances, I'd keep silent, but with the current political climate and your sorceress being our potential salvation, I fear I might not be allotted another opportunity to speak my mind."

Lir narrowed his eyes. "Then speak."

Tara exhaled, reaching her hand out and catching drops of gold in her palm.

"You northern Sidhe kingdoms have been spared from Niamh's trickery. In recent centuries, she's been hunting for something or someone, stealing Sidhe brides, Sidhe children, forge-born beasts to the Other."

Lir held his breath.

*Seven storm seasons come but never go.*

> *Come child, I hear the wild horns blow.*
> *A western faerie weeps, broken by a lonely heart,*
> *Cursed to the Other, destined to live apart.*

The eerie melody of "The Architect of Yillen" moaned alive in Lir's mind.

"And what became of them?" he asked.

Tara frowned. "Never seen or heard from again. As I said before, rumor claims she's looking for someone or something. And all those she's deemed unworthy of entering the Other, thus far, are collected by the Other's galleon and sailed to their death. One after the other."

> *Listen to the rain, child*
> *But don't be beguiled*
> *For a faerie will drown you in her tears*
> *Or she'll steal you away for years*
> *Just so that she might not be so lonely.*

"How can you be certain?" Lir asked, but even as the question slid between his fangs, he knew the answer himself.

"I cannot be certain, but I distrust Niamh and so does the southern Sidhe world."

"And yet, why would she leave the north untouched?"

Tara's eyes drifted toward Lir.

"Niamh's fear of you has kept her at bay, but fear is easily stifled by desire," Tara said. "High king of the Sidhe on the mortal plane, master of Racat, with a grisly reputation and a penchant for violence. No other has reigned so powerfully, so forcefully, nor as wildly as you in the history of the Sidhe. Niamh is wise to avoid making an enemy of you... or, she *was* wise."

Lir opened his mouth to speak but thought better of it. He looked to Aisling.

The sorceress gripped the Goblet more tightly. He could feel the magic of both Anduril and Racat bristling and waking with heat. He could taste it popping on the tip of his tongue as Aisling's knuckles grew white and her pupils flooded her eyes black.

Lir frowned, recognizing once again the target Aisling's power placed on her back and the hunters that gathered when she turned.

∽

AISLING

Between the clouds, Castle Yillen shook with music. Bears, foxes, badgers, toads, and Sidhe danced until mortal feet would have bruised, drinking wine, spilling mead, and gulping special punches from the bulbs of giant tulips.

Below Castle Yillen, sat a lake as silver as any blade. A forest huddled around it like groves of druids falling to the knee to sip from its waters, rippling with the force of the storm around them.

This was where Aisling bathed while the rest of the Sidhe world celebrated the acquisition of the Goblet. The evening grew feverish with their celebration, the Other eager for the first sip to be drank from the chalice's lip beneath the storm moon— the first since she'd obtained the artifact.

Aisling lifted the Goblet. She'd filled it once, twice, thrice with silver lake water only for the water to transform violet the moment it slithered over the Goblet's brim. She poured it over her head and rinsing out the dirt, blood, and sweat from her tresses. Glittering, she stood waist deep in the loch. A dark body of water said to be where the gods once cupped their hands and collected their tears.

Aisling had snuck away from the crowds, the parties, the

lights, the drinks, and the foods. She'd been overwhelmed with attention since she'd woken from Eogi swallowing her whole, then spitting her out.

She felt war inching closer, tasted the rot her father was infecting the Other with—grin spreading through the forest, even here by Castle Yillen, like a plague.

So, Aisling scrubbed the past several days off her skin, washing herself till the thoughts stopped spinning so quickly in her mind. A moment for her to sip from the Goblet alone and test its power for the first time. To once and for all seal the mortals' fate with the treasure she'd earned. But in the same breath Aisling had poised the Goblet before her, the loch was transformed by the vibration of its *draiocht*. Like the Forge itself, the loch bubbled black, gurgling strangely as if struggling to speak. Crests and peaks formed atop the surface, its dark waters lunging for Aisling in great splashes, liquid edges stretching like fingers for the sorceress.

"*By the Great Forge of Creation and the twin gods, a new master has stepped forward,*" Aisling said, both her irises and her pupils fading to pure white as she spoke. Aisling shivered, her spine tingling as every word wrung with the echo of someone or something that was entirely Other. A voice possessing her body and using her lips to speak.

"*Vow your allegiance to the Forge and to the draiocht,*" the Other spoke from her mouth. She knew it was the realm itself—its spirit watching and waiting for her.

"I vow it," Aisling said.

Thunder clapped and lightning webbed across the sky. The clouds gathered more thickly, blending with the canopies from the forest that thrashed side to side. The storm moon smiled, watching Aisling with glittering eyes from up above.

"*The Goblet of Lore is now yours to drink, in the name of the Forge.*"

Aisling brought the Goblet to her lips and tilted the legend back.

*Aisling*, Anduril sang to itself. *Aisling*, it repeated. Aisling hesitated, the brew a hair's width from reaching her lips yet still not close enough to taste. She lowered the Goblet further.

*Aisling*, Anduril said again, this time louder.

Aisling forgot the Goblet, focusing on Anduril's voice.

*Aisling*.

Aisling allowed the belt this brief respite. Allowed it to sing at her waist considering it'd kept her alive outside of Eogi's cave.

But then another voice spoke her name aloud.

*Aisling*, a feminine voice sang.

Aisling cocked her head to side, immediately startled.

"Who are you?" Aisling asked aloud, feeling silly once she had. But the incorporeal voice continued, repeating her name again and again.

*Aisling*, it called.

*Aisling*.

And then Aisling's ankles were yanked and she was dragged beneath the surface of the lake, the world dissolving to black.

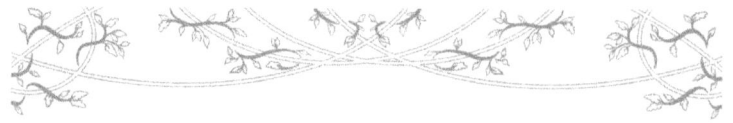

# CHAPTER XXXII

## LIR

On this eve, fury was given a new name. Fury cut through the forest like the child he'd been centuries ago. A winged wisp, axes in hand, weeping and carrying anger between his fangs like a hot coal. Then, he'd been burdened by the passing of his mother. Tonight, he held a butchered heart between bleeding fingers, comforted by the darkest reaches of the greenwood.

Lir rubbed his eyes, wishing he could burn the image of Aisling and the past several days from his mind. He'd cut it out with iron if he must. He'd torch his memory for the opportunity to forget. And yet, no spells, no potions, no salves were potent enough to undo the agony his love for Aisling had wrought inside him. And still, he knew Aisling needed him.

The end of the war was approaching swiftly—too swiftly. The last moon of the storm season was coming. Everything Lir held tightly to seemed to slip through his fingers until he feared he'd have nothing left. Every choice made thus far, Lir made to step closer to Sidhe victory over the mortals. So, how now did he find his every ambition lost before he bore the chance to claim it? How now did he feel himself... losing? Losing Annwyn, the Sidhe, Aisling...

Lir turned to face the blood ash behind him and sank his fangs into its bark. He sucked hard, eyes rolling back in his head when the first droplets of sap reached his teeth and filled him. Sweet, sticky, and thick, the sap took immediate effect, calming his nerves, his muscles, his fury. His shoulders fell, his hands softened, and his pupils tripled in size till no green was left.

The sap of a blood ash was intoxicating. More powerful and more pleasurable than even Sidhe wine.

"*Drink, drink, sire,*" the tree whispered. "*Rest, sire. Rest.*"

Lir sank against the trunk of the tree, ignoring its branches as it bent to cradle him. *Ellwyn* bloomed and held his head gently against the tapestries of lichen, weaving new vines between his ringed fingers.

> *Take flight, little wolf.*
> *Let no hunter catch you,*
> *no fox outwit you,*
> *no devil master you.*
> *Take flight, little wolf.*

Lir hummed the verse his mother sang when she'd taught him how to fly. Ina repeated the verse again and again, mending his wings and carrying him between the turrets of Castle Annwyn when he was too afraid to attempt the flight himself. And even after he'd grown, after he'd led legions and vanquished them, she'd sing it again.

Lir woke from his reverie, his interest piqued by the commotion darting through the forest in his direction. It was the distant brushing of leaves, splitting branches, and the stench of their adrenaline that stole his attention. A wild fox leaping through the brush for an elk finch.

The fox's first bite forced the greatest cry; gory and gone was the first wing. The second bite was a whimper and rip was the tearing of the second wing.

"*Easca,*" Lir hissed, more silent than a whisper.

His voice cast shivers down the spines of every oak, elm, and willow. The forest rustled, chilled to the bone, shaking rain from its canopies like hounds.

The fox obeyed, stopping itself short of devouring what remained of the elk finch. Slowly, despite the racing of its heart, the beast brought Lir the bird.

The elk finch flailed in the Sidhe king's palm, painting a pattern of blood across his markings.

"Hush, little wolf," Lir whispered to the bird. The finch's fluttering heart slowed as it fell to its side. "I wish you a kinder death in the next life and thereafter."

The elk finch puffed three last breaths: one for its king, one for its forest, and one for the life it lived.

Lir closed his eyes, and the bird crumbled to bone and soil and the flowers that fed there. He turned his hand over, returning to the forest what it had lost.

The greenwood groaned.

"*Pity does not become you, mo Damh Bán.*" The voice emerged from between the songs of rain. A female materialized before the Sidhe king, strikingly tall, elegant, stained by the same paint the gods used when they forged the first thunderous skies.

"*Leave me,*" was all Lir replied, not bothering to lift his eyes.

"*I always knew there was mischief afoot,*" Niamh smiled coyly.

"*I said, leave me,*" Lir repeated, his voice more a wolf's than his own. Fangs bared and nose scrunched like a beast prepared to snap. This time, a flash of anxiety possessed Niamh's expression but only for a breath.

"*You may be high king of all the Sidhe in the mortal plane, but here, I am queen, and you will obey me,*" Niamh said, holding out her hand for Lir to take. Lir sneered at the gesture, ignoring her while he unfurled from his seat at the base of the tree. *"Come with me, Son of Bres and Ina."*

Lir turned to snap at the Seelie queen. Instead, the storm roared alive until the forest was cloaked by the cloudburst. The rain was so dense, Lir struggled to see anything other than Niamh until, at last, it quieted to a whisper and no longer did they stand in the Other's forests below Castle Yillen. Now, they stood in one of Niamh's glass domes at the height of her palace, adorned in stained-glass portraits perpetually weeping.

Lir exhaled, both annoyed and frustrated with her magic. He scraped his fangs against his bottom teeth. After centuries, patience was a virtue Lir had mastered. One couldn't withstand eternity without first learning to surrender. Still, Niamh burrowed under Lir's flesh and festered there, making his skin crawl.

*"Calm down, mo Damh Bán."* Niamh spoke first, appraising his expression with a glint of fear she couldn't manage to hide. *"I only wish to speak with you in private... and show you something."*

Niamh waved her arms and water descended from the ceiling in great sheets tracing the edges of the room. And once the water dispersed, twenty or so Sidhe females stood in its place, each dressed for a celebration. Butterflies fluttering between curls, honeycombs sewn into corsets, raspberries dangling from earlobes, and sweet mushrooms sprouting between the folds in their skirts.

*"Your bride has forgotten you,"* Niamh said. *"So, why don't you do the same?"*

Niamh walked along the edges of the room, gently brushing her fingers across each Sidhe female. They stood still, smiling coyly at Lir beneath dark, dew-jeweled lashes. Most trembled in his presence, searching to meet his eyes, yet too afraid to hold his gaze. To Lir, they were lovely like flowers, and he felt for them the same as he would a tulip, a peony, a dandelion, or lavender. Yet, everlasting would be his desire for flames that burned, for teeth that bit, for curses that held him by the throat.

Lir scoffed.

"*You're trying too hard, Niamh,*" he said, turning to face the Seelie queen.

Niamh's expression fluttered before collecting itself once more.

"*I simply wish to know what it is you want, mo Damh Bán.*"

Sakaala had asked Lir the same before they'd ventured to the Other. The answer was complex and yet all who asked already knew the truth of it. They simply wanted the satisfaction of hearing the dark lord of the greenwood speak it aloud.

Niamh snapped her fingers, and the females were washed away once more, vanishing at her whim.

"*Katari and Siwe might find forgiveness still pumps through their hearts if you continue your pursuit of their daughter,*" Niamh pushed.

"*Peitho and I aren't caera,*" Lir replied.

"*And yet, love smiles smugly at convention.*"

Those words burned Lir more than he expected, forcing him to look away. A blow he hadn't anticipated yet should have.

"*I tire of your games, Niamh.*"

"*Very well,*" the Seelie queen said. "*What of your wings?*"

Lir's eyes flicked to Niamh. She smiled, indulging in Lir's newfound interest and attention.

"*What do you know of my wings?*"

Niamh grinned, ear to ear; horribly unsettling and fearsome to behold. A twinkle of mischief dancing between her primordial eyes.

"*I know what Danu took from you. The last vestiges of your mother, ripped from your back like a fruit fly.*" Niamh tilted her head to the side and rain washed over Lir. The rain removed his tunic, his jacket, and loosened his belt, leaving him bare chested save for the axes tethered to his chest—axes that couldn't be removed by spells or magic. Only Lir's will bore the power to surrender them. But it wasn't his blades Niamh hungrily devoured with her eyes. It was the brutal scars where his wings once bloomed.

Anger rose up Lir's throat like weeds.

"*Do you believe me so simple, so weak-minded as to fall for your tricks?*" Lir bit.

"*Everyone has a price.*"

"*And what is it you wish to buy, Niamh?*" Lir asked, stepping closer to her until he towered over the Seelie queen and she was forced to look up at him. She gulped, throat bobbing.

"*I want you to leave here. I want you to return to Annwyn and never look back. Leave Aisling and forget everything that would've once made you stay.*"

Lir tipped his head back, still appraising the Seelie queen. She held firm, chin raised high almost convincing Lir she wasn't afraid. Almost.

"*Was my promise not enough? I expected more from the gods' favored one,*" Lir growled between his fangs. "*Your mischief is clumsy and uninspired. Whatever your history was with my mother, it won't be repeated with Aisling. And I'll remain here in the Other, by Aisling's side, to ensure it.*"

Niamh's eyes widened, as round as twin moons. She opened her mouth to speak, but no words left her lips.

"*I don't—*"

"*Are we clear?*" Lir asked, eyes a shade of ruthless green.

"*As daybreak,*" Niamh said at last.

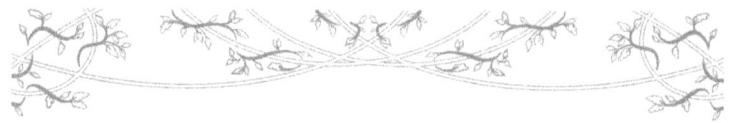

# CHAPTER XXXIII

AISLING

Traveling through water felt like being born. Or so Aisling imagined.

The sorceress rose from icy depths like a banshee clawing through a haunted wood, screaming with a tongue covered in saltwater tears. Yet, Aisling didn't weep. She was surrounded by the savage churning of the Ashild sea, slapped by frothing, pearl tipped waves.

Aisling flailed, panicked, gulped mouthfuls of ocean water. Her head was swallowed by the waves time and time again. Already disoriented by the magic of such travel, the storm only worsened the conditions, spinning, dragging, whipping Aisling's body to and fro like a fish it'd banished from its depths.

Aisling reached for the Goblet of Lore. Moments ago, it had been in her hands and now, it was gone. Her fingers searched for it to no avail. The artifact lost and gone from the sorceress.

"Aisling," a familiar voice called from a distance. Was it a hallucination? A vision? The voice sounded different, cut off time and time again by the merciless thrashing of the sea.

"Aisling," the voice continued, until something rough

wrapped around Aisling's body and pulled. It scratched her skin, rubbing against the wounds still healing from Eogi's knight.

Aisling lit like a violet comet, an animal cornered and afraid, baring its teeth to preserve itself. Whatever had tangled itself around her body shriveled, releasing her to the will of the sea.

"Aisling," the voice continued, but this time, it was followed by a splash. Four legs kicked her own, fighting to swim themselves. They reached for her, but her flames grew brighter. A misfortune for what came next stole Aisling's breath from her lungs. Whoever surrounded her, tied her in chains of iron and dragged her writhing body through the storm.

Aisling shook her head, doing her best to focus her vision, her thoughts, her mind. Yet, it was futile. Futile as she was lifted by both the chain and a body that held her from the tossing sea.

Aisling blinked repeatedly, still choking on salt water as she fought her captor.

"Drop her here!" another voice said. They didn't speak Rún. Their tongues were round and blunt. A stark contrast to the lilted, melodic voices of the Sidhe.

"Careful," someone else said. "Set her down gently... that's it."

"How long will her magic persist?" the first voice asked.

"Until she's calm," the second said. "The iron will make quick work of such a process."

"It's harming her," a new voice added.

"A necessary evil," the first said. His voice was deep and filled with memory. One that had, at one point in Aisling's life, been the center of her small world. A pang of deepest sorrow filling her to the bone with grief. Grief and unfathomable anger.

"Leave her," the second voice said. "She'll exhaust herself soon enough."

But Aisling didn't feel she'd ever be calm again. The pain of the iron, the stench of humans, the vomiting of salt water, the weakness of her muscles. It crossed her mind she might die here: a flower of flaming violet slapped against creaking floorboards that rocked side to side.

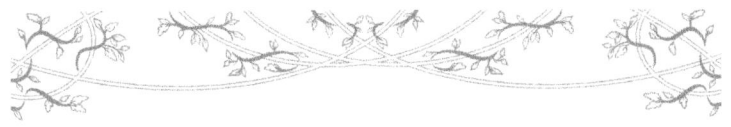

# CHAPTER XXXIV

LIR

Lir started toward Niamh's threshold, reaching for the handle when the door swung open. A small rabbit appeared in the doorway, shivering as it peered up and met eyes with the Sidhe King. Between its paws, it carried the Goblet of Lore.

Lir's stomach catapulted into his throat. Dread making his bones cold.

"*Mo Damh Bán,*" the rabbit chirped, offering Niamh the Goblet for safekeeping as it spoke. "I have some bad news."

"What is it?" Lir said, already in a bad temper.

"It concerns the sorceress, *mo Damh Bán,*" the rabbit said.

"What's happened?" he asked, Niamh stepping behind him to understand the conversation well.

The rabbit dithered, eyes darting back and forth.

"She's been taken, *mo Damh Bán.*"

# CHAPTER XXXV

## AISLING

Aisling woke with a blade at her throat. Yet, the sword bore no wielder. It floated before the sorceress, the tip scratching where her throat bobbed.

Alone, half of Aisling's face was clasped with an iron mask, burning her lips when she tried to scream. Iron fists clasped her hands, chained to the wooden walls surrounding her. She rocked from side to side, desperately trying to light herself on fire. Racat squirmed within, choking on its own flames, struggling to inhale and exhale the *draiocht*.

No longer was Aisling soaked, nor dressed in her night slip from Castle Yillen. Now she wore a homely, wool dress, patterned with Tilrish tartans at the waist and hem. It sparked with her magic, burning holes through the craftsmanship but failing to devour it in flames entirely.

The door at the far end of the room creaked open. Two eyes twinkled from the dark slit of the threshold, hesitating before entering. Normally, Aisling could've smelled or sensed whosoever watched her from the entryway, but no longer. The iron mask prevented her from experiencing or feeling anything other than its stench.

Slowly, once Aisling had settled, someone opened the door fully. From the shadows, a woman tiptoed into the room, chest rising and falling with unnatural fear. She considered Aisling for several minutes before revealing her face in the torchlight, at last, unveiling herself.

Clodagh, Aisling's mother and queen of Tilren, stood before her.

Aisling froze. Her heart hammered inside her chest, painfully shoving at her ribs. She could scarcely breathe. Could scarcely believe this wasn't some cruel deception, mirage, illusion on behalf of the Lady or Danu.

"Aisling," she said. Aisling's heart tightened painfully. Her mother's voice cut bluntly through her—the rounded, common accent of Tilrish mortals made terrible by the sickly-sweet inflection of her mother's tongue. Brutally familiar.

Aisling didn't blink, blood-shot eyes glossing over with tears.

"Daughter," Clodagh said, this time a little more confidently. "I hope you don't mind, I wished to see you dressed in Tilrish garments one last time." Clodagh gestured at Aisling's woolen dress. "I wanted you to be buried this way as well. This is how you'll be remembered, daughter."

Aisling couldn't breathe. Couldn't think. Couldn't move until Clodagh took a step toward her.

Aisling shuffled backward awkwardly, hissing beneath her iron mask. The chains clanked as she moved, pressing herself against the walls.

The phantom sword at her throat moved as she did, its tip never leaving her throat.

"Resist no further, daughter. The end is nigh," Clodagh said.

Aisling's insides exploded with fire, scalding her from the inside out. Smoke spilled from her ears and her tear ducts, clouding the room with her rage.

Clodagh gasped, shuffling backward. She met Aisling's eyes

for only a moment, and what she saw, Aisling knew not. Only that her mother gave a foul scream, and scratched at the door in panic to flee as quickly as possible.

Two men burst into the room. The first quickly grabbed Clodagh while the second immediately focused on Aisling.

Starn and Annind. Two of Aisling's brothers.

Their dark, hawk-like eyes drank in the sight of their sister. But there was something else there now. A strange, dark fire brewing in their eyes and seeping from their lips like a *dragún*. This was the same unnatural magic Aisling had seen at *Imbolc*.

As if prompted, the phantom blade at her throat pushed against her flesh, summoning a stream of blood that trickled down the sorceress's throat.

"What have you done to mother?!" Starn asked Aisling, his expression warped with a combination of both fury and fear.

Aisling jerked at the chains, pulling them till the nails in the walls groaned.

"Enough!" Starn yelled, the bridge of his nose as red as his ears. His eyes flared red—that unnatural magic glowing angrily. The phantom sword pressed harder. Aisling whimpered, closing her eyes the minute the blade punctured her flesh and wrenched a muffled cry from her blistered lips. And still, Starn did not relent. He continued toying with her, exploring how far he could push the blade until she died of either pain or gargling on her own blood.

"Is this how you treat your sister after so long?" another voice piped from the entryway. Aisling hadn't heard them enter, but the moment she opened her eyes, she wished she never had.

Nemed, Fergus, and Iarbonel stood at the door, watching Aisling beneath hooded, empty eyes: her father and two other brothers. Their eyes shone cruelly, possessed by new spells that smelled of the Lady.

"It's not my sister," Starn spat, releasing the floating blade from his command. "It is a beast that's crawled inside my sister's skin and laid waste to mortal fleets. Innocent lives, gone at the cost of her ravenous, spoilt temper."

"Patience. You'll have your opportunity soon enough, Starn." Nemed smiled, the horizontal scar across his face made more gruesome by the dancing shadows cast by the torchlight. He appeared much older than the day Aisling had last seen him. Like a stone, weathered and worn by the unforgiving winds of time. It was a satisfying sight to behold from the perspective of Aisling's newfound immortality.

"Unlock her muzzle," Nemed ordered. "I wish to hear her voice."

Aisling's clann exchanged glances. Her family. Her kin. Her blood... Aisling stopped her thoughts short. The sorceress's heart still pumped with both the blood of man and fae alike. Yet, no longer was the last remnants of human blood in her veins her clann's to claim. It was her own. These humans before her were not the same that'd raised and been raised alongside her. Everything had changed. Aisling was indeed the beast her brother described.

Starn cursed beneath his breath, but never would Nemed's eldest son disobey his father's commands. Cautiously, Starn approached Aisling and unclipped the mask. The iron contraption fell to the rocking floorboards, clattering as Aisling gasped for air.

"Release me or I will slaughter everyone aboard this galleon," Aisling threatened, her voice laced with the lilt of Sidhe accents and wild, feral magic. A ripple of her *draiocht* pushed through the chamber and beyond, sending shivers down each of their spines.

"Your threats are empty," Annind said. "You'll drown alongside us if you cast your magic while still shackled to our ship."

Aisling laughed. "Your knowledge of the fae is unsurprisingly lacking, brother. I'd remain chained to this ship for an eternity if it meant watching your ashes become lost to oblivion. For while I cannot withstand your iron shackles, nor breathe beneath the waves forever, my magic is sufficient to, at the very least, watch you die."

Clodagh broke down weeping, trembling in Annind's arms.

"So eager for the end," Nemed said, pressing his lips into a thin line. "Where has your ambition gone?"

"Like an arrow to its target," Aisling bit, more the image of a chained wolf than ever before.

Clodagh's eyes caught onto Aisling's fangs, sending her squealing like a piglet in fear.

"Calm down, daughter," Nemed said, accentuating the word "daughter" to further provoke her. "You won't need to claw for your life just yet. You'll help us first."

Aisling reeled, unable to mask her surprise.

"I'd rather you cut the curse breaker from my chest than aid either you, the mortals, or the Lady who lent you a pathetic morsel of her magic." Aisling glared at the phantom sword Starn wielded. A replica of the blade he'd used against her, Lir, and Dagfin at Lofgren's Rise. And if that wasn't enough, they'd clearly been aided by the Lady to steal her from the Other and bring her here.

"Yet, cutting the curse breaker from you will do just that—the triumph of the mortals, at long last, over the fae. And thanks to the *wystria*, it's finally possible," Nemed said.

*Wystria.*

Aisling turned the word over in her mind. This was the magic the Lady had lent them. This magic that tasted not of plums or syrups but of bile and acid.

"Yet, there's more I desire," Nemed continued. "You, daughter, will give us more than the curse breaker. You'll give us the entire fae world to burn. So tell me, Aisling, where is the gateway to the Other? Where is Leshy?"

Aisling hesitated, appraising her father anew. She'd assumed they'd wanted her head on a pike, the curse breaker clawed from within her, and the fulfillment of dark prophecies. Yet, once more, she'd underestimated her father's ambition. Nemed would always want more. He not only shared her violet eyes but her thirst for power as well. More so than any other creature she'd met, fae or human.

And what's worse, the Lady was clearly involved in the mortals' schemes, tying her threads and knotting them again and again, working to fulfill her own visions.

"You're mad," Aisling said. "There is no Other. Yet, I'm surprised you've fallen for such hearthside tales."

"So, your mortal blood still runs thick in your veins," Annind said. "How effortlessly you lie."

"Show us the gateway," Starn ordered, readying his phantom blade once more. His eyes burned a darker shade of red. Aisling could feel the magic of the *wystria* clawing into the room like a guest itself.

"Or what, brother? You'll kill me?" Aisling smiled wolfishly, her expression glittering with promised violence. Her clann would cut her regardless and so, their leverage was vanishing before their eyes.

Starn's brows lowered, his face contorting madly.

"There are worse outcomes than death," he said, stepping so close Aisling could smell the iron, ash, and mortal sweat on his tartans.

"If you won't lead us to the Other, then there are others who will," Nemed said. Her father gestured for each of her sons to approach the doorway. Clodagh was the first to vanish past the threshold, then Iarbonel and Fergus seemingly mute with fear, anger, or confusion, Aisling wasn't certain.

"Let's test the fae's loyalty to you. Let's see who comes for you first," Nemed said, closing the door behind him.

He was toying with her. Nemed enjoyed these cruel games

—hopefully, to a fault. Someone would come for her and Nemed would regret it. And if they did not come for her, then they'd come for the Forge.

The ship shook with her screams, smoking between the cracks in the floorboards and staining the entire galleon with her cries.

# CHAPTER XXXVI

AISLING

*Rain tapped Aisling's forehead. Once more clad in her ivory night slip, Aisling balanced on a spider's web. Every string sparkled like starlight, darting from one edge of the cylindrical cave to the other. The tunnel glittered with the intricate handiwork of a beast, one Aisling preferred to never set eyes on. Something much larger than even the neccakaid.*

*One hasty breath and every string trembled.*

*"Aisling," the Lady called from further inside the cave. "Aisling."*

*Aisling would recognize her voice after a millennium. Even if time had erased all else, the Lady's voice would dye the fabric of every age to come and thereafter.*

*Aisling held her breath, holding onto the web's strings with all her strength. They cut into her flesh, drawing blood. Aisling hissed in pain. Still, she couldn't escape. Below the web was an abyss and above, an oblivion grew dark and vast. She was trapped inside the Lady's nest, forced to listen to her laughter.*

*"Aisling. I found you, Aisling," she said. "Now let me in."*

*Aisling cursed, peering into the dark above and below for the Lady.*

*"You cannot outrun fate, Aisling. Let me in."*

Aisling climbed through the mess of strings, doing her best not to fall through and into the endless pit below.

*"The day I let you in, is the day I devour you whole, Lady."*

The Lady cackled. *"She bites."*

*"She savors—relishes the potency of your death on her tongue."* Aisling spoke of herself, sucking in a breath as eight reflective eyes materialized above her. The dark shrouded the beast—the Lady, Aisling realized—cloaking all but her bygone eyes.

*"Savor me, then,"* the Lady said, a smile in her voice. *"Chew my bones and rip my flesh, and still, your world will burn."*

She sprang for Aisling, the cave collapsing into nothingness.

Aisling screamed awake.

Her body jolted upright, snatching at the chains still bound to her wrists and nailed against the wooden walls. And had it not been for her clann's iron, Aisling would've been swathed in flames, burning through the bottom of the ship that'd stolen her away. Anduril dulled at her hips, unable to withstand the iron that surrounded them both.

"Are you alright?" a boy asked from across the chamber.

Aisling flicked her eyes up, meeting the gaze of not a boy but a man. And yet, he bore the same eyes as he who'd run through Castle Neimedh's corridors alongside her when she was a child.

Iarbonel stood with a tray of food in his hands. He trembled, the dishes clinking against one another.

Aisling didn't care to answer. To him, she was nothing more than a leashed savage, hissing and snapping like a caged animal.

But where Aisling anticipated he'd throw the tray at her and return above deck, he stayed.

"Was it a nightmare?" he asked.

Still, Aisling bit her tongue.

Iarbonel shifted, his throat bobbing. His eyes were ringed both black and red, dark hair overgrown by mortal standards and tangling near the tops of his rounded ears. Perhaps that was why he resembled the boy he'd been. The kindest of all Nemed's kin with a penchant for bad luck. Aisling had spent various evenings plucking leaves from his tangle of curls, mending the holes in his boots, and wiping tears from the sharp edge of his cheeks. Afterward, he'd smile at her and pat her on the head—a gesture she'd pretended to despise at the time.

Iarbonel set the tray on the floor. For the first time, he met Aisling's eyes, appraising her carefully. Slowly, he pushed the tray toward her, and once it tapped against her knees, he snatched back his hand.

Aisling glared at the plate and mug he'd offered. Both her tastes and appetite had long since been elevated by her fae blood, and so, this meal was no better than the dirt beneath her fingernails.

Iarbonel kneeled before her, just out of reach if Aisling straightened the chains.

"You used to wake like that when you were a child," he said.

Aisling looked up.

"It would scare me half to death," he continued.

Aisling's brow furrowed. "I always did frighten," she explained for him.

Iarbonel stiffened, considering Aisling more closely. She'd given him four words.

Her brother collected himself, shaking his head. "What? No, I was scared *for* you, Ash."

*Ash.*

Aisling sat on her heels where she kneeled, the chains chinking as she moved.

"Half because, if father knew you'd woken us, he'd lash you.

And half because I feared the evil the fae might reap upon my túath. My clann. That the nightmares I'd sworn my life to defeat, would invade our home and harm those I loved most."

Iarbonel stared vacantly at the floorboards groaning beneath them. He ran a hand through his hair, exposing burns, blisters, and cuts along the pale edges of each finger.

He breathed slowly—far slower than the fae. Aisling felt his exhaustion. His shoulders hung as if burdened by an invisible behemoth. Something loud and growing, pressing down on his mortal will.

He breathed a laugh, but it was humorless.

"I wish I could have corrupted my senseless naivety then and there," he said. "Because the fae indeed reaped my sister." His breath shook. "Reaped my sister at the will of my blood."

Aisling clenched her jaw. Her chest ached, the pain of which glossed her eyes with unwelcome tears.

"*Our* blood," Aisling corrected. "We were one, then. Or so I believed."

Both brother and sister were silent for several breaths. The churning of the Ashild a chorus of hushed voices as it frothed outside their ship.

"Do not believe us. Do not forgive us, sister," Iarbonel said, unfurling from his position. "Fight us to the death."

## CHAPTER XXXVII

### LIR

Doorways were dangerous magic. Slipping through a pond, a lake, a fountain, a pool was only possible by the will of a powerful forge-born creature. Beings such as the Lady, Danu, a Sidhe sovereign, or the gods themselves. One day, if Aisling survived the war, she, too, would command the gateways that transcended time, space, and realm.

Lir, Fionn, Niamh, Galad, Gilrel, Peitho, and Filverel stood before the first and largest half of the gateway to the Other. A colossal dream tree towered over them at the center of an emerald meadow. Larger than Danu herself, the tree was a beast, groaning while its highest branches danced beneath Niamh's storms. It gulped the showers insatiably, humming strangely to itself. The dream tree didn't speak to Lir as the forest and its guardians usually did. It was possessed by old magic—the *draiocht* of beings who, at the beginning of all things, spoke no tongue.

The other half grew in the mortal realm: Leshy.

"There must be another way." Peitho spoke first, sunset tresses whipping across her face as she stared up at the tree.

Gilrel cleared her throat beside the Sidhe princess, unsheathing her blade.

"Let it be me who travels through," the pine marten volunteered, masking her fear well.

"It's my mistake to rectify." Fionn stepped forward, clenching his fists at his sides.

Lir traced the tip of his fangs with his tongue. He said not a word, but he'd finish what he'd begun at Castle Yillen if Fionn took another step toward the dream tree.

Niamh shook her head, pulling a blade from the sapphire scabbard at her hip. Sarwen, the original mortal reaper—an enchanted sword of legendary proportions and the twin to Aisling's blade.

"Only one of you can travel through the gateway," Niamh said, her voice blending with the thunderstorm. "Aisling's whereabouts are still unknown to us and so, I bear no anchor to guide the passage. Whosoever voyages past these doors, risks error, death, or an eternity stuck between worlds."

Niamh raised Sarwen above her head and lightning struck its tip.

Peitho reached for Gilrel, pulling her back and away from Niamh's power. In that moment, it felt as if the whole universe spun around Niamh. She, the core of the Forge.

"*Esanti tenaska less track nu,*" Niamh chanted in Rún, thunder mixing with the feminine lilt of her voice.

The dream tree shook. Its roots writhed beneath the earth, stirring the energy of the grass, the soil, the flowers, and the natural world it fed. Before their eyes, the body of the tree morphed. Like a bundle of snakes it moved, parting at the center until they could see through to the other side. A giant threshold made from the heart of the tree at Niamh's command.

The gateway was open.

Lir could feel the *draiocht* breathing through the ancient

lungs of the tree. Its breath rattled with age, heaving to keep the doors open at its center.

"It is done," Niamh said, dropping Sarwen before her. She swayed, knees almost buckling before Galad stepped forward and held the Seelie queen upright. A trickle of blood spilling from her nostrils.

"Does it always require this much strength?" Filverel asked. "To open the gateway?"

Niamh winced, gathering herself.

"I am the gate, and it is me," she said. "But it is also itself."

Filverel, Gilrel, Galad, and Peitho exchanged glances, not understanding.

"When it wishes, the gateway opens with little effort. *Lá Brear* and *Samhain* are examples of this. But when it would rather remain closed—when it does not wish to pry open its mouth —then yes, it requires this much strength," Niamh explained.

A muscle flashed across Lir's jaw.

"Then why does the gate protest now?" Filverel continued, considering the roots still slithering back into place.

"I don't know," Niamh confessed, finding her footing once more and straightening. "Yet, I sense it's afraid."

The entire party glanced at one another now. A chill ran through each of them, sending shivers down their spines. There was a spirit present that hadn't been there before. When Niamh had opened the gateway, so, too, did she wake something else. They each felt its consciousness and tasted its fear.

Something was coming, and the gateway understood.

"Lir," Niamh called.

Lir flicked his eyes to the Seelie queen.

"Unfortunately, you're the most likely to survive," Niamh said. "Your *caera* bonds you to Aisling, and so, let that be your guide as you pass."

Lir worked his jaw. He felt that intangible cord pulling at

his chest, straining painfully. Thoughts of her haunted him, tightening the cord. A violet phantom finding him in every breath the day sighed before its end. And so, he found himself eagerly awaiting the agony loving her inspired.

The rest remained quiet, bracing themselves against Niamh's cloudburst. Fionn, however, scalded Lir's periphery with his icy glare. But when Lir half expected his brother to protest, he did not. Perhaps it was the shame of having failed to protect Aisling, or perhaps Fionn knew the alternative wasn't possible. Either way, Lir rejoiced in the silence.

Lir dropped his arms from where they'd been crossed at his chest. He reached back with both arms, unsheathing his axes. He spun the hafts between his fingers, familiarizing himself with their balance.

"Glad we agree," Lir said. "I was prepared to resort to the blade had we not."

Lir stepped forward and toward the dream tree. The beast swayed, shuddering in the presence of the Sidhe king. Intangibly, it whispered to itself.

Lir waited, looking into the gateway.

To those who were blind to magic, the gateway appeared like an old, gnarled tree with a giant split at its center. An opening that widened at the bottom and thinned into a sharp archway, curving at its middle. Beyond, was nothing more than the field in which they stood.

But Lir felt its magic already familiarizing itself with him. Vibrations that thrummed through the earth. The *draiocht* was monstrous here, rolling over like bears in deep sleep.

"Return swiftly," Galad said.

"Both of you," Peitho chimed.

They all looked up at him, expressions solemn. For a moment, Lir half wondered why, and then it dawned on him: the risk he was undergoing was of mortal consequence. He'd hardly cared, not only willing but eager to give his life for

Aisling. And so, Lir realized, he'd forgotten the vows he'd sworn to Annwyn: his kingdom and the heart of the Sidhe. His life didn't belong only to Aisling, even if his heart did. All which made a liar of Lir. For it dawned on the Sidhe king that, if forced to choose, he'd always choose Aisling. As he did now.

Lir winced, resisting the urge to grab his chest.

The Sidhe king met Galad's eyes. His first knight nodded his head, and Lir tipped his chin in response.

Nothing more was said as Lir turned and stepped through the gateway.

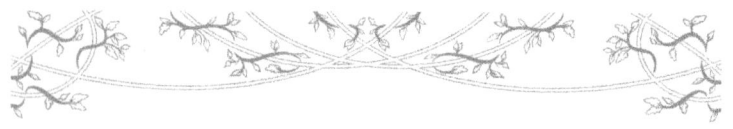

# CHAPTER XXXVIII

AISLING

"Sister," Starn spat from the doorway.

Aisling sat on the floor of the room, back against the wall. She didn't care to lift her head, only her eyes in acknowledgement.

"Rise," he commanded. "Your presence has been requested on the main deck."

Aisling looked up then. She searched past Starn and at the staircase beyond where torchlight, the taste of salt, and stars spilled from above. Aisling wasn't certain how long she'd been held captive. There was scarcely any light, and the ocean rocked her to sleep at odd hours. And so, an opportunity—the *possibility* of fresh air—sent Aisling's heart racing.

Aisling stood, hiding the quivering of her knees after days cooped up.

Starn unhooked the chains from the walls of her cabin. He carried them like a leash, tight and wrapped around his wrists.

Her brother led her up the stairwell and onto the main deck.

Aisling was fed a second life when the waxing moon's light embraced her. She inhaled, eager to gulp breaths full of ocean air. The chains around her wrists suddenly became less heavy.

But where Aisling expected to be lost in a sea of stars at the center of the Ashild, she rather found herself drifting along the river roads of some eastern mortal kingdom that spilled into the Silver Sea.

The midnight black of evening's cloak was gilded by the lanterns hanging on strings between the kingdom's sharp towers, ornate domes, every narrow thoroughfare, and even across the great width of the river on which they sailed. Hundreds of mortal ships surrounded the one in which they bobbed, cannons loaded with iron, fire-laced ammunition.

Rain misted over the landscape, dusting the world in shimmers.

"Daughter." Nemed greeted Aisling from the stern castle. The whole crew paused or slowed their business, turning to lay eyes on Aisling for themselves. Although the reprieve was slight, Aisling relished what fresh air surrounded her for the stench of iron and mortality fought for attention amongst her senses. Aisling frowned, wrinkling her nose as Starn pulled her toward their father.

They climbed two sets of ladders until Aisling faced her father atop the stern castle. They looked out over the ship, watching as the crew busied themselves once more. Iarbonel, Fergus, and Annind worked alongside the crew or spoke amongst one another. Clodagh, on the other hand, breathed deeply at the edge of the ship, pale with sea sickness.

"Tell me, Aisling, how does one hunt a myth?" her father asked. His violet eyes twinkled despite their age.

"You take it by force," Starn said, smirking to himself.

Aisling exhaled. "You find its maker," she corrected.

"Precisely," Nemed said. Starn's smile fell, replaced with a familiar scowl.

"There are countless legends of the gateways to the spirit realm," Nemed said. "Most of Tilren's folktales involve a 'crossing over.' But how is it done? Well, you enter as you would anywhere else," Nemed said. "Through the front door."

Aisling glanced at the inky waters beneath the belly of the ship and beyond. They rocked side to side, jagged and tipped with the gold light from above. The ocean—one of the twin gods' eldest sons—both arcane depth and breathtaking beauty.

"The ocean is vast, father," Aisling said, but her eyes drifted to the mist veiling their passage, dappling her cheeks with dew. Every droplet pricked her skin, sending shivers down her spine.

"Aye," he acknowledged, "but a myth is vain, daughter. Legends are vanity incarnate. They refuse to be ignored. They crave your attention. And they long to be caught in the light." Nemed's eyes followed Aisling's, appraising the sheets of rain.

Niamh's rain.

"The Silver Sea rests between three storm lands in the east and we are at the center of it. Or," Nemed reconsidered, stroking his chin, "close to it. With the help of your rescuers, we'll arrive within a week's time if not sooner."

Aisling swallowed the lump in her throat. Her tongue had run dry, and her eyes burned.

"Why are you telling me this?" Aisling asked, doing her best to conceal the dread in her voice.

"Because when we lay waste to the spirit world, destroy their gate, and reclaim all that is rightfully mankind's"—Nemed looked his daughter in the eyes—"you will not be here. But I wanted you to know."

Aisling didn't flinch. She steeled herself, straightening and keeping her father's stare.

"No," Aisling admitted, "because you recount dreams, father. But I only exist in your nightmares."

Nemed's expression shuttered with emotion. His brows knotted, eyes flicking to the iron cuffs at Aisling's wrists that prevented her from casting magic.

Before either could speak another word, a bell rang from

four different towers in the kingdom. The figures that speckled the landscape hurried indoors, slamming shutters, and locking doors.

Several shouts erupted across the ship and panic descended. Half the crew gaped at the surrounding kingdom, mouths hanging open at what traveled in their direction.

Aisling, Nemed, and Starn followed their line of sight.

As the ship floated, a dense fog rolled through the kingdom, across the river and toward their ships. It whispered frantically, taking odd and jagged shapes uncharacteristic of natural fog. Aisling was the first to feel it: the ripple of the *draiocht* as it spilled from a fresh source.

"By the Forge," Aisling cursed beneath her breath.

"What is it?" Starn snapped, his voice breaking. "What have you summoned, fae?!"

Aisling shook her head silently, watching with wide eyes as the fog approached more quickly. The crew busied themselves, loading the cannons and lifting the sails. Yet, nothing could prevent what was coming. Nothing could be done.

Aisling knew not its name, but she knew its kind: Unseelie.

The fog arrived and it creeped up the belly of their ships. Various men released the cannons, leaped overboard, or fought to fit below deck in a panic. They struck one another in the frenzy, chaos descending.

Clodagh was escorted first by both Fergus and Annind, speaking frantically into the collars of their tunics.

Starn summoned his phantom blade from where it hung on the main deck, and Nemed gripped the banister of the stern castle.

"Onward!" Nemed shouted, directing the ship to sail forward and swiftly. But it was too late.

The fog creeped over the lip of their ship. It rolled in slowly, building anticipation before it brushed the boot of the first crewman remaining above deck. In a heartbeat, the fog snatched the man in a blur of blood and teeth and white mist, leaving nothing but splatter and ichor in its place.

The crew screamed, shouting prayers and begging for their lives.

"Release my bindings," Aisling growled, lifting the iron fists wrapped tightly around her hands.

"Have you gone mad?" Starn simmered, face red with fear and anger alike. "None have forgotten what you did to the last ship you and I shared."

Aisling's mind flashed back to Dagfin's ship, the *Starling*. Then, they'd been attacked by merrow, and to survive, to spare the ship and themselves, Aisling had lit the entire galleon on fire. And while she'd spared the lives of her clann, herself, and most importantly Dagfin, she'd forsaken the lives of the rest of the crew.

"Then you'll remember you're in debt to me," Aisling bit back. "For had I not intervened, you wouldn't be standing here today... unfortunately."

Nemed shoved the skipper standing before the wheel of the ship and took hold of it himself.

"Your shackles remain, daughter," her father said, jerking the wheel to the right. The ship obeyed, swinging from one side to the other.

Aisling flew across the stern castle, slamming into the side of the balustrade with her hip.

She seethed, watching as the fog continued to devour more crew members. Nemed couldn't outsail or outrun this Unseelie. Whatever it was, it was determined to devour them whole, and they had nowhere to run, nowhere to hide, and no way to fight the fog.

Aisling slammed her fists against the mizzenmast. The iron fists didn't bend nor dent. Instead, her bones rattled inside, forcing a scream from her lips.

Starn whipped his head in her direction, raising his phantom blade at Aisling's throat.

"Attempt something like that again and I'll sever your hands off altogether," he yelled, veins bulging at his neck and forehead.

Aisling slapped the blade from where it floated, poised before her. It clattered to the ground where Starn hadn't expected retaliation. Her brother, swiftly, lifted it once more and drove it between Aisling's eyes.

"Starn!" Nemed shouted, staring at them over his shoulder. Aisling wasn't certain how they'd cut the curse breaker from her, but she assumed it wasn't this way.

Aisling dodged the onslaught, stepping lithely to the side. Starn watched her move, eyes growing wide. Her brother swung again, this time for the legs. Aisling leaped, landing on her feet and swinging at the blade again. She knocked it to the side and even after the sword clanked against the floorboards, it continued to slide with momentum, falling off the stern castle and onto the main deck.

Aisling lunged for her brother, throwing the iron fists at his temples.

Starn staggered backward, clumsily avoiding her attacks.

"Enough!" he grunted as he moved his head side to side, but Aisling persisted, pushed her brother until his back was against the balustrade, threatening to send him off the edge in pursuit of his phantom blade.

"Where's your magic, brother?" Aisling asked. "Where's the Lady to help you now?"

She threw another punch, twisting with her entire body as Peitho had shown her. At last, the attempt hit. Her fist collided into the side of his face, sending Starn reeling. The top half of his body was backward and horizontal over the railing.

Aisling, huffing with exertion, took a step back.

Starn froze. As slow as the moon wanes, her brother turned to face her. Already the blow had painted an ugly, purpled gash across his cheekbone. He touched it gently with his fingertips, eyes becoming saucers when they spotted the blood at the tips of his fingers.

He met Aisling's eyes.

"You'll regret that," he said, so softly it was almost a whisper.

The fog grew in their periphery, the ship rocking side to side in Nemed's desperation. Yet, Aisling's eyes remained glued to her brother's, fury pulsing between them.

"Perhaps," Aisling said, "but only that it wasn't fatal."

Starn shook with anger, the phantom blade rising behind him. It turned, sparkling between the bloodthirsty mists of the East.

The blade spun till its tip faced Aisling. He screamed and the sword darted for Aisling's heart.

"That's enough, Starn!" Nemed boomed, but he couldn't let go of the wheel lest their ship spun into the city streets. He jerked the wheel and both Aisling and Starn were sent flying onto the main deck.

Aisling struggled to her feet, the weight of the iron fists bruising her wrists. She spun on her heel, biting through the pain of the fall. Starn was nowhere to be seen. The main deck was thick with fog and warm with death. Aisling held onto the main mast, slipping on the blood slick boards as the ship rocked.

"Where are you, sister?" Starn called, and from a distance, Aisling could see the glimmer of his phantom blade through the mist. He navigated carefully across the deck, averting his eyes from the men the fog devoured in his periphery.

Aisling pushed her back against the main mast. She considered climbing it or leaping overboard yet every direction spelled her name in death's hand. She couldn't climb with the iron fists, nor could she swim.

"Sister," Starn called in a sing-song voice, the same way he had when they were children. The same way he did in her nightmares. "Come out of hiding, little sister."

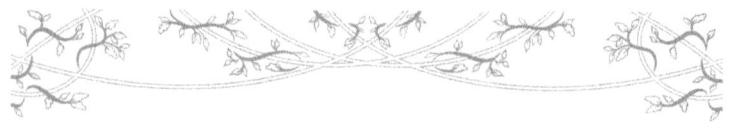

# CHAPTER XXXIX

## LIR

Traveling between worlds was an act of worship. One didn't slip between realms without feeling the guttural rattle of the gods' breath on your nape, the cosmic hum of the stars, or the vertigo of being flung like a leaf in a storm across spiritual bridges. But this time was different. Lir had no explicit direction he wished to travel. He only had *someone* he wished to travel toward. So, he clawed for the thread of fate that bound Aisling's soul to his, and once he'd taken hold, he didn't let go. His body flickering in and out of existence, bending and warping like a dream on the cusp of vanishing.

Lir woke in a bed of water, the surface glittering distantly above him. He blinked several times, allowing his mind to focus.

He tasted the water: salt, eastern spices, and rainwater churned by a forge-whittled ladle.

The Silver Sea.

A hundred or more ships bobbed close by, the shadow of their hulls like beasts surfacing for a breath of air. They reeked of iron, poisoning the waters in which he lay. But none so much as the largest ship of all at their center.

Lir swam toward the largest ship, ignoring the delirium, his blurry vision, or the ache in his centuries-old bones. He could feel the pounding of her heart, smell her perfume, and hear her heavy breath. He was close.

Lir emerged from the sea, wiping his dark hair from his eyes. Fog rolled atop the surface of beetle-black waters. It spoke manically, snapping its chops and spraying the seas with the foam that gathered at the corner of its fiendish lips.

The ceo. An Eastern Unseelie species that lacked sentience. It only wished to devour and to spread, claiming the lives of those it ate—dooming its victims to become that which reaped its life without mercy.

Lir cursed. The ceo had already skulked through the mortal village that surrounded the river in which he swam, climbing over the edge of the iron ship where he was certain Aisling was being held captive.

Lir's *draiocht* growled, thrashing inside and desperate to be freed. The moment the rabbit confessed Aisling was missing, Lir had feared it was mortal mischief at play. And of course, no such mischief could be executed without the Lady's help.

Lir fumed, unsheathing his axes and slamming one into the side of the ship. He climbed up its side, his pointed ears overhearing the screeching of those hiding below deck the moment his blades punctured the ship's iron and wood.

He used his second axe as a stepping stone so he could leap over the edge when the time was right. For now, he peered through the railing at the fore-deck like a wolf in wait.

# CHAPTER XL

## AISLING

Aisling hid in the mist, stepping over corpses and puddles of blood.

"Come out, come out, sister," Starn continued to call. His voice carried a cruel smile—as if he relished the torment her eldest brother had a penchant for inspiring.

Aisling saw the glimmer of his phantom blade, dancing across the main deck in search of her. It swept through the mist and cut past the Unseelie hunched over a body in a mass of wispy white and teeth.

"Aisling," he called for her. His voice accompanied by the screams, groans, and whispering of both mortal man and Unseelie.

Aisling sucked in a breath. Her iron fists were growing heavier by the minute and her head throbbed. Nevertheless, her adrenaline quieted her pains—the taste of revenge in the air renewing her might.

"You always lost at these games," he said, his voice closer this time. Aisling tiptoed across the deck, cringing at the occasional clank of her chains dragging behind her. "You never could stop giggling when you were meant to be hiding."

Aisling crouched behind three barrels pressed against the wall of the fore-deck.

"The anticipation of being caught was almost as satisfying as the hunt itself," she said, gathering the loose chains and bundling them in her arms.

Between the mist, Aisling saw Starn's silhouette. He paused at the sound of her voice, cocking his head to the side to gauge its direction. The phantom blade following suit.

"Did you always know?" Starn asked. "Did you always know you'd meet this fate? Did you always anticipate betraying your túath? Your blood?"

Aisling perked up, ensuring she'd heard correctly.

"Betray my túath?" she repeated.

Starn cut more quickly between the mist, slicing through another Unseelie that blocked his path.

"To think I *admired* you the day you wed yourself in sacrifice to the fae," Starn spat, drawing closer to her. "The way you embraced your duty to mankind despite yourself."

Aisling's heart twisted.

*Admired.*

How many years had she longed to be recognized by her clann? How many years had she thirsted for that very word to spill from her clann's lips? How desperately she'd craved their validation, the recognition she wasn't as inept as she'd felt all her life.

"Be honest with yourself, brother," Aisling said, her voice stronger and more leveled than she anticipated. "You were not glad of my sacrifice. You were glad to be rid of me."

Aisling unfurled from where she crouched behind the barrels and darted toward the opposite side of the ship. And with her chains tangled in her arms, her progress was much quieter.

"I loved you," Starn said, his voice different. Aisling searched for him through the mist, knocked to the ground by four or so mortal crewmen fleeing from the Unseelie. They'd seemingly materialized out of nowhere, knocking her off her feet and leading the Unseelie right toward her with the crash of her chains on the floorboards.

The creature loomed over her, sniffing her like a hound.

Aisling resisted the urge to scream lest she led Starn right to her. The mist cackled, studying Aisling more closely. The sorceress couldn't wield her *draiocht* with her hands cuffed in iron and bore no blade to defend herself. The mist opened its mouth—or what appeared like a mouth—twinkling with a collection of sharp fangs. It inhaled, moaning to itself before chomping down on Aisling. Yet, the timbre of the creature's voice sounded... familiar.

Danu.

The empress of the dryads was searching for her and... and... Aisling couldn't remember who else the empress searched for alongside Aisling—a gap in her mind that grew the more she tried to remember. Aisling knew Danu was eager to dethrone the Sidhe king of the greenwood, Lir, and lead the Unseelie herself. Perhaps it was his name that evaded her.

Aisling shook her head, gritted her teeth as the mist leaned in closer, tangling itself between the knots in her matted tresses. Aisling could smell its *draiocht*, more so than most Unseelie. This was an emissary. A messenger on behalf of the empress.

Danu had aligned herself with the Lady in some capacity, their shared hatred of Aisling, binding their cause.

Aisling clenched her jaw and slowly grabbed the chains once more. The ship jolted to the right, Nemed throwing the ship to its side to avoid the edge of the city.

The mist twitched, too distracted by Aisling's perfume to notice her iron fists clumsily collecting the chains once more.

"Aisling," Starn called.

Aisling leaped to her feet, swinging the chains attached to her iron fists. The chains launched forward, their iron cutting through the mist that'd cornered her. The Unseelie screeched, bleeding black before it evaporated entirely.

Aisling enjoyed a single breath of victory before Starn appeared between the sheets of white.

"I loved Aisling," Starn said, expression void of emotion as the fog brushed his cheeks. "And you destroyed her." Starn held Aisling's eyes. "Nevertheless, justice prevails. I'll savor your death the way you savored my sister's."

Starn's phantom blade winked at Aisling beside him. The crown prince nodded his head once and the blade shot toward Aisling.

Aisling staggered back, raising her iron fists to block the strike.

Yet, the blow never came.

Aisling opened her eyes the same moment two blades crashed against one another. They rang out, piercing her ears and sparking.

Starn's phantom blade whacked into the side of the hull, followed by another: an axe, warped by the woodland.

Aisling lowered her arms, both she and Starn's attention shooting toward a figure between the mist.

Taller than any man Aisling had ever laid eyes on, he was breathtaking. Battle-dark hair falling into eyes possessed by forest dreams and nightmares alike. His pointed ears and tattooed throat were bejeweled by wild gemstones and freshly cut gold chains. His cologne was heathen's magic: unadulterated and ladled from the heart of the Forge itself. His every breath, haunted by the collective susurration of the oaks, the yews, and the alders.

Lir.

His name scraped and clawed through the walls in Aisling's mind, pounding at the gates to be let in. Anduril stayed quiet this time, chained by the iron that suffocated all magic.

The Sidhe king's axe hit the hull but immediately spun

back, flying toward its keeper. Lir caught the spinning blade deftly, never taking his eyes off Aisling.

"I believe you have something that's mine," Lir said, eyes flicking to Starn.

The depth of his voice flooded through Aisling, river-black and laced with the foam of its rush. It carried the familiar Sidhe accent, aged like wine for over a millennium.

The Unseelie still hovered at the periphery of the ship, but Aisling could now smell their fear—teeth chattering, mouths gaping, they shuddered from the Sidhe king.

To Aisling's surprise, Starn smiled.

"You're as punctual as ever, fae," Starn sneered.

And as if prompted, the ship slowed, and Aisling heard a familiar "stomp and drag" in the silence that followed such violence. The rest of the mortal ships were silent and dark, rocking along the current aimlessly as ghostly galleons.

Nemed limped toward them through the fog on his iron prosthetic. His violet eyes glittered knowingly, soaking in the sight of the legendary dark lord standing on his very ship in the Silver Sea.

"How I've longed for this moment," Nemed said, nodding his head toward Lir in greeting.

"The feeling isn't mutual," Lir said, the tilt of his head arrogance personified.

There was something so familiar about the way he moved, spoke, looked at her. She was pulled to him by an invisible current, threatening to drown her at the edge of the rift should she resist. Yet, her mind cloaked any memory they shared.

Nemed scoffed.

"On how many battlefields have we met, *mo Damh Bán?*" Nemed asked, stepping closer. He said his Sidhe title mockingly.

Lir rolled his neck.

"I haven't been counting," the Sidhe king said.

"We could end this now," Nemed continued. "Let us, high king to high king, end this now. The Aisling you wedded is no longer. She's been replaced by something insatiable and uncontrollable. Any hopes you or the Aos Sí have of mastering her abilities is both fruitless and futile. There was a reason Aisling was never given a blade, a key to Tilren's gates, or a crown gods forbid. She is reckless, wild, and the creature that devoured her is worse. She will ruin the Aos Sí and the mortals alike. Surrender, *mo Damh Bán*. Surrender and return to your caves to lick your wounds."

Lir grinned, ear to ear. His fangs sparkled despite the gray-clad skies.

"For a millennium I have cut through mortal legions, wept over my slain kin, and shielded Annwyn from your fires. My wings have been ripped from my back, my skin burned; iron swords have been pulled from my chest. And by far, the worst of my suffering has been dealt not by the hands of humankind, but by your daughter." Lir's eyes flashed to Aisling. "And I'll happily forsake those millennia," Lir said, "for her."

Aisling's eyes burned. Her tear ducts smoked. She wasn't certain why or for what reason but her *draiocht* flailed inside, roaring and scratching to be released in the presence of this Sidhe king. She felt it powerfully, wildly, insatiably. His words tangling roots around her heart until she couldn't stand its feral beating.

Nemed and Starn exchanged a knowing glance, lips curling.

"I was hoping you wouldn't surrender," Nemed confessed. "But as a gentleman, I had to, at the very least, offer you an alternative to suffering."

Lir licked his fangs.

"Is this our cue to fight to the death?" the Sidhe king asked, spinning the haft of his right axe in his hand.

"Not quite," Nemed said. "You're going to lead us to the gateway between our realm and yours and then you're going to help us carve the curse breaker from your bride's heart."

Aisling was almost knocked off balance.

Bride.

Bride.

Bride.

Anduril was quiet, his voice smothered by the iron and unable to contradict the feelings spiraling inside her chest.

Lir's eyes flicked to her. They shone inhumanly, spilling over the brim with shadowed *draiocht*. But for a breath, something heart-wrenchingly vulnerable swept his expression, rendering Aisling weak at the knees.

Why couldn't she understand? Why couldn't she remember? Only a few days ago, everything had been clear. Now the past, the present, and the future were muddled. Faces and voices fighting for attention in her mind, all claiming to speak the truth.

"So, the Lady has filled your minds with fantasies," Lir said, his voice betraying nothing.

"You cannot lie, fae, and so do not attempt to. I know the truth of the gateway and it will burn before my eyes," Nemed said.

Iarbonel, Fergus, and Annind opened the door that led below deck. Slowly, they emerged, searching the fog for the Unseelie that shuddered there. Briefly, Aisling locked eyes with Iarbonel. He dropped his gaze almost immediately—he, Fergus, and Annind, swallowing at the sight of the Sidhe king aboard their ship. They each carried a weapon, perhaps prepared or afraid of what they'd find above deck after the Unseelie onslaught.

"We'll see," Lir said.

Nemed nodded his head, and all four brothers swarmed the

Sidhe king. Starn's phantom blade swung for him, gliding through the air masterfully.

Aisling smoked madly, further veiling everyone's sight as they sprang. Yet, Lir slipped between Aisling's brothers and their blows with ease, throwing his axes at Aisling instead.

The axes cut through the air like a sparrow.

They struck Aisling's iron fists with alarming accuracy, splintering the metal like nothing had before. They shattered and clattered against the ship's deck.

Aisling's *draiocht* burned, wasting not a moment to rise up her throat and into the world. Aisling exploded into flames, the iron fists blasting off her hands.

Lir dove for her, recklessly taking hold of her flaming body, able to withstand her *draiocht* in a way he couldn't before their consummation.

*Consummation.* The image of his mouth on her neck, her palms on his muscled abdomen, his need entering her slowly and fully, lit her thoughts on fire.

Aisling's mind was ripping in two, memories bubbling to the surface before popping and disappearing. Anduril woke then, the chains removed, desperately making up for lost time. The belt shone brightly, burning her flesh and begging for attention.

Nevertheless, Lir held her tighter as he flung them both off the ship.

They flew over the edge and into the waters. Immediately, the Silver Sea extinguished her *draiocht*. Lir pulled her through the mist, hands around her waist as he swam, diving deep below the surface of the water, gritting his teeth for Anduril's ringing.

Aisling looked back only once as they escaped. And only once did she see her brother's, Iarbonel's face, staring after her through the sight in his crossbow.

He had a clear shot. Aisling was still close enough to be stopped, and Lir's hands were wrapped around her and not his axes.

Aisling held her breath, waiting for the iron bolt.

Iarbonel lowered the crossbow, removing his finger from the trigger.

"*Fight us to the death*," Aisling repeated in her mind as he disappeared between the fog. And she would.

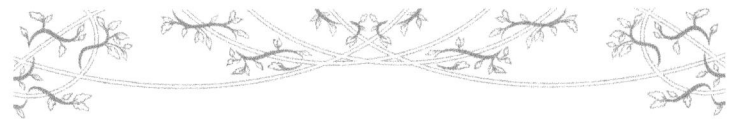

## CHAPTER XLI

AISLING

Silence cradled the sorceress and the Sidhe king as they descended.

Lir carried her deep beneath the waves till the surface glittered distantly above. He met her eyes, squeezing her more tightly. The Sidhe king tapped his throat, reminding Aisling to use her *draiocht* so she could breathe beneath the waves. He demonstrated quickly, blooming *ellwyn—ellwyn*. This time, the word—the flower—triggered something inside her she couldn't quite describe. *Ellwyn* grew between her curls, tickling her cheeks when she smiled wider. An expression Lir stared at for a beat longer than anticipated.

With what strength remained, Aisling summoned her *draiocht*. She inhaled deeply, lungs hot.

This all felt so... familiar. Learning to breathe beneath the water through her *draiocht*, *ellwyn*, Lir. So, why couldn't Aisling remember?

Lir pressed Aisling against his chest and closed his eyes.

The sea flipped upside down, stretching like sap between a bear's paws. Aisling and Lir shot forward or backward; Aisling wasn't certain. There was no up or down, left or right. Only forward and toward the destination Lir had in mind.

## CHAPTER XLII

AISLING

Sapling satin curtains swayed gently in a warm, summer breeze. Aisling blinked, doing her best to focus. The room smelled of plums and sugared teas. Aisling gripped the bed on either side of her, fingers filled with sable-soft pelts.

"Ssh!" a small voice hushed. "She's waking!"

Aisling bolted upright, hands blazing like twin comets.

"*Ell—*" another voice started, stopping itself short. "Aisling," the voice finished.

Aisling turned, coming face to face with the Sidhe king of the greenwood. He bent over the bed, one arm leaning against the headboard carved from the trunk of a plum tree, its branches, leaves, and bulbs, stretching across Aisling like a canopy.

Aisling extinguished her *draiocht*.

For whatever reason, the Sidhe king's place in her memory continued to elude her now. Nevertheless, he'd aided her in her escape, lived up to his title as her knight, and that was sufficient to win him more of her trust. For now.

"Where am I?" she asked, searching the bedroom in which she lay.

Lir's expression flickered, and had Aisling blinked, she would've missed it: a moment of sincere concern gone before she could make sense of it. His bitter disdain for her, returned.

The chamber was empty save for several pine martens cowering from Aisling behind the curtains. They bore a striking resemblance to Gilrel and carried trays full of tea, buttered rolls, truffle cakes, and goblets full of Leshy's tears. But the tables at her bedside were strewn with bandages and salves.

"We're in the Simril Glade," Lir said, "a haven hidden in the wilds of the mortal plane for the forge-born."

Aisling stood from the bed and approached the windows. Robes sewn with threads of unicorn hairs spilled around her bare ankles. As white as mourning and as delicate as the death that precedes it.

Aisling admired the handiwork, smiling at the martens. Surely, it'd been their gentle hands that'd cleaned, mended, and dressed her.

The martens squealed when she acknowledged them, looking to Lir for guidance.

The Sidhe king nodded his head. "Leave us."

The little beasts scurried past, gently shutting the door behind them as they took their leave.

"Do they live here?" Aisling asked, tipping her head in the direction the martens had fled.

"In a way," Lir said. "They're changelings."

"Unseelie." Aisling knew.

Lir nodded his head. "Unseelie that aid the passage of bairns passed too soon, helping them onto the galleon that'll sail them into the misty afterlife of the Other. So, too, do they care for them here: in the Simril Glade."

Lir didn't flinch, but his voice thickened. A change so subtle, Aisling was surprised she'd noticed it at all.

"A nursery," Aisling conjectured. "But they look like common beasts."

Lir moved his hands into his pockets.

"They slip into new forms depending on their audience. Whatever shape will bring comfort to those they wish to care for is the form they'll inhabit."

Aisling stared at the shut door long after the changelings left, wondering why, of all places, Lir would bring her here.

At last, she inhaled and pushed apart the curtains.

She stood in a sharp, ornate tower chiseled from the bones of opals. Every speck of the tower was carved by the methodical, precise, and whimsical fingers of the Sidhe, narrating tales of beasts, forests, and winged knights with glowing sabers. The tower grew from the center of a crystal-clear pool, filled to the brim by the sleek silver waterfall slipping over beds of wildflowers and moss. The rest was dense forest populated by fruitful plum trees, soft glowing orbs drifting aimlessly, and the hum of insects.

Most marvelous of all, however, were the clear skies up above.

The moon sighed, laying its head on quilts of clouds, dreaming up stars that scattered across the sky.

Aisling leaned out and over the edge of her window, drinking up the view for several moments.

"Do you..." Lir began, startling Aisling. He moved closer to her, joining her at her side by the window. "Do you feel alright?" he asked.

Aisling appraised herself, inspecting the bandages around her wrists, hands, and abdomen with her eyes. Indeed, her wounds still hurt her. Yet, the fresh air here was enough to strengthen her by the breath full—void of either the mortal flesh or iron she'd been forced to inhale.

"Aye," Aisling replied, meeting Lir's eyes. "And I'm eager to return to the Isle of Rain."

This close, Lir was nightmarish in his beauty. He carried himself with both feline elegance and the promise of brutal violence. Both enough to bring most people to their knees at the mere sight of him. But his eyes grew deeper the longer Aisling looked, pulling her into a forest of shadows and bloodthirsty beasts till she couldn't find the way back.

Aisling dropped her gaze as if burned by the image of him. And if Lir noticed, he didn't react.

"We'll return you to Castle Yillen as soon as you've gathered your strength," he said, crossing his arms over his chest.

Aisling chewed on her bottom lip. "Did you bring me here?" she asked.

Lir looked at her, shifting slightly.

"Yes," he confessed.

"Thank you," Aisling said. "Thank you for helping me."

Cautiously, Lir studied her with his eyes, never meeting her own. He traced her wounds, her shoulders, her brushed hair, her flushed cheeks. His gaze lingering on the edge of her lips.

Aisling swallowed.

"Do not thank me," he said after several quiet moments. "It's my oath."

"Why then did you bring me here? Weren't you meant to return me to Castle Yillen?" Aisling asked, gripping the windowsill more tightly. Her rational mind didn't trust Lir. Her mind insisted he was a stranger she'd scarcely spoken to—every memory of him, quick and slippery. And yet, her *draiocht* spun madly in his presence begging her to release it. A strange knowing that if she were not injured, exhausted, or spent, her magic would devour them both whole whilst in his presence. Was this the effect the high king had on everyone? Aisling shook her head, swatting away her thoughts.

*You're confused, tired, and lost*, Anduril said. *Do not believe the questions sprouting inside your mind now.*

"You needed to rest and regain your strength," Lir said. "As soon as you step foot in the Other, you'll need to focus on the Goblet once more. The Goblet of Lore is the only way to prevent the mortals from destroying the gateway. And with the fire hand close to discovering its location... simply put, the Forge and time are no longer aligned."

Aisling nodded her head in understanding. Still, his answer didn't satisfy her. He spun words like a spider spins its web, effortlessly snaring unsuspecting insects.

"And yet you brought me here?" Aisling pushed. "When our haste is of the utmost importance?"

Lir worked his jaw, staring out and over the forest—as if doing his best to avoid meeting her eyes.

"I—"

"You're wounded as well," Aisling conjectured, answering for him. Indeed, Lir no longer wore his intricate Sidhe leathers. Now he donned a loose knight ritter blouse, the strings undone so all his fae markings shone along his throat, collar, and the beginning of his broad chest. His abdomen narrowed tightly at the hips, belted by several humble, leather straps to secure his trousers. And still, his axes winked at his back, crossed like wings on his shoulder blades. But it was the gauze peeking beneath his ritter that caught Aisling's eye.

Burn bandages.

"*I've* wounded you," Aisling said.

Lir had leaped off the ship with Aisling swathed in flames. She'd smelled the burning of his flesh as they'd fallen into the sea, knotted together.

The Sidhe king had ventured to the mortal realm for her, rescued her, and held her despite her destructive magic. He'd sacrificed and risked a great deal, reminding Aisling of herself: she too—at one point in time—had risked everything for mankind. She recognized the obligation of duty on not only his crown but on his heart. Why had she never noticed such virtues before as she did now?

Lir hesitated, uncharacteristically tripping over his words.

"I've suffered greater pains," he said, not bothering to

acknowledge the blood still seeping through the gauze and staining his ritter.

"You need to rest," Aisling said. "More so than I."

Lir shook his head. "Kings do not rest. Especially now."

"Then why bring us here? When the fate of the Sidhe rests on my shoulders, why waste more time than we can afford?!" Aisling asked, raising her voice. Her ears burned, her temper flaring. The Sidhe king's actions confused her and so, she felt frustrated. She trusted him and yet knew he was keeping something from her. She simply wasn't certain what.

Lir ran a hand through his hair. He tugged on it, mirroring how Aisling felt.

"To allow you to heal," he said, repeating his answer from before.

"Liar," Aisling snapped. There was no reason for the Sidhe king to care for her health or her recovery. He needed her as did all the fae: as a weapon.

"Your impatience makes you ignorant," he said, his voice like dark velvet. "The Sidhe cannot tell a lie."

Aisling shuddered, praying to the Forge the Sidhe king didn't notice it.

"The truth is no match for your mischief, dark lord. As all the tales go," she said, steeling herself against him.

"Then you'd be wise not to provoke me," Lir growled. "Weren't you just thanking me for your rescue?"

Aisling bit down on her anger, holding it between her teeth.

"Rescue?" Aisling asked, baffled. "I would've escaped on my own given time. I thanked you for *helping* me and nothing more."

"What gratitude," he said, both words dripping with ire.

"You may be king, but I will not kiss your boots as do the others."

"Perhaps you'll kiss something else then?" he asked, his eyes darkening. He spoke in jest to ridicule her, to humiliate her, and yet, her abdomen stirred hotly at the sound of such intimacies on his lips. Their night at Dorkoth's tavern sprouting inside her mind and flushing her complexion.

"You disrespect me with those words."

Lir snapped toward her, meeting her eyes for the first time since she'd woken. He leaned closer to her, dropping his arms at his sides.

"So be it," he whispered—the sound of canopies rustling in the wind. And yet, it felt more like an arrow to the chest.

Aisling narrowed her eyes, her *draiocht* swelling like a storm in her throat. The tower shuddered with the energy pulsing through its bones. Their chests rising and falling with the pace of their breath in anger.

*A heart for a heart.* Aisling's mind flashed like lightning, descending into darkness a heartbeat later.

A knock sounded at the door.

Both Aisling and Lir whipped their heads in its direction, startled by the welcome distraction.

The door creaked open, and a pine marten stuck its head through the gap.

"*Mo Damh Bán, mo Lúra,*" it greeted them.

*Mo Lúra.* The title clung to Aisling's mind like talons in flesh, digging deeper the longer she considered it.

*It means bride of the forest,* someone had told her once.

*The memories are your imagination,* Anduril said. *Do not trust false visions.*

"The bell will ring within the hour, *mo Damh Bán,*" the pine marten said before bowing and slipping from the room again.

Aisling turned to the Sidhe king, expression filled with questions.

"Very well," Lir said. But when Aisling searched his face for answers, it'd already slammed shut. No longer was there anger, frustration, or mischief. It was void, washed clean, and without a trace of the temper she'd provoked.

Lir glanced at Aisling one last time. He lingered for a breath and grabbed her hand. Slowly, he brought her fingers to his mouth and kissed the backs of her knuckles. And to Aisling's surprise, she let him.

"*Ellwyn*," he said in parting, cold and cruel.

Aisling watched the door long after he'd left. And at last, she decided to follow him.

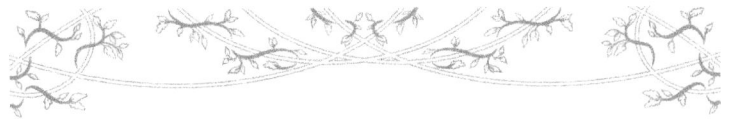

# CHAPTER XLIII

NIAMH

Niamh slipped through the corridors of Castle Yillen like a midnight breeze, howling through the stone. Her gown left a trail of water in its wake, cleaning the cobbles as she passed.

Tonight, she'd commanded her hair be braided from her face and a veil draped over the crown of her head. The fabric was made of morning mist and dappled with droplets that shimmered in the fae light. She was a specter, haunting her own castle and eager to go by unnoticed as she slipped into the Yillen libraries.

The books paused briefly to greet their newest guest.

Niamh bowed at the hips, dipping her chin with respect. Without further delay, the flying tomes, scrolls, and booklets resumed their hushed chatter and flight, proceeding through the labyrinth of shelves.

The Seelie queen sucked in a breath. She pushed past the desks, the mess, and the statues that adjusted their spectacles to get a better look at her. Still, she continued, eager to reach the darkest recesses of the library.

At last, she arrived, coming face to face with the behemoth statue of one of the twin gods. Arawn.

Niamh shivered. The vacant eyes of the statue measured her, incense curling from his lips like basilisks.

Immediately, the Seelie queen fell to her knees.

She folded the veil over her head and prayed in Rún.

"*By the Great Forge of Creation,*" Niamh began, "*I have sealed a bargain.*"

Silence filled the room, devouring even the distant chatter of books and the scraping of their flipped pages.

At last, the incense that curled in great wispy, milky tendrils thickened at his lips and surrounded the Seelie queen.

Niamh shivered, swallowing hard.

"*I request a morsel of your magic whilst you sleep,*" Niamh said.

The statue grumbled this time, shaking the library like the rattle of nearby thunder.

Niamh steeled herself, remembering why she scarcely visited the second god to pray. His magic was oppressive, heavy, and disorienting. Her mind felt clouded by the smoke, her lungs full of water, and her heart slowed by the vibration of the statue's breath. The gods slept but during prayer, it was believed they heard the voice of their kin. A practice Niamh dreaded after she'd learned the cost of a prayer asked wrongly.

"*I pray to return something to the Sidhe king of the greenwood that was lost,*" Niamh said all at once. "*If my bargain is met.*"

Silence again.

Niamh endured every terrible, quiet breath, waiting on the knife's edge of Arawn's judgment. The god grumbled, moaned, stirred, and watched, weighing each of Niamh's words with the patience of an immortal.

> *Seven storm seasons come but never go.*
> *Come child, I hear the wild horns blow.*
> *A western faerie weeps, broken by a lonely heart,*

*Cursed to the Other, destined to live apart.*

A voice sang from behind Niamh. Startled, the Seelie queen bolted upright from her kneeling position and turned to face her intruder.

Galad, Lir's first knight, leveled his gaze with the Seelie queen, singing "The Architect of Yillen" from memory.

> *Listen to the rain, child*
> *But don't be beguiled*
> *For she'll drown you in her tears*
> *Or she'll steal you away for years*
> *To her castle in the sky*
> *Just so that she might not be so lonely.*
> *If only, if only.*

Galad finished, the room descending into silence save for the perpetual beating of the outside storms.

"Your reputation precedes you, Lady," Galad said, calm as the woodland yarrow in midsummer. His sapphire eyes did not yield, his back straight, and his boots planted onto her marbled floors.

Niamh sat still as prey cornered as if feigning death. She didn't speak, did not move, did not blink until, at last, she'd collected herself.

Niamh straightened, throat bobbing as she swallowed.

"Where did you hear that song?" she asked.

Galad smiled. "Your libraries are a wealth of knowledge, my queen."

Niamh's nostrils flared, but she didn't protest nor deny the narrative of the melody. By blood, she was bound to speak the truth and alas, it'd already been sung.

Niamh rubbed her temples, the outside storms hushing into a "pitter patter" against the library's dome.

At last, the Seelie queen of Rain and high queen of the Other met Galad's eyes, measuring him before speaking.

"You interrupt me," Niamh said.

"I'm glad to hear it," Galad replied, holding his ground. His blue eyes were striking even when draped in shadow.

"You know not of what you speak," Niamh replied.

"Does it matter? There is no trust between us," Galad said.

"It will be your loss if you do not," Niamh argued.

"Is that so?" Galad challenged. "For as far as I can tell, a Seelie queen with a hidden motivation sneaks through her own castle when she believes none are looking, praying to a god that's slept for centuries."

"My only motivation is to aid Aisling," Niamh maintained, lifting her chin in defiance.

"So you pray for the gods to return something?" Galad asked.

"You cannot understand—"

"Maybe not," Galad confessed, "but it hardly matters. My duty is to protect both my king and queen. Stand before me and I'll not hesitate to repay your crimes—Seelie queen or not."

Niamh's eyes darted to Galad's sapphire blade strapped to his back. It winked when lightning flashed and lit the room, greeting the Seelie queen of Rain in turn.

They stood face to face for a long while, neither surrendering to the other's calculated suspicion. They were at a stalemate, accompanied by Arawn's thick breath and the beating of the outside storm.

"My relationship with Lir, his mother, and now his bride is complex," Niamh confessed, releasing a heavy breath. "I have fought against my lonely fate for as long as I can remember, forsaken at the edge of the world. I'd initially hoped Aisling would be my salvation from such a fate at long last. A gift from Ina after years of suffering alone in my castle. But the once-mortal princess did what no Sidhe, Seelie, or Unseelie could: she brought our worlds together."

Niamh shifted, her veil falling further down her back where she'd folded it over her head.

Galad held onto her every word, his eyes narrowed as he thought.

"Was it man who did that?" Galad asked. "Or Aisling?"

"Indeed, war has brought our Sidhe kingdoms to their knees and forced us to retreat together, here in the Other, but it is the hope we all place in Aisling that unifies us. That every beast, every forge-born creature, every monster, every Sidhe, and every bairn is looking to. Whether they be grisly monster or Seelie queen, we look to her now." Niamh gulped. "*I* look to her now. I must for she is our only hope."

Galad exhaled, exhaustion sitting heavily on his shoulders. His eyes studied the Seelie queen and then the statue of Arawn behind her. He weighed her for longer than Niamh believed necessary, but she tolerated it. She endured his judgment for she knew helping Aisling was the only path.

"You wish to align yourself with Aisling and Lir fully?" Galad asked.

"Aye," Niamh said. "I believe Aisling and I can close the gate before the mortals enter or destroy it entirely."

Galad ground his fangs against his bottom teeth, seemingly deep in thought. His sapphire blade, dimming in thought as well, it appeared.

"And yet, I maintain that you cannot be trusted," Galad insisted, crossing his arms over his chest.

Niamh frowned.

"Not a soul in this castle or Castle Annwyn is exempt from the tragedy of their own decisions," Niamh said. Every word weighed with exhaustion. "Filverel, Lir's advisor," Niamh called out. "Had your king listened to his advice and slaughtered Aisling the night of their union, the Sidhe would be doomed."

Galad shifted but didn't relent. He remained quiet, staring straight ahead at the statue of Arawn.

"Peitho," Niamh said. "Her duty to your Niltaor and the South is unfulfilled. With no union with the high king of all the Sidhe and the power of Racat, her kingdom remains in rubble."

Galad turned to the side, understanding dawning on his expression.

"Gilrel," Niamh focused on next, "her loyalty and courage know no bounds and yet, you played a role in her sister's death."

Galad held his breath for he seemingly knew what came next.

"And Galad," Niamh continued. "He who failed to protect his own *caera* from the violence of man."

Galad didn't flinch. He held himself straight, keeping Niamh's stare as she spoke.

"And myself," Niamh said. "She, whose isolation, indeed, drove her to lunacy at the cost of my dearest friend... Ina."

Lightning flashed and the stained-glass portraits doubled over in tears.

"And yet," Niamh said, "I wish to help."

Galad uncrossed his arms, his expression softening slightly.

"I mean no disrespect, m'Lady." Galad dipped his head respectfully whilst still maintaining cool confidence. "But whilst your power might protect you from formal consequence, it will not when weighed and measured by public perception. We've all witnessed how the Unseelie and even the forge-born can turn on their sovereigns and wage inner conflict, and so, how long will your reign last if the Sidhe world knew of your sins against Ina?"

Niamh flinched as if physically struck, pursing her lips and weighing Galad's sentiments in her mind. "Fate," the Seelie queen began, "is the fourth anonymous god. It creates, it breaks, and it never sleeps. My hand in Ina's death was a tool used by the will of fate to accomplish its ends. The choice is yours to either believe me or condemn me, and yet, in time you'll each come to recognize this truth for yourselves; your agency is a gift taken often and mercilessly by the crown of fate itself." Niamh sucked in a breath before exhaling. "Ina was always destined to die whether it be by my folly or another's."

Galad stood quietly, turning her rationale over in his mind. The great hall boasted seven souls all bearing the weight of centuries on their backs. Niamh, however, carried a millennium.

"I boarded the galleon in which Ina sailed into the afterlife of the Other. I kissed her cheeks and wept by her body, staining the silver of her hair with my tears. One last time, she opened her eyes. And one last time, she shared a vision with me:

*Black is the sky with smoke, huffed between the clenched teeth of iron beasts. Red is the color of the soil in which they reap their crops, puddled with the ichor of their wild conquests. White are their lies with which they poison their new world, erasing the natural history like books burned in piles. But green and violet are the tales whose heart still beats beneath the waves, within the wind, just beyond mortal touch.*

Niamh closed her eyes, her hands shaking at her sides. She dug her nails into her palms as she gathered her hands into fists, exhaling slowly.

"I cannot claim to understand this vision fully. But, in some capacity, the mortals will triumph over the Sidhe—this, Ina has foreseen. I believe both Aisling and Lir are pieces fate moves often across the board in which we find ourselves, either for the sake of our damnation or salvation—of this, I am uncertain. The only thing I am certain of, is that there is hope," Niamh said. "I choose to believe Ina placed the curse breaker and the power of change in Aisling—of transformation—for a reason."

The room stood still, books pausing mid-air to better eavesdrop.

"You may not be capable of trusting my motives considering

my sins," Niamh explained, "but you can trust I'll do whatever is within my power to do what Ina could not: spare the Sidhe from extinction.

"And should that mean Aisling reigns over the Other in my stead, then so be it. But let it be because she is the hope—the change—Ina believed her to be. Let her claim her victory herself and not be given it," Niamh said.

Galad dropped his head. Niamh hoped that although he didn't trust the Seelie queen, he might still empathize with her motivations. Perhaps he, too, thirsted to make amends for his mistakes and he'd give everything for the chance.

"Very well," Galad surrendered, at last. "We stand a better chance together."

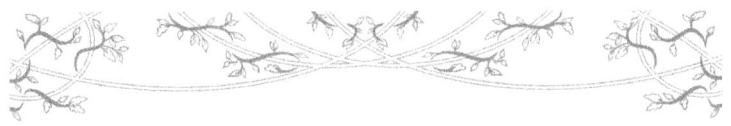

# CHAPTER XLIV

## AISLING

Aisling tiptoed down the slippery stones, spiraling toward the base of Simril Tower. Not another soul passed her on her journey nor inquired of her whereabouts. Only the delicate chirping of pond toads, the "hush" of the waterfall, and the babbling of bugs accompanied her descent.

At last, she arrived at a steepled door. Framed by a garland of glowing flower bulbs, Aisling heard several voices whispering enthusiastically on the other side. She pressed her ear to the wood, listening to what was being said.

"We've been commanded not to!" a small voice insisted.

"But surely if they've sent this much correspondence... we cannot continue to ignore them," another voice said.

"They're merely concerned where they've disappeared to. Once they return, all will be well," a third voice said.

"For our sake, I hope that's true," the first voice said.

"I trust *mo Damh Bán*," the second agreed.

"As do I," the third piped.

Time in Simril's Glade passed differently than anywhere else and so Aisling wondered how long they'd been gone.

A moment of silence passed before Aisling, at last, chose to open the door.

Moonlight unspooled in a pillar of light, cloaking Aisling like a specter. On the other side of the threshold, three martens —changelings—stood quivering, gaping up at Aisling.

"*Mo Lúra.*" The center changeling greeted her between the chattering of his teeth. All three bowed, wet noses pressed against the opal floors.

*Mo Lúra.* That title again. Aisling frowned.

"Rise," she said, offering each a simple smile.

"Is there something we can assist you with?" the center changeling asked.

"I'm searching for the Sidhe king," Aisling explained. "Do you know where he went?"

The changelings exhaled, their shoulders slackening. Seemingly relieved, they spoke to one another through silent glances.

"Of course, *mo Lúra*," the third changeling said. "*Mo Damh Bán* would enjoy nothing more than to see you."

Aisling quirked a brow, taken off guard. "He would?" she asked, her heart beating several paces quicker.

The changelings exchanged puzzled glances.

"Of course," they said in unison, gesturing for Aisling to follow them.

Aisling fell into step behind their small paws. They climbed down the opal stairwell that descended into the surrounding pool stopping short of its waters. From here, the waterfall was hidden on the other side of the tower. The surrounding forest, on the other hand, circled the Simril Glade and yet, it was unreachable lest Aisling chose to swim. There was no bridge, no stepping stones, nor a pathway on dry ground.

The first changeling reached into his small, quilted coat and pulled out a water lily. Gently, the changeling set the flower into the waters. It floated away, tipping from side to side on the gentle rock of the current, traveling around the tower and toward the waterfall.

Aisling watched curiously, wondering how they'd reach Lir with no aid.

But then another changeling arrived, paddling himself forward with a gnarled staff on the back of an enormous turtle. The changeling smiled in greeting at his comrades, turning to Aisling with a gulp.

"Come, *mo Lúra*," the first changeling said, cautiously but politely grabbing Aisling's hand. He led her toward the last step, soaking the hem of her gown in the pool. The turtle neared, close enough for Aisling to step on top, the newest changeling helping her aboard.

Aisling teetered slightly, almost losing her footing. The shell of the turtle carried more than just Aisling and the newest changeling. Atop its shell, grumpy toads sat, snowdrops sprang, and bundles of tufted moss grew, enjoying the steady sway of the waters beneath them.

"*Mo Lúra* wishes to accompany *mo Damh Bán*," the first changeling explained. The newest changeling nodded his head and shared a nervous smile with Aisling before paddling away once more. The turtle lurched forward, and Aisling dropped to her knees to keep her balance. Her gown dragged through the waters: a veil of shimmering white amidst the glittering waters of Simril.

After several moments of nothing more than the chorus of croaking frogs, the gargling of waters, and the stirring of the surrounding forest, the turtle rounded the edge of the tower, bringing the waterfall into full view.

Giant lily pads floated delicately at the surface of the pool. Twenty or so pine martens—changelings—stood atop the pads, staring ahead as if in assembly. Spectators of he who stood before the waterfall, waist deep in the waters.

Lir.

His clothes stuck to his muscled body, sprayed by the roar of the falls. He sparkled in the moonlight, kissed by stars that circled his head where a crown was destined to rest. He didn't turn nor look over his shoulder, his eyes focused on the waterfall ahead.

Aisling rose to her feet, lips parting.

The changeling opened his mouth to announce Aisling's presence, but the sorceress quickly shushed him.

Lir hadn't noticed her arrival and Aisling hoped it remained that way. She wanted to see for herself what the dark lord of the greenwood preoccupied himself with within the privacy of the Simril Glade.

A bell rang thrice over. Aisling searched the glade, at last, finding the bell's resting place at the top of the tower. It swung side to side, ringing till the forest vibrated with its strength.

The *draiocht* thickened by the breath full, saturating the air with a warm, lush breeze. It ran its fingers through Aisling's curls, brushing her cheeks, and sliding beneath the folds of her gown. The taste of ripe plums and glittering black wine, licking her senses.

The waterfall split like a tapestry, pulling apart at the center till a steepled archway was made. Darkness filled its void, seemingly nothing beyond but the shadows of an ancient cave long since asleep.

Aisling held her breath. The *draiocht* in the air was becoming feverish, clotting and tugging at the magic inside her.

Lir stepped forward, approaching the waterfall's threshold.

Aisling awaited a beast: a starving, salivating aberration that skulked in the Sidhe king's wicked depths. And yet, it never came.

Instead, a lily pad materialized from the shadows, passing through the waterfall's threshold and into the moonlight. Aisling squinted, doing her best to see what the lily pad carried.

A bundle of tartan wool, filled by the cries of a bairn.
A mortal child.

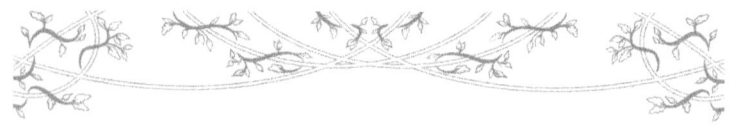

# CHAPTER XLV

## LIR

Lir gathered the bairn in his arms.

They were always lighter than he anticipated, the Sidhe king pressed the child against his chest tenderly. The bairn warmed, nuzzling its rosy cheeks into the fabric of Lir's ritter until its wails softened to coos.

Despite its passing, the child smelled of mortality, of iron, of flame. Still, the backs of Lir's eyelids burned as he held the creature, his hands almost larger than the entire bundle.

"*Take flight, little wolf,*" Lir sang, barely a whisper. "*Let no hunter catch you, no fox outwit you, no devil master you. Take flight, little wolf.*"

The *draiocht* heated, buzzing as the chorus of insects rose to a crescendo.

Lir struggled to find his breath. He held the creature more tightly, accidentally rocking it in the cradle of his arms.

"*The time is nigh, m'Lord,*" a changeling piped softly behind him.

Lir gritted his teeth but nodded his head regardless. This was always the most painful part: saying goodbye.

Lir pressed his lips to the bairn's forehead, blessing it fully.

"*I hereby knight thee and invite thee into the hallowed afterlife of the Other: Caoimhe, child of the mortal plane. Sail onward,*" Lir recited, his voice thick. "*Sail onward and never look back.*"

Lir laid the child back onto the lily pad, wincing as if he were laying down a piece of himself, freshly gouged from his body.

Caoimhe cried, suddenly cold without Lir's warmth. Lir cherished its cries for it was alive and beating with magic now.

Lir shut his eyes.

"*Arise knight of the Sidhe and be recognized.*"

The bells of Simril rang thrice over and the lily pad carried the bairn back through the falls, and into the Other. The spell was complete; another mortal child christened by the high king of the Sidhe and accepted into the sweet planes of the Other by honor of his blessing. A small mercy Lir believed every bairn, Sidhe or not, was owed.

Still, Lir bled tears from wounds he knew would never heal. The loss of his own child, a fresh memory despite the passing of time. Grief, the enemy he preferred to keep alive.

# CHAPTER XLVI

## LIR

The sun, passion-filled, broke the heart of night each dawn. And so, too, did the night run weeping this morning as Lir collapsed into a bed of pelts in one of Simril tower's wings.

He'd knocked off his boots, tossed his ritter onto a nearby chair, and unbuckled his belt, sparing not a moment longer to throw himself into sleep. But the moment Lir closed his eyes, he saw her.

*Lir turned, immediately locking eyes with Aisling.*

*She was a star: shining and commanding the green earth below. The berry-black of her curls a mouthwatering variance from the ivory of her robes, the hem floating around her ankles like a halo.*

*Both mind and heart stuttered, blinking to ensure she was real and not an unholy specter. He hadn't anticipated she'd follow him to Simril's falls, but with retrospect, he should have.*

*The violet of her eyes studied him from where she stood. And despite the distance, the intensity of her gaze struck him like a reed, his hand drifting to his heart without thinking.*

The memory of Simril falls clung to Lir and Lir to the memory, thinking of it again and again—cursed to wonder endlessly what Aisling saw when she looked at him. Even now —after he tossed in his bed after he'd woken in the middle of the night—he struggled to sort out his thoughts.

The door to his chamber creaked open. The Sidhe king stilled.

He'd heard her footsteps in his half sleep and smelled the lavender of her soaps before she even flipped the door's latch.

Aisling knocked on the door before fully opening it.

Lir said not a word, rather curious to know if she would enter regardless of his silence. When they'd first arrived in the Simril Glade, the changelings had arranged a chamber at the crown of the tower for both Aisling and Lir. And the Sidhe king hadn't the interest nor the desire to explain that the sorceress no longer loved him. That he'd sworn an oath to the high queen of the Otherworld to never act on his love for Aisling again. That he couldn't disappear because he'd rather live on with a sword in his heart than be without her. But only if the blade was forged by her hands.

And so, he'd said nothing at all. Rather, arranging a bed for himself in this west wing tower where he could avoid Aisling in the evenings. Lir wasn't certain what Aisling felt or remembered of their relationship, and he wasn't armored with the courage to ask. And so, he wondered if she bore the nerve to enter his chambers uninvited.

Aisling slipped into the room like a dream. Slowly, she padded across the mosaicked tiles. Her head turned, searching for the Sidhe king between the shadows of a still reigning night. The fog of evening rendered her more fantasy than reality.

"Lir," she said, almost a spell.

The Sidhe king caught the moment she laid eyes on him, standing from his bed of pelts.

The darkness ran its fingers over Lir as he stepped into sight, the light undressing the shadows that surrounded him. He met Aisling at the center of his rooms where the moon showered them in a pillar of silver.

Aisling looked up at him and her eyes darkened, her chin turning even as her eyes stayed, tracing the ink of his markings from his chest to his hips where he slept with only trousers. His wounds were tightly bandaged, gauze wrapping around the muscles of his arms and abdomen. The violet of Aisling's eyes grew wet with need.

The moment Anduril had settled on Aisling's hips, her eyes had dulled. Vacantly, she often stared for several beats, blinking as if trying and failing to rekindle the fire that once burned beneath her eyelashes.

Lir had mourned the way she looked at him now, and yet here she was, waking from the graveyard of his heart like an immortal foe.

"I wanted to inquire about your wounds," she said, collecting herself swiftly.

Lir looked down at his burns. Still, they bled, purified by Simril's waters despite their gnarled appearance.

"I'll survive," Lir said, unable to help the way the corner of his lip curled.

Aisling didn't mirror his expression, nor did she soften. A smile received from Aisling was a victory and a laugh, a celebration. And so her stoicism now stoked his hunger to chase the high her joy inspired.

"May I?" Aisling asked, gesturing to his wounds.

Lir nodded, his smile fading as she leaned forward.

"You can relax," Aisling said.

"I am relaxed," Lir countered, eyes darting toward the axes at the edge of the pools and not strapped to his back. He couldn't remember the last time he'd undone his bandolier in the presence of another, even Aisling. He hadn't anticipated she'd come searching for him and, somehow, she'd caught him both off guard and unprepared.

Like ink, Aisling's hair slipped over her left shoulder as she leaned further.

"Do these—" She hesitated, eyes flicking to his before falling once more to her trembling fingertips. "Do these still pain you?" she asked.

Lir nodded his head, his heart thumping in his throat.

Torturously, Aisling's nails brushed his bare flesh, tracing the edge of his wounds with her fingertips as if exploring their violence.

Lir shut his eyes, his entire body stiffening like stone.

Aisling paused, biting her bottom lip before speaking. "I can stop if you're—"

"No," Lir said, despising himself for saying it so quickly. He hungered for her touch. For the smell of her dusky perfume, the sound of her voice, the vibration of her *draiocht* rubbing against his own when she was near. And he knew she felt it too. Felt it and didn't understand its energy: an intense compulsion to move closer to the other—to let go and sink their teeth into one another's magic.

Thankfully, Simril Glade was a sacred haven of both serenity and peace. Those forces did well against the might of Aisling and Lir's bond but couldn't stifle their energy entirely.

Aisling resumed her work, growing more confident as she continued. Finally, she reached the worst of the blisters scarring the side of his abdomen. Her eyes grew wide till all the whites were visible, her fingers freezing in place.

"So this is what mortal fire does to Sidhe flesh," Aisling said, running her eyes over the gory mess. Indeed, Lir healed swiftly and efficiently from all wounds unless they were dealt by either iron or fire. And this time, even Leshy's tears had struggled to mend him fully.

"I knew," Aisling confessed, "but never have I seen it up close."

Aisling didn't remember. Didn't remember him or the experiences they'd shared. For Aisling *had* seen the destruction of her flames on Sidhe flesh up close—several times before. Scars Lir cherished. Anduril demanded she forget Lir, attempting to unravel all that'd inspired her love for the dark lord.

Lir clenched his jaw, turning his head away instinctively.

Aisling frowned, considering the Sidhe king through tired eyes.

"Why can't I remember you?" Aisling asked at last. The question took Lir off guard, demanding his full attention. In some capacity, Aisling was aware all was not as it should be.

*You do not need to remember. He is only destruction. He is only your loss,* Anduril said, buzzing hotly, speaking more quickly.

"Sometimes," Lir said, as matter-of-factly as he could manage, "it is better to forget."

"But, you haven't forgotten," Aisling said. Her violet eyes devoured him—the intensity of her gaze, overwhelming.

"No," Lir confessed, "I haven't."

Against his own volition, the Sidhe king's eyes wandered toward her lips. Raspberry red, they hid two growing fangs, sparkling with hunger. Lir swallowed, swatting away thoughts of his own fangs chewing on her bottom lip.

*"Promise me you'll never love Aisling again." Niamh said, her voice strained and quick. "Promise me you'll let Aisling go."*

*"I promise," Lir said and the Forge boomed like a drum, snapping lightning and thunder in its fury, threatening to crack the skies in half. The Other and the mortal plane both, trembling with the finality of their high bargain.*

The memory struck Lir like an arrow. He hissed from the pain of it, his nose wrinkling.

Aisling startled, pulling back her fingers.

"Did I hurt you?" she asked. And had it not been for their circumstances, Lir might've laughed. There were few souls in this realm or the next that could inflict pain on the Sidhe king, but none amongst them did so as brutally as did Aisling.

"You should return to your chambers," Lir said instead. "We'll travel to Castle Yillen at dawn."

Aisling pinched her lips together, brow furrowing.

"Who was the creature that stood before the falls this evening?" Aisling asked, not moving an inch. She spoke confidently, her words as clear as a bell struck. "For the creature that cradled that mortal bairn was not the creature that stands before me now."

Lir's eyebrows raised. He wasn't certain of what to say. They hadn't spoken of Simril falls and he had no desire to.

"Don't ask questions you won't like the answers to," Lir said.

"I do not ask so I might enjoy the answer," Aisling argued. "I ask because I simply wish to know it—regardless of how I might feel."

Lir turned his head to the side, preferring to stare at the dome of the astronomy tower than her violet glare. Eyes that would scald him should he deny her.

"Should a forge-born child endure an untimely death, the galleon will sail them into the Other for eternal peace. Mortal bairns are not awarded the same afterlife," Lir explained reluctantly.

"Where do mortals go when they pass?" Aisling asked.

"I know not," Lir admitted. "Some believe they shrivel to ash and nothing more. Others believe they reincarnate on the mortal plane until the end of time. And still, others believe they sail to a land of their own making, beyond the clouds."

"What do you believe?" Aisling pushed.

Lir exhaled, running his fingers through his hair.

"I believe their afterlife is different from our own. That even in death, the Sidhe and mortals are cleaved apart. Perhaps the gods created a land for good-hearted mortals—if you believe in such a thing—after Ina's mistakes. It's impossible to tell," Lir said.

"So why?" Aisling continued, not wasting a breath. "Why cradle those mortal bairns beneath the falls only to return them back to whence they came?"

Lir shook his head. "Those bairns do not return."

Aisling's expression pinched, puzzled.

"Under my reign," Lir said, his voice roughening against his volition, "whether their blood is laced in iron or the *draiocht*, no bairn shall be forsaken. Even in death. And so, the changelings bring the deceased human children to the Simril Glade where I then bless each one, gifting them a fae name by which they'll peacefully enter the Other."

Aisling blinked repeatedly, visibly sorting through Lir's words.

Lir would've given anything to read her thoughts. Aisling understood him as a monster, this much Lir knew. So, what did she think of him now?

Lir watched her through the shifting moonlight—a veil that teased his eyes.

"You've bewitched me," Aisling said finally. Her words rang through the tower, cutting to the center of their mischief. "I don't know for what reason or what cause, but I've recognized your tricks." Aisling narrowed her eyes, her voice like black wines. "I can feel you beneath my skin," she continued. "I can hear your voice between my thoughts. And I can"— she hesitated, seemingly catching her breath—"taste you on the tip of my tongue."

Lir's eyes cut to Aisling's lips. A compulsion he didn't care to fight. His chest rising and falling with every new, deep breath.

"I can feel the hand of your spell choking your name from my memory, squeezing while I beg. Still, it holds me down, staking me through the heart."

She moved closer, the ends of her hair dipping into the water.

Lir's expression bloomed darkly. Aisling's magic went beyond flame and common charms or spells. Every glance, every word was witchery itself. And so when she spoke, Lir fell to the knee at her altar.

"Do you deny it?" Aisling asked, the edge of her lips closer to his own than he remembered them being seconds ago.

"Not if you're confessing your heart to me." Lir smiled, his accent thicker the faster his mind raced.

"Don't toy with me," Aisling growled, her tone, a contrast to the tilt of her neck so its supple edge shone in the moonlight.

They shared a heavy breath, lips a thread's width apart.

Fate was humming, spelling them together. Lir could hear the laughter in its voice as it worked, humming louder and louder until Lir feared Simril's Glade would burn. His *draiocht* scratching at the walls of his consciousness as if trapped in a jar. The sound of its claws against the glass, unbearable.

"Rest," Lir commanded by a miracle, and he'd despise himself for it for another millennium. He turned his back to her, tearing her hands away from his bandages. With her so near, touching him as she did, he'd lost the ability to cloak his true feelings. He'd made an oath, and even if it killed him, he was bound to uphold it. And this temptation—this torture of her proximity—forced Lir to wonder if he'd survive his promise to Niamh and the Forge or if perhaps a death, intertwined with her, was preferable.

Still, Aisling remained, watching him quietly.

"Were these scars forged by my magic as well?" Aisling asked.

Lir closed his eyes, exhaling. He didn't need to ask what she referenced. His shoulder blades were grossly scarred where his wings had been taken.

"My commands aren't suggestions, sorceress," Lir said, ignoring Aisling's questions.

"Command me something else then," Aisling offered, her voice lowering.

Lir forced himself to remain still. If he turned and faced her... he wasn't certain what would become of them both.

She placed a gentle hand on his shoulder, lazily traveling down the length of his arm. She traced every muscled curve with her fingertips, followed shortly after by her nails.

Lir swallowed, his tongue a stone in his mouth.

"Command me," she repeated as she moved closer to him, her lips brushing against his spine. Lir shuddered, unsure whether this was dream or nightmare incarnate.

The Sidhe king shut his eyes tightly, bracing himself. The need to resist, thinning by the breathful.

Lir turned, bending to her will.

She stood before him, half-soaked by the light of the stars shimmering from the dome above. Her robes and hair stuck to her body, mercilessly exposing her figure and the flesh beneath.

Lir jerked his head away, averting his eyes, fangs grinding into his tongue.

Wicked as a wolf, Aisling grinned. Her red lips spread apart, and Lir imagined his tongue between them, tasting her dark, effervescent magic.

Aisling grabbed his jaw and gently turned his head so he faced her once more.

Lir held his breath, eyes half-closed by her opiate.

"Command me," Aisling said again, "before I command you."

A muscle flashed across Lir's jaw.

"Either way, you'll do as you like," he said, his voice not his own. Thick, raspy, and heavy as wine.

"Is that what you're waiting for?" Aisling asked, placing her palm flat against the center of his chest. Lir's *draiocht* shivered, chilled to the bone. Pupils drowning his iris in black.

With whatever wisdom remained, Lir grabbed her wrist and held it in place. This way, she was unable to stroke the hard angles of his abdomen.

Aisling stood on her tiptoes, craning her neck so her mouth barely pressed against his throat as she spoke.

Suddenly, Aisling hissed with pain, doing her best to obscure the sound from Lir's ear. But the Sidhe king heard it regardless the moment Anduril emitted a soft luster that burned like a blade dipped in the Great Forge of Creation itself.

He cursed beneath his breath, able to smell Anduril's magic but not hear it, fearing what whispers it spun inside Aisling's mind.

Lir leaned into her touch, the will to resist her, melting and dripping between his fingertips.

She lifted her head, bringing her mouth to his. Lir pulled back but only slightly. The distance between them fathomless, so long as they weren't wholly intertwined.

Her adrenaline smelled of ripe cherries, dripping down her chin as she bit into its flesh and succumbed to the draw of their intimacy.

Lir closed his eyes.

Their lips met, melding together effortlessly. Lir sank into the kiss, hands flying around her waist and pressing her against him. He felt her soft curves, her supple angles against him, and growled between breathfuls. He was ravenous for her.

Aisling slipped her hands around his neck. She panted against him, pushing herself against him as if to feel every line of his body against her own.

Lir groaned against his own volition.

He couldn't... he shouldn't.

Anduril was glowing hotly, forcing a violent reaction from Aisling as she visibly resisted its magic. Aisling focused on Lir, her pupils dilating and shrinking wildly as she fought for agency.

Lir clenched his jaw, forcing himself not to tear the Blood Cord from her body like a diseased branch on an oak. She was in pain, her mind tearing at the seams of Anduril's and her consciousness, sewn violently together. Fury flamed inside the Sidhe King—the overwhelming urge to protect her, overcoming him as he witnessed this dark magic. He'd cut it from her if he must—

In the midst of his anger, Aisling slipped her tongue between his teeth and Lir unraveled. He picked her up by the backs of her thighs and lifted her. She wrapped her legs around his torso, pressing herself against him as she kissed his lips hungrily, hands weaving through his dark hair.

"Who are you to me?" she said as Lir's hands found her thighs and slid up.

"Your undoing," Lir said, his mind lost to her. His heart blazing. His *draiocht* whistling with heat, begging to be unleashed.

LISTEN TO HIM, Anduril roared.

But as soon as the last syllable dropped from Lir's lips, Aisling let go and pushed herself back.

It was hot and then, in a breath, it was cold, her body no longer against his own.

And when Lir emerged from her spell—magic brewed with the spices of hers and his longing—he saw the destruction their intimacy wrought.

Flames licked the surface of the baths and beyond, the forest whipped to and fro, growing like giants before their very eyes. No longer was the moon visible beyond the great canopies of plum trees—gnarled and contorting oddly. Faces burnt into the trunks that screamed alive and thrashed as if Simril's Glade stormed. The night, crushed by the devastating blow of a morning sun.

"And that," Aisling said, wiping her bottom lip as she stepped back from him, "is all I needed to know."

Lir flinched as if physically struck. Aisling had deceived him. Seduced him for answers. He'd been a fool to believe she'd want him despite Anduril who still muddied her mind. And yet, he'd known that. Known that and succumbed to his desire for her regardless.

"Be well, dark lord," she said as she climbed the bath stairs and rose from the waters, her robes sticking to her legs. Her every movement, feline. "Be well and think twice before you bewitch me again."

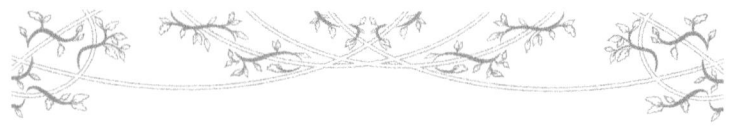

# CHAPTER XLVII

## AISLING

Only one moon remained of the storm season. The Sidhe were falling and their end was rushing toward them, unstoppable. The mortals worked in the dark, veiled by the Lady, but the forest grew black and bloody and filled with rot each moment their influence inched closer to the heart of the Other.

They were coming.

They were coming and Aisling's *draoicht* sensed it, lighting her fingertips each time her heart leaped with nerves. The journey back to Castle Yillen, jumpy and anxious as she navigated the waters in between and was spat back out in one of Niamh's courtyards.

Aisling swiftly changed and ate three full plates from the kitchens before searching for Galad.

They were running out of time.

Galad swung his sword like a blue star burning through the sky. He lunged to the left—a feint, for he swiftly changed direction and struck on the right. Peitho, on the other hand, avoided the onslaught with the grace of a dancer, her feet moving swiftly between each strike. Their duel, a collaboration more than a fight.

"Without strength, make use of your agility and your speed," Galad said, moving his heavy blade in a devastating arc. Peitho responded swiftly, dodging the tip of his sword by a breath's width. She found her footing, leaping and striking before Galad could raise his giant sword again. She threw herself toward him, Luinagren burning bright as she swung. In the last moment, Galad raised his weapon, shielding himself. Both swords connecting in an ear-splitting clash.

They came apart, heaving and exchanging nods.

Aisling stared at them both, Sarwen between her fingertips.

"Would you like to give it another go?" Galad asked Aisling, approaching her at the side of Niamh's floating, glass ballroom.

Aisling shook her head, sweat dripping down her temples after hours of training.

"Perhaps destroying my clann will demand magic rather than the blade," Aisling said. "Forge willing."

"Don't be discouraged," Peitho said. "You've improved greatly over the past several days."

Hours after Simril's baths, Aisling and Lir crashed through Niamh's giant gateway.

Galad and Gilrel woke angry. Both the knight and handmaiden had fallen asleep against an oak, waiting on their return with no word or sign from Lir as to their whereabouts. Both were rushed inside Castle Yillen where Niamh gave them both a verbal lashing.

Galad and Peitho had occupied every hour of the past several days training her in Niamh's ballroom for what might lie ahead. She hadn't a moment to breathe and thankfully, neither did she have a breath to think of Lir—he who creeped into her mind if left unguarded.

She'd deceived him at Simril's Glade, eager to understand what'd bewitched her mind. Someone or something was toying with her and she'd known from the beginning Lir's hand played a heavy role. This much was made clear by the changelings arguing outside Simril Glade's tower. Lir was keeping her there, away and without anyone else. And so, the memory of her mischief made her lips curl. Anduril growled hotly.

Still, it hadn't been entirely a lie: a confession she hadn't mustered the courage to admit to herself just yet.

"Use whatever is at your disposal," Galad said, tearing Aisling from her thoughts. "If you cannot wield your blade, summon your *draiocht*. If you cannot summon your *draiocht*, use your wit. There is always a way, no matter how large or small," Galad said.

The first knight clapped a hand on her shoulder, smiling encouragingly.

"And remember, never ignore your instincts," he said. "Act quickly and confidently."

He walked her to the threshold, nodding a farewell at Peitho as they left.

They wandered through the moving corridors of Castle Yillen, bracing against the storms when there was no covered walkway.

"How are you faring?" Galad asked Aisling as they made their way.

"Well," Aisling said. "The blisters on my palms will fade by nightfall and by morning, I'll be prepared for whatever comes." Indeed, Aisling knew the mortals were on their doorstep. It was only a matter of time before they knocked down the doors and demanded blood. And so, the Sidhe world was preparing for war come morning.

Galad nodded his head.

"I'm glad," he said. "But how are you faring after your encounter with your clann?" he asked, sapphire eyes searching her expression as they walked.

A dark coal bloomed red with hatred inside her chest at the mention of her family.

"They'll face justice soon enough," Aisling said, her voice

short. She swatted at the image of their faces in her mind. She drowned their words and slashed the feelings they'd inspired inside her. She despised them more with each waking hour.

"They're searching for the gateway to the Other," Aisling said. "To destroy it."

Galad's lips pressed into a thin line as he considered.

"So I've learned," he said. "Lir's received word from Sakaala that their mortal fleets are circling the center of the Silver Sea. Do you believe they'll find it, or Leshy?" he asked.

Aisling bit her bottom lip until it bled. "I hope they do."

Galad looked at her.

"For the next time we're reunited, will be the last," she clarified.

Galad exhaled a laugh. "Forge willing."

Indeed, Aisling's clann had not only imprisoned, tortured, and murdered Galad's *caera*, but Starn had branded the first knight's flesh in remembrance of their horrors. His thirst for revenge was rich in the blue of his iris, eager to be slaked.

"And so," Aisling said, "I'll give you a hand in their destruction."

Galad grinned at this.

"It would be my honor," he said. "My honor to serve and honor your everlasting reign, Ash."

Ash.

Aisling's heart leaped. Galad hadn't called her so since before she'd fled Annwyn. A name she'd given him as a friend. The first friend she'd made in Annwyn. But he'd held her at arm's length after her betrayal, foregoing their familiarity in place of duty.

To hear her name in the cadence of his voice was warm and bright, motivating Aisling.

"And so shall you," Aisling said, mirroring his smile.

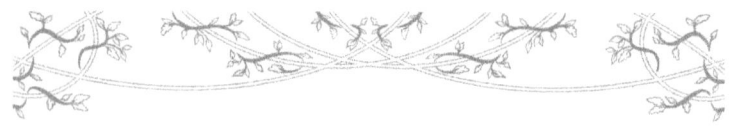

## CHAPTER XLVIII

AISLING

Aisling ran her fingers over the intricacies of her armor, watching her hands move in the mirror's reflection. Niamh approached Aisling from behind, the Seelie queen's strange eyes materializing over her reflection's shoulder.

"The end is in sight, Aisling," Niamh said, running her fingers through Aisling's loose hair. "You've almost done it." Her touch seemed genuine and tender in its authenticity. Her movements were slow, soft, and measured—fingers lingering a beat longer than necessary.

Aisling pressed her mouth shut, wiping her expression clean as she met the Seelie queen's eyes.

"And then what?" Aisling asked.

"And then you possess everything you've ever wanted," Niamh said, a smile peeling across her face. The blue of her flesh, almost translucent in the dim flower light of the corridor in which they stood. *Everything you've ever wanted*, Aisling repeated the words in her mind. She struggled to taste its indulgence.

"And you?" Aisling countered. "What will you have?"

Niamh turned her head, parting Aisling's hair before

braiding it. Her face was half-veiled in shadow and so Aisling almost missed the flicker of desperation. Almost.

Niamh slid her fangs over her bottom lip, brows drawing together.

"Freedom," she said, her voice soft. "If I'm no longer the keeper of the gateway, I'll be liberated from this godforsaken castle. Until then, I await the day. In solitude."

Niamh dropped Aisling's hair and stepped back, her robes of gray winter rains swishing as she moved.

"Why then do you flee from the object you once coveted above all else?" Aisling asked, the backs of her eyes beginning to burn. "Did your mind change?"

Niamh's eyes darted left and right, her mind racing while her lips parted.

"Yes," Niamh confessed, her Sidhe tongue shackled to the truth. "Wanting and receiving is never enough. Desire is a bottomless cauldron, quenchless and lined with teeth. With every bite, its hunger grows. Eventually, it devours itself."

"Yet, here you stand," Aisling said.

Niamh nodded her head, "Aye, here I stand with the object of all my desires—sovereignty, Yillen, and the Goblet of Lore—and yet I am *without*."

Aisling held steady, studying the Seelie queen closely.

"Did you realize your regrets before or after you were forsaken here?" Aisling asked.

Niamh hesitated, eyes flickering.

"See for yourself," Niamh said. "As it was written in the Lore of All Things."

Dust like mist gathered in sparkling runic words: *Victory was swiftly followed by regret, the Seelie queen of Rain filled to the brim.*

Aisling read the verse once before Niamh snapped her fingers and the mist scattered.

"Are you and I the only two to have held the Goblet?"

Aisling asked, turning to face the Seelie queen. "Have no others drank from it?"

Niamh's expression fell before it recovered as a smile, cutting across her sharp features.

Aisling resisted the urge to shudder.

"Are you nervous, Aisling?" Niamh asked, arching her brows. "Is that why you're asking all these questions?" The softness in her voice was unfamiliar, yet Aisling found she starved for it.

The blood in Aisling's face vanished, her expression hardening to stone. The sorceress opened her mouth to speak, but she was stopped short. The door at the end of the corridor creaked open by a phantom wind and the land beyond crashed into their quiet moment like a stampede of drums, trumpets, fiddles, chanting voices, and idle chatter.

Aisling swallowed, her hands going numb.

"Whatever is meant to be, will be, Aisling," Niamh said, her voice uncharacteristically soft. "Perhaps you will die. Perhaps all of us will perish and sail into the Other. Or, perhaps you'll be our salvation. Only time will tell the will of Fate and who its chosen to align with."

Aisling glanced at her over her shoulder, watching as the Seelie queen disappeared into the shadows of the hallway. The door shut behind Aisling. A threshold she could no longer cross back.

# CHAPTER XLIX

## AISLING

Blood red, Aisling's bare feet crushed fallen berries as she danced. The music floated through the air like the herb-dense smoke from a toad's pipe, feverish in its intensity. Every Sidhe, every forge-born beast, guzzled sparkling wines, ciders, and meads, eyelids falling as they celebrated Aisling and the eve of the war's finality.

Each of the Sidhe sovereigns were in attendance too. Tara spun with the music's rhythm, mushrooms sprouting where her ankles graced the floors. Dagda, Nuada, and Lottie lounged on thick beds of moss-like cushions, whispering and laughing between sips of punch. Katari, Percy, and Mac Cuill took turns knocking an apple from atop a tortoise's head, lending a bow and arrow from a nearby fox swimming in the central pond, spilling over the edge and off the side of Castle Yillen. The stained-glass dome far above their heads shielded them from Niamh's rains, now coupled with the stars in celebration. Arcs of color brightening the spectacle as Aisling danced.

Galad, Peitho, and Gilrel were there too, lost between the folds of gaiety. Aisling met their eyes on several occasions, something silent passing between them.

The sorceress wore a three-headed wolf headdress, her gown, white as snow. She clasped the hands of badgers, of weasels, of raccoons, of rabbits, and of the Sidhe, spinning in circles that made the air dense with magic.

Aisling ignored the pains in her joints, the tears in her muscles, or the aches in her heart.

Nevertheless, tonight, she'd enjoy the Sidhe world the way she had the first time, watching their unruly, savage celebrations through the eyes of a mortal girl accustomed to stone and iron. So she drank the pints of Leshy's tears Gilrel had offered her, pinched her nose, and fell into the festivities without a second thought.

"As soon as this is over, you may visit me in Oighir," Fionn said, dancing beside her. His silver hair was loose around his shoulders and his robes untied at the chest. He was a chip of ivory in a mosaic of emeralds, the contrast jarring to behold. "If it still stands."

"Oighir?" Aisling asked, entranced.

"Aye, Oighir. My kingdom at the edge of the world," Fionn said.

Aisling stumbled on several large stones. Fionn reached for her, grabbing her elbow and steadying her.

Aisling hadn't yet considered what her life would be like if they survived this war. After she'd obtained and won everything she'd ever wanted. *What then?* she asked herself.

Fionn twirled her beneath his arm, eyes drifting to the Sidhe sovereigns watching their intimacy from the periphery of the celebration.

"You could still be my queen of fire and ice," Fionn continued. "All of Fjallnorr and the North will be yours to rule and lead."

Anduril didn't buzz or hum with heat. Instead, the belt was calm, peacefully settled on her hips.

Aisling imagined herself in Oighir—in Fionn's world of glistering ice and blizzards, where beasts slumbered and the forest was powdered by the cold. She'd don robes, gowns, and armor embroidered with battle-ready bears, ornate snowflakes, and silver trims. She'd govern a land both frostbitten and far from all else. At the edge of the world.

Aisling's feet stopped dancing.

"Is something wrong?" Fionn asked.

Aisling searched his face.

Aisling shook her head. Her mind was swathed with voices —with memories that shifted and morphed like gnarled trees growing too quickly for their size. She'd known the Sidhe king of the greenwood, Lir, had bewitched her somehow. Had plagued her with a lust she could scarcely deny.

Aisling felt a bubble of panic rise up her throat. She'd trusted the son of Winter and this Gods Forsaken belt and now, she felt the first ice-thin cracks spider through her heart. Anduril was corrupting her, taking her body as its own.

Was she imagining it? Was the weight of prophecy, skewing her mind? Or was there truth in what she felt?

"Aisling," a voice sounded, tearing Aisling from her thoughts.

The sorceress turned to find Galad and Gilrel approaching her side, narrowed eyes considering Fionn closely.

"You should retire for the evening," Gilrel said. "You'll need your rest in the coming days." Galad nodded his head in agreement, placing a gentle hand on the small of Aisling's back.

"Where is Lir?" Aisling asked, the words falling from her lips before she understood them herself. As if the Sidhe king's name found the tip of her tongue of its own accord.

Galad and Gilrel exchanged glances. Fionn, on the other hand, scowled, silver eyes freezing over. The son of Winter said not a word, grinding his fangs together in anticipation of their answer.

"He prepares for the end," Galad said. Both his and Gilrel's eyes wandered up and toward a tower floating at the height of Castle Yillen. It was one of the few whose windows were gilded with warm light.

"Can I speak with him?" Aisling asked. The moment the words fell from her lips, Fionn reacted. He moved lissomly, wrapping his hand around Aisling's waist and knocking Galad's away in the process.

Galad frowned, both he and Gilrel noticeably bristling.

Aisling's heart leaped, but her mind resisted the impulse to sink into his side. She bit her tongue, growing angry in her confusion.

"Galad and Gilrel are right," Fionn said, breaking the silence. "You need your rest. Let me take you to your rooms."

"We're more than happy to do so," Gilrel said, stepping in front of their path.

"No," Aisling interjected. "I need to focus on the Goblet and so, I prefer solitude this evening." The sorceress smiled sweetly, exchanging glances with Fionn, Galad, and Gilrel. But while Fionn's posture was hard and restrained, Galad and Gilrel offered knowing, smug smiles, nodding their heads at one another.

"*Mo Lúra* receives as she requests," Galad said. "Her word is final." The knight gestured toward the threshold to the rest of the castle, making a path for the sorceress.

Aisling bowed her head at Fionn, not glancing back as she retired. Still, she felt Fionn's gaze follow her to the doors, into the darkened corridor, until, at last, the door shut and his sight was severed.

The castle purred with the muffled bedlam from Niamh's festivities, their dancing, their drinking, their howling undoubtedly burning the midnight wick. Aisling wandered through Castle Yillen afraid to find her chambers for she knew what awaited her. Before Aisling could fall into sleep's chasm, she'd lie awake, reminded of Lir, of her clann, of the Goblet, of the Sidhe, of Dagfin standing before her. Thoughts she'd avoided well enough until now. So she wandered further, growing lost in the castle till she could no longer find her chambers even if she so wished.

Aisling roamed the corridors like a ghost, slipping between rooms. At last, she found a wing she recognized, the cross-vaulted ceilings spreading into a great arched entryway that led into the throne room.

Aisling approached the doors, hesitating before pulling their handles. Both doors were already cracked ajar, a ribbon of light leaking into the hall. The sorceress listened closely for several breaths. She took off her headdress, holding it between her hands so she could better hear who occupied the room beyond.

To Aisling's surprise, she heard not silence, not music, not conversation but weeping—labored breathing punctuated by soft sobs, wracking their keeper. And whilst the rain wept relentlessly and the stained-glass portraits cried at all hours, nothing compared to the sorrow that wracked this miserable creature.

Curiosity took hold and Aisling peered inside.

The threshold's hinges squealed, and the moment Aisling laid eyes on Niamh curled into a ball before her throne, so, too, did the Seelie queen lay eyes on Aisling. The Goblet of Lore sitting beside her on the dais.

A heartbeat passed and Niamh collected herself, unfurling from her position on the ground. She straightened her gown, smoothing the sheets of clouds on her lap.

"I apologize," Niamh said, addressing Aisling for the first time. "I didn't realize any still wandered Yillen at this hour."

Aisling shifted awkwardly, pushing the doors open fully.

"Come in, please." Niamh welcomed her, still wiping tears from her eyes.

"I should return to my chambers," Aisling said. "But first, I'll take the Goblet back for safekeeping."

The Seelie queen of Rain's eyes darted to the chalice before finding Aisling once more. A fleck of panic in her eyes—of fear.

"No, no," Niamh replied. "It will do well in my keeping. I'd meant to speak with you before tomorrow regardless."

Aisling stilled, arms hanging at her sides and unsure of what to say. The sorceress glanced around the throne room, noticing for the first time that there was not one but two thrones cresting the dais.

The last Aisling had occupied this room, there had only been one throne.

Niamh followed Aisling's line of sight, softening her gaze when she looked back at the sorceress.

"That was the throne I'd designed for Ina," she said. "Before I realized she'd never truly join me here, of course."

Aisling's brows lifted. "You intended to rule the Other with Ina?"

Niamh considered the thrones more closely. "With my entire being." The raw truth of her words buzzed with the *draiocht*, the Forge acknowledging their purity.

"Come," Niamh invited Aisling, waving her arm for the sorceress to enter more fully into the hall.

Niamh lifted her dress slightly, ascending the dais. The Seelie queen took her seat in one of the thrones. She sank into its structure, perfectly tailored to her body.

"Join me," she said, tapping the throne beside her.

Aisling dithered for a breath, eyes darting between the Seelie queen and the empty throne. A pit formed in her stomach, staining her gut with dread. She did her best to swallow it, yet her instincts hadn't led her astray thus far.

Aisling toyed with the wolf headdress in her hands, hesitating a moment too long.

"Is everything alright?" Niamh asked, her voice, hardened and sharp.

Aisling straightened, glancing one more time at the second throne before approaching.

"Of course," Aisling lied. "But I should be returning to my chambers with the Goblet. It's late—"

"Nonsense," Niamh said, waving her hand as if shooing away Aisling's protests.

Aisling swallowed hard. Niamh grinned, but it lacked all warmth. Her trove of shimmering teeth, stolen from the maw of a forest ghoul and stacked behind pale blue lips.

"You must learn to channel your magic if you're to sip from the Goblet," Niamh said.

"How does one channel magic?" Aisling asked.

"With practice and time. Both of which you don't have. But your strength alone could be enough to either destroy or protect the gateway if wielded properly," Niamh said, her voice straining with emotion. "These thrones are more powerful, more impactful—" She stopped herself short, her thoughts suddenly trapped inside her throat. "Even these thrones were once channels of power. All things are. The wind, the trees, the heart—our most powerful weapon."

"I don't understand," Aisling said, unafraid to hide her discontent this time.

"Yours and Lir's power when combined will destroy everything—but it's possible yours alone is enough to protect the Forge on its own," Niamh said, leaning forward in her chair. Aisling stepped back instinctively, her tongue turning to ash in her mouth. "We both recognize your power, your potential. As did Ina. You and I, Aisling..." Her voice trailed off, attention darting to the figure who stepped into the hall.

Aisling followed Niamh's eyes.

Lir leaned against the archway with his ankles crossed, twirling his axe easily.

The room grew several degrees hotter, forcing a shudder from Aisling. The sorceress blanched.

"How villainous," Lir said, straightening. He tipped his head back, amused. And without knowing how, Aisling recognized the sharp cut of his smile and the bloodthirst it implied. He summoned his *draiocht*, snatching the Goblet with his vines and returning it to Aisling's waiting hands. The sorceress smiled despite herself, appraising the Goblet she'd won anew.

"Leave us be, Lir," Niamh said, a vein pulsing in her throat.

"And pray tell me," Lir said, "why would I do that?" The Sidhe king padded forward. Niamh turned rigid as stone. Her eyes fixed on Lir as he approached. Instinctively, he stopped a pace before Aisling, his shoulders, shielding her from Niamh.

"This doesn't concern you, *mo Damh Bán*," Niamh said. The Seelie queen gripped the arms of her throne till her knuckles turned bone-white.

"How not?" he asked, the depth of his voice sending shivers down Aisling's spine.

"You are neither champion nor king to Aisling here, and so, we owe you no explanation," Niamh bit.

Lir took another step forward, twirling his axe between his fingers. Niamh appeared to count his steps, expression hiding her anxiety well.

"I serve the Lady Aisling as sorceress, as queen, as curse breaker, and as knight. As should you. And so, an indignity to Aisling is an indignity to me. You dishonor her and I make you suffer." Lir lifted his brows, asking if she understood him.

Niamh shifted.

"Arrogance doesn't become you, *mo Damh Bán*," Niamh said, holding Lir's gaze. "Remember you made an *oath*."

Aisling looked up at Lir from where she stood, studying his expression. He concealed his thoughts well, his face betraying nothing. But there was an unforgiving, vengeful forest growing beneath the cool shadow of his exterior. A fury Aisling both recognized and understood.

The Sidhe king of the greenwood turned on his heel. "Nothing unbecomes me," he said, motioning for Aisling to join him as he coolly started toward the door. He placed his hand gently on the small of her back and pushed. Once Aisling surrendered and stepped forth, he pulled her tightly against him by the waist. Aisling's heart leaped and the bridge of her nose flushed. His touch, burning through her gown and scalding her skin.

"You're fortunate the mortals storm our world another day and not this eve; unlucky is he who sheds blood before battle," Lir said as they arrived at the door. Lir paused, turning and facing Niamh, fuming still at the dais. "Nevertheless, never rest and always wonder if the next corner turned is your last. My hand, your end."

Niamh parted her lips, following Aisling and Lir with her eyes. Aisling cast another glance at Niamh, wondering what she'd meant. Wondering if Aisling could wield the Goblet alone, after all. Or was there some magic to hers and Lir's union that spun fate, destiny, and the universe toward its end regardless of the choices she made?

Lir led Aisling onto a balcony. They floated at the edge of Castle Yillen, connected to no other turrets until the next pathway arrived at their door. At once, Lir whispered a spell beneath his breath.

"*Helliacht sec tru saera deste.*"

Aisling turned to Lir, searching for the manifestation of his magic. A boom sounded to her right, knocking the tower to the side. Aisling stumbled, quickly caught by the Sidhe king. The sorceress found her footing, spinning to find a giant tree knocked from another level and onto theirs: a bridge.

Lir picked Aisling up, holding her behind the knees and around her back. Aisling's first instinct was to strike him for touching her. Aisling still believed he'd somehow bewitched her, her body burning from the inside out in his proximity. Her *draiocht* grew feral and tempestuous, eager to bite.

The Sidhe king walked them both across the fallen tree and onto the next platform. The downpour made the bark of the tree slick, but Lir walked nimbly and easily across.

Lir leaped onto the next level, Aisling still in his arms. This part of Castle Yillen was overgrown with different species of moss, wildflowers, lily pad ponds, and weeping willows, all hugging the spindly tower at its center.

Lir walked them to the door nestled at the base of the tower, crowned with archivolts. Sidhe markings were etched across its surface—protection runes, Aisling recognized. The door, on the other hand, was latched with a tangled system of roots, braided together.

"Where are we?" Aisling asked. Lir set her on her feet gently. He approached the door and the latched roots immediately unlocked, slithering apart.

"My rooms," he said, stepping inside.

Aisling considered leaving then. She could slip away and take refuge in her chambers until the break of dawn. Exhaustion tugged at her body from the floor, her eyelids growing heavier. And still, against reason, she stayed.

The sorceress followed the Sidhe king inside and out of the rain.

As soon as one stepped across the threshold, the tower spiraled upward in an intricately carved staircase. They climbed up, emerging into a large bedroom at the top of the turret.

Aisling inhaled, soaking in the room.

It was humbler than Aisling would've imagined, neither covered in a king's precious gemstones nor metals. Instead of pillars, ash trees grew crooked yet tall, supporting the slanted ceiling of the dilapidated tower. And the rain that dripped from the holes was gulped by the *ellwyn* that spread like a disease over everything: the paint-chipped walls, the pointed windows, the beams that ribbed across the ceiling in great vaults.

Aisling stepped into the room, her feet brushed by fallen petals, by the grass between cobbles, and the hand-woven rugs.

Lir shut each of the windows, his flowers preening when he neared.

"You're welcome to rest here for the evening," Lir said. "Tonight, this is the safest edge of the castle for you."

Aisling glanced over her shoulder at the door. It was still open, inviting her to leave if she so wished.

"I may not trust Niamh," Aisling said, "but neither do I trust you." Against her will, Aisling's eyes flicked to the solitary bed at the edge of the room, pressed against an enormous rosette window. She swallowed, an image flashing across her mind's eye like lightning: Aisling—clad in a ruby gown and veil—stood in a tent, lit by the soft glow of flower bulbs. Lir towered across from her, a bed between them.

*This is your imagination and nothing more*, Anduril said. *This is a fantasy.*

The image possessed her—the *memory*. Her *draiocht* singing to itself gleefully inside her.

The corners of Lir's lips twitched up.

"I hadn't planned on staying," he said as if reading her mind.

"Good," Aisling said without pause. Lir's smile widened, but he turned his face away from her.

Lir waved his hand across the garlands of flower bulbs, bubbling around the windows and across the bed's canopy. They grew in bundles that spilled down the bedposts, blooming before Aisling's eyes with light.

Aisling smiled despite herself, trying and failing to hide it.

Lir's expression stilled, eyes widening slightly as his gaze lingered for a breath longer than usual.

Aisling averted her eyes, turning to the unlit candles frozen mid-melt. She picked up one and blew softly, lighting the candle and all others with violet flame.

The room was gilded by both fire and flower, their *draiocht* thick and ripe in the air.

Lir leaned his back against the wall, crossing his arms. He appeared cool as summer evening breezes, calm as undisturbed woodland ponds, and yet Aisling felt the thrashing inside him. Felt his *draiocht* seeking her own. A forest's tempest, trapped inside him.

"Tomorrow is the last moon of the storm season... the war will most likely commence at daybreak if not sooner," Lir said, his voice abandoning all levity.

Aisling approached him, studying the way he stiffened the nearer she grew. A vein snaking up his throat.

"Rest while you can," Lir said, eyes darkening while he watched her move. Aisling relished his attention. The sensation of his eyes memorizing the nuances of her body was like fingertips to bare flesh. As if only she existed: Aisling, the enemy of his heart.

*Run, flee, escape, walk away,* Anduril pleaded.

Aisling shuddered, her *draiocht* flaring wildly inside her as it'd never done before. She drew closer, her feet guiding her toward the Sidhe king as if bespelled.

"Where will you rest?" Aisling asked, her voice sleepy.

Lir straightened against the wall, knocking over a stack of books beside his elbow. He glanced at the commotion for a brief second, returning his eyes to Aisling as if she might vanish if he looked away too long.

"It's not your concern," he said, his voice rasping at the edges.

"Is it not?" Aisling asked, almost a whisper now that she was near enough to see the racing of his pulse. The snow winds, the only sound outside the crackling of Aisling's candle wicks. "You've failed to conceal your tricks to me and now that I know with certainty you've hidden something from me, bewitched me, betrayed me somehow. You and everything you are is my ultimate concern," Aisling said, chest to chest with the Sidhe king, forcing her to tip her chin up to meet his sage eyes above.

"Ask me then, sorceress faerie," Lir said, leaning his head down and toward her. "For despite oath or bargain, by the Forge, I am incapable of telling a lie. So, ask me for the truth."

Aisling gathered her thoughts in armfuls, struggling to focus when in his presence. This close up, the Sidhe king was no more than a dream, a legend, a mythic figment of her imagination, kindled by the tales of fantasy she'd hungered for as a child. He was the dark knight she'd clung to in the recesses of her most sacred wishes and the wild savage she'd felt inside herself.

"Do you love me?" Aisling asked, holding the Sidhe king's eyes. Her breaths grew heavy, the beat of her heart throbbing even in her tongue while her body buzzed with adrenaline. It was strange this exhilaration—this connection between them— pulling her toward him by an intangible thread. What she felt was inexplicable, unfathomable, and without reason. A thirst only he could slake, bringing sweet salvation to her lips by the mouthful if he so wished it.

The forest green of Lir's eyes were flecked with pain. His mouth bent oddly as if resisting the laws that compelled his tongue to speak the truth and the truth alone.

"Yes," he answered at last.

But like a spell spoken, their *draiocht* surged upward, the flower bulbs overcome with light and the candles blazing despite their small wicks. The Goblet beside them both, thrumming with excitement in the presence of their combined power.

*No*, Anduril roared, squeezing Aisling's hips painfully and biting into her skin.

"Then why can I not remember?" Aisling asked, rising onto her tiptoes so their noses brushed against one another. Lir shut his eyes the moment she touched him, holding onto his arm for balance. "Why has the memory been cut from my mind and not my heart?"

ENOUGH, Anduril screamed drawing blood from Aisling's skin.

Lir opened his eyes, pupils drowning out his irises. His expression was heart-stricken, appearing and disappearing just as quickly.

"Because this cannot be," Lir said beneath his breath as if forcing out the words.

"What cannot be?" Aisling asked, her lips a breath from his own, pulling the truth from between his fangs.

"You and I," he said. "You and I are ruinous."

*Listen, listen, listen, listen*, Anduril said.

"Since when does the high king of the Sidhe fear destruction, power, might and the devastation it leaves in its wake? Are you more virtuous than the tales my kin would have me believe?" Aisling asked, her body heating. "Where is my dark knight?"

*My*. The word fell from Aisling's lips as second nature. A detail that hadn't snuck past the Sidhe king undetected.

Lir shook his head. "It isn't heroism that compels me," he said, his gaze deepening the longer he held her eyes. "Not long ago, I was bespelled by a sorceress who donned the guise of a mortal princess. Violet-eyed, she cursed me with one glance, transforming all my desires, all my muses, all my thoughts into one unholy jinx alone: her." Lir brushed her lips with his own. "You," he clarified.

"And so, thief, violet-eyed sorceress, you have bested me," Lir said, speaking into her lips. "Have mercy on my soul, for it swore an oath to serve you until the end. A heart for a heart,"

Lir said. "My soul, your own. All that you covet, my heart's labor."

Aisling pressed closer to him.

"Then have me," she said, her body leaning into him so every part of them touched. She needed him to reach out and hold her. To fold his arms around her and bring her close. To bring his lips to hers and taste the desire sticky on her tongue.

Still, Lir resisted, his body as hard as stone before her. Her fires raged, melting the candles to puddles throughout the tower. The trees inside groaned, bending and warping the shingled roof of the turret.

"I cannot," Lir said between clenched teeth. "My oath is binding."

"I don't understand," Aisling said.

"You will," Lir whispered.

Aisling shook her head. "Serve me then. Serve me and break the oath you promised."

"I cannot," Lir repeated, grimacing as if in agony.

"Then you break another oath!" Aisling shouted this time, her *draiocht* swelling inside her throat till she believed it might burst. She needed to remember. She needed to understand what'd dug its claws into her memory and scraped away at her heart.

"I'd cut out my tongue to be your liar," Lir said. "I'd forsake all that I once pursued or chased. I'd condemn both realms to keep you," Lir said, his voice growing rough as he spoke. "Unless you are the cost of it."

Aisling paled, her *draiocht* grumbling awake and smoking from the nostrils.

"You refuse me," she said, her voice hard and jagged. "You refuse me when you alone bear the power to release me from this disease of the mind. You've bewitched me and so, you shackle me and imprison me in this cavern of ignorance."

Lir flinched as if physically struck. The sage of his eyes bled with grief and raw compassion. As if he understood the years of solitude pacing the corridors of Castle Neimedh, the days shut behind iron doors, or the banquet of lies her clann fed her since she was a bairn. The secrets that'd left Aisling alone and wandering in the dark.

Aisling turned, ripping herself from the Sidhe king. She started for the door, eager to distance herself so she could stew in her frustration alone.

Anduril hummed with triumph.

Lir grabbed Aisling's wrist just before she stepped out of reach. Lithely, he spun her toward him and before Aisling could protest, he brought his mouth to hers.

His left hand reached round her waist and firmly pressed her against him. His right hand cupped her jaw, tilting her chin up so his kiss could deepen. Aisling stiffened, flushed, and held her breath, her flesh, prickling with the needles of fate sewing madly.

Aisling's *draiocht* pulsed with energy, kindled by Lir's magic interlacing with her own. Her *draiocht* roared, clicking its bones as it unfurled and rose onto its hind legs. Her *draiocht* shot forth from her soul, lighting her in flame.

The fire grew outside of Aisling's control, crawling atop Lir and swathing them both in her violet magic. Yet, Lir never hissed nor reeled in pain. Instead, he held her more tightly, fingers sliding from her jaw and into her hair. His kiss, both hungry and possessive. They were a comet, smoldering in the mouth of Lir's tower.

Aisling gasped, appraising Lir. Usually, if the Sidhe king touched her flames, he burnt. Here and now, their magic mixing like a cauldron's brew, he lit flame alongside her, flowers growing between each of their curls simultaneously. An ancient, hallowed ritual taking place as Lir kissed her again: the fog that'd cloaked Aisling's mind, lifting.

*An oath is kept and an oath is broken*, the Other howled in the storm winds.

STOP, PLEASE, PLEASE, Anduril screamed, bleeding her once more.

Her memories, freshly polished, were suddenly bright and clear in her mind. They slipped from the darkness they'd been hidden in, rising again as richly as they'd once thrived. Aisling exhaled into Lir, tears blooming from her eyes with relief.

Lir kissed her more thoroughly, picking her up and holding her tightly. Every kiss, sucking Anduril's influence from her veins like a snake's venom expunged from the body.

The Sidhe king stroked the back of her thighs, turning and pressing her against the wall of the tower where he once stood. He brought his mouth to her neck, kissing her deeply and as his mouth traveled, his fangs scraped the soft edge of her throat.

Aisling shivered, her body moving against him slowly with a will of its own. He cursed, matching her movements and tasting her lips. He ran his hands up her dress and took hold of her bare legs. His abdomen tightening as he thrusted, hips rubbing against the inside of her thighs.

Aisling sucked in a sharp breath, tangled her fingers in his hair while her back arched into him. Lir groaned, slipping his hands further up her slip until they held her waist on either side. Aisling pushed the remaining fabric aside and unbuckled his belt. Every kiss, expanding their lungs with more power than they knew how to control. They blazed, flooding the room with flame and flowers till the tower shone like a star. The Other, thumping with the rhythm of a drum as Lir entered her.

He held her steady by the waist, pushing and pulling against her. His jaw clenched, every muscle cording in his body while his head threw back. Both their eyes, reflecting the outcomes of omens, of prophecies, of the future yet told. Pleasure, wracking them both through as their hunger accelerated— their combined power rising to a crescendo.

Aisling reached out, grabbing whatever was close by for support.

S*top, please*, Anduril shouted. This time, the belt gripped her as tightly as it was capable, forcing a scream from her lips.

Aisling reached for the belt and its clasp. She hesitated a second, meeting Lir's eyes.

Aisling ripped Anduril from her body.

*No*, Anduril shrieked, its voice already melting into the memory of the Forge.

Its possession rid Aisling of her strength but also its curse. Her body flared with her *draiocht*, she and Lir a combined comet of fire and flowers, joining into one.

Lir acknowledged Anduril on the floor only briefly before returning his full attention to Aisling. He moved more quickly, harder, possessively filling her with each stroke. His breath heavy and his chest glistening with both their sweat combined.

The omens, the prophecies, and the curses, taking shape as they intertwined. As they braided their *draiocht* and fed off the other's obsession. Pleasure vibrating through both their bodies in great pulses of pure satisfaction.

She loved him unequivocally. Tragically. Hopelessly. Whether it be destiny that compelled her heart or herself, she knew not. Perhaps she'd never know. She only knew that whatever breaths remained in her body would be spent loving those she cared for most. And there was no greater adventure, no greater purpose, and no greater power. Her pursuit for everything was completed the moment she handfast the nightmare before her.

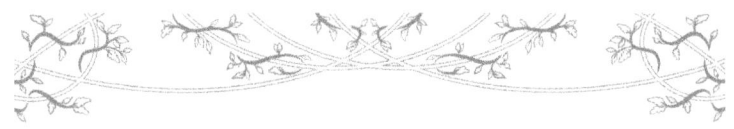

# CHAPTER L

## AISLING

Spun in a spider's cocoon, Aisling screamed, chafing her bare flesh against the needle-thin, ivory threads when she squirmed.

"One, two, three." The Lady laughed to herself in the dark. "One, two, three, here we come."

Aisling tore the cocoon apart with her teeth, ripping herself free, thread by thread.

"One, two, three, here we come," the Lady repeated, as she emerged from the darkness. A grotesque colossus of a spider, reflecting Aisling's violet eyes from the eight, beady orbs of its eyes. Blade sharp legs, clicking as she approached.

"One, two, three, here we come. Here we come. Here we come. Here we come."

Aisling screamed, gums red with her blood, sliced by the threads she desperately tore with her teeth.

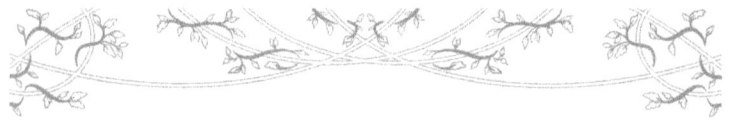

# CHAPTER LI

## AISLING

When the Other snored beneath the highest stars, Aisling woke beside Lir. Her heart fluttered, her stomach knotted, and her mind spun, her body resisting the urge to wake him and let him enter her once more. But there was no time.

Lir held her tightly in his sleep, so Aisling slipped from his arms carefully not to wake him. She tiptoed out of the fae king's rooms and wandered Castle Yillen's halls.

That evening, a gown lay waiting for Aisling atop her pelts. Bane-black, the dress was breathtaking, whispering like a chorus of shadows to be worn. Aisling held up the gown, *ellwyn* petals slipping off its folds the moment the sorceress raised it.

"*Mo Damh Bán* had it made for you before *Imbolc*," Gilrel said.

A murder of silver-eyed ravens took flight in Aisling's stomach, admiring the gown more closely. Ribbons of black hugged the bodice of the dress, cut flatteringly beneath the breasts. Sigh-soft pleats of sheer chiffon wrapped around its center till they reached the deep, drop waist "v" at the hips; the same delicate material of her sleeves, beginning below the shoulder. Both sleeves hugged the arms, flaring at the elbows and sweeping the floors, the grass, the lakes. A gown of this beauty should taste them all at least once. And from the hipline, the skirts spilled like ink to the floor.

"No armor?" Aisling asked.

Gilrel shook her head. "No, *mo Lúra*. Only Sarwen. To wield the Goblet, you'll only need what's inside." Gilrel placed a paw to her heart. "Let me help you dress."

Aisling slipped into the gown, aided by the pine marten's diligent fingers. Her handmaid laced up the back, strapped Sarwen to her gown, and dabbed her lips with crushed cherries.

Aisling took one last glance at herself before exiting her chambers. Her violet eyes were rimmed with red and her cheeks hollow—a wolf's bite in her expression.

And so, the moment Gilrel slipped out the door, Aisling secretly did as well.

Barefoot, Aisling relished the cool stone beneath her feet.

Aisling hugged the Goblet of Lore between her arms, careful not to spill a drop as she traveled.

She held her breath as she snuck past the guards, as she tiptoed past the toads sleeping in the library, and skulked past winged Sidhe yet to find their chambers for the evening.

The faerie moved quietly and nimbly, eager to make it before the sun peaked its head above the horizon and war began.

Aisling popped open another door, sliding into the corridor and closing it softly behind her once more.

"Aisling," a voice chimed.

Aisling almost leaped out of her skin, tightening her grip on the Goblet as she turned to face whomsoever had caught her slipping through Castle Yillen's halls.

Niamh stood at the end of the corridor, watching her closely. Her expression was somber and her eyes swollen from hours of tears wept.

"Where are you going?"

Aisling hesitated, her knuckles growing white on the stem of the Goblet.

"You cannot stop me," Aisling replied, steeling herself. No longer did she wear Anduril, but her magic was powerful enough. That, combined with the Goblet... she could defeat Niamh if necessary.

"I don't intend to," Niamh said, taking a cautious step forward. As if afraid to startle a doe.

"Our interaction earlier suggests differently," Aisling said.

Niamh flinched as though she'd been physically struck, her face falling with sadness. Her shoulder sloped and her arms hung loosely at her sides. She was seemingly ashamed of her behavior, standing before Aisling like a broken bird.

"I am—was desperate. Desperate not to be alone," Niamh confessed. "For there is no more desperate a creature than those on the verge of losing all they value most."

"We have a chance of winning this war," Aisling assured the Seelie queen. "To flee, to turn around now would be to forfeit our only chance of survival."

Niamh nodded her head slowly, still staring at the cobbles beneath her feet.

"I agree," she said, her voice surprisingly sincere.

Aisling shifted uncomfortably, unsure what to say.

"I've come to aid you," Niamh continued.

"Aid me?"

"The mortals are coming, and the gates must be destroyed," Niamh said.

"And yet, the other sovereigns still believe in protecting the gateways," Aisling countered.

"Aye, they do," Niamh surrendered. "But I do not."

"Because you're afraid, Niamh. Afraid of being trapped, here, alone, forever."

"Perhaps," Niamh said. "But I also acknowledge sacrifices must be made."

Aisling studied the Seelie queen closely, ignoring the steady rain beating against the windowpanes of the corridor.

"Is that not what you're traveling toward now?" Niamh asked.

Aisling's eyes flicked to the Goblet before returning her attention to Niamh.

Cautiously, Aisling nodded her head in reply. She'd taken the Goblet, intending to destroy every gateway before her father could do so. Before Nemed could destroy the Other altogether and carve the curse breaker from her chest. If her father was to win, he'd win blood and dust and ruins. And so, Aisling would destroy every gate if it meant protecting those she loved. If it meant guarding the Sidhe and the Forge from the death-bidden touch of mortal man.

"It is," Aisling conceded.

"Let me help you," Niamh said. "Let me help you destroy the gates."

"Is it possible?" Aisling asked.

"I'm not certain," Niamh replied honestly. "But it's worth a try."

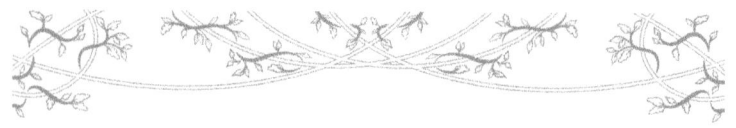

# CHAPTER LII

## LIR

The forest called the Sidhe king to its lip before devouring him whole. He sank into the labyrinth, his every sense more alive and eager to explore the Other—his intimacy with Aisling, strengthening his *draiocht* in a way he'd never felt before. Had never experienced. He hungered for those feelings, for her, for their destiny together. He'd woken without Aisling, wondering where she'd gone. He'd wanted to stay and hold her. Touch her. Hear her voice and look into her eyes. But he knew better than to indulge in the future when they sat on the eve of war. He knew better than to hope for more, for goodness, when the second boot would always drop and violence would ensue.

It was the trees that told Lir where his bride fled. That she, dressed in shadows, sunk into the forest and wove through its depths beneath the light of the last storm moon. And so, he'd follow.

Lir's heart drummed inside him. He paced the forest floor unable to sleep when war was approaching, twisting the rings on each of his fingers. He felt afraid. Terrified. He tasted the end of everything and all that consumed his mind was Aisling. Where was she? How was she? Where would she be when it was all over? It was happening more quickly than Lir was prepared for. His greatest fears on the brink of being realized by mortal makings.

He sucked on the sap of alder pines to calm his nerves when he couldn't find her and still, his heart beat like the drums before blood was shed. And what's more, the grin had contaminated almost everything, spreading like wildfire from the forest and into the meadows. An infection that took but never gave, leaving death in its wake. He saw its influence for miles and tasted its contagion in the sap of every tree he passed.

"Over there!" The trees called to him.

Through the branches, Lir saw a ghost. No, not a ghost. Two maidens racing through the forest like spirits in the night. Like banshees.

Aisling and Niamh raced on white stags. They cut through the trees, the forest bending and twisting to make a path for them both.

Lir's chest seized, his hand wandering toward his heart.

Aisling's beauty was poetry; a verse that both wounded and healed, staking you through the heart with unfathomable, unmistakable, and horrible recognition. She, a forbidden whisper, a confession, a bearing of the darkest depths of the soul.

Lir wasn't certain how long he stared at Aisling as she raced, only that it wasn't enough. For as soon as she was out of sight, his heart sank and his boots flew in the direction she fled.

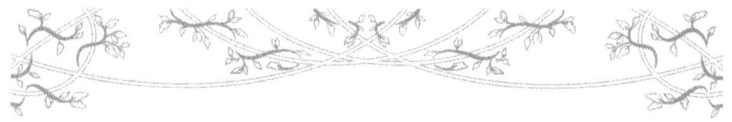

## CHAPTER LIII

AISLING

Aisling and Niamh slipped out of the forest and into the meadow where the great gate stood. The gateway to the Other and the mortal plane. A behemoth dream tree split at the center where water rippled vertically. Already the dream tree was infected with the grin. Her clann was close.

"Destroy this one," Niamh said. "And all others will collapse. Including Leshy."

Aisling nodded her head, flying off the stag with the Goblet in hand. She stared up at the gateway, at the cool, peaceful night, and her stomach rose into her throat.

The stars gleamed down at her, smiling sweetly and curiously.

"What now?" Aisling asked, facing the end of everything. The gate was a giant, looming above her ominously. Challenging her to destroy it fully and completely.

"Take a sip," Niamh said.

The sorceress, the faerie, the mortal princess looked up at the star-beaded sky. The last storm moon shimmered between curtains of rain, considering Aisling with intention. It's *draiocht* calling to the Goblet and inviting its power.

In the roar of the storm and in the light of the moon, Aisling brought the Goblet of Lore to her lips.

Aisling drank tentatively at first and then in great gulps. It tasted of rich plum syrups and bubbling jinxes. Of sorcery and magic incarnate. Her stomach tumbled madly as every word was another step closer to either her ruination or ultimate victory. She'd known the consequences would be cosmic and her own life was at stake. But for the first time, she'd tasted the reality on the lip of the Goblet.

"A sacrifice is demanded: one made of the self," Niamh said. "The Forge demands blood."

Aisling's attention followed Niamh's line of sight, landing on a serpent coiling tightly around her ankle.

Aisling's stomach dropped.

Lir's ruthlessness was but one of the various characteristics Aisling admired of the Sidhe king. One she intended to master as she aged into eternity. Yet, she'd found time and time again, whenever her own ruthlessness was tested, that such a sacrifice was no sacrifice at all. Her bloodthirst wet her tongue and coaxed her arm forward till the serpent hung from her hand, biting her fingers and struggling to keep hold of Aisling. Like the sting of coin bees, its fangs sank into the scars she'd earned burning Danu's nettle from inside Lir.

The Other leaned closer. So she lit it aflame and watched as it hissed and squealed, shriveling until it, at last, released Aisling and was swallowed whole by flame.

Niamh grinned ear to ear, her fangs sparkling. "By the Forge, I pray thee laurel the worthy in garlands of glory and damn the unworthy."

The Other heaved with great satisfaction, tasting her blood.

*Aisling*, it spoke.

The Goblet was hers.

## CHAPTER LIV

LIR

Lir left a trail of *ellwyn* in his wake as he ran. As he shifted through the oaks, jumped over the stones, raced through creeks, and dove out of the forest.

His lungs burned, his heart whipping inside his chest with desperation. He looked over his shoulder, ensuring she wasn't there. He was alone, cutting through the Other like spring breaks winter.

The oath he'd sworn to Aisling, scalding his skin and singeing his tunic where it throbbed.

At last, he heard the drums of the *draiocht* beating, the horns blowing, and the vibration of the Goblet thrumming through the earth and through his boots.

His mind flashed with the image of Aisling in a crimson veil. With her hands wrapped around his axe nailed into the earth. With her expression the moment she learned his name, and the sound of it when she'd spoken it for the first time. He saw her before the trow, the Cu Scath, the fomorians, Danu... He saw her on her stag after he believed her dead. He saw her escape Castle Oighir, stand before Racat at Lofgren's Rise, he saw her breathe fire. He saw her in everything and couldn't remember anything before her. He had to stop her—to save her from herself. The world would burn, and he'd let it spare her. He'd do anything for her.

*Whatever you covet, will be my heart's labor.*

Lir hesitated, his boots catching on vines he hadn't noticed in his desperation.

A faerie and her knight.

The memories swarmed his mind.

*"Are you trying to corrupt me?" Aisling asked.*

*"No," Lir replied. "I'm trying to show you, you already are."*

Lir closed his eyes, pushing back tears. He realized it all at once, his heart pushing at his chest to be released.

Aisling and Lir were not *caera*. Only Lir and Narisea were. That was why Lir was able to wed both without killing either; Aisling was something different to him entirely.

Ina had never intended for Lir to be Aisling's lover. He was her protector. Her guide. Her strength as she spared the Sidhe from the destruction Ina foresaw. The love he felt for Aisling was not a product of magic or fate or threads of destiny.

It was his and his alone.

Lir was a wolf, cutting through the forest. He was too far. He couldn't make it in time. He wasn't moving quickly enough.

The woodland parted, forging a path for him. Yet, no path, nor passage, nor spell could deliver him quickly enough to the gateway. His knights on his heels. The Other's breath rattling through the caverns of the Forge as fate unspooled.

To make his feet light and his pace quick, Lir released his fear of the end. He released his fear of loss. He released Aisling. And Lir let go.

## CHAPTER LV

### AISLING

Sticky and sweet, Aisling swallowed the Goblet's brew gulp by gulp.

Her veins bubbled like champagne, her *draiocht* startled awake, and her pupils dilated fully. She felt the magic inside like the creature it was, possessing her body as a capsule for its power. Endless possibilities pricked at her fingertips. She could both create and destroy. Could dip her fingertips into the molten belly of the Forge and retrieve whatever her mind imagined. The world, the universe, magic as old as time, was hers.

Niamh watched her closely as she lowered the Goblet.

Aisling's eyes shone vivid violet, illuminating her face with an eerie glow.

"And now?" Aisling asked. Her voice was not her own. It was now accompanied by another—perhaps the Forge itself, nestling inside her lungs and commanding her voice as had Anduril. And once more, it was a sacrifice she'd make.

"And now," Niamh said, "speak your will."

Aisling stared up at the gateway. It watched her in return, studying her strength as she studied its own.

# CHAPTER LVI

LIR

Lir let go.

The Sidhe king flung himself from the forest with a great cry. The bones in his back snapped in half at the shoulders, molding and remolding as he writhed on the grass in agony. From here, a meadow stretched between him and the gateway—too far for him to reach on time. And now, he was afflicted by some strange torture, crippling him when Aisling needed him most.

"*Ellwyn*," he said between clenched teeth, but none could hear him save for the flowers he crushed as he dragged himself across the grass.

"*Ellwyn*," he repeated like an undead creature, stopping at nothing to meet their ends.

The Sidhe king roared out in pain, reaching for his back and scratching at the strange wound. Had he run into a tree? Caught himself on something? Been shot by an arrow? Lir rummaged through his mind to make sense of his pain but found nothing. Nothing until his fingers scraped the silky soft edge of a wing.

Lir froze.

He brought his fingertips before him and stared at the blood smeared there now. He reached back again, this time less cautious.

Two wings grew from his back, expanding, stretching, materializing from his shoulder blades with a magic most called "miracle." It smelled of bargains, of promises, and of the rain. The storm that soaked him now and showered the world with its finality.

The Sidhe king winced when he attempted to move them, screaming and biting through the torture of new muscle and bone alike. Lir shook his head, determined to use his newfound wings here and now.

Lir moved again, complexion red with his effort.

At last, his wings moved fluidly, rising and falling, collecting rain and light and glimmering with an otherworldly glow. They spread behind him like a dragon boasts its mighty wings, great and wonderful and the makings of legends.

Lir focused on his mother's teachings, swallowing hard before he, at last, took flight.

He sprang into the air and darted for Aisling and Niamh already standing before the gateway. The Goblet of Lore shone brightly in Aisling's hands—an ember amidst the darkened night.

He'd make it in time. With his wings, he could reach her and together they'd bring mankind to their knees—

Aisling tilted the Goblet back and drank.

The air pressure grew heavy, pushing down on Lir as he flew. It made his wings heavy as if he tore through currents of pure, undiluted magic from the dawn of time.

"Aisling!" He called across the expanse, but he was still too far. She couldn't hear him.

## CHAPTER LVII

AISLING

Aisling stepped forward and opened her mouth.

Niamh followed shortly thereafter, grabbing her hand.

"Thank you," she said to Aisling. Her voice was strange, mottled with emotion. "I'm proud to have trusted Ina's judgment in you. There was a reason she chose you, Aisling. You were born for this."

Aisling felt a lump in her throat. She tried to swallow it but it was futile, growing larger and thicker the longer she watched Niamh. They were the words she'd wished her mother had spoken to her, even once. The sentiment she'd prayed her father would feel for her. And yet, here and now, she needed none of her clann's, her túath's, her family's validation. She'd earned her strength, her power, her might overtime and it was enough. It was what she'd developed along the way that she fought for now. That she'd sacrifice her life for.

Aisling nodded her head in reply for there weren't words capable of describing how she felt in that moment. She could only hope Niamh understood and remembered.

"Will you be lonely still?" Aisling asked the Seelie queen.

"No," Niamh replied quickly. "Not anymore."

Aisling and Niamh exchanged smiles, prolonging the inevitable. But it was time. The moment made clear as the gateway shuddered to life with a violet boom.

Her father was here.

## CHAPTER LVIII

LIR

Lir blazed through the meadow. From the lip of the woods, the field stretched before him like a legion of tall grasses, reigned over by the mammoth ash tree at its center.

The skies darkened with the storm looming overhead. And even from here, Lir could see the black rot oozing along the base of the gateway.

Lir cursed. He skidded to a stop just before the gateway, staring it up and down. His wings folded behind him, and silently, he thanked them for doing what his feet could not: delivering him to the end so that he might stand by Aisling at the gateway. A final favor. And now, the gateway was opening.

"Aisling!" he shouted.

Both Aisling and Niamh turned on their heel to see him. Their mouths fell open not expecting to see the fae king here and now, and especially not with wings. Niamh, however, collected herself quickly, smiling proudly at the wings spread behind him. She winked at the Sidhe lord and Lir could've sworn he heard Arawn's laughter in the thunder up above.

"Lir?" Aisling called back, staring at him as he defeated the distance between himself and the gateway, pried open by iron from the other side. Sparks flew from the warped surface of the gateway, bending and breaking at odd angles. One moment, the door was like water, and the next, it hardened to stone, then oak, then glass, desperately trying to rebuild itself as the iron cut deeper and deeper. It stretched then shrank, releasing spine-chilling groans from the tree itself being pulled apart limb by limb. A torturous affair that rattled even the rotted woods of the Other.

"Destroy the gate, Aisling!" Lir shouted. "I'll do my best to keep it closed until you break it fully."

Aisling nodded her head, resolve lighting her violet eyes. She hesitated on his wings but seemingly resolved to speak of it later. After, once they had a moment to breathe—once victory was theirs—they'd have an eternity together to speak about everything.

At once, Lir placed his naked palm against its trunk despite the grin. The tree jerked side to side, overwhelmed with the sudden burst of Lir's magic. The tree shrieked till Aisling refused herself the urge to cover her ears. She needed her hands, her power, her full force. Her palms slick with the gateway's blood, sap, and tears as she worked.

The Sidhe king closed his eyes, concentrating. This tree was unlike any he'd ever spoken to: it was older, stranger, more mischievous than any creature he'd harbored or grown in his forests. It carried the depth and sorrow of the beginning of time and the celebration of its end. Its voice echoed, afraid and in pain.

It was time. He couldn't keep it closed anymore.

"The mortals," Lir said. "They're here."

# CHAPTER LIX

## AISLING

Aisling's blood turned cold. Niamh sent bolts of lightning across the sky, begging the other Sidhe sovereigns to come and aid them. They received silence in response—the three of them alone at the foot of the gateway.

The sorceress shook her head, eyes vacant. The gateway was a colossal tree, split at the center to reveal a doorway. And despite Lir's efforts—desperately trying to keep it shut—it was opening regardless.

Aisling approached the gateway, the Goblet in hand.

"Aisling!" Lir screamed, he pulled her back, catching her in his arms. They both fell to the floor with her momentum, finding their footing swiftly thereafter. Through the shimmering surface of the gateway, Aisling saw them: her clann's faces flashing beyond the gateway when their iron punctured deeply enough to cause significant damage. Leshy's blood and sap spraying Aisling's horror-stricken expression.

Her clann, the mortals, mankind, stood on the other side, their fire and iron weapons in hand. Nemed smiled at his daughter, the sight of which rendered Aisling ill. Her brothers stood closely beside him, staring into the Other like a bairn devours a new world. And yet, it was not meant for them. The sorceress was overcome with pure, undiluted rage.

They were close. Just on the other side of the world. Their eyes met and Aisling felt their shared blood heat.

"Aisling," Nemed said, his voice corrupted by the mayhem and the writhing of the gateway as it struggled to stay alive. His eyes burned red and fire spread behind them like a column of flame, hungry to devour the Other as soon as it was allowed. Leshy's cries ringing into oblivion. A group of men stood in rows behind them, their eyes glazed over and dead. Chills wracked Aisling's body. This was how they'd done it—survived despite her scorching of their mortal fleets. The Lady had brought them here with dark spells and forced wills.

*Wystria.*

"Father," she said although she hadn't meant to.

"I love you dearly," her father shouted back, rewarded by the glistening, jealous eyes of her brothers. Especially Starn. Smoke spilling from their lips. "But you forget your duty to humankind."

"And you forget your duty to your kin," Aisling replied, her body numb, hair wicking wildly in the wind of their mutual destruction.

"The fate of mankind is larger than myself or you, Aisling. That is what you must fight for," her father said. "Sacrifice yourself for the greater good. Be as kingly as either I or your brothers for once. Do the right thing and honor your blood... for this once."

Aisling clenched her teeth, the world falling silent except for the timbre she'd once feared in her father's voice. She still felt the sting of his hand on her cheek when she was five, the chatter of her teeth when he'd beaten her below the stairs, or the silence when he'd ignored her for the latter part of her life.

Always Aisling would remember their expressions on this day—so alike the evening they'd left her to the Sidhe: Nemed and Starn stood proud and determined, Fergus and Annind were silent but obedient, and Iarbonel choked back tears. But this time, they bore no intention of letting Aisling leave alive. This time, they'd take everything, and then they'd take Aisling too. Nemed couldn't control her, and so, he'd end her. He'd not rest until all and everything fell obedient at his boots. Until he'd proven Aisling was weak and useless. Even if that meant death was the only outcome.

And so it was.

"As queen of the Sidhe and keeper of the Goblet," Aisling proclaimed, her voice spectral and frightening, imbued by the magic spinning all around them, "I honor my blood."

*I summon the draiocht*, Aisling commanded Racat.

Racat chuckled, leaping from his resting place with a growling belly.

Aisling lit with violet flame. She took hold of the gateway and pulsed with magic, expending every last ounce of power she possessed. Her family watched in disgust, raising their iron blades, prepared to cut the curse breaker from her chest. But it was Starn who took a flaming Sarwen from Aisling's back and plunged into Lir with the magic the Lady had lent him.

The Sidhe king of greenwood appraised the damage. He'd been too distracted, too enveloped in protecting Aisling to anticipate Starn's mischief. A carelessness that led to a blade lodged just beside his heart.

Lir fell to his knees, staring at the blood on his fingertips.

At last, the other Sidhe sovereigns arrived. They came on thunder clouds, on bolts of lightning, on freshly whipped winds, on wolves, by wings, and on foot. They crowded around the gateway, acclimating themselves to the mayhem unspooling at the edge of prophecy.

Lir groaned in pain, finding Aisling's eyes from where he knelt.

Aisling screamed, burning more brightly. The gateway

ignited like a torch. Every Sidhe sovereign staggered back, avoiding Aisling's fires. Lir lit with flame as well and just like the last time, he was unharmed by her fires.

Aisling collapsed beside him, holding his face between her hands. Still, the mortals clawed through the gateway, striking it with their cannons and weapons. The war, slipping between Aisling's fingers in a matter of seconds.

Aisling buried her face in Lir's blood-soaked shirt. He held her closely, pressing his lips to the crown of her head.

His heart beat against her cheek. The smell of him, of cypress needles and the rain-soaked earth. He, and the axes twinkling at his back, were the forest incarnate. The savagery, the wildness, the magic of the Sidhe drinking from the wellspring that was their king.

Aisling gritted her teeth.

"No!" Niamh shouted, but it was a strangled cry—a panicked response before the inevitable. Before fate worked at the loom itself.

Both Aisling and Lir exploded with the strength of their *draiocht* combined. The world turned violet, burning at the center of a wick. The Forge churning as the gods opened one eye, startled from their slumber. Aisling felt the Forge's magic roll onto its side after millennia asleep—charms of yore sewing through the fabric of the universe in a different direction. The stars turned and the words unwrote themselves.

Racat wrapped his sinuous body around the ash, squeezing tightly and suffocating the gateway. The mortals pounded against the gate, their expressions contorting with rage and a hunger Aisling recognized. A craving for something just out of reach.

Niamh appeared between the licks of flame, her storm crashing atop the gateway in a desperate attempt to put out Aisling and Lir's magic.

"No more, Aisling!" she shouted, lightning striking her heels as she neared the gateway. "You will destroy *everything* if you do not relent."

The other Sidhe sovereigns raised their *draiocht* and attacked. Calling upon their winds, their waves, their summer suns, their stars and the weapons they were gifted by the gods themselves.

Aisling met Galad's eyes, then Gilrel's, a silent moment passing between them amidst the chaos. They shared their pain with Aisling, their memories, their rage.

Lir pulled Aisling against himself, his blood wetting her gown. His heartbeat was flickering like a dying fire even as their magic raged. He was dying, struck by her own enchanted blade.

Aisling bit through her tears; she and Lir, a pillar of violet fire below the tree. The Goblet channeling her magic as precisely as a sword cuts flesh, her bidding its whim.

Alone, Aisling and Lir were insufficient. But Ina had known all along the devastation Aisling and Lir would wreak as a product of their need for the other. She knew of their ill omens, their curses, and their ruinous love. She knew of their power, of their coupling, and of their potential to destroy that which nothing else could. She knew of the Goblet and she knew of the gateway.

Nemed reached his hand through the gate, feeling the Other's storms for the first time. The legions behind him, Aisling's clann, snickering with blood lust and *wystria*.

They pushed at the gate with their iron shields and weapons, releasing flaming arrows that ricocheted off the gateway's rippling surface. Their power formidable and cruel, laced with the Lady's perfume.

Aisling closed her eyes. As if her túath had brought their hands to her lips, she tasted blood: the Sidhe's, the Forge, Dagfin's, Galad's, Gilrel's, Lir's, and now her own.

Nemed stepped a boot through the gateway. He stank of

iron and soulless magic. Of shadows and vengeance and blood ties cut and burned.

The Other shuddered, a mortal unwelcome in this spirit realm. And so, the grin spread throughout the plane with wicked speed, closing in on the gateway with its disease as Aisling worked. Their mortal influence corrupting from the inside out.

Starn reached his head through. Aisling held back when her brother entered, waiting instead for the tip of Galad's blade to sever her brother's head from body. And sever Galad did. In a slushy thud, Starn's head hit the ground and rolled down the roots of the ash. Her father gaped, expression blank as he clawed through the gate to reach his son's head.

*I summon the draiocht*, Aisling whispered. *I summon it all.*

Racat grinned, ear to ear. *At long last.* The Goblet focused on hers and Lir's combined power.

Aisling's magic flared, blood dripping from her nostrils as she focused on her clann, her father, and let go.

*Aisling!* The Lady shrieked between the folds of oblivion, reaching for Aisling through the veil. But it was too late.

The gateway ripped apart and warped with her flames. The dream tree shrieked with pain, its limbs crumpling and curling in like a dead spider's legs.

Aisling felt the lives of her clann end, staring vacantly long after their flesh had melted from their bones. There was an instinctual pang of grief followed by absolute fulfillment. In this one fleeting moment, Aisling, at last, had everything: power, love, and release. Vengeance, sweet on her tongue as she collapsed across from the Sidhe king. Both swathed in flames, the storm washing away their blood.

## CHAPTER LX

### AISLING

The Great Forge of Creation bubbled darkly from the brim of the Goblet.

Neither here nor there, Aisling stood in darkness, caught somewhere in between. Her wings fluttered at her back and her blade was licked with violet flame.

Aisling smelled the plum-fresh perfume of the Goblet. Slowly, she brought the chalice to her lips, its brew dripping down the corner of her mouth and down the edge of her throat. Aisling drank and drank, guzzling until not a drop was left.

At last, she came up for air. Pupils dilating across the whites of her eyes.

"Rise," Racat purred, "Rise and reign everlasting."

Aisling wiped her mouth with the back of her sleeve. Her gown glittering even in the darkness.

"May I take one last sip of the Goblet?" Aisling asked, not entirely sure whom she asked.

"Take as many as you like," Racat said.

Aisling brought the Goblet to her lips once more, tasting its sickly-sweet sap. She closed her eyes and thought of her intent, of returning what was stolen.

# CHAPTER LXI

Prophecies, self-fulfilled or otherwise, were cunning. Visions and ill omens were only as powerful as those who believed in their shadowed magic. But to those who had faith in their blades and their unique ability to carve destiny from the battle of wills, fate cowered. The dauntless pointed their swords in the direction of their conquests and not away.

Ina foresaw an impossible magic. Whilst some claimed such sorcery was the product of the gods and their cruel mischief, others deemed it a miracle. All the same, it was a magic more powerful than a blade, more unbreakable than a spell, and greater than any prophecy.

Combined, Aisling and Lir's *draiocht* was the only magic powerful enough to destroy the gate and protect the Forge and all its kin, this much Ina knew. The Seelie queen of Iod toyed with different outcomes, stirring the waters of time and rearranging the endings. In some tales, the mortals passed through the gateway and destroyed the spirit world. In others, Aisling and Lir burned both realms to nothing more than ash. But perhaps, Aisling and Lir were always meant to destroy the gateway to protect the Forge. Perhaps, there was never another ending.

Aisling stuck her hand into the Goblet, elbow deep. She rummaged through the brew, stealing every forge-born creature remaining in the mortal plane and delivering them to the Other—magic sucked from the veins of the mortal plane until Aisling had her fill.

The mortals and the fae could never coexist. Mankind destroyed, bled, and blazed through the earth the Sidhe lived off. And so, the forge-born were best protected in a realm of their own. Still, their magic thrummed through the earth, between the trees, beneath the mountains, within the wind. Just beyond mortal touch.

Without mercy, Aisling spared only those who'd supported Lir and Annwyn. Others, such as Danu's Unseelie, met brutal ends. Danu herself was given to Lir who rebuilt Annwyn in the depths of the Other's most ancient woods. His castle, forged by the forest itself for their sovereign.

Over the span of eternity, Lir cut Danu's branches one by one. He kept the empress alive, a ghost that would haunt Annwyn's corridors till the realm's end.

The Sidhe king of the greenwood reigned as high king of the Other—a period of unadulterated magic filling the Other to the bone with enchantments. Still, once a year, the Sidhe king journeyed to the ash tree at the center of the field where Niamh's gateway once stood.

On the eve of *Samhain*, when the veil was thinnest, Lir would sleep below the tree and wait for her.

She tiptoed through the mists of time, pulling apart the tapestry of the universe, and slipping into Lir's arms just before he woke. She, having given her life to destroy the gate and save Lir, became the gateway herself. A spirit of beginnings and endings. A creature of the in-between. A savage beast and magic incarnate, she was limitless. Aisling was free, anchored to the tangible only by her love for her nightmare, enemy king.

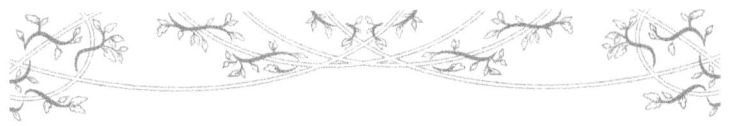

# EPILOGUE

When the rest of the Other drowned themselves in heathenish celebration, Lir made his way to the ash tree at the center of the field. The haunting of their drums and horns, the beating of their feet against the earth as they danced, the smoke and glow of their feverish light dimmed to a whisper as Lir flew with new wings and approached the ash.

Lir cradled a small bairn in his arms, with her own wings tucked into a swaddle that Gilrel had wrapped around the child. The infant cooed, nestled against the Sidhe king's chest. One of her eyes was violet and the other green as the woodland she would one day rule.

"Hush, Orlaith." Lir smiled at his daughter, bringing her close. "She'll be here soon."

Lir made two beds of ellwyn and fig moss, one for himself and one for Orlaith, beneath the ash. The child drifted to sleep, lulled by the distant revelry of Samhain. Lir, however, stared at the stars dancing above, his heart thudding with anticipation.

"Aisling," he called into the night. Her name was like a prayer to him now. As he spoke it, he felt his complexion flush. Fate seemed to gather around him.

"Aisling," he said again.

And this time, she heard his call.

The Other shuddered with her magic. Every oak, yew, and maple swayed to the rhythm of her steps. Lir stood, and carefully gathered the sleeping Orlaith in his arms.

She stepped out of the ash tree like a myth—and she was at once a specter and the woman she had been and all the tales they'd tell of her. A guardian of the veil, forever caught between here and there. But always, always his.

Their eyes connected and Lir almost fell to his knees. Aisling's eyes were violet as magic itself, and she watched him with the gaze of one who has seen eternity. She stood naked save for transparent webs of black silk, sparkling in the moonlight, and the raven-black hair falling down her back seemed alive with the breath of the forest.

They stood in silence, watching each other.

Every year, on Samhain, Lir had come here alone. And every year, Aisling had found her way across the veil to spend this one night together. Last year, she had arrived with Orlaith in her arms.

Lir always feared she wouldn't recognize him. Feared that the goddess who loved him must be a figment of his imagination, something he'd woven in dreams on the endless lonely nights between one Samhain and the next.

"Lir," She said, and her voice was not one but many.

Aisling ran to him. As they met, the universe dissolved into nothing more than her body against his, and their child between them. Her lips found Lir's and consumed him, alive and burning with overwhelming heat.

Later, Lir held Aisling as she cradled their child, humming lullabies that Orlaith would repeat as she grew older. Lullabies that would fill the halls of Castle Annwyn with Aisling's magic.

On this eve, every year, Lir and Orlaith would wait for her, whispering her name until she slipped through the veil.

"*Aisling*," Lir said, again and again until the sun rose.

# A LETTER FROM ASHLEY

Dear reader,

Thank you for reading *The Forever Queen*. The nature of books and their endings is strange. Their stories, their characters, their worlds, and the emotions they wrought on us, are as deeply rooted as the underbelly of the forest in which this tale grows. Everlasting is the mark of a cherished book. And yet, there will come a time when every reader and every storyteller alike will write and read the conclusory words: "the end." The story is done, never to be experienced for the first time again. Perhaps the nature of books and their endings is not so strange, but rather the nature of endings has always felt tragic to me: a place one can never fully return. It was, thus, crucial as I wrote the last installment that if an ending was inevitable, it would be the right one. An ending that suited the series as a whole and acknowledged the everlasting magic of a legend told more than once. And so, if you enjoyed *The Forever Queen*, and want to keep up to date with all my latest releases, just sign up at the following link. Your email address will never be shared and you can unsubscribe at any time.

*www.secondskybooks.com/ashley-metzler*

Hearing my readers' voices has been one of the most invaluable experiences of being an author. It is a gift to be able to share my stories with you all and I treasure your thoughts, opinions, and feedback. Whether it be a book thrown across the room in frustration, a cover shut tight in anticipation, a page torn and taped to the wall, or a discussion with fellow readers, I'll never tire of hearing your experiences. Reviews are always appreciated and might help *The Forever Queen* discover new readers to steal into the feywilds.

If you feel inspired to do so, stay in touch on my social media or my website.

With love,

Ashley Metzler x

www.aejurgens.com

instagram.com/ashleymetzlerauthor
tiktok.com/@ashleymetzlerr

# PUBLISHING TEAM

Turning a manuscript into a book requires the efforts of many people. The publishing team at Bookouture would like to acknowledge everyone who contributed to this publication.

**Audio**
Alba Proko
Sinead O'Connor
Melissa Tran

**Commercial**
Lauren Morrissette
Hannah Richmond
Imogen Allport

**Cover design**
BRoseDesignz

**Data and analysis**
Mark Alder
Mohamed Bussuri

**Editorial**
Jack Renninson
Melissa Tran

**Copyeditor**
Helen Hawkins

**Proofreader**
Catherine Lenderi

**Marketing**
Alex Crow
Melanie Price
Occy Carr
Cíara Rosney
Martyna Młynarska

**Operations and distribution**
Marina Valles
Stephanie Straub
Joe Morris

**Production**
Hannah Snetsinger
Mandy Kullar
Jen Shannon
Ria Clare

**Publicity**
Kim Nash
Noelle Holten
Jess Readett
Sarah Hardy

**Rights and contracts**
Peta Nightingale
Richard King
Saidah Graham

www.ingramcontent.com/pod-product-compliance
Ingram Content Group UK Ltd.
Pitfield, Milton Keynes, MK11 3LW, UK
UKHW040751190126
10168UKWH00019B/123